Blue Blood

Yellow Jacket

Clayton Roscoe

Copyright © Clayton Roscoe 2019

All rights reserved.

Clayton Roscoe has asserted his right under the Copyright, Designs and Patents Act 1988 to be identified as the author of this book.

Although the setting is very real, as are match officials and players, all characters who feature in this story are purely fictional and any resemblance to those people on the scene at the time is entirely coincidental.

No part of this publication may be reproduced, distributed, or transmitted in any form or by any means, without the prior written permission of the author, except in the case of brief quotations embodied in critical reviews and certain other non-commercial uses permitted by copyright law.

For permission requests, contact the author.

ISBN: 9781670681263

Typesetting & cover design by Socciones Editoria Digitale
www.socciones.co.uk

Prelude

The First Part

She says that football is the greatest game ever played on the surface of this earth, or any other planet, and she'll argue the toss with anyone who says different. Athleticism, teamwork, drama, the most exquisite personal skills, it's all there – although she hasn't seen an awful lot of any of that inside Goodison Park these recent games.

Once the pure girl of the church, inclined to clutch a Bible to her heart and recite passages from the psalms, she did grow quite naturally into restlessness and, singing to herself the popular songs of love and desire, migrate to the land of experience. From there, after finding herself lying in a vale of unbelief, she found her way to Goodison where she discovered for herself a place among the faithful. So she slips into her little blue car and heads there once again – another matchday in that grand old stadium, another afternoon wearing the yellow jacket.

She steers towards the Dock Road that will take her into the north of the city, her thoughts shifting between last night's soap opera, in which some rather startling revelations occurred, and this afternoon's match in which a convincing victory against opposition considered inferior should not come as a surprise – but unfortunately it will, for this is one of those seasons.

She does like to sit down and watch a soap in the evening after her regular shift on the hospital ward, because despite all the bickering and betrayals and occasional body under the patio she reckons she sees some real life there – and she does know a lot about real life because she's been a nurse since she left school. And life can, she reckons, occasionally turn into what seems like an episode from a soap opera.

A woman of a little over average height, she steps away from her car which she has parked just off the Netherfield Road, a Protestant stronghold in the old days of sectarianism in the city when they and Catholics would hurl at each other half bricks, bottles, abuse, accusations of abomination and devilry and all manner of other nonsense until in the Sixties lads with girly hair and girls with a pack of contraceptive pills in the back pocket of their jeans, who found sex and drugs and rock n roll far more interesting than the bigotry of their forefathers, were heard to ask: What the hell was that religious argie bargie all about?

Loathing, resentment, animosity, hatred – where did all that go? Blown away by the salt wind from the Irish Sea or still lingering in the dark depths of some psyches?

A trim woman moving with a purposeful stride, a certain energetic grace, she cuts through to St Domingo and down to Everton Valley, on along Walton Lane, glimpsing the old blue stadium up ahead as she follows the edge of the old park that divides the Country of Blue from the Dark Side: Anfield.

After crossing the road she arrives at the statue of Dixie Dean, the greatest goalscorer to leap from the green turf of Goodison, or of any other stadium, and head a football, power it with every muscle in his neck, beyond the goalkeeper's fingers and into the net. But he stands alone just now. There is no throng here yet, no massed gossip and gab, no sign yet of bustle in the streets around the stadium. The rush and push is still to come. It is all so muted. But there is a sense that some event might soon take place here. A few early boozers hang around the doors of the Blue House. The big truck that transports the police horses goes past as the first cops are arriving on the scene. The matchday traders are just beginning to set up: badge sellers and fanzine hawkers, the merchants of the colour blue.

She turns into the short terraced street that brings her to the club's almost empty car park, moves across at an angle towards the coatroom where all crowd stewards sign in and take on the yellow.

Margaret Maynard made the decision that she would devote her life to helping others at an early age. She has served on many different wards in her time as a nurse, and in other countries too. So she's pretty much seen it all: black and white, thick and thin; naked man and woman. She is part, as she is very well aware, of a great singing and dancing, smiling and suffering, loving and yes hating, humanity. But to what in particular, within the billions on earth, does she have a sense of belonging? With whom does she have affinity, fellowship? To what might she feel she truly belongs, this figure that can now see to her left the big blue gates of

Goodison Park?

She reaches for the handle to the door of the coatroom where she will become Maggie May to all the lads; a nickname plucked from the city's old myths that doesn't displease her despite its association with Lime Street harlots and all of that. For she is of this place, the city of Liverpool, and she does feel it – this old settlement by the sea, once of almost a million people but now only half that. Yes, she is a local girl, a Scouser, and proud. But even at only half its old size the city with its Garston and Bootle, and Old Swan and Norris Green, and all its other districts and areas, feels to her too big for that powerful and very personal sense of belonging.

Once, it is true, she was of the church, a girl in a pretty but sober frock going punctually to Mass, but that is now a long way behind her for she had slipped the grip of the priest long before priestly scandals rocked that monolith, the Catholic Church, all the way back to Rome. And if she can no longer feel any belonging with the church she chooses to stay out of the mucky pit of politics and does not, despite some encounters with fellas that she would prefer to forget, wish to retreat into those rooms reserved for women where the man-haters sharpen their tongues.

So what of family? Yes, there is that. But her family is too small. It is so much reduced, with uncles and aunts and cousins moved away to Adelaide and Toronto, only a rump left as this city has shrunk from a heaving rough and ready old trading port to an agreeable sightseer town doing its own line in tourist tat. The city's poor, her family, migrated to Australia and Canada and in their place Nigerians, Somalis, Lebanese, Jamaicans were taken in and found themselves, some of them, at times, on hospital wards where Nurse Maynard took good care of them. Her mother's family, the Gallaghers, came from County Mayo in the West of Ireland, and one female, on her father's side, was the daughter of an Italian immigrant, an organ grinder and ice cream seller who settled in a hovel off Scotland Road, but Maynard, a name which hints, not inappropriately, at hardiness, has travelled from Germany via Norman France to the North of England.

And so, after all that migration, here she is as Maggie May stepping into the Goodison Park coatroom, this big box full of yellow jackets and mantalk, where she does once again begin to sense within herself that feeling of belonging. For she is, by and large, a popular lady in the coatroom – Our Maggie. She is known for a competence and reliability that is allied to a very winning cheerfulness, and she is known also as one who likes to step on to the dancefloor at weekends and go wherever the music might take her: a dame who likes to have fun. Once that girl who read the Bible with a proper studiousness, and recited from it whole rich and resonant passages, the realization that she had more in common with Eve or Mary Magdalene than with the eternally virginal was her turning point, and she did, some say, go astray. So there are those who will regard her narrowly and with a judgemental eye.

She acknowledges the greetings of two lads who work in Section One as she steps in, and is as pleasantly evasive as ever in the face of uninvited flirtatiousness. John Sanger is in early as usual – Solid John. Bulky, square-shouldered, upright, he's like they say: Solid as a house. But he's no flirt; although, having worked alongside him on one occasion, she considers him to be as conscientious as she is herself. There's something stiffly military about him, she reckons. And he has indeed been a soldier in his time. Not her type, and anyway he's married.

As she waits her turn at the counter to collect her jacket Mark McColl enters, crosses the room without noticing her. Scholar McColl, the Ginger Scholar, he's one who gets his share of verbal stick from the more mouthy blokes. She watches him pass as he lifts the counter flap and moves through to the back of the room where the senior men – for they are all men – claim their own jackets. He's an outdoor man, a gardener, in his other life, so she's heard, and she can see how the winds and the sun have touched his skin. He slips into his big jacket, the yellow contrasting with the weathered bronze of his face, the redness of his hair, and then moves through to the office where the briefings for the bosses take place; for Scholar McColl is a deputy.

Reaching the front of the queue, she signs her name in the appropriate place beside her number on the sheet for Unattached Stewards. 'You're on Section Three today, Mag,' says Mick Molloy, a wide man with a narrow smile, a binman who on matchdays rises to the role of Head of Jackets, as he slides hers across the counter.

Section Three this afternoon – next game? Who knows? But there is no part of the ground in which she has not now worked during her years here filling in wherever there were gaps left by absentees. So she knows, it now feels, every inch of Goodison Park, every stretch of concrete and iron and wood, for she has been in her time here up and down every staircase in the old stadium.

She does not linger and gab like some in the coatroom. Dressed for the job, she makes her way out and as she approaches the big blue gates, now, as ever, she really does have that feeling: here she truly belongs; she is a part of this and always will be, for she serves this institution and has fellowship with those who gather here. She bangs on the blue iron and hears the latch clunk and then sees the little inset door swing open. 'Hi Joe, you okay?' she says as she steps through, and the large man in the large yellow jacket, a firm but affable former carpenter and club doorman who this season has taken over as gateman from the firm but affable big bear of an ex-cop who had guarded it for years gives her the nod.

Instead of stepping on along she pauses. 'How's the back?'

'It's not complaining – yet.'

'Well when it does, my advice is: ignore it!'

'Thanks nurse,' he says flatly, 'where would this club be without you?'

'And you Joe. And all the rest of us. How's your lad these days, by the way?'

'He's permanent on Section Two now – where I started out.'

'The generations, Joe.'

'That's what it is in this place Mag, you're right: the generations. He's taken my place over there. You never thought of settling down yourself?'

'They've never thought to ask me, Joe,' she says as she begins to move off.

Inside now. This is it. This is the place: the pitch, the running track, the terraces; so familiar yet somehow ever fresh to her. She looks up at that old blue crisscross ironwork set against the white of the upper stand, and feels that this, yes this, for better or for worse, is her place of belonging: Everton Football Club.

Whenever she arrives her response is the same: Yes, I am here again and would not be anywhere else, I am part of this great old thing. And if Everton Football Club is not a big box full of diamonds, nor a place where she will ever see her own name lit up in bright lights, nor a setting for a knight on a white horse to appear in order to show her the way to Paradise Park, even if it is not any of those things every time she walks through those big blue gates she gets this feeling, a feeling she carries as she walks the red running track down towards the section in which she will attempt most diligently to do her duty this afternoon.

The Second Part

Maggie May

Watching a great goal scored in a football ground can be like having an orgasm. It can. In the excitement of the moment your voice escapes from your body. It does. Sometimes. Your voice breaks out, out of language altogether, goes beyond words into pure sounds – as if it wants to get up there where the angels are and tell them what they're missing.

If you still believe in angels, that is.

I've seen too much down here on earth to be able to do that any longer. Nine months working in a refugee camp in East Sudan was plenty of time to rid anyone of fancy thoughts. But I was well beyond all that anyway. By then I was. Football is what I preached out there. I arranged to have a proper ball brought in and organized games – a little bit of relief, for me as much as for those displaced and desperate people, from the hard, hard facts of what life was really like. I was a true convert by then, a Gwladys Street Girl with blue blood in her veins. And even if I was no longer the fair and innocent maiden of my early years, even if I had by then seen a thing or two in the emotional circus we sometimes find ourselves attending, I was getting a hard lesson in what life was like for others.

What some of those women had to put up with, you wondered how they found the strength, trying to hold everything together, to keep those around them from starvation and from despair while in their homeland, over the border, the conflict went on and on, the Eritreans fighting to expel the Ethiopians, and fighting between themselves as well, as the villages were destroyed and the crops failed, and yet more people set out in search of refuge.

The University of Life? I was back in primary school – and I didn't grow up in any green and cherry blossom suburb of Liverpool either.

There was one, Aatifa, a young widow who had walked across the border and the desert with her two children to escape the fighting, and had even gathered in an orphan on the way – because that was her way: to look out for others. She had come from a place of palm trees and elephants, fields of corn and pumpkins, beans and oranges, to this place of dust and tents and ramshackle dwellings but still she talked of sharing and of hope while others saw only darkness ahead and even talked of death as the only likely destination. I showed her a picture of Goodison Park I'd taken with me for when I felt far away from home, told her how wonderful it was to be there in the crowd on a matchday, everybody singing while they watched the beautiful game. If only everyone just played football, I said to her, there'd be no more wars. Sounds silly now, I know, so naïve. But you'd have to be there, where I was, as a young nurse all that way from home for the first time, to understand.

She taught me how to ululate, Aatifa did — that loud, high-pitched, rhythmical sound that African women make by moving the tongue very fast from side to side while doing a big soprano vocal. But she did it while she danced to show that it wasn't just a sign of grief — although there was plenty of that around in the camp. Even the idea of joy, of dancing at a wedding, gave you a boost out there. And I had another one to add to my repertoire of female expressiveness!

She was no bigger than me, Aatifa — a very calm lady with big dark eyes, the eyes of a dove, looking at you from out of a red patterned shawl — but it made you feel so small just watching someone like her cope, even though you were the white girl who was there to defeat disease and heal wounds. Because you knew that when your stint out there was over you would fly away home — to those cramped but orderly old streets of the Dingle, and to the Grand Old Lady of Goodison Park.

Actually, because I was asked and couldn't say no, I flew west from Khartoum, went on to Ghana, spent nine months among the fishing people of the coast. There are bits of English even in the dialects over there — what those colonial chaps, the empire builders, leave behind when their treasured monolith falls apart — and enough old architecture to remind you that here was once the centre of the slave trade. You stood before *The Door of No Return* through which so many had unwillingly passed and then, stepping through it yourself, looked out on a bay into which ships with Liverpool crews once sailed to haul away their human cargo.

Our lads from back in the Pool, when the city was young, doing the dirty work, and earning for some Prince of Castle Street more filthy lucre. Vexation of spirit, as old Ecclesiastes would say: I felt some of that alright as I stood there. But my own work kept me from dwelling in the gloom of dark thoughts. I was based in the cleanliness of a hospital and dealing with people who at least had homes of a sort, even if some of them had little else. And then I did come home. Yes, home to the Grand Old Lady herself, to see the resurgent Blues showing the rest how the game should be played: with precision and with style, and a little bit of swagger. Howard Kendall, he of the Holy Trinity, had returned to his home in Goodison Park to recreate the glory days of the Sixties.

And me? I put on the yellow jacket for the first time.

That's a few years ago now, more than a few. All those seasons I've been looking after the crowd, watching them celebrate when the Blues bang one in – and having to stop my own voice from escaping.

I was going out with Robbie Ryan at the time, when I first started working for the club. A lad from the Gwladys Street, he was. And one time – talking of orgasms – one time I was with him up in the bedroom. I was living off Cockburn Street then, when I came back from Africa, one of those little streets that slope gently down towards the river and, back then, what used to be the old oil jetty, and the remains of the Herculaneum Dock. Dingle girl, me, born and bred, I am. And proud, in a way I am. Oh, yes.

Even if I was once a little Catholic growing up in a big scrum of Protestants: the Clarke bothers, Frankie Owens and his loudmouth little crew – hardfaced lads who knew no better, calling me Ragarse when actually I looked rather pretty going to Mass in my Sunday frock. Ragarse little papist, yeh. What you had to put up with as a girl. And that wasn't all. One time – I'd be about eight years old and we'd just moved house – me and my Ma went into the corner shop at the top of our new street for the first time and these three women who were already in there turned around and one of them said, 'You are Protestants, aren't you?' So my Ma explained that no we weren't but we were Christians. I still was at the time, obviously. But, fellow Christians or not, we were looking then into the faces of the purest hatred as the daggers of their eyes were flashed at us. They could have trampled us into the floorboards, those three women, if it wasn't that the good old Protestants who came in later for a bag of sugar or a few of slices of streaky bacon would have had to step around the mess. But it's all finished, that nonsense. Now it is. It was dying out then, actually. I just caught the arse-end of it. As they say in those earthy old streets I grew up in. Rather appropriately in this case.

So... me and Robbie Ryan, we were bang at it on the bed, in our naked glory, doing that old procreation jig like no creatures on this earth ever did. And I was just getting there, almost, almost, the way it is, like any second, any second now, the special effects are *really* going to be switched on down in your belly, and you're waiting for it, waiting for it, Oh, Oh, Oh how you're waiting, and your voice is breaking loose, the way it does. But it was high summer, so the window was wide open, and my voice must have been all over the street. Because suddenly there's a hammering on my front door. And my voice wasn't rising any more. Nothing makes you groan like when you get interrupted just at *that* moment. As I'm sure many will understand. Ohhhhhhhhhh!! What?!

But the banging on my door went on so I had to put something on and go down. It was the old lady from a few doors along. I'm trying not to look really, really, pissed off. And she's saying, 'Are you alright dear, it sounded as if you were in pain, or being attacked?'

Florence Beatrice McLelland had obviously never made the big trip to the funfair at bedtime. Poor dear.

'Pain?' I said. 'Attacked? I said, 'I was having the time of me life, Mrs McLelland.'

So then I had to try and explain. And then I had to go back up and start all over again. Robbie Ryan was having to play extra time. And he had a Sunday League game the next morning. I was soon back on the Big Dipper though, but keeping my orgasmic vocals down a bit this time.

I'm used to it now, biting my tongue. At the match I am. When you've got the yellow jacket on your back you have to keep your voice zipped up tight while all the others break free. Can't join in any more. Much as you might feel inclined to when a special one hits the net.

My first game at Goodison I saw one of them. Martin Dobson hit it from thirty yards out – a proper screamer it was, and my voice went with it, rising above the roar of the many. That was the winner, that day. And me, I was won over. Totally. Standing there in the middle of the Gwladys Street End, in the midst of all those voices, right in amongst it: life, people, togetherness, excitement – this is the place for me.

It was supposed to be an Easter treat, being taken to the match. But after that I said, 'The fellas aren't keeping this game to themselves any longer, no chance.' After that I was back on the Gwladys Street every match whether that lad Barry wanted me to be there with him or not. I was only fourteen then but I worked in a fruit and veg shop Thursdays and Fridays after school, and on Saturday mornings too, so I had no problem paying my way to get in to watch the beautiful game

And it is that; at its best it is. When the game is at its very best you see beautiful patterns out there on the pitch, players gliding into space, the ball zipping between them at different angles until a player with fantastic skill clips it between the white posts and triggers that explosion of voices.

He was that kind of player, Martin Dobson, a classy player. He was in there with the most elegant players you've ever seen. So graceful, such beautiful balance, he would truly glide across the green in his royal blue jersey; but he had a sharp eye for a pass too, and the ability to deliver it. Lovely player to watch. Looked like a man who could waltz or do the foxtrot. You could easily imagine him waltzing: Sir Dobbo. But not out on the pitch, you wouldn't want to see him making a show of himself in front of all those people.

I do like a man who can dance, though, who knows that his feet aren't just there to stop him toppling over or for kicking a ball. And I have known one or two very decent movers who danced me all the way down to where the delights are handed out.

Football and sex, though, where would we be without them? A question for the wise men and sages? Oh yeah.

If you want to hear some earthy wisdom talk to a nurse. But preferably not when she's covered in the overflow from somebody else's urinary tract. And definitely not on a Saturday night down in Accident and Emergency when she's got a mob of idiot fellas, a crowd of boozed-up, coked-up lads on her hands who have only just left off kicking the blood and the shite out of each other outside some club where they supposedly went to enjoy themselves.

How would we cope without football, though? What could replace it now – the world game that brings so many of us together? Is it something precious like an old building that needs protecting from those who might damage it? It does make you wonder.

You have a little bit of time for that when you don the yellow jacket, when you're standing around in the early afternoon before the turnstiles begin to click the first fans through; those turnstiles that are now polished from generations of Blues pushing through, brushing past. You notice odd little details like that when the stadium is empty. And sometimes when it's at its most empty you realize how full it is of lives, all those lives that over so many seasons it has brought together – more than a hundred years – all those human hearts beating together, decade after decade, the dock workers and the factory hands, the binmen and the bakers and the bus drivers, all that shared longing for the goal that will give release from the cares of the week that is just ending and those of the one that is soon to begin.

Then it starts: click-click-click as those turnstiles begin to turn once again. And before you know it an early punter is approaching you, bringing you her problem.

'There's no paper in the women's toilets,' she informs me gravely.

Somebody hasn't been doing their job properly. But I must do mine. 'Oh, I am so sorry about that,' I tell her. 'I'll sort that out straight away.'

The things you have to do for this club, the true drama of being a crowd steward in Goodison Park. It might seem weird that you could, in a funny little way, feel proud playing Lady of the Bogrolls – but you do. Sorting out little problems. What you're there for. But the fact is: they could put the best players in the world out on that pitch but without us, doing what we do, match after match, season after season, the game couldn't go ahead. Not now it couldn't. So you do feel proud. Especially when you look around a proper old stadium like Goodison Park and feel part of the blue and white and think of all the ones who've been here through the years, the Blues of now and generations past, and feel like the Grand Old Lady of Goodison Park has taken you also to her heart.

Part One

1

Stepping on to the End of a Story Line

I know her: Maggie May. And I knew all the others at the time that this happened because as well as having royal blue blood powering my heart, and having been up on the mountain top with the blue masses and done time with them down there where the demons lurk, and obviously having had to deal with the old foe from across the park in Anfield, I also served the Grand Old Lady of Goodison Park.

I first wore the yellow jacket for Everton Football Club soon after I came out of the university with a degree in Law. My uncle Eddie was one of the boss stewards so he put in a good word for me and I became a matchday crowd steward as well as a weekday lawyer. And as it happened I was duty solicitor attached to Admiral Street cop station the day Billy Whizz was brought in – so I got that story very hot. But I'm jumping way ahead of myself there.

It was my uncle Eddie who started taking me to Goodison. In nineteen sixty-five, that was. And I was both dazzled and seduced by the Grand Old Lady. Not only that, we went on to win the Cup that season. He got two tickets for the final so I was the lucky boy. There I was, only seven years old walking down Wembley Way, taking my place inside that wonderful old stadium – and watching us concede two goals. I looked up at Eddie for an explanation that never came. The response was delivered out on the pitch. What a fight back. What a victory. I can still see Shirley Temple racing clear, only the goalie to beat, and leaving the man in green spread-eagled on the deck staring back to where the ball sits pretty in the corner of the net.

The winning goal – what a moment: what a fantastic, unforgettable, moment for a young lad to experience. It's like gravity suddenly loses it power. It's like you're floating through a royal blue universe. And it stays with you too, that does, like a dream you'll never forget.

Old Arthur Blockley, the Archie Block of this tale, he was there in Wembley that year. But what he recalled most vividly, as this story will demonstrate very clearly, was a fan who'd been standing near him, running on to the pitch when we scored the equaliser, and dodging all the cops until he was finally rugby-tackled to the turf. If Archie hadn't been there to witness that incident so closely would things so many years later have happened differently – would I not have had this story to tell, this tale of how a bunch of ordinary, or maybe not quite so ordinary, Scousers get themselves in quite a tangle?

From where I worked I'd seen that crew, season after season, going about their matchday duties. Archie Block, close now to retirement, he was boss down on Section Six. And Billy Warlow, known throughout the streets of the city's South End, the downtown alehouses, the karaoke dens of the Crazy Quarter, as Billy Whizz, he'd worn the yellow jacket there long before I started on the job. A one-time flying winger of the Sunday leagues, he was a roofer by trade, but a man who, when the need was there, would turn his hand to whatever might put cash in it. In contrast to him stands the very upright former soldier Solid John Sanger, and somewhere leftfield Sanger's childhood mate Mark 'The Scholar' McColl, a wordy type, so they say, who gets referred to by various names but most mockingly as The Ginger Scholar.

Back in the day, more casual times, some stewards didn't get paid – a match programme, that's all they got for carrying their responsibilities through an afternoon in a packed Goodison Park. Some got paid, some didn't. Quite illogical. So Scholar McColl, who from his armchair had ventured into the dry zones of logic, stood up at a meeting and told the big bosses how ridiculous it was that some men had worked for the club for twenty years and never been paid a penny while others got a fiver from their first shift. He asked them to explain the logic of such a practice. The response of the bosses was to hum, or to stroke their chins, or to study something of great interest on the back wall. But by the next home game *everyone* was being rewarded with a fiver. So some lads had a little extra dosh in their pockets – but it didn't stop them calling

Mark McColl opinionated.

I knew Frank Brigstoke also, but he'd thrown in the yellow jacket and turned away from the game. He'd turned into a do-gooder, some said – although they weren't saying that by the end of all this. After thirty years of watching football he'd decided that it had become both a plaything for billionaires and an opiate to keep the masses from thinking about serious matters that really did require attention. I'd see him in the Albert sometimes because like me and Maggie May and the others from that Section Six crew he lived in the South End of the city. I'd half listen to one of his sermons when what I was actually there for was the music. I get up and play harmonica sometimes with some of the guitarists. I still see Mark McColl there occasionally. The Ginger Scholar plays classical guitar mostly but can turn his hand to boogie-woogie and even some surprisingly punky riffs when the ale's flowing. He's a big reader like me. We still swap books, pass on a good read and warn each other off the ones that turned out to be a bundle of hyped-up trash. But I see more of Maggie because we work together now on matchdays, for right at the end of this tale I became involved in a way I wouldn't have expected, and I don't mean sorting Billy Whizz out for his appearances in court. What I refer to is what happened after that. But it was a promotion, and after all those years working with the crowd I could see no reason to shy away from it. I was invited to become the boss of Section Six and someone had to take the job on after what had happened, so I did.

Then this woman walked into the law office; a novelist she was, and a very interesting lady too. She'd been falsely arrested returning from a night out in town because the cops claimed she looked like someone on their wanted list. Now she wanted apologies and she wanted paying. Not because of their mistake, because she knew we all made them, but because they were rough and rude with her.

She got what she wanted. And then sometime later she turned up again. But she wasn't in trouble this time. She showed up wearing a bright flowery T-shirt and pastel yellow trousers, semi-high heels with a sparkle on them, breezed in as if she were Queen of the Summer, saying, 'That court case of mine, the story is too good to waste. I'm going to make a book out of it, but at the moment there are parts I can't get into. So what I want is…'

What she now wants, what she needs, is my side of the story –

the legal inside of the case, the detail – to make it work as she envisages it. I have the feeling that she thinks it will be exciting for me to be the living person on whom a fictional character is based. But while she talks, while she entices me into this project, I have an idea. While she goes on talking about her book I am thinking about another book entirely – it's a habit of those involved in the law profession to think very quickly around any situation.

I thought: Okay you're a tough lady so now I'm going to cut a tough deal with you. Then I told her, 'Okay, I help you and you help me. I'll give you all you need for your book, but I've got a story too. What I need to know is how to tell it, so…'

So I told her. And then I said, 'I know hundreds of Evertonians, they get up for work on Monday morning, they put their shift in through the week, they pay their taxes, they do their duty as citizens, voting at elections and attending for jury service when called; they obey the speed limit and stop at red lights, they teach their children respect – they've never got themselves in a terrible tangle – but I couldn't write a three page story about them.'

She said, 'That's why they say the devil has the best tunes: if nothing goes wrong there's no story.'

2

The Crew on Section Six

Section Six: this tale begins with a man dancing there, dancing a little jig in the gangway he is charged with keeping clear of spectators while those all around him, the thousands of them, leap and shake and roar and slap their palms together to celebrate a goal by the players in the royal blue jerseys. If you look at it one way it begins there, yes. But there are other ways to look at it, there always are, for where can anything truly be said to begin or end? So – a man standing in a gangway in Goodison Park does a little jig when Everton score a goal, a dance he is forbidden to do as he wears the yellow jacket of a crowd steward.

That man is Billy Whizz. He's a sharp-featured character, kind of ferrety, built strong but light, for speed; although now he carries that little bit of overweight of a small ale gut.

In his life outside football Billy Whizz was a character that got around. If business in the roofing trade was slack he'd turn his hand to something else, anything else: car mechanic, delivery driver, decorator, wheeler-dealer, whatever would turn an hour of graft into a handful of notes and coin. He was by nature a chancer, checking the odds, trying his luck, and if at times he'd find himself scratching and scraping, snatching at bits, grabbing at pieces, he always managed to get by some way or other. And if, on occasion, he'd had to live by his wits he would tell you that his wits had served him well, not brilliantly maybe, but well enough. As a lad knocking about in the cobbled back alleys he was hardly ever skint. He'd be out helping the milkman in the dark before dawn, selling the odd pint on the side. He'd hang around the market in search of odd jobs, and get them. He'd dodge school if there was a couple of days' skivvying with a local building crew to be had. So he usually managed to put his hands on a bit of coin. One way or the other. He always had ciggies when he was at school, almost always, and if he didn't he knew who to go to in order to cadge one. So he was the King of Smokers' Corner, a tasty dogend in his blazer pocket – a blazer from which he had ripped the school badge and tossed it out the back window of the 82 bus. He was Mr Bubble Gum, Coca Cola Charlie. For he always had things other kids wanted, like a penknife with a polished bone handle, a magnet as big as a horseshoe, a proper professionals' football that he'd nicked from Goodison Park when it got kicked into the crowd but never got thrown back. But he didn't need to depend on possessions for his popularity because he had his football skills, he was an ace dribbler, and speedy with it, and, like John Sanger and Mark McColl who were also at that age very decent players, he could hold his own, do his stuff, in games with much bigger and older lads. And then in addition he had his monkey tricks: he could go up a drainpipe quick as any chimpanzee, piss as high as the highest cistern, spit right over a ten foot wall. William Dixie Dean Warlow, when he left school a teacher, Rickety Rickaby, said to him, 'Goodbye Warlow, and whatever you do don't ever come back and visit us.' For that Billy treated himself to one final prank and hurled the front wheel of old Rickaby's pushbike on to the bike shed roof.

Billy Whizz, a man who's game: game for a caper, a giggle, a round of cards, a song, or yeah, a dance. And it is with his little jig that events begin to develop. Although it will be useful, necessary perhaps, to take a look a little further back, to the final day of the previous season, for example, when an incident occurs that will take on extreme significance as one thing follows another and this story nears its conclusion.

It is May 1998, the final game of what has been a turbulent season, another season of torment, and this promises to be an occasion of yet more footballing frenzy as the heartrate doubles and the voices rise, as a huge and relentless crowd tries to roar its team, the Blues, to victory and therefore, hopefully, safety. Amid the hubbub of it all – the chants, the screams, the almost hysterical exhortations to clear the ball, to pass it quicker, or to shoot – Archie Block, Billy Whizz, Scholar McColl, and Solid John Sanger, stand in their positions and watch over the crowd; though their eyes are inevitably drawn to the action on the pitch.

It has for them all been a busy afternoon in a packed stadium; packed with needs and wants, and tension too. There is a dreaded presence lurking around this scene, one known throughout the football universe as Relegation. And all week the doomsters have been making their dismal prophesies: The End is nigh, prepare to meet thy doom oh ye cursed Evertonians.

Oh yes, the mockers and the taunters have been having their sport. The Blues, apparently, will soon be down among the dead men where they deserve to be. But this big blue crowd – they who have endured the jibes, the barbed quips – has pushed the team to survival before and why could it not do so again? So today the thousands have the passion for the task.

And the players have in their turn imbibed the spirt of hope – they battle the opposition wherever the ball may bounce, they chase and press, hound and snap. This might be rough and ready hurly burly football undecorated by talent, skill, poise, but nevertheless, for all their shortcomings – and they have come up so very short these recent months – the players are today possessed of a mighty will to make amends, to atone for all the sins of the season.

Only seven minutes of this very tense game have gone when, out on the pitch, the wounded old warrior Duncan Ferguson nods the ball down and this lightweight lad in blue, who all season has looked like he couldn't score if the goal was as big as the stand behind it, sends a wonderful half volley flying past the gaolie and in off the post. The stillness in the surrounding stands is shattered: so many leaping forms as the collective voice box breaks, e-e-e-e-e, o-o-o-o-o-o, and the jumbled vowels of affirmation soar beyond the roof to swirl about the sky above. All around the yellowjackets, who must not join in such celebrations, people are up out of their seats, jumping and jigging, doing wild tribal moves – some may never have looked so ridiculous and yet felt so happy. The stadium is rocking and bouncing – such stamping of feet and slapping of palms. And how the multitudes in blue now sing as they glimpse the word *Salvation* illuminated in their visions.

They are still in high voice when one of the spectators, a small overweight man who seems to walk on wobbly shoes, approaches John Sanger where he stands in the gangway behind the blocks of seats and, lifting his hand to show something small and round, says, 'Some people sitting near me have been hit by these.' He drops the little pale green missile into the hand of the yellow-jacketed figure who stares at the dried pea on his palm: a puzzled man.

John Sanger is a steady man, a tidy man, an upright man with a lot of shoulder and a close-trimmed full black beard – an imposing figure perhaps. As befits a man of strong views, a citizen of very firm opinions about how we all ought to comport ourselves, he looks at this stone-hard little vegetable and shakes his head in not only puzzlement but in annoyance. After checking out where the wobbly man is sitting he says with a well-practised conviction, 'Okay, I'll get on to that. I'll sort that out.'

Solid John Sanger, a machine fitter on weekdays, a former engineer in the British Army, a man who buys the best tools, the very best, and takes very good care of them because that is the right and proper thing to do, is a man who expects of himself, and everyone else, what is right and what is proper. When the complainant has wobbled back to his seat the sturdy man, that ex-soldier long ago trained to be mindful of ambushes, firing lines, and all that sort of thing, makes a considered guess as to where in the crowd the culprit most likely lurks.

Sanger picks out two lads, proto-teenagers sitting on the end of the back row of one of the blocks of seats – something not right about that pair. He figures them as hardfaced hangabouts, the kind he views with disdain as he walks the streets around his home pushing his unfortunate son Stephen in a wheelchair. He calls on Billy Whizz to join him; and then, guided by the crafty Billy, they position themselves so that they have a clear view of the suspects without making it obvious that they're observing them.

'Only a matter of time and vigilance now, if I'm any judge of scallywags,' says Solid John as he nudges Billy whose eyes may have wandered by now back to the game. And then sure enough they watch as the lad on the end drops his right hand down by his feet and flicks something, some tiny object that causes a figure in the next block down towards the front to slap a hand on the back of his head and then turn in vexation while the two scallyboys swap smirky looks.

'I'll take the smile of that face,' mutters a determined man as he moves most purposefully along the gangway until he's looking into the faces of the young villains who, having seen him coming, have arranged their looks of innocence.

'I saw you do that,' John Sanger points a stiff finger at the main culprit.

'What's goin on?' the big man from the seat beside the offenders is leaning towards Sanger. His tone is aggrieved, his look is angry, challenging. 'That's my lad you're talkin to!'

'Well he needs to learn how to behave himself,' Sanger replies, speaking firmly but evenly.

'Eh?' The man broadens his chest, shifts his muscles into gear.

'This is a missile, small as it is,' Sanger informs the expanded man, raising the dried pea, 'and this lad of yours needs to understand that you don't throw things like this at people in this ground and that if you do you'll very quickly be shown the way out – which is what I intend to do if it happens again.'

The man leans further over, 'This lad is stayin here with me, worrever you say.'

'He stays if, and only if, he behaves himself from now on,' says Sanger, and no man ever spoke firmer.

The father just stares at the steward for a second, turning up the heat, as if he could make the other man melt. 'If yer know what's good for yer you'll reali-i-i-ze yev made a mistake.'

John Sanger shakes his head, but before he can speak Billy does, 'No mistake!' And this one, who himself can be so ready with the pranks, the banter and the backchat, but who loves Everton Football Club no less than his fellow steward, adds, 'And ya can't be throwin things at people in here. Thas no good. Can't be allowed.'

Sanger warns the man, 'Make no mistake this boy will be leaving the ground if he's not careful. If you are his father you could choose to go with him, that would be up to you, but the boy would definitely go. If you were to try and prevent this happening I'd call for assistance and if that didn't work we'd involve the police.'

John Sanger looks at this person, this figure who seems to represent so much of which he disapproves, straight in the eye and sees one who isn't perhaps quite so sure of himself. 'And now,' he states, 'I'm asking you to either sit down or leave the stadium.'

'It's you lot that's goin down,' the man says, leaning further and speaking into Sanger's face in a grunty kind of whisper. 'Ain't gonna miss this. Weeve paid to enjoy this.'

Billy Whizz and Solid John Sanger look at each other in puzzlement, each then realizing at the same moment that they are dealing here with the old enemy, representatives of Liverpool Football Club, the Reds.

'But weeze winnin,' Billy Whizz tells him, 'Or maybe you hadn't noticed.'

'Not fer long. You watch,' says the man sinking back into his place.

And sure enough, all around the two yellow-jacketed figures the crowd now gasps and twitches – and continues to do so until halftime brings fifteen minutes of relief. But after that more and more shrieks and groans and desperate commands rise from a worried silence. For, much as the players in blue try to stand firm, the opposition is starting to look as if they might nudge them off balance and snatch the prize; a robbery that would send forty thousand people, who for more than an hour have sat willing their team to hang on, to cling on by whatever means, to that single goal and the three points with which they could survive, tumbling to that dreaded place. Out there on the green stuff the will might not be weakening but the legs, after all that chasing and harrying and trying to hurry the ball forwards, surely are. And on the terraces the marker on that great invisible stress gauge edges up, up, up through the high numbers towards that band marked *Unbearable*. Rising, rising, rising…

Oh how slowly, how painfully, the minutes pass, the seconds even, for those, and there are many, who have become obsessed with timepieces. Still ten minutes of this to endure. Seven more minutes of agony. Five. And…Penalty !!! Yes, the Blues, with a single sure shot, have a chance to burst the balloon of tension that this afternoon has become. But, no, the effort lacks power, the necessary precision. As the opposition's goalie feels the ball strike his gloves so many of those watching are groaning like the dying. And with so much apprehension in the stadium who would be surprised if at least one heart gave out?

Billy Whizz, a sharp-eyed character, has seen something of concern in the crowd and is on his way, and though he no longer plays on the wing for some alehouse team he is still speedy on his toes. He pauses in the aisle frantically gesturing, waving in two directions at the same time, as if he might be playing at directing traffic, some prankster routine by the lifelong scallywag, but he has perhaps never looked so serious.

Two other figures in yellow jackets get the message. Scholar McColl hurries towards him along the main gangway while from the opposite direction comes his childhood mate Solid John.

Billy by now has shuffled halfway along a row of now upstanding punters and is struggling to hold up a heavily slumped figure. McColl, the deputy, takes one look, pulls out his walkie-talkie, 'Section Six to match control, calling match control, need the medics, got a collapse, could be cardiac…'

Working fast, Sanger starts to clear the row, getting punters out of their seats and into the concrete aisle. Then between them the three yellowjackets manage to haul the comatose figure out and lay him in the gangway as a stout, creased, clearly older man in a blue coat arrives: Archie Block, the bossman. 'Looks like a mouth-to-mouth job to me, that,' he suggests. And then, crouching, he pulls the fallen one's jaw down, while John Sanger, on the other side of the collapsed figure, places a finger on the man's neck. Without looking up, he announces, 'Got a pulse!'

At the same moment the prone figure twitches, one eye half opens, the man grunts.

'Wasn't havin that, Arch!' quips Billy Whizz. 'Not the big kiss. Not from you!'

Cackles and snorts of relief – today these four men will not be dealing with death.

'You okay? Sanger asks the man into whose body the life is ebbing back.

'Blackouts: I get them. I'll be alright in a minute. What's the score?'

'We're still winning,' Archie Block informs him. 'Just about.'

'Hanging on,' says Sanger.

'We're clinging on like those three points are covered in grease,' says McColl with that clever look on his face, the one that Archie Block, among others, detests.

'Take no notice of his smartarse talk,' Archie Block tells the prostrate man as he jerks his thumb at his deputy. And the eyes of the two senior figures on the section briefly clash as an ambulance crew appears: sprinters in uniform, racing up the gangway.

'Okay, stand back lads,' orders the lead medic slamming down a metal case.

Old Archie Block bristles at being ordered around in his own domain, 'What dy mean stand back? The job's done. You can go back and finish ya crossword.'

But the men in yellow jackets, leaving the fallen one in the care of the professionals, smiled too soon. For out on the pitch, as they move back towards their positions, a tall black man in the colours of the opposition rises in the goalmouth and heads powerfully through the goalkeeper's grasping hands – and that oh so precious lead is lost.

Solid John Sanger mutters curses, Archie Block winces, Billy Whizz stamps a foot and throws up his hands, Scholar McColl closes his eyes for a second: a mix of reactions repeated thousands of times around this old stadium.

Here now is a people shock. How could that have been allowed to happen? First they miss a penalty, now this! So if they concede again the Blues are gone – down to the dreaded place. And even if they don't: if Bolton get a point at Chelsea, the Blues are gone – simple, and painful, as that.

And to add to the collective inner turmoil a punter with a radio to his ear is announcing, 'The reporter at Stamford Bridge is saying the Chelsea fans are cheering for Bolton, they want them to score so that Everton go down. He says in thirty years of reporting on football he's never heard anything like it!'

In your most difficult hour it can seem as if the whole world is against you.

Sanger turns to look at the interlopers, those three figures on a family day out in the back row. Such glee on those faces, such utter malicious delight.

Billy Whizz also cannot resist a glance in that direction. 'We can't let them leave here laughin,' he tells Sanger, 'we can't let that happen.'

Sanger winces at the thought of such an ending to the day. Billy takes a deep breath, smacks his hands into a loud clap-clap, 'CmonnnnnEverto-o-o-o-nnnn!!!!' Such a large voice rising to float above the many heads.

Sanger lays a big paw on the other man's neck, 'Wrap up, lad. Or you'll shout yourself into trouble.'

'Ach!!' Billy mock-spits at authority, at stupid rules, as he has done so many times in his life.

Archie Block reappears, tells his men, 'If there's a pitch invasion at the end of the game the instructions from up top are to let them go. But any sign of trouble get in there and clear it.'

The final whistle – and the word goes round: Bolton Wanderers lost at Chelsea. The Blues are saved. Again. They're staying up! And the crowd, leaping, cannot be contained: such roars, such screams of jubilation, as it bursts across the pitch.

The yellowjackets stand and watch the thousands of merrymakers cavort on the grass, diving into it, swimming through it, some bouncing on it, doing cartwheels, as the players dash to escape this celebratory invasion. For some that remain on the terraces there are the hugs, tears even, of those a little bewildered at being suddenly released from that terrible tension. Others have slipped into some kind of delirium and are gibbering in their joy.

Solid John Sanger and Billy Whizz, stood in the gangway, observe three figures approaching: all three faces wearing the expressions of those who've been cheated, and had their special day out ruined.

As they arrive before the two stewards the father stops, addresses himself to Sanger, 'I'll tell ya what, Bluenose: Don't be surprised to find that y've walked into a fist one of these days: right, smack, on the nose. And when ya gerrup don't be surprised to find that y've had yer fokin ear ripped off.'

His pair of lads snigger in unison.

The world in which he has travelled so widely still at times baffles John Sanger – and his expression says exactly that as he addresses the man, 'How will these lads ever learn respect listening to that kind of talk?'

The man doesn't take questions. 'And al tell ya somethin else,' he says, about to move off but pulling back. 'Yer goin down next season. Yer goin down where ya belong. And don't forget,' he jabs a finger, 'I know your face.' He leans his head even closer to Sanger's, like players sometimes do when they're acting silly out on the pitch. He taps the side of his head. 'Av got your picture up here.'

Sanger, the responsible man, cannot quite manage to let that pass. Looking firmly at one who, though built so large, he reckons to be an overgrown adolescent he replies, 'And I've got yours. Unfortunately.'

As the family moves away the lads turn, raise fingers of abuse. But the two in yellow turn their backs on them. And as they do so

Sanger observes to Billy, 'You can't tell with that type. Do they mean it or was that just bravado fuelled by too much booze?'

Billy is untroubled by doubt, 'Ad say that's the ale talkin – talkin shite.'

Sanger, a man who has travelled a far wider world than that of his fellow steward, remaining thoughtful, adds, 'You never know. But I've always reckoned that the ones who talk most are the ones who do least, that it's the fella who does his talking with his eyes who's much more likely to be waiting for you in the dark with a knife up his sleeve.'

Billy is in no mood for such serious reflections. Billy Whizz is laughing, 'They come to gloat, but they ain't gloatin now are they? Not now they'll be realizin how much money they wasted.'

And anyway, the Jamboree of Relief is rocking and rolling on the pitch, to which he and Sanger now move.

'That was too close for comfort. We can't go on having seasons like this,' Archie Block mutters with his hand on his chest as he steps on to the grass where some fans are now kneeling, offering thanks, worshipping the green stuff on which they found salvation. Some continue with the slapstick gymnastics, while others, calm now, are perhaps wondering what they're doing out there on the pitch.

Solid John, seeing a kid running while waving a corner flag, jumps in front of him. 'What you doing with that?'

'I'm waving the flag for Everton.' The boy's teeth illuminate his smile.

'No, you're not!' Sanger yanks the flag with such force from the other's grasp that the lad half stumbles after it.

That smile shrinks into a pout. For a moment he studies the sturdy man in the yellow jacket who has dispossessed him so fiercely. 'Why?' he demands.

'Why what?'

The boy now gives him a look he doesn't like. John Sanger, bending, shakes his head at the kid. 'You're not fit to carry the flag.'

'Why?' The lad looks so puzzled. 'Why aren't I?'

'What do you think?' Sanger demands as his stare shifts from the lad's green eyes to the darkly-shaded skin. 'Look at yourself.'

Mark McColl stands watching as the lad begins to wander off into the joyful mix and then turn back as Solid John Sanger, holding the corner flag like a trophy, says to a yellowjacket standing beside Archie Block, 'Trouble is: if he looks in the mirror in a darkened room, that lad, he won't know he's there!'

Part Two

3

Sanger and McColl, Some History

The Fence

They are eight years old, and they're with a mass of other kids in the Boys' Pen up in the back corner of the stand – two lads who are growing up together in the Dingle and playing for the same school team and the same Sunday League side, and going to Goodison together to watch the Blues. They are very alike in some ways, although not in others. But their attitude towards playing is the same. They'll play anywhere with any gang of lads who've got something round and bouncy and somewhere to kick it. On concrete or tarmac or grass, they don't care, in the scruff or a team shirt, they're not bothered, although the young John Sanger, like the man he will grow into, is never scruffy.

 The Boys' Pen is a mixture of scallywags' den, the monkey house at Chester Zoo, and a stage on which the Squeaky Choir of Goodison Park perform on matchdays. It can be rough in there at times with some cockeyed little villain and his cousin the schoolyard bullyboy on the prowl, but for Sanger and McColl it's no worse than the rougher parts of the South End of the city which they negotiate regularly without problems as they go from one game of football to another; John Sanger, well-built for his age, walking proud and upright, like he's practising for life as the strong and silent type, and his smaller mate at his side moving light-footed and watchful like a scowly fox that's learned a few tricks peering round the door of the Golden Gloves Boxing Club. And anyway, there's always a little Dingle crew in there so they all stand together and the lumpy loudmouths and apprentice pickpockets, and other borstal boys who've got black pudding for brains, give them a wide berth. But it's just like a normal day up there this particular afternoon as Ginger McColl looks at the fence that separates the boys from the men on the terracing on other side: the way that barrier soars above him, the way it turns into spikes at the top – spears of denial and forbidding that fail to prevent the daring boys from going over. He stares through it, the iron of prohibition, confinement, and says to himself what he says every time he is here: One day, one day I will go over. And then he looks around at the faces of the kids already gathered in the Pen. Which of those faces shows the signs? For one, he is sure, is thinking of going over, is preparing himself for the dash and the leap.

As he turns to face the crowd of kids behind him, trying to spot the wild boys before they go over, he picks one out – a lad in a jacket like a cowboy's, an outlaw, for sure – for there's a certain way a jumper's eyes will slide between the fence and the lawman who patrols it. McColl notes how this lad watches from the corner of his eye while pretending to look somewhere else altogether. There's a certain way a smart scallyboy's face will crease up as if he's working out some extremely complicated puzzle or equation: adding and subtracting; times, distances, heights and speeds. And this is one, this lad who stands with his hands in the pockets of his cowboy jacket, his elbows tucked in like wings that might very soon begin to stretch, having positioned himself close to where he'll have reckoned the bold and dashing lads who have gone over before him in this and seasons past have loitered, he is very clearly awaiting his moment. But he is not alone in his daredevil enterprise. Today there are two of them, Ginger McColl guesses. The lad beside him is surely his mate, for he too is clearly a young desperado of the streets. Ginger notes how they begin to speak in a language of grunts and little growls while their lips hardly move. Yes, they are biding their time, like crafty banditos, waiting for a particular moment – as he knows they must do if they are not to be caught and face the risk of being ejected from the stadium. They are waiting until the terraces over there are three quarters full so that the bodies make a forest into which they can disappear – too few and there is nowhere to hide, too many and there is no space in which to land. And when that moment comes they will go like the wild boys do, up and over, and once they've jumped, once their feet are on the deck over there, the fellas will close around them and protect them from the lawmen and they will dart away through the massed bodies and watch the game as if they've grown big inches in less than an hour. And these fence jumpers, these daring kids, he knows, are the divils, the rascals, the hard-faced boys his mother warns him to beware of. But why would he steer clear of them? Why should he not want to run with them and make the jump? It's as if they are saying: No matter how high anyone builds them barriers they'll never fence us in. It's like they're telling him: All rules are there to be broken.

And why would a lad like him not want to listen to that?

So Ginger McColl bides his time while he's growing, until it is his day to be the daredevil, the bold one, who steps out when the lawman's back is turned and scrambles for the top of the fence before leaping the spikes into that place which is stuffed with wide shoulders and workboots, with sideburns and sturdy belts, overalls and donkey jackets, or jackets from what used to be Sunday best, or maybe a flash suit from London Road that makes a fella who lives round the corner and drives the binwagon look like a movie star. Of course he craves a place in there, that manly region which rings and crackles with curses and laughter, that whiffs of tobacco and booze, of strength and the big world and life beyond short trousers and schoolbooks. Why should he not want to be in the middle of something vast and powerful, something that can suddenly throw out this massive sound that's like one enormous voice made of thousands? For what is in there can make the afternoon explode, it can make the stone beneath your feet feel as if it's quaking, as if it really is about to start breaking up.

What is over there is a hint at something he doesn't yet understand. It is a glimpse of what people from tight streets and tower blocks, from long avenues and leafy estates might do in combination. It is an image of faith, belief, loyalty, and occasionally sheer joy, for they love Everton Football Club these big lads, these men with spiky chins and beery breath and fingers stained dark with smoke. They gather, this mighty congregation of the rough and ready, and they sing with such devotion on Saturday afternoons in this their blue and white church. And, listening through the fence, before the game, to their banter and their gab, their curses and crosstalk, why should not any kid, any lad with scabby knees and skinny arms, want to join and be accepted, to mouth as they do the myths and narratives, the quips and wisecracks, that show their team up as the best?

The mysteries of the big world – one day he will go in search of answers. But for now there are lots of things, as teachers keep reminding him, that Ginger McColl doesn't know. He doesn't know where Timbuktu is or how far it is to the moon or where electricity comes from; and when he did a test before Christmas he didn't even know, for he does not pay attention to what does not interest him, which one was the prophet out of Joseph, Isaiah and Judas Iscariot; but he does know how, breaking from midfield, to score goals for the school team, and he knows plenty about jumping the fence that separates the boys from the big lads and the fellas.

There are the ones who go over fences and there are those who don't, and who never will, ever. There are those who dare and the others who don't even think of it; for of those left behind by the fence jumpers some are too slow or awkward or flatfooted to follow, some too roly-poly from scoffing too many chips and chocolate bars and seconds of school fly pie and custard, and some are too fearful, too shy of defying the rule makers: they can't bring themselves to make the run, the climb, the jump, for there is always a cop patrolling that fence and so to be a jumper is to go against the law, it is to break the rules of good and proper behaviour, and some lads will not do that. There are multitudes of kids like that who will never quite manage to do the daring thing. They might be fingered or collared, they might get their hide tanned with their old fella's belt or be locked up by the lawmen or they might be sent down to the fiery zones where the preachers say all bad boys must eventually go. But none of this holds back Ginger McColl, only his smallness does that. For he has observed that the ones who succeed in scrambling up and over the fence are always older, bigger than he, so feels too undergrown yet, and is indeed no more than bones in a bag of skin that's topped off with a tuft of red curls. He looks at his mate Johnny Sanger and knows that he will never go over – he's not that type of lad, for nobody ever calls John Sanger, stocky for his age and very upright, always very upright, a divil, a scallywag, a hardfaced young buck.

But one day, McColl reckons, when he's got more inches, more beef and gristle, he will go over, go over like the ones who must guzzle risk and sing a song called Defiance. Because if you wait till you're big enough and you time the run just right the cop will have no chance. That lawman is like the sentry patrolling some fort in the Badlands – he's the one who gets the first Apache arrow in the neck, the one whose name you don't even know.

No, the cops won't trouble him then, he will go over into that big world he can see through the bars; in there where a particular gang of men always gathers just the other side of the fence; men who will swig from some small bottle of firewater that makes them suck their tongues and breathe out hard, or light up ciggies and speak the names of the players in smoke, or utter remarks from a hoard of the choicest curses, profanities and blasphemies, and assorted verbal filth that Ginger has already appropriated, that he keeps now in his memory book and throws into the vocal mix of the squeaky-voiced Pen boys; but one day his voice will be part of the big noise – over there – as he tells the linesman what he can do with his flag or makes a smart comment that sets all the other fellas laughing.

And now he sees it, sees the outlaw go. Ye-e-e-esss.

The one who dares is dashing, leaping out of the crowd.

Ginger McColl sees a sudden explosion of arms and legs that turns a lad into a monkey scrambling for the jungle roof. Hand over hand he goes, reaching the spikes, setting one foot in position to kick himself airborne, way clear of the kids' zone, as a cheer goes up from some watching boys. And then he falls to land like a gymnast, without a stumble but with a glance back at those he is leaving behind, and then darts away to disappear into the mass of men before any cop has even got a sniff of him, never mind a handful of collar.

One outlaw gone over, and soon, Ginger knows, his mate will follow him. Just as one day he himself will follow. He will watch and wait. And then one Saturday afternoon – Go, he will tell himself, yeh-go lad. Go-go-GGGoooo!! That's it. One day, yes one day it will be him. Him. And those who know him will say, 'Ginger McColl jumped the fence at Goodison, he gave a two fingered bye-bye to the cop who tried to nab him: See ya later, masturbator!' And then he realizes; the thought comes to him – he will be over the other side and then he will look back and see that he has indeed left his mate Johnny Sanger behind.

4

The Penny Lane Final

And this is their big day. And already the bigger one is called Solid John – because, playing as a centre back, this lad Johnny Sanger is never anything but dependable in the middle of any defence. He is the resolute defender policing the penalty box and, with great spring in his heels, heading dangerous crosses away; while the other, Ginger McColl, prowls much further up the pitch – that peppery carrot-head ever ready to dash from midfield, to dart between opposing centre backs and flick the ball beyond the opposing goalkeeper's fingers.

So now here they are together at Penny Lane where the stars of Harry Catterick's great Everton team of the Sixties had played in big games as schoolboys: Labone, Royle, Whittle, Wright and Morrissey. And now it's their turn: Sanger and McColl.

On this slab of green behind the houses, inside the tall red walls, they will play on a pitch with straight white lines and proper goals before a crowd of sorts – teachers and schoolkids, dads and uncles, the local codgers – and will surely win and maybe one day become professional players; with Everton perhaps. But like the oldsters have told them, there are two kids on every corner in this city daydreaming of football stardom, so Solid John thinks he will more likely go away, join the army and travel, while Ginger hasn't a clue what he might do and can't see why he should have. But today they think only of one thing.

Both are a year younger than the rest of the team but one through his presence and the other through his mouth and his hard running in midfield have got themselves promoted, and neither of them feels like he should hang an excuse round his neck for being here. The older lads need them no less than they need the rest. The tall, the squat, the reticent and the mouthy, together they make a tight unit, together they know they can pick up that little silver pot.

In the dressing room – a space that smells like some mix onions and ointment, old socks and sweat, dampness and dust – they go in for some ritual banter, some last minute re-statements of the old tactical plan: to hound the opposition into giving up the ball, to use it well and then get into space ready to receive it. They stamp their studs on the wood and the concrete and then they step out on to the grass and clap their hands and rub their palms and spit and swear – all the manly rites of an adolescent little tribe in black and white stripes.

They have entered here a special place, their other life is hanging on a hook in the changing room. Out on the pitch Solid John stands square and statuesque feeding on air, feeling his chest grow bigger, and looking down the pitch in a way that makes the opposition seem smaller. Ginger is jogging and jumping, shaking his swelling muscles around, loosening up the wire that has grown into his limbs these recent years.

And then the referee's whistle sets the game whirling.

And it's a close-quarters tussle with little space given, but if one side is forcing the other back it is them, the black and whites, the stripes, so at halftime they speak only of victory and how it will be achieved.

A fist is raised and shaken as they get set for the restart – it is the large youthful fist of Solid John Sanger. And to complete the duo's little kick-start routine Ginger McColl shouts, 'Come ed, let's gerrin to em!' And then they're away and Ginger is running through the midfield, darting, dummying, doubling back. He is trying to be always available, not to hide in some other kid's shadow. If one lad can clinch a victory here, why should it not be him? Why should he not shape the moment with his own sweaty hands as he works back and forth from box to box? He passes the simple ball and seeks the return. He blocks off the space that maroons would slip into. He is talking team-mates through this game, lads who in turn are bolstering him.

And nothing gets past Solid John at the back, he breaks up the opposition's high moves with his leaps and his headers and hoovers up the bits with those speedy boots of his, and nobody, no player ever, knocks him off the ball. He is thirteen years old and will never be so commanding on a football pitch. And everything he does is calm and neat, well inside any rule that was made for the game.

His smaller mate is perhaps not quite so respectful of the rulebook. He jumps into tackles, leaves his foot in, comes away with the ball, is given a finger-wagging by the ref. But this is his day too and he knows it – breaking from deep as two players tussle he sees the ball roll into his path and smacks it. The goalkeeper scrambles it past the post. But the black and whites are winning the midfield where he is running into space like a creature that will never be caught. He is some feral thing, part ferret part fox, that will never see the world from inside a cage. And he will surely get another chance, and that one, he tells himself, he will take.

The opposition, the maroons, are arriving too late or making the wrong moves. Take a look at the manager, their teacher, Mr Something with a boxer's nose and Hitler moustache – a loser for sure – you'll see the lines of despondency deepening in his face. He is watching something slip away, quite out of his grasp – because the red-haired one is pulling hard on the other end while Solid John stands square and vocal backing up his mate, telling him how good he's doing, telling him to go all the way if a space opens up.

One of the maroons tries to dive in on Ginger but both the ball and the curly head have gone long before that would-be ballwinner arrives. For McColl, skipping and dancing with the ball at his feet, is quick today, far too quick for any lad who would nail him down on some muddy spot.

He drifts out to the right and sees a pass coming his way but a defender gets a toe to it. The ball spins off that boot and bounces behind the full back into a nomansland in which Ginger, if he puts all his scouse dinners and bacon-butty breakfasts into one sprint and gets first to the ball, might do Adolf Crookednose and his maroon army some serious mischief. There is nothing else, only the orange ball. His whole world is that bouncing sphere. He has never heard of acne, he has never been given the cold eye by some starlet schoolgirl, he will never again have to pass an eternity in a classroom listening to the mechanical drone that emanates from some grey-suited dummy while he inks EVERTON into yet another desktop. There is only this football which his boot chivvies and caresses into the penalty box as he leaves that defender looking at his back, pondering perhaps his, the defender's, entire future: a life of chasing shadows or shunting boxes destined for nowhere.

But Ginger McColl sees no such potentiality. What he scans immediately ahead of him is two centre backs, twin stooges, a pair of pillars in a creaking defence, who try to make themselves taller and tighter by chewing each other's words.

On a wider view he glimpses black and white stripes flashing to his left. He makes to dart past the defenders with the ball but, without breaking his stride, releases it with a neat sideways tap, and swerves them until he is running free behind their backs ready for the return ball when it comes, letting the other full back, Jimmy Ballwatcher, who maybe never did fully grasp the rules of the game, play him onside. So he's in behind their centreboys, he's pulled down their shorts and exposed their backsides to the entire universe – so many moons rising above the grass of Penny Lane – he's flying through forbidden space like a lad who never felt the drag of gravity, the constricting force of rules and prohibitions, the weight of those grave looks elders turned on him as he was lectured on his foolishness, his fecklessness, the essential silliness of the free-spirited nonsense he has picked up in some dustbin of backstreet philosophy. He is a bird with a bright crest, a kind of exotic magpie, a fly-by-night midfielder who's finally got free, who's through into the light – and flying surely is what he was born to do. He wasn't meant to get tangled up in a net of explanations, to be caged by convention; there is just him and the air he drifts through, and the beat of his wings says all there is to say about being a kid in a football kit and knowing that only one side will win the game.

So he knocks the ball on, takes a look up as he closes on the goal, and clips it with his right, the outside of his boot, giving a bit of bend and not too much weight, low towards the left hand corner and it looks to be going just inside the post until the goalie, who he reckons looks like too much of a schoolroom swat to be a good keeper, does a diving dash and, his arm lengthening like some great octopus limb, gets a bit of his glove on it and sends it spinning up and on to the post from where it spins back into play over his now falling body. He throws himself up and forwards on the bounce as Ginger, lunging and stretching, feels the knock, the blow of the ball on his instep, and goes tumbling, rolling on damp grass and bald mud, feet over head, hip and shoulder taking the impact, red hair in the green stuff. But he knows without seeing, without watching the film of that afternoon that he's buried the ball and the whole maroon team. The sound of the place tells him all before he scrambles up and sees, over the goalkeeper's corpse, and to the right of the waxwork leftback, the orange ball in the great bag of the net, and he is skipping from the grasp of teammates – all those would-be lovers who would smother him with praise – to dance in a corner, a disco caper, a solo team-breaking instinct that he doesn't yet understand but cannot feel to be something to correct, let alone frown on in himself, until sensible John Sanger arrives to haul him back into the embraces of the team.

And it has to be him, the lad from the back, who snatches the second, the clincher. And it has to be Ginger who waves him up for a free kick, who sends in the bending cross that he rises to meet – soaring above all others – that he head-hammers into the top corner of the net.

And if already the paths of this pair have begun to diverge, today that does not matter – for with a medal in one hand and a handle in the other, together they lift that little silver trophy.

5

Something Jagged Starts to Show

Sunday afternoon in late April. John Sanger stares as Ginger McColl approaches along the street. As he gets closer Sanger says, 'What happened to the eye?'

McColl automatically puts his fingers to the purple bruising. As he halts before the other lad he says, 'Got jumped outside the match yesterday. Some bunch of lunatics who call themselves the Headhunters.'

Sanger's own head jerks back.

McColl continues, 'Yeh. Some hooligans from the Chelsea Shed attacked us.'

'Why?' John Sanger needs to know. 'Why was that?'

McColl shrugs, 'Weren't very happy about being relegated, maybe.'

'Even so,' says the appalled young Sanger – Yobs bringing violence to the streets of the capital?

'But they didn't seem like the type who needed much of an excuse to kick the shit out of someone,' McColl explains. 'Especially a band of Scousers strolling down the Kings Road with smiles on their faces, chatting up the Cockney birds.'

And it is possible to smile about it once again – for Ginger McColl it is.

John Sanger doesn't do a lot of chatting up of birds, Cockney or otherwise. He knows a nice girl called Mary from Mossley Hill – a girl who's already been offered a job in an office downtown for when she leaves school. On Friday he'd taken her to the pictures to see *The Apple Dumpling Gang*, because she liked Walt Disney, she was a nice girl who enjoyed a nice comedy.

McColl had spent most of Friday night hitching down to London for the last match of the season: a 1-1 draw at an unhappy Stamford Bridge, surly boys up in the Shed watching their team fall through the trap door into the Second Division while Everton finished in a comfortable fourth place. To get back home he dodged onto the train without a ticket. It was a laugh, going to away games, even if he had just had his initiation into the unfunny side of things in some other crowd's city.

'What you doing now?' asks Sanger.

'The usual.'

The *usual* now that proper football is finished is to walk down to the park to see if there's a kickabout game going on.

As they head down the Eggy Road Sanger announces solemnly, 'I went down to the Army office yesterday. When I'm fifteen and a half I can apply to join. And then as soon as I'm sixteen I'm going in for basic training.'

'Attensho-o-onnnn!!' calls McColl, suddenly halting and stamping down his right foot, as he jerks his mock-salute up towards his bruised eye socket.

The soon-to-be Private John Sanger, not amused by such clowning, keeps on walking. Her Majesty's Forces are an important part of the British Nation, he now believes, and soon he will play his own small but important role in what they do to protect the British people. Disrespect – it was unfortunate that his long-time mate carried rather a lot of that around with him these days: arguing with teachers in school, with referees during matches, talking in a loose-mouthed scornful way about all forms of authority. And now at Goodison he thought nothing of paying to go in the Boys' Pen and then climbing over the fence, and acting not only as if it was his right to do it if he wanted to but also as if it was some kind of joke played on Authority. It was starting to seem as if there was no end to it – bunking off school through a hole in the back fence, riding on trains without a ticket. And now he's coming back from an away game black and blue after fighting in the streets of the capital – and you wouldn't know with him nowadays whether it wasn't his own big mouth that had started the trouble.

Ginger McColl carries his disrespect – and his amusement at his own antics – in silence for several hundred yards until they turn down the Lane.

They emerge from the other end and cross into the park. Over on the Big Field there is indeed a gang of lads having a kickabout, coats for goals.

The pair are recognized, welcomed – as decent players would expect to be – and then split up. Sanger takes his familiar defensive position in his team. McColl goes up front for the fun of it, and is soon closing in as his old mate brings the ball forward. Against a sturdy lad like Sanger you have no chance of taking the ball off him unless you go for it with great purpose – unless you go in hard. So that's what he does: very purposeful, very hard. And succeeds in winning the ball and running clear with it, or would have done if the other lad hadn't given him a hefty shove in the shoulder to knock him off balance.

The aggrieved ballwinner rocks back. And shoves back.

'Watch yourself there, lad!' Sanger warns.

'Oh, aye?' McColl scoffs, gives the other a look that he knows he won't like. But the ball is in play, the other lads aren't hanging about to view *The When Mates Fall Out Show*.

The game goes on.

And soon brings them back into a similar situation – because Sanger with his large but quick feet is so comfortable with the ball, bringing it from deep. And is McColl going to hold back now, shirk a tackle? Why would he?

He hurls himself forwards, a true tackle, his foot on the ball, going right through his big mate, who is dragging him back with one fist and raising the other ready to swing it.

Until the intervention.

'You'll have another one of those eyes the way you're going,' Sanger persists. 'I'll give you one to make a set.'

'You might try,' McColl taunts.

The other lads are pushing them apart, laughing at them, 'A right pair of mates you two are!'

And it is kind of funny, when you think about it. Ten minutes after turning up together they're snapping at each other's throats, growling dog-nonsense. Wuff-wuff!

You have to laugh.

And then get on with the game.

6

That Damned FA Cup Semi Final

Today they confront the old enemy, Liverpool Football Club, at Maine Road and as Mark McColl hands John Sanger the ticket he sees the floodlights switched on in the other lad's eyes. Private Sanger, after managing to get leave from his army unit, has only just arrived back in Northern England and now he's holding a piece of printed card that will gain him admission to a semi-final – so you could illuminate a whole stadium with that gaze of his.

And why not? This is as big a Cup game as you can get short of the final itself and the whole city wants to be there, to decamp to Manchester and be a witness, a participant. This struggle with the Reds is in the centre-circle of their culture and this duo will take their rightful places amid the travelling horde.

It has been a damp few days and the pitch will be heavy but by half past one they are light-headed with ale and expectation. They are squeezed into the Manchester City Supporters' Club with a thousand and one other Scousers, Red and Blue, back to back, elbow to elbow, voice to voice. The walls are bulging with the din, the hot beery breath and banter. The building itself could be the waiting zone in some station or airport – shiny surfaces, plastic and steel, tough low grade materials for mass use. It's the kind of place to which you have to bring your own atmosphere – so okay, no problem, the place is certainly full of that.

After two years in the army Sanger seems sturdier than ever. He looks like he could stand on a table and hold up the ceiling with one hand – or push the whole building down if he had the mind of a vandal which he most certainly doesn't. He is, like they say, like they've been saying for years, a solid lad. He's upright as a stone pillar and regular as Sunday, and he never in his growing years stood on a railbank and dropped his kecks to flash his arse at the occupants of a passing train or told a teacher where to stick his homework. He's a big clean lad with deep bronzed skin and around his neck he wears a brand new silky-looking blue and white scarf knotted up like a thick shiny tie.

Naturally he talks about foreign places he's visited: Cyprus, Brunei, Belize, Germany; which young adventurer ever could keep his mouth shut about a world he had just discovered singlehanded? And he's also spent time in Norway where in his leisure hours he had learned to sail on the fjords, so he is now a sailor as well as a trooper.

While Sanger talks in snapshots McColl recalls the time when his mate wanted them both to join the forces together. That idea never meant anywhere near so much to him as it did to the other – all that marching and saluting. No, if he was looking for anything, and he probably was, it was something else entirely. And, anyway, why would he do one thing just because someone else was doing it? No, he carries with him still the idea that he walks his own way and that when the paths divide he waves people goodbye.

But today – *semi-final day* – they are reunited, they are there together deep in the mix of the red and the blue, there amid the booze and the wisecracks, swapping opinions as to who will crack open the Reds' defence, a fissure through with they will glimpse the final, the twin towers of Wembley Stadium. McColl reckons it will be Magic McKenzie, that free spirit in blue. Some don't rate McKenzie, say he's a maverick, an individualist. But for Ginger McColl he's an original, a rarity, who refuses to be locked into any system. He might not be a tireless Alan Ball or an angelic Alex Young but on his day he is a magician who can bamboozle the opposition with his cute thinking and tricky footwork, and he surely will be the one to rise to this massive occasion.

Solid John disagrees. John Sanger is a team man, he is growing into his chosen position as a military engineer and next to high workmanship he rates teamwork. For him McKenzie is a poser, a fancy Dan, and such a type, he insists, cannot be relied upon to turn up and shoulder the collective burden when he is needed.

McColl objects: it is exactly on occasions like this that the magicians of football show their worth.

Around them the high noise subsides to a moody rumble as the tale goes around of how a pair of scoundrels, red or blue, a mix of both maybe, nobody is sure, have snatched the takings at the entrance to the club and dashed off into the cover of the crowd outside – a commonplace kind of caper for some maybe but especially shameful here where a foreign club has opened its doors to them. John Sanger shakes his head while muttering of the embarrassment, the disgrace. He shares his dismay with two men on the next table. Suddenly the three stand and stride to the bar. They return with an empty beer glasses. 'Throw something in there, lad,' John Sanger says to his mate as he reaches in his own pocket. 'Let's see if we can't replace what those toerags have robbed.'

When they've both dropped a note into the glass he moves to other tables – as do the other two men: a pair of Reds. John Sanger's presence, his tone, is persuasive. Every man he approaches puts his hand in his pocket. Is this a step out of character? It doesn't surprise the lad he's with. The young professional soldier does it utterly naturally, without fuss or show, and sets such a striking example that McColl finds himself grabbing another empty glass and joining him.

After completing a full circuit the four collectors have full glasses. And by the time they've tipped out all the coins and notes, and added them up, and handed over to the Manchester men on the door more than was stolen from them, it's almost time to make a move. And while they drink up one last pint McColl says that maybe this is the time for them to beat the Reds again, that he's got a feeling they will, it's a buzz, a tingle, he can feel it in his bones, his balls.

'I hope so, lad. I want something good to take back with me.' Sanger hasn't come all the way from Germany to watch a shower of redsnouts shove his team aside as they head for Wembley. 'Anyway, come on, get that ale down you. Let's go.'

So they push through the clicking turnstile and climb the high terrace. They clap and they chant up there amid the blue and white throng; they sing the battle hymns up there where you feel the power of the mass, its huge body and surging voice, and you realize, if you didn't already know, that this is the kind of day that separates the game of football from all others.

But this will be a day when they share with many others disappointment, disbelief, a distinct feeling of having been cheated by a dodgy decision from that damned referee, Mr Clive Thomas. For much as Magic McKenzie does to give them tickets to the FA Cup Final, and he does a very great deal, scoring one goal, creating a second, and also playing his part in the third that is so unjustly disallowed, he cannot correct a bad ruling by the man with the whistle.

But McColl at least has, at the end of it all, a scrap of consolation that he might wave around. He'd put his faith in that dazzling individualist McKenzie, and that man, unlike the referee, did not disappoint. Like one occasion when, through speed of thought and quickness of feet, he stuck the ball in the net and left the Reds' goalkeeper on his knees in the mud nagging his defenders like Old Mother Hubbard the day she lost her pension book and found mouseshit in the frying pan. With his feints and flicks, his combination of vision and precise passing, his willingness to take the game to the opposition in the Manchester mud, McKenzie did more than anyone in royal blue to try to snatch that elusive victory from the old enemy. That he did not succeed is something for which only one man can be blamed.

'I was right about McKenzie then,' McColl proclaims as the pair move away from the Stadium of Disappointment. 'Best player in a blue shirt.'

His solid mate turns and stares at him. 'Ohh, spare us, please!' There's a buzz in his voice as his words swarm at the other. 'Well done with the pre*diction*, lad! You're wasted out there on them terraces! You know that? You should be sitting in a television studio!'

McColl's eyes dart, they hit the spot, the bullseye, and hold there.

Like that pesky wasp at a picnic, something has intruded here, and somebody, if they're not careful at this little reunion, might get stung.

Solid John Sanger waves that invasive insect away.

'Tell you what, lad: Why don't we just forget your maverick man and that damned referee,' the sturdy one says, raising his big fist, 'because if he walked past here now, that bastard ref, I'd give him that. I would. For what he's just done to us. I would. So why don't we just forget them both for a while and go find somewhere that does a decent pint.'

'Just the one?'

'You planning on getting drunk then?'

'Not drunk, nah…very drunk.'

'Now that does sound like a plan: a fitting end to a day like this.'

7

D–Day 1994

Deputy Head Steward Mark McColl stands in his big yellow jacket watching the ground fill up with those who could possibly be facing the most dreadful day of their lives.

The Day of Destiny – yeah, another one.

And the Crazy Gang of Wimbledon is in town. So it's beat them or be relegated. And you couldn't face more difficult, more awkward, more combative opponents than these who are, in addition to their notorious peskiness, it is said, on a large bonus to send Everton down. Yep, once again, it seems, there are those about the country as well as the city of Liverpool who would delight in seeing Everton Football Club dumped out of the big time.

But the faithful are there as ever. The ground is full and many are locked outside. The thousands within are a constant chorus of encouragement. In this coliseum of football they will play their part. But within twenty minutes they begin to sense that rather than attending the theatre of high drama they are down at the circus. The clowns in blue are tossing goals away like slapstick jugglers. Two down and tumbling into tragi-comedy, the clowns for sure seem doomed. But a goal from the penalty spot pops into the script. Is that the line by which they might haul themselves back from the edge? Hope, a small one, reappears in bright costume, but those peering into the shadows on this judgement day will still see a sinister figure lurking.

At the interval a worried murmuring pervades the place as the many shuffle towards the teabars.

McColl, surveying the crowd from the gangway, spots a familiar face, but bearded now: the solid lad, become now the solid man. Hasn't seen him for years, not since the wedding when John Sanger wed that one girl he was always going to marry – loyal as a man as he was as a lad. But it wasn't difficult to lose touch, not with one stationed abroad much of the time, and the other out of the city to study landscaping and then settling over the water for a while with his own new wife, his now ex-wife.

McColl makes his way along the gangway. 'Alright, lad!'

John Sanger: the surprised man. After the big handshake he pokes at the big yellow jacket. 'Never thought I'd see you in a uniform.' His finger moves up to the deputy's badge. 'Officer too. Now that is a surprise.'

'It was offered,' says the former fence jumper and street fighter. 'So I accepted.'

'Less work next season for you then. Smaller crowds if we drop out the big league. Unless something dramatic happens in the second half – and we score a couple of goals.'

'It'd better happen.' The alternative doesn't bear thinking about. So McColl changes the subject. 'How long you home for?'

'Permanent. Finished in the army a couple of years ago.'

McColl studies him, 'Was that a hard decision or..?'

'Had to be made. Family reasons. Living over Mossley Hill way now. Got a job on maintenance, working in different places.'

'I heard you had a kid.'

'Two, couple of lads. But one is…he's erm…not erm…wheelchair. He's not stuck in it, but his legs don't work properly. Needs help to get around sometimes. That's why I gave up soldiering. Mary couldn't cope with me away a lot of the time. She managed for a few years, but then it became too much for her, so…So here I am.'

Is there something a little bit shrunk about him? Is it his facial expression or maybe the way he holds his substantial body? Around the black beard, that seems to be concealing a scar across his cheek, he's still got the remnants of a tan and, despite that old facial wound, looks healthy enough. But has having to give up his profession, his calling, whacked him hard in the guts, or is it perhaps just the years, those years past the age of thirty, that have begun to weigh on him? The life he wanted, the life he chose, a life in uniform, doing his duty, shouldering the nation's burden, is behind him now. Being a professional footballer was mere dream, but soldiering, the comradeship, that shared sense of playing your individual part while giving each other support: that was real. As was the ocean going yacht, *Britannia Princess*, in which he held a share, along with a bunch of marines and soldiers; a vessel on which, over the years, he voyaged out across the Mediterranean, the Atlantic and the Pacific, even into the Indian Ocean, and on one occasion, after flying out to Australia to join the boat, the South China Sea. Oh, what days they were: shipping out for the seaports of the world on a long leave. And all they are for him now is the fabric of memory: all those places he visited, in uniform and out, are names he will chant to himself or anyone who'll listen. They are scraps he will carry through his old age. For he'll never go back to his unit now, he'll never go back on the high seas. His uniform is hung up now, his share in *Britannia Princess* sold on. He has stood on deck, out there in the middle of the Pacific, gazing into the water with a pain in his gut as he tries to digest the hard fact that this is his last voyage, that his sailing days like his soldiering days will soon be over, that he has no choice now but to go home for good.

He says, 'I promised Mary right from the start that if she ever needed me to be there that I would be. So here I am.'

McColl says, 'You've made a big sacrifice there, John lad, and people will respect you for it.'

Sanger considers that for a moment. 'I could have stayed in uniform as long as the army wanted me – and they did want me, they had me lined up as an instructor. But if that lad of mine needs me to be there day and night and if his mother needs me to be there to help her cope then that's it, that's the end of other things for me.' Punters walk past in both directions but nothing is going to interrupt his flow. 'But I had a good run, though. I've been all over the world, far more places than most manage. I was where I wanted to be the best years of my life. And they were good years too,' and then he adds, 'mostly.' And after a distant moment he goes on, 'But that's all finished now. So I've been watching regular football again. Picked the wrong season, unfortunately. I'm usually across the other side, using a season ticket borrowed from a mate who's been in Oz for six months. But he's come back for this one – a game he couldn't miss. I was lucky to get a ticket for in here. If you can call watching this shambles lucky.'

There's a pause. They stand looking at ground staff out on the pitch replacing divots, stamping them down.

McColl says, 'I could fix you up here if you want to work on matchdays.'

'Me in a yellow jacket?' John Sanger is trying to see the picture.

'You'd be good at it. If they could find a jacket wide enough.'

A big yellow jacket? That he might zip himself up in it and truly feel that he has found a new life. 'I wouldn't mind having a go.'

'I'll put in a word for you as soon as the right ear comes along.' And it's as if he sees the other man growing back to his full size, beginning to look like the Solid John of old, his whole body filled with muscle and confidence: that lad who was the rock-like centre back who held the rearguard together in front of the goalie, the youth who returned from his first trips abroad talking as if the whole world now was his.

'Just hope we're still in the top division when you put on that yellow jacket,' says McColl as he takes a step away to resume his duties.

'We better be,' says Sanger, as if he might exact retribution from those who fail him.

But they don't fail him. The Blues come out for the second half and push, push hard, to topple the wall between themselves and survival; to stand, at the final whistle, victorious on the rubble of a season. But the telling strike, the one that makes the breach in that wall, is in truth a weak one: a poke, a toe-jab at the ball, that somehow fools the goalie and delights the faithful. A fitting end to an underwhelming campaign. Yet a powerful enough shot to destroy all doubt and trigger a joyful pandemonium, a rapturous lunacy – as if men are trying to shake off their arms or burst open the earth beneath their feet, or to swing a contemptuous punch at some invisible fiend who has been fiddling with their fate. And when the game is over they quite naturally surge on to the pitch. Who could stop them? Certainly not Deputy McColl who seeks out his old mate to tell him, 'I'll let you know about the jacket, I'll be in touch.'

Part Three

8

New Year, Old Story

This is the present, the now of January 30th nineteen ninety-nine – the beginning of the end of a century, a century in which Everton Football Club has achieved much of which to be proud, yet known also times that are best forgotten – if only present circumstances would allow that: nineteen thirty, relegated but promoted back up the following season; nineteen fifty-one relegated until they returned after three seasons; nineteen ninety-four, avoided relegation by two points; nineteen ninety-eight, avoided relegation on goal difference. And now here they are in fifteenth place looking down once again at the old demons.

Deputy McColl stands in the gangway with the crowd mostly settled in anticipation of kick off. And he reckons we can win this game – or rather, that we'd better win it. We're up against the Foresters this afternoon, and if we can't defeat them then who can we beat? Nottingham Forest are way down in the pit of the division where they've been all season and where they've damned well deserved to be – that hard stony bottom where the rats of relegation lurk, creeping through the darkness and the dead leaves of the season to gnaw on your boots and your bones and yeah, your balls.

But a win will keep us clear of those dark depths. So even if the sun isn't going to shine on Goodison today that victory, and three sparkling new points, will bring a little brightness to the place. Big silent gulls, however, gather on the roof of the stand opposite. The scavengers are beginning to mass. The doom birds are back, immobile against the darkening blue of the sky, casting their cold eyes over our green turf. And our future?

A bad omen? Before the game kicked off McColl would have dismissed such nonsense talk. But as the ball is shunted up a deadend yet again he hears from the crowd the first grumbles of the day. A wet rag has already fallen over the flames of expectation.

And as that sense of dampness and chill becomes more insistent the grumbles grow louder, turn to scolding and cursing.

The Ginger Scholar's feelings have to be kept hidden inside the yellow jacket. So he does not lambast the players like so many around him are now doing, he does not offer simple advice tinged with abuse, he does not curse and castigate and cajole – much as he might feel like joining in; for most moves break down before they get going, and those that do reach the penalty box end in shots that are well wide of the goal's white woodwork. But the mountain that daunts and frustrates those boys in blue is a mere sandhill – they won't be given a less demanding task than this all season.

The players do *try* to put on a performance. It's not that they lack effort – they have the strength and they have the stamina – it is guile and self-belief they are in need of. In their clumsy determination they bump into each other, run the wrong way, try to give what will never be received.

Figures in the crowd that surrounds them are beginning to wear the expressions of grass-eaters who are catching a whiff of lion in the wind. And the predator here is a big dark rebellious Dutchman in a red shirt. When the ball drops he fires a range-finder that's not so far off-target. We have to get tight on him, cut off his supply and hustle him beyond the fringe of danger – or pay the full toll.

Our Italian centre back, Signor Marco Materazzi, gliding out of defence as if he has olive oil on his boots, releases a missile that has the Forest goalkeeper groping and flapping – and the crowd applauding, doing the big handclaps of hope and renewed belief. But the Foresters have picked up the loose end of this Everton attack and their wideman has taken a firm grip on it. He's away down the flank unhindered by anything that might resemble organized defending. Space and time? He's got as much as he could ever wish for. So he delivers the ball once again at the feet of the big Dutchman who once again – what? WHAT?! – nobody has bothered to mark.

Wham!

Unstoppable. The net is shocked by such power: it bulges, trembles, sags. Nil-one. And the majority must now endure the celebratory antics of the red-shirted riffraff from the dregs of the division as they go wheeling and waltzing, as this bunch of no-hopers pose like prima donnas. But averting their gaze from such galling capers they are seeing perhaps the spectres that lurk in those dark places beyond the grass.

Here is a mass silence, people shrinking into silent incomprehension – until anger punches its way out of the shock zone. How could these players have let this happen? As the tongues begin to lash them those who wear blue out on the pitch are left in no doubt as to what they must now do. Although, there are those among the spectators who accept, as always, that it is their duty not to chastise but to encourage. A punter springs up in his seat and flings his voice far. And then another, still seated, flexing his elbows, hurling his palms together, sets off a chant. The faithful try, as ever, to rouse the players to some kind of effective and telling response. But no, somehow you can sense that it's going to be one of those days. As the big songy chant shrinks to a mumble – the crowd is no better at getting things together than the players today – McColl notices a man standing in the gangway further along. That man is a foreign body in a space that should be vacant. Spectators cannot watch the game from aisles or gangways, all emergency exits must be kept clear at all times – the Scholar's training has told him this because that's what the ground's safety certificate says and without that certificate there can be no events here. It's the kind of regulation that annoys punters, maybe, but it is very simple and very clear and it has to be enforced. And the jacket on his back means McColl is the one who has to enforce it.

So, looking purposeful in case of resistance, he moves towards the standing figure. The man is burly, but his brown hair is thinning and fading and his flesh is pale. He's fortyish maybe, but he looks as if the years weigh on him: the creases in his forehead; that bellybulge and the birth-signs of a second chin. He wears a faded jacket to match his jeans; his shirt also is blue, a slightly washed-out blue. McColl notes the sad and somewhat pained expression on that pale and rather damp-looking face. But what's new or special? The Blues have just let the worst team in the division stick a goal past them. There's plenty of sadness and, yeah, pain around the place.

When McColl gives him the message that he must return to his seat the man looks at him in a kind of puzzled way and then back at the pitch, but shows no signs of moving. No indication of defiance, though. Rather, this man seems somehow bewildered, distracted. A tricky little task, perhaps, for the one in yellow.

Out on the grass the team's response to going behind is a frantic form of fragmentation, passing the ball into spaces where they have no players, shooting when there is no gap through which for the ball might pass. And through the gaps in this team you cannot now help but view the future with alarm.

McColl places his elbow on the rail at the back of the seats and lounges a little, so that he seems unthreatening. He looks into the eyes of this man and sees a haunted space, one that becomes a place where some mental earthquake is occurring; for this man is beginning, ever so slightly, to shake.

McColl shifts his hand on to the man's shoulder and lets a little of his own reassuring bodyweight steady him, so that whatever demons he is staring at might begin to withdraw. When the words fail what else is there?

But quite suddenly the man will speak, 'Everything I do turns out wrong. So every time they let in a goal I feel like it's my fault.' He speaks in a kind of half voice that turns his words into sighs.

You put on that yellow jacket and then you just do not know what manner of human frailty you will be called upon to deal with. McColl tells him, 'You can't blame yourself for what's happening out there, lad. The finger should be pointed at somebody but that certainly isn't you.'

Out of the blue comes a surprise: a whizzbang of a shot that near blows the goalie's fingers off. The Blues aren't dead yet, not quite. But this trembling man fears the worst. 'I'm gonna faint or die or somethin. If this goes on I'll jump off a buildin someday soon.'

'It's a Cup game next week, mate,' McColl tells him. 'You could end up missing a trip to Wembley.'

'This team at Wembley?' Contempt rouses this man. 'No chance, norra chance.'

What has this man's life been? An endlessly twisting path that leads into the ever darkening woods? You do not look after thousands of spectators season after season without learning something about the vulnerability of humankind. So McColl will keep on talking to give this man a chance of finding some kind of equilibrium. And gradually, he senses, the man is calming. As if the tremors have ceased and those demons that haunt have at least partially withdrawn.

'I can't sit in this crowd today,' says the man, 'in case they think it's my fault.' He sidesteps away, looking towards the exit.

'Nobody thinks it's your fault.' McColl must reach out once more and touch. 'Just stand back a bit, so you're not so obvious, and watch from here where you've got space around you. If anyone says anything tell them the deputy said it's okay. And whatever you do don't ever think that what happens on that pitch is your fault.'

Sometimes, McColl reckons, the only thing you can do with a rule is bend it. So he leaves the man standing in the forbidden space with whatever peace is available to him.

But what is really happening here? Are these people being punished for something or in the Grand Casino that is football is it just that the present dealer has placed before them a very poor hand? For there are those here who have seen Everton as the power and the glory, the force that could not be stopped. They have felt their entire bodies tingle as the team wove beautiful patterns out there on the green stuff. They have witnessed to rising of the Golden Vision as Alex Young glanced another one into the net. They have seen Alan Ball launching the showboat, piloting that sleek and speedy craft that was the great side of the late Sixties. And twenty years later they saw Sharpe and Gray demolish teams, leaving the rubble of defences in the goalmouth as they wheeled away, their arms aloft. They have watched Kevin Sheedy pass that ball so sweetly that he must have dipped that left foot in icing sugar before he pulled on his sock and his boot. They have seen Peter Reid, the man who would never hide, stand with arm raised and call for the ball again and again, and then go darting towards the penalty box like a pig that's spotted a fruit shop door left open – and in doing so inspire those around him to rise to the heights. They have seen the glory – grace mixed with power and sublime invention – both here and elsewhere. They have roared their defiance and sung their own anthems and raised their glasses as they lit up the night streets with the glow of their victories and still been there to watch the sun rise on their celebrations as new chapters were being written in the Great Blue History Book. And they have, as is obvious and natural, paid plenty of visits to the Vale of Frustrations and the Valley of Defeat, but rarely, very rarely, have they seen a shambles such as this.

It is as if there is a force acting on the club now, sucking it downwards towards some pit full of darkness and gunge. So those who can affect its fate need to get a grip on something solid and they need to do it quickly. All the old fears return. A shape that the faithful can hardly bear to look at comes sneaking over the horizon and squats there. Memories of the bad times flash back: all those nervy end-of-season games – too many, far too many. Is this to be another grim chapter from that story? Are all these fans to be exposed to the chill wind they have felt too often on their necks in recent seasons; they who have learned the art of suffering together? One man in the third row holds his head in his hands. And all the rest of the people? It's as if you can hear a long and very deep collective sigh.

Out on the pitch the ineptitude is continued. On the terraces the sigh becomes again a grumbly discontent which turns into disgust and begins to build, to swell until it bursts: Boooo!!

These thousands and thousands of patient sufferers boo with such zeal, such unity, such collective passion. Here is frustration, anger, hurt as the multitudes in blue give vent to what has been building up for months. McColl gazes about him, he has never heard a crowd in the old stadium of myths and legends boo their own players like this. Boooo-oooo-oooo!!!

As he moves down the gangway Solid John Sanger inclines his own look of disgust towards him, almost growls, 'How can you lose to these: a team of dogs – hounds!?'

The broad man, big shoulders twitching, is set to sing an angry song. But McColl will aspire to objectivity, 'The most dangerous forward on show scored the goal. And that centre back of theirs, that Carlton Palmer, has been the best player on the pitch.'

'Him?!' John Sanger is, predictably perhaps, not impressed. 'Second Division player! Always has been. And that's what he'll definitely be before long.'

But McColl will insist on truth, 'He's very sharp for a big man, today he is: sees things coming, gets them long legs out there and clears the danger.'

Sanger continues in denial. But McColl is persistent also, 'We've got nothing past him all afternoon. Nothing. Tell me one occasion when we've got past him.'

McColl thinks he's shut the sturdy man up but as he walks away he hears him say to Archie Block, 'That Palmer, he's like some spooky African...'

But the renewed booing drowns out this angry voice. So many rounded lips and up-tilted noses – Boooo!!! Have so many people ever said so much with one single prolonged vowel? It's like the first note of a grand opera called *Derision,* one long seemingly-endless vowel of contempt. Delivered with such intensity and brought to such a resounding crescendo, it is a sound that comes from deep down, the darkness within, where the effects of so many past hurts have lodged. Boooo-oooo-oooo!!!

The final whistle. The Blues 0. A bunch of no-hopers 1.

Boooo-oooo-oooo!!!

The joys of the beautiful game. But it's over now. The players flee the scene, exit the stage on which they have performed a show whose central theme was *failure* as the crowd, upstanding now, turn their backs, begin to push and press, anxious to put this flop of an afternoon behind them.

McColl observes, as he is required to, the muted exit – the long slow grumbly shuffle down the aisles and gangways to the gates that will open on the ordinary day these masses left behind when they entered this old stadium that has been the setting for such glorious and rousing footballing events. Subdued and discontented, they will disperse, spread through the city, back to the everyday cushions of home, the pots of tea and the distracting dramas on the screen, the pints of anaesthetic brew in the Blue House or the Winslow or The Brick or the Dark House, or some local in the centre or the suburbs.

Those in yellow jackets must remain at their posts until the whole disgruntled crowd is gone, gone back to lives whose gloomiest corners will most definitely not be illuminated by the events they have witnessed. And the weight of this defeat will have to be borne through at least half the coming week.

If life sometimes turns into a soap opera, the season so far is not so much a story about lack of desire or failure of will as a tale of ineptitude told without invention or inspiration. But with what climax, what conclusion?

The Blues are not in trouble yet, but they're not too far away from it. So something is going to have to change very soon or those scavenging birds that gather on the tops of the stands will be picking at the bones of a fallen giant.

9

The Workaday Week

The weight of defeat begins to ease as other concerns reassert themselves. Mark McColl must earn his coin, his daily bread. And in doing so finds himself pleasantly distracted by this woman whose garden he's been working on.

Ms Natasha Molyneaux's house is up in the leafy far North End of the city and McColl has been wrestling with the overgrown shrubs she inherited when she moved in. It's a muscle and sweat job, ripping out the thick roots, to make space, to allow light through her windows. But eventually he wins the contest. How could he not with such an attractive dame watching him?

'That's why I put in all those hours in the office, so that I can pay someone else to do these jobs,' she tells him in a voice that not only sounds cultured but which also combines, for him, warmth with seductiveness.

What does she get up to in her free time, Ms Natasha Molyneaux? Karen McMullin, who McColl has been seeing for the past year and a half is away visiting her sister and his mind is wandering. He can't help wondering about Ms Molyneaux. In this line of work he's used to peeking into other people's places, other people's lives. And this work doesn't make him miserable. It seems to him not a bad way to earn your coin. He's out in the air. He knows the seasons, the habits of birds. He breathes the rich and natural odours. And he meets people.

'I'm not sure about that one either,' says Ms Natasha pointing her painted finger nail at another large shrub.

'The forsythia? It'll look glorious in a few weeks when those buds flower,' he tells this one who already, without her gladrags, looks pretty splendid.

'You don't think that's too big?'

'Looks fine to me.'

'I'll give it another year and then decide. Maybe call you back.'

And he would so willingly come. She, like her forsythia bush, has a kind of mature attraction, nothing woody and straggly, nothing shapeless about her. She stands framed by the French doors and he could look at her for a long time. For she's a modern classic: slim but not skinny; straight, sheeny hair; finely-sculpted features: a nose and mouth crafted by some Florentine, some contemporary of Michelangelo. She's so naturally attractive that she probably doesn't need to bother. And in addition she's quick and learned and apparently successful in her career. But there's nothing showy about her. She wears that black hair long and simple. She's neat but unfussy in her dress. And she seems so busy, so connected, so full up with life. She's a bright, pleasant, and rather alluring woman, no longer young, in a comfortable set-up, who maybe hasn't yet settled for what she's got. And maybe what she hasn't got is a man. And maybe Mark McColl could be that man. Ha!

The working man's daydream. Okay. But sometimes you never know.

What he would, oh so dearly, love to do is lie in her bed and introduce Ms Natasha Molyneaux to the joys of the beautiful game: the perfect pass, the nutmeg, the quick one-two.

But if he can't consider her as available there must be another who is. After the problem of Karen has been sorted out, of course.

It's starting to feel that Karen McMullin is his biggest critic. And throughout his life he has not been short of them. And his usual response has been to walk away.

But there is work to be done here, and when that is complete he says goodbye to Ms Natasha Molyneaux and takes his daydreams and frustrations away with him. And there are distractions to look forward to. There is the next match. There is always the next game to look forward to. Sunday. Away to Derby County. And it's on TV. A few pints in the Albert and maybe an away win to watch. But before that he's got other work to do.

So it's Friday – one of those days when the wind and the sun and the greyness are all mixed up – and he's spent the best part of it laying a garden path and now he's heading south through the city, picking the team for Sunday as he drives. When he's almost home he realizes he's out of bread so he pulls up outside Ali's Bazaar. The corner shop has a small queue. There's a woman in front who

Ali is serving while behind her are three lads getting rather loud with adolescent stupidity. Behind them, and in front of McColl, stands another man.

McColl picks up a small granary loaf and then wonders about buying a newspaper. There's a Times and a Guardian left. It makes him grin how the lads at Goodison call him The Scholar because of what he reads and the way he talks. It's intended to be derogatory. But, apart from the short landscaping course he attended, he had no more formal education than they did so he takes it as a skew-whiff complement. So, to buy or not to buy? Some days now it feels as if he's read it all before. The location, the toll, the government line – details change but the storyline seems ever more familiar. There is an ongoing squabble in Parliament, the great icecaps are cracking up as the world boils, some revolution has finished by turning on its own people, there is an unstoppable movement taking place of countless refugees looking for a haven in which to begin again… Odd days he feels that same small excitement he experienced as a kid when he'd come down in the morning and see the paper on the mat and sense that it was full of stuff he didn't know, that it was a big mixed bag of subjects from which he would pick what was new and surprising and informative. Naturally the football page was where he always started – was there any breaking news on the Blues: had we made a surprise swoop in the transfer market overnight?

As he decides against a newspaper the loudness from these lads is becoming something more than irritating noise. You can see at a glance that they're loose-end kids, the perennially bored and frustrated, lads who pass many hours lurking and loitering, stagnating already, their young lives becoming ever more stale, growing mouldy, turning rancid. They are getting louder and more obnoxious and it's becoming one of those unpleasant, unpredictable situations. Ali, a man who needs to make a living, acts as if he doesn't hear and goes about his business. Okay, they're just local surly boys with their identical cropheads and footwear, their immature shoulders and curling lips, playing that adolescent game of provocation and reaction, so do you blank them totally and deny them the attention they seek, or what?

The man before him – he must be roughly the same age, and at a glance he seems just like any other unremarkable fella you'd pass in the street or see in a shop – jerks his head back and McColl senses a certain toughening in his stance.

One of the lads grabs a tin of dogfood from the shelf and sends it sliding along the counter towards Ali saying, 'Here's your dinner…'

Adolescent laughter bubbles up. And then here is the man's voice surprising them, the rowdies, surprising everyone maybe, his words clear and precise, 'That's enougha that!' His eyes shift from one youth to another as they turn in surprise. He shakes his head, 'Nobody wants this sort of nonsense around here.' His voice is local, clear but heavily accented. He doesn't carry a huge amount of physical bulk, but he does have a certain solidity about him.

The woman at the counter turns, nods agreement to what he has said. So, McColl wonders, is he going to be drawn into this now? There are so many reasons for not wanting to be: he's had a long day of muscle-work and is now in a mood to rest; he only came in for a loaf, not a scene from some inner city drama. Nevertheless he steps forward, stands at the side of the man who has spoken, and shifts his eyes across three adolescent faces now shaped by puzzlement, letting the provocateurs know that now they face stronger opposition. 'What this man says is correct,' he tells them.

But he is ignored. 'Oo are you?' one of them demands of the man who spoke up.

The lad doesn't wait long to find out. 'Am the person oos tellin you to leave this shop if you can't behave yerselves.' And it's as if he draws some powerful chemical from the air deep into his lungs. For he wears no badge, no protective uniform, he has no document of status to hold them back, he offers nothing to deter an attack, only the resolution of his bearing, the steadiness of his gaze.

As their eyes shift from him to the others and then back again the malcontents make a calculation. Four witnesses to whatever happens now. These sums are wrong for them.

They shuffle their feet, looking for the most solid ground from which to retort. They don't seem to find it. Rather surprisingly, but giving those who watch them some very fierce looks, they shift towards the door. As they file out one of the youths, hands in pockets, elbows wide, deliberately bumps a rack and sends a couple of tins tumbling.

But fallen objects are mere props in this scene.

When they are all out one lad turns and aims an upraised finger at the man who was most vocal. 'Yoo ain't seena last of uz.'

The man says nothing. He has said all he needs to say.

'Weell find out where ya live,' another lad warns him, speaking like an apprentice gangster who'll never make the grade, but like one who intends to do some damage on his way to nowhere.

Will this man be a target now for some underhand plot, or was that threat just bluster and swagger? If there is concern about that it is not evident. He stands his ground watching them leave. And when they are gone he steps towards the rack and stoops to pick up the tumbled objects while giving no sign that he has just done something not at all ordinary for a man who went out to do a bit of shopping. Does this man, perhaps, surprise himself sometimes?

'Clowns,' is all he says, and the four in the shop share a small laugh, as if they have indeed just watched some circus routine that went a bit wrong – when they know very well that they haven't.

You walk into a place looking for a loaf of bread and then what? Boom. A small urban explosion. Nothing too melodramatic, no shock appearance by gangsters or other terror-merchants, but it might be one of those experiences which reverberates down the long corridors of the mind. And thus it will be for the Ginger Scholar: Deputy Mark McColl.

It's still there in his thoughts when he heads for the Albert on Sunday afternoon. In the bar he bumps into Woody Woodburn, an old face from way back in the Street End. In those days when he was a travelling Blue he would bump into Woody Woodburn in Birmingham, Manchester, London. West Ham: he recalls one Saturday afternoon when side by side amid the travelling Blues they had to battle their way along Green Street and away from Upton Park; for there were times back then when that was the only way home. Oh, aye, there were some battles in them days: Chelsea, Arsenal, but especially West Ham.

Yes McColl has been there in his day, down in the wild places where the heavy crews lurk and ambush. Once he followed the Blues everywhere. He was always going somewhere, coming back, about to set off. Out on the road, sometimes alone, he soon learned that *The Traveller's Story* was not a tale littered with corpses but that there would be scary moments when it paid to have your wits about you and to be able to look after yourself. And sometimes, for sure, after the game Trouble would come looking. You'd find yourself surrounded. You'd be stood there facing a mob that had its heart set on crucifying a Scouser: they'd fetched the hammer and nails with them, and if they couldn't manage to cobble a cross together any tall gate would do. What else could you do but fight your way out? You carried your bruises home with you, and of necessity you left a few behind. Maybe you even brought back stitches if you hadn't been quick enough on your toes. Or maybe like the young McColl you brought home a blue shirt stained with your own blood, for that nose of his only needed a single bang before it began to leak the red stuff.

But it never seemed to be an issue of large importance. He'd had the odd scrap in the schoolyard or the park or some alleyway, and plenty of smouldering niggly feuds on Sunday League football pitches. He was no urban warrior but he wasn't a saint either. He was certainly no disciple of a philosophy of meekness. No kid in a claret scarf or a black and white one or a red one was going to use his arse as a doormat if I could help it. If a tussle started, then so be it. If it happened, it happened. If Trouble passed him by that was fine. He would never be out scouting for it. Others, he was aware, were constructing narratives that would nourish or shame them for the rest of their lives. He knew of those crews, he knew some of those lads: Apaches of the north, scalp-takers, bare-knuckle scrappers, ambushers extraordinaire, the royal blue irregulars of Dingle Vale and Lee Park and Everton Valley, ever planning new strategies for engagement on their own ruthless terms, ever putting together new myths of the ruck: how the dim Geordies came on, came on into the trap; how the young Cockneys were lured into the blue valley of their greatest defeat where no prisoners were taken, not a single one.

For the rest who were recruited by no militia, no band of irregulars, it was just a hazard you viewed as part of the everyday world. Wounds heal; bruises, cuts, black eyes: they come, they go. At that age life is a fast flowing river. Lads like Ginger McColl were not disposed to meditate, to philosophize and moralize. You had to survive, and that's what you did, up north, down south, wherever.

And West Ham was always a place where you had to be geared up for survival. You were on foreign territory and you were well outnumbered and the only protection you were likely to get down in the badlands of the Smoke was what you gave yourself.

Back in the day, yeh. When we were young. When we were young and reckless.

When he's heard enough of Old Times from Woody he moves back to the bar and sees Sammy Arnold standing there stiff-backed, hands in denim pockets, staring deep into his glass – at a preview of the game perhaps. From the expression on his face the Blues aren't winning.

McColl waves a banknote at the barman. When Sammy looks up he asks, 'You hear any news about your job?'

'The worst. They're movin out East. And if you're not makin anythin here you don't need machines and if you don't have machines you don't need men to look after them…'

McColl has heard all this before. The late Seventies, the Eighties: he's familiar with the crash and clatter of old industries collapsing. What can you do but listen? As a bookman he has spent time with Charles Darwin, he knows that there is a constant struggle going on, that no living thing has a fixed or permanent place, that nothing is guaranteed, that something is changing, always there is change, movement, a critical shift. Maybe it is ourselves who change, maybe the place we are in, but he knows that in the struggle that has gone on since a bolt of lightning first sparked the earth's chemical stew into life that there has been a struggle for survival going on in which those who cannot or will not adapt are doomed to extinction.

'So it looks like it's come down to a choice,' Sammy goes on. 'What do I need more: work or the Blues? I have to use me hands. I have to be doin somethin. So if the work's gone I'll have to go too. I've got family out in Oz, Adelaide, who could fix me up with work.'

Adelaide? He hasn't missed a match for the last thirty years. And he's only thirty seven.

'Emigrate?' asks McColl. 'When?'

'As soon as the season ends. If I hang on through the summer the new season will kick off and then I'll never get away and then…'

A life without the Blues. Could that be him – the Ginger Scholar of Goodison Park? Others do it. Frank Brigstoke turned his back on football saying it was a con trick that deceived the common man. Now Sammy Arnold is getting set to fly away and leave

Goodison Park behind. Always there is change: so what will be the next?

McColl moves away with his pint to find himself a seat before the screen. And then he watches a match that is best forgotten. The players look awkward and uncomfortable all afternoon and he feels the same watching them. Everton scored their first goal in six hours' play but it still wasn't worth a point.

So, after the game: what now? Have another beer or head straight to Karen's?

A pint of bitter, two, the barroom banter, the crack and the jangle of beery voices – and life seems not so bad after all.

The coin-snaffling bandit winks and blinks like a maniac just inside the door, keeping a pair of the local rascals mesmerised. And the corner crowd beckons. Their noise invites him. Maybe he just won't go to Karen's. A mixed bunch of boozers, drifters, loudmouths, chatterboxes, self-schooled lawyers and alehouse philosophers makes space for him while their squabble goes on. Rob the Rabbit, one of the more wordy ones, asserts, 'Men domesticated horses, and women have been trying to domesticate men ever since.'

And Mike Donovan, who does enjoy playing the mischievous one, must add his tag, 'That's the horses' revenge.'

The ladies aren't taking that in silence. Jean Radford must intervene, 'Civilize, I think, is what we mean here. Women have civilized men, or tried their best.'

And her friend Allison also: 'A thankless task. Like cleaning the bathroom. But someone's got to do it.'

And why should Scholar McColl be left out? 'Another important move we made was to stop following herds of animals and build cities, because without cities there would have been no football grounds.'

Ah, that predictable chorus of female groans. But the Rabbit will not be intimidated, 'Football's where men used to go to get away from being domesticated until women started moving in there, and then the seats were put in and the atmosphere went out the window.'

Voices explode: shrieks and moans as verbal shrapnel is flung through this beery mayhem. So nobody is listening while McColl tries to say that for humans to have taken over the planet from the big beasts was a bit of a triumph of the underdog, a bit of a giant-killing act, because we're slow and vulnerable compared with tigers and big apes, it's a bit like a lower division team winning the FA Cup. And if we had never started hunting bison and other powerful creatures, working in teams to some tactical plan, we would never have invented the great game. We perfected our techniques and brought home the bacon. The next step was warfare. The next was artificial warfare – sport: *football.*

When the ceasefire is declared Sam Rogerson, this old would-be prophet, says he stopped going to Goodison after he was punched in the face during a match there. And Louise Boath says that she went once and was struck by how all the faces around her were twisted and disfigured by anger and rage and hatred.

Sam Rogerson is like a big shambly house covered with an ivy beard: The House of Wisdom, he'd like you to think. But he spills words like some fruit machine its jackpot. He says, 'Wherever there are people there'll be force and aggression, animosity towards others. It's there in sport, maybe under the surface maybe not, but it's there. Everywhere. Always was. We evolved from animals…'

The Catholics and the pacifists are raising their voices at the same time, uniting to trash such a gloomy view, and Scholar McColl, relishing the ruck of argument, would continue to have his say, but Karen calls. It's time to drain the glass and seize the door by the brass handle.

When he arrives at her place they embrace in their usual way and sit and talk in their usual way of everyday matters: her trip to her sisters, anecdotes from his working life – though none which feature Ms Natasha Molyneaux. And then, in the absence of more to say, they make their way to bed where they find familiar positions and release the animal that feeds not on words but on flesh. And then, gorged, they must rest.

They lie there, seem to doze, Karen begins to talk in that quiet bedvoice of hers, he makes occasional sounds like a man who is trying to remember how to hum properly. And then they subside once more into silence. And then she is rolling and reaching, taking her turn in the riding seat, astride him, upright, eyes closed, thrusting, thrusting, taking what pleasure she can, greedy for it, grabbing handfuls of manflesh, stuffing herself, thrusting, female on male, fluid yet hard, thrusting on, on and on and on, desperate almost, to sing at the endpoint, to arrive there and fall back into a world of feathers, to get there, to be there, to know it, and feel it, there, there. There.

That point beyond desire.

But.

But where did the passion go, the real passion, the true passion? For it was most definitely there – once. When did they fall into this sequence of more or less predictable actions – like athletes at a routine event? It isn't unpleasant but neither is it in any sense wonderful – it is, has become, just…what they do.

It happens. And then you realize. That's how it is, how it's been other times with other people.

When they rise for a drink and a break from bedsports they find themselves not in that calm and clear place which they once would visit but in a tangle. She has somehow found her way into what he would call: one of her moods; pouting, glaring, staring sideways at something or other. But this old routine produces from her a hot question, 'What does love mean to you? Do you love anything or anybody? Have you ever really loved anyone?'

Coolly, he sits. Unimpressed with her tone, her look, he says nothing.

But if she has to repeat herself she will, 'I mean, what means anything to you? What really matters to you, eh? Hmm?'

Still he says nothing.

She says, 'Have you ever been really excited about anything? Hmm?' she demands through a mask that some Grand Inquisitor might have loaned her, 'What do you get really excited about? Hmm?'

Does he have to sit meekly and be treated like a freak? By now he's had enough, so he says, 'I'll tell you what got me really excited once.' Why this, he's not sure, for he surely knows that this will provoke her, but the words are in his mouth, 'One night the Blues were losing in a big, big, game against these Germans. Bayern Munich in the Cup Winners' Cup.'

She gives him *that* look. She's got a face on her like a plate of offal, is how he would describe it. But now that he's begun why should he not go on? 'It was the semi final and we were losing at halftime. We had to score goals or we were finished.'

She blanks him now. She finds her wallpaper so much more

attractive. As if that will stop him. But it was her who initiated this little scene and now he is in no hurry to terminate it. He goes on. 'We came out and ripped through them…' But while he speaks he hears his own questions: Have I been coming here too long, and if so when will I do something about it?

His voice continues, 'Three goals we stuck past them. And they were done for. And the ground was throbbing…'

That was some night: real tribal stuff. The drums were beating way, way back down the line. The massed braves in blue roared and stamped and earth trembled beneath them.

Through the words he can see it, feel it, 'The iron and the timber were pulsing with the power of it. It was like no place on earth I've ever been in. It was like – '

'Oh shut up! Shut up your stupid nonsense!'

'As it happens I've finished. We won three-one.'

'When a man gets to your age and that's all he's got to offer then that's sad, that's bloody sad.'

'Maybe. Or maybe not.'

'You're weird,' she says. 'Has anybody ever told you that you are really *weird*?'

'Yes, you have. The week before last.'

But when the years have worn him back to the bone, and the future is a closed door a little way along the passageway, he will, he is sure, remember the big games. He will recall his travels – the desert regions, the rainforest, the old cities – and perhaps even a few high points of a patchy lovelife. But he will also remember those big games and talk of them to whoever will listen. He was there. This was his life. He wouldn't have wished to be anywhere else.

She demands, 'Why can't you just be - '

So he tells her, 'I am what I am Karen. Just like you are. And I can't see that either of us is going to change very much.'

So there they are together – unchanged. The same old Karen and Mark.

And when he stands at the door the following morning, set to go, work on his mind, she says, standing on the doormat but stranded somewhere between a sigh and a smile, 'So will I see you on Friday when I get back from London?'

He pauses. He has to think for a second, does he want to come back here on Friday, does he really want to?

She waits for an answer.

'Okay,' he says, 'Friday.'

But when he arrives back at his own place to change into his work clothes, still wondering whether he regrets not saying to Karen what really needs saying, he finds a letter on the doormat – from the Club. There is a training session for all stewards on Wednesday evening.

10

The Disaster Plan

They are gathered inside a silent Goodison Park. But tonight the yellowjackets are dressed as themselves. The surrounding streets, those that on matchdays throng with the thousands, are deserted. The stadium is a dark shell. But the big lounge bar deep inside is fully peopled with club stewards called in for a session entitled: *Dealing with Emergencies – Fire.*

Out front, beside a screen, is a long table. Behind it are men, important men in suits and uniforms, who sit doing the manly chat of important men in suits and uniforms while a microphone is being tested.

At the back of the room, by the door, Archie Block is exchanging quips, some more barbed than others, with those who do not concern us. He's a squarish, thick set, weathered stone of a man with a bristly little moustache. Formerly a tradesman who spent his working life amid the racket of hundreds of shipyard hammers and drills he is himself a loud man on occasion; popular though, with some.

Billy Whizz is stood in a space to the side of the rows of seats laughing at something, yakking and guffawing, for Billy can spiel with the best of them.

John Sanger, that sturdy and righteous man, is seated in the middle of the room speaking with another former soldier about the old days: the places and the people and the problem situations into which they were once pitched.

Mark McColl, the Ginger Scholar, just arrived, sits on the end of a row, on the edge of things, quietly watching and waiting. That so-called know-all, who is said to be never short of an opinion, or two, seems quite comfortable sitting in silence. If his bookishness has taught him nothing else it is to observe the world through unblinkered and, sometimes, amused eyes. Thus he will smile in the face of derision, though not all forms of ignorance.

And then there's Maggie May who is just arriving, exchanging smiles and chitchat as she makes her way to a seat; for after working all over the ground, filling the gaps wherever required, she knows many of the lads here and is by nature easy in company, lively and chatty. Seeing an empty seat next to Mark McColl she says, 'I'll sit here.'

Looking up, his own face brightens, 'Do. Be my guest.'

'Oh, are you going to entertain me?' The flirty girl, it seems, is at it again.

But it's as if he is noticing her for the first time. Entertain Maggie May? 'Well…' he says looking at the figure settling in beside him. But at that moment a figure rises from the line of senior men at the long table out front and calls the meeting to order.

The rumble of voices descends into a mumble which shrivels into silence. Bert Butler, Head of Operations, rises, introduces, for the sake of any new recruits, his important colleagues: Harry Cluny, his personnel man, Bob 'The Builder' Burnside, the stadium manager, and George Gnomes, the man from the council: a thin but influential man who has the power to issue and also to cancel the stadium's safety certificate. On the far left of the table sits Len Knox, the security expert, and on one side of him is Fred Gutteridge, an ex-cop who works in the main office with the head of Liaison, Communications, and something or other. He's got a safety brief, so on matchdays he's the link with the emergency services. On the other side of Knox is a bunch of high-rank cops, stern-looking characters with pretty little decorative bits on the shoulders of their uniforms. At the other end of the table are a senior ambulanceman and Fireman Gee, representing the brigade. For *Fire,* yes, is the topic of the evening. And the big questions are: What do we do in Goodison Park in the event of a major outbreak? What can we learn from previous disasters? And the answers? Well we can start by watching this film.

The lights go out, and immediately everyone sits silent.

On a screen in front a disaster, a very, very real disaster, is being replayed. Nobody speaks, nobody moves, nobody makes a sound. We watch Bradford City's ground begin to burn as the game goes on. The camera focuses on the smoke that drifts easily upward, swaying and slowly turning, a light-footed interloper there to mess about, not interested in watching the match, like one of those kids who crawl in under the turnstile. At this point it could be ejected with relative ease, it is not yet a beast, a monster, that cannot be controlled, but it is swelling, heaving itself up into something bolder, brawnier, something altogether more powerful.

As the smoke thickens the players escape to their dressing rooms and attention turns to the flames that can now be seen like little red fingers waving the fleeing spectators goodbye.

Who's got the key to the gates down below? asks a Bradford voice through old radio crackle, and the seconds are clocked on the bottom of the screen as a fist of flames swells up to seize hold of the stand. And then the question is asked again: Where's the man with the key?

This monstrous thing rises to the roof and spreads, flexing its dark muscles, sending out, underneath the seats, its fingered tentacles, shifting more punters, pushing them away down the stand and over walls on to the pitch.

The Everton stewards sit on, silent, watching it in their still rows, they who must be trained up for their own potential Disaster Day. You could wrap all the Hollywood disaster movies into one and they would not watch that fiction with a fraction of the attention they give to this. It is an old wooden stand that burns before them, similar in some ways to the old stands in Goodison which are decked with chunky timber, arranged with wooden seats. Those figures on the screen could be themselves.

But where was the man with the key, the key that could let people out, allow them to escape the smoke and the flames that pursue them? We don't hear the answer to that while we watch the flames move upward and outward and the seconds trip over into minutes and the minutes double up.

This thing, this powerful and sinister interloper, is revealing its true self now, it is beginning to brag. Its crackling tongue says: I am a thing that cannot be controlled, try me and see. It grabs another row of seats, consumes it, seizes what remains of the roof, sends more people fleeing. But some are dragged back, some are not allowed to escape. And yes, it could be them, *it could be us*, this could be Goodison. Here is the truth of what some ordinary Saturday match might turn into.

But where *was* the man they spoke of, the one with the key? And where, in other football grounds that day, or any other matchday in nineteen eighty-five or the preceding years, would the men with the keys have been? Busy with one of many duties, or what?

When I first worked at Goodison Park in the early Eighties, on the stand where I was based the man with the key to the wicket gate down below would always, when the match kicked off, come up to watch the game. Often he stood at the top of the steps, key in hand, but sometimes, if there was a spare seat nearby he would sit in it. He was a big man, an ageing man, a rather slow man, not where he was supposed to be. If the beast of flames had crept into Goodison on such an occasion would he have got down those steps ahead of a mass of panicked punters? There were other ways out down there, but what if for whatever reason they were blocked, or curtained in toxic smoke, and the only way out was through this man's gate? Would those terrified punters crowding the stairway have been faced like those in Valley Parade by an unmanned and locked gate? But it was not only the big slow man with the key who sat down. I also sat, if there were empty seats, once the game had kicked off. I and the other yellowjackets who worked with me.

But all that changed after Bradford.

In Valley Parade this thing is a beast come out of some old myth that speaks of terror and destruction, loss and despair. And when that beast is almost dead, having quite consumed the main stand, as it is being finally vanquished, as we approach the aftermath I am seeing, on the edge of the scene, this man who wears the red jacket of a steward, some guy like ourselves, standing quite still out on the pitch, his gaze cast down at the grass – as if some explanation might be found in the undamaged green.

Elsewhere the dead are being removed to somewhere more suitable, the injured are being treated, and the plain-clothed cops are waiting to take over, to sift for evidence to feed the legal process, and this man continues to stand alone, as if there is nowhere he might now go, no one with whom he might speak. As if there are no words that can give a shape to, or even begin to get a grip on, what it is that's in his head and in his heart.

This one in the jacket – he could be myself or John Sanger or Mark McColl. And his worst nightmare has come to him at work, here in the ground on a Saturday afternoon. So he stands there now in the middle of it, immobile as a statue: a monument to all of us who are there to look after others – and fail to do so. All his certainties have gone up in flames; that which should not happen to anyone has happened to him. And so he stands. And so he will stand out there until somebody approaches, sends their voice echoing down the long cavern of his skull and calls him back, leads him away to a place in which he might sit down and weep while around him in the corridors, the passageways, there is a muted chorus saying: We should have known, we should have realized, somebody should have cleared all that paper out from underneath the stand, somebody should have seen that one day it would catch fire.

For how could all that litter have been left to lie there, building up, sitting there like some amorphous malevolence that was biding its time, knowing that one day its time would come, that one day it would be tossed a small flame and that when that happened it would be sure to catch it and shove it down into its many pockets made of old bags, newspapers, programmes, and that then it would be up, climbing through gaps to seize its moment, to grab the whole stand and lives it contained?

Why? Why? Because we are what we are. We do not think. We let each other down. We are not there when we are needed.

But now we know.

And here is more for those who serve Everton Football Club to think about. They must imagine a light aircraft crashing into the roof of Section Five, bursting into flames and then bouncing over to the roof of Section Three. Wreckage falls on the fans below. Fire spreads quickly through Section Six. The seats are in the grip of something fearsome as the thousands scramble to dodge that grip.

There are points which we who must aid them have to grasp: we must not flee, must hold our positions; nor must we tackle the blaze. Our priority is to get the people out. We must guide the fans down the normal escape channels, using our master keys if necessary, or on to the pitch, according to instructions or perhaps our own initiative.

I, they, everyone here must remain calm amid the chaos and beware the deadly effects of smoke. We must not touch any personal effects left lying around, we must leave those for the plain-clothed cops who will move in when the fire is out. We must eject the press if they come snooping and get in the way. We must bring the casualties to the concourse where they will be tagged, colour-coded for medics: the dead, the needy, the walking wounded. The church on the corner has been designated as a mortuary. The bars will be set aside for grieving relatives. It has all been worked out now, planned for.

All this they must take in and consider. But what problems lie ahead for them, for Archie Block and John Sanger and Billy Whizz, and the popular Ms Maggie May who sits with Mark 'The Scholar' McColl on the end of that row, what awaits them – a disaster involving fire, or something quite other?

Part Four

11

The Build Up

Maggie May

On my way back up to the ward, heading for the lift, when I get this sudden tingle – the way a thought will suddenly come to you and set things off. It's a Cup game on Saturday. I'm getting glimpses of us on the Glory Road, the way you do. But then the part of me that isn't tingling is saying that we need to show a big improvement if we're going to go very far in that direction.

Nurse Galloway appears, walking next to me, my friend Sarah, 'So are we going out on Friday, then?' she wants to know. Sarah hasn't got a very long concentration span where football's concerned. Show her some Samson of clubland, though, and she's all there, she's taking everything in, she's Delilah in her Friday night frock. Myself, though? I'm not so sure about that any more. I'm really not.

'Yeh, we'll go out,' I say. Well I won't meet anyone sitting at home will I?

When I arrive at the lift Blue George, the security man, appears and as we wait I tell him, 'The trouble is, Everton have been playing the long ball for so long that they've forgotten how to play the game properly. But it would help if we had a proper centre forward up there!'

He says, 'Aye, you're right. You're quite right Maggie.' He always was an easy man to talk to.

I say to him, 'We hoof the ball goalwards from all over the park as if the big man is still there. What use is that? Pass and move: that's how the best teams operate. Close the opposition down, get your foot in, dig the ball out and then pass and move.'

He says, 'Sounds like we could do with you in the dressing room, luv.'

'But someone needs to tell those players, George: Lay the ball off and then find space, get the ball back, give it to a blue shirt and then you go again. Simple.'

'Watch out,' he says, but too late. I fling my arm out and nearly knock over the one that the girls call Dr Twinkletoes.

'Oh, I am sorry,' I say, 'but you shouldn't be on the pitch.'

He looks at me like I'm mad. But he's a Red. And anyway I know a thing or two about him playing Doctors and Nurses in his free time that Mrs Twinkletoes might be interested to hear about.

When the lift arrives Carla the cleaner steps out and tells me, 'Old Ada was asking for you.'

So I have a patient to attend to. Ada has woken. It's always me she calls – in that thin faded voice of hers that's like the sound of old material tearing. But if I don't go and see her she might be gone for ever by the morning; and then who won't be able to forgive herself?

I put on my cheery nursey voice, 'Hello Ada, shall I do your pillows for you before I go?'

Her mouth shows the effort required to move the remains of her body. She can't weigh much more than a big novel now. A long story: Ada's life. But now she seems like an old book nobody reads any more – except me and an elderly neighbour who comes in to visit. But she has her memories; and very good ones they are too.

I might have known she'd start talking football, or try to. What she does is to direct a rather whispery croak towards my ears. Those illnesses, three of them in quick succession – like a hat-trick scored by some opposition striker late in the second half – have left her looking worn and more than a little dazed.

She says, 'It's a worry isn't it. When a team can't score goals.'

Hours have passed since we had that conversation. But what are hours to Ada? And she is correct. And after that shambles of a performance against Forest I have felt the cold hand of worry on the back of my neck. You could weep over such woeful performances. But the worry is: you might be in need of a big box of hankies.

I say, 'We play like a charity side Ada, as if we've got points to give away.'

Ada looks now as if she's arranging her thoughts – slowly and with much effort, as if all weigh as much as a brick. I give her my sympathetic, encouraging look. Her eyes shift towards the cabinet. 'I asked Mrs Donovan to bring something in for me. It's in there for you.'

A purse: a little tawny zip-up leather pouch. The narrow zip parts to reveal paper the colour of peaches.

When I was a girl, in between reading the Bible, I hid the map to a secret island in an old purse; and later on the names of boys, along with my secret undelivered messages to them. But by then my religious phase was coming to an end, and I was heading for the country of doubt, and also of sex, and of course, of football.

'Take them out dear.'

The peachy paper is folded. Inside: a ticket stub saying *Wembley Stadium, Final Tie* – one from the distant past. And lifting that up I see scrawled there the name of one of the old blue gods of Goodison Park: *Alex Young*.

'I got him to autograph it,' she manages to tell me. 'He was such a nice man. He spoke to me so softly.'

Did anything ever please her so much? There is a little brightness still down there in the old bones.

'You can have them. If you want them,' she says. 'I don't know who else I might give them to.'

If she must pass them on to someone then it seems that I must accept. Could I let her die thinking they'd get thrown out with the other useless odds and ends?

'He was a beautiful player,' she informs me dreamily. But memory of the man has given her energy. 'He was an angel. When you saw him jump, floating through the air, you knew he was an angel. He was so graceful. It was a joy to watch him. I used to worship him…'

How she loves to talk of Alex Young. And I do see him through her words, see him once again rise like some royal blue spirit in the penalty box, soaring there, glancing in goals with just a touch of his head, letting the ball brush against his golden hair to send it just beyond the goalie's grasp into the net.

But after so many words she must now rest. She is not done yet, though. She says, leaning ever so slightly nearer, 'I've got something I'm going to tell you.'

We sit in silence as I wait. I look at the peachy paper and the ticket stub. Who will I pass these and my own precious bits and pieces on too?

Her old voice returns, 'There's something I should tell you before I go Maggie.'

I am ready. I will never be so ready. I have ears like a baby elephant. 'About what, Ada?'

She sucks on her lips and rummages around in her old body for the breath she needs. But it has all been expended on Alex Young, the Golden Vision of Goodison Park.

And who doesn't hate not knowing? Like having the dessert trolley wheeled up and then pushed away before you can order.

She lies there as if she's been playing practising being dead and the game has gone too far. But what if she is slipping down into the darkness? What if she doesn't last through the night?

What is it that I should know? All her life's wisdom in a couple of sentences? A few lines to guide me? Was Ada ever caught out doing what she shouldn't have been? A warning for me? Advice? What? That she wishes she had had children; that although she was never restricted by parenthood she came to wish in the end that there was a young one she could call her own?

Who will listen to my stories? Who will I tell?

But she's going to tell me nothing of it today. Tomorrow maybe. But tomorrow I may not have the time or she might not have the strength. You look at them, the fading ones, and you know, like folk have been saying for generations, you have to make hay while the sun shines, you have to sow your seeds in the season of fruitfulness. But to do that you need a good man.

Scholar McColl

I head over to Karen's. This could be the last time. It may be the last time, I don't know. It's like I'm walking through the verses of an old song. But beyond them, at the end of the week, is a Cup match, a game, at last, surely, that we will actually win.

Karen opens the door, lets me in. We sit down and talk, but again I have that feeling that we no longer have much to say to each other. Her mind is a territory that I've explored already, and mine is still a mystery to her. Eventually, if I remain here, we will, as is our way, make our way upstairs. She won't let go of this, or can't; we are a sort of cracked unit that she seems determined to hold together no matter what the evidence of inevitable further fracturing. But me? I lack the will now for patching up and repainting the dull artefact that is us.

Things wax and they wane, love and power, the glory days. We enter each other's lives, we pass through them, and then we are gone: a memory; less than that perhaps. And if we're lucky we find something fresh, something better, maybe. But who knows who'll be the lucky one and who will not?

It goes on all the time. And why would it be any different?

And so this goes on as before. Or seems about to.

But if we go upstairs we will undress and get into bed, and begin as we have often begun before, and we will find the familiar, the known, the too well known, the too familiar clefts and curves. We will employ certain techniques of the tongue and lips, certain dexterities, certain finger-skills, and we will go on, keep on going on. We will push through to the end and fall apart. And then I will wonder why instead of coming to her bed I did not say what needs saying.

Once there was something that is no more. We are like a pair of figures crossing a field in the summer dusk – behind them in the far, far, distance are the heights they will never scale again, never even see again.

We have so little to say to each other and yet there is so much that needs saying. One of us sooner or later will have to say it. Seems as if it will have to be me. And why put it off? What is gained by procrastination?

So I say it. I say what needs saying because one of us must.

Because in my life the only thread that doesn't get broken is attached and firmly knotted to Everton Football Club. Still, after all those seasons, a victory opens the gates, releases me briefly into a land where the travelling is light and easy. Yes, defeat can lock me into a room that's damp and dismal, and that can seem a dark and lonely place at times, but there is always the next game to bring you back, back into the sunlight that brightens the grass of Goodison Park, back into heart of things, the royal blue masses.

But I have paid for my loyalty. I've paid in bruises and I've paid in what you suffer in the banter-room when your team keeps on losing. My entire family are Reds: brothers, uncles, nieces, and of course my old fella. He couldn't understand it. Because once the

Holy Trinity broke up and the rest of Harry Catterick's team of champions faded the Reds kept winning. It was one long party on the Kop, so how come his own son was stood outside in a blue and white scarf, how come his lad had defected? It made no sense to him. But to me it was just something that was meant to be.

Just as this does now – that I should walk away from Karen McMullin. But she is saying, 'You mean you don't want to see me any more?' Karen looks like a kitten I'm about to dump on the hard shoulder. 'Is that what you're saying? You don't want to see me any more?'

Miaaaoow. Damp eyes looking up.

But if I weaken I will do neither of us any good. So I do what I can to explain, repeating myself, leaving sentences unfinished, but trying to get over to her that when I entered her life I made no promises that I would reside there for ever, that once it was good, once, but…

But it is no good now and cannot be made better. Like a plant that's bloomed, that's had its day, if this is left to go on now it will just struggle and grow ugly. Like a footballer who's best playing days are behind him – and I have seen them in royal blue shirts – he becomes with each passing game more and more a sad reminder of what he once was. Without the energy, the sharpness, the spring in the step, he is a ghost of himself, and, yes, a sad one. And so an old player must step aside so that somebody new, who can do what he once did, can take his place. Players must move on. Fresh seeds must be planted where the old plant withered. Affairs must end, people must part, just like they always have, and no doubt always will.

I say, 'I'm saying it was good while it lasted Karen. But nothing lasts for ever.'

And now I need to get out of her life and look for someone else.

Maggie May

On the beat now, moving to the pulse of night music, dancing down the lines that will lead, I hope, to Pleasure Land. I can do no more for old Ada. If she will not emerge from her slumber then I am doomed to never know what it was that she would tell. The working week is done. Shifts, tasks, duties, the onerous, the irksome and the rewarding: all done now. The earning time is over. Here is the spending, the squandering. Here is lager and make-up and the sound system throbbing, the rhythm hammering through me, beating back everything that shouldn't be there. I'm on the beat, with the beat, moving to it, shifting with it, round and back, to this side and that. I'm all hips and shoulders and elbows. I am free now of all that irks me, all that makes demands on me. My clothes are scanty and my flesh is free. The rhythm is a tightrope on which I balance knowing I will not fall, it is a path made of stepping stones that I tread with total assurance. I rave on, rave on, will not be still, must have a ball, and will. I am at one with the dancers, with those who know how to live, those who see that this is our moment, that if we have wasted other nights we will not waste this. And so I boogie on, boogie on, in air that smells of hot bodies and scent and beer and fun and then I meet this fella. 'Hi. Great atmosphere, yeh. My name's Margaret, Maggie to you. I like your shirt. I'm a nurse but I also work for Everton on matchdays. Of course I'm a Blue, is there any other colour? Don't tell me you're a Red and ruin everything. No I'm only joking…'

And through the mist of music and alcohol, through the laughing and dancing, he looks smashing, he looks wonderful, he looks like *it*, the thing I've been waiting for all week whether I've realized it or not, and it seems like there's no limit to the fun we can have together.

'Ooh, I'm just in the mood,' says Sarah.

We chuckle and we sparkle, for the mirrors in this place make us look like stars. So we touch up our beauty and go back to the men. And I believe that I too am in the mood for…yes, I'm going to have that man. Connor. Kind of pretty but handsome with it. I will have him naked and full of need for me. Yeah, I'm going to shag him. I know I'm a bit drunk but…

But I wake up six hours later. One of those mornings. Your thoughts heavy in your head. You've gone and done it again. The curse of the random shag. Fukkkk!

Lust. That's all it was, lust, just plain naked lust. Sheer, unadulterated lust. Rank lust. Stinking lust. We dress ourselves up, wrap ourselves in powder and silk and sweet little sounds and then the animal breaks out lusting for meat. I will place my hand on the autograph of the Golden Vision of Goodison Park and vow: Never again. But for now there are clothes everywhere, my bedroom looks like the back room of a charity shop. It is a box of yesterday's odours, last night's leftovers: nicotine, old sweat, stale beer breath.

I move my eyes, fix them on a mouth that hangs open, gormless, as he begins to snore. Is this, can this really be, the gorgeous one with whom I danced? What do they put in that lager that makes men look so wonderful?

If only he would get up and dress and leave without speaking. I want my bed, my room, my house, my day back; I want to start fitting the bits of myself back together. But he's obviously not an early riser. That's not a joke. My head feels as if it's got a crack in it. The last thing I'm in the mood for is jokes. I make the first move, wrap myself up and then am ready to loudly clear my throat and speak, 'My mum is coming round first thing in the morning but you can stay and have breakfast with her if you like.'

The shock of word-sound in his ear makes him swallow his own snore. He grunts. I repeat myself. My words sink down to the bed of his brain. When they have all settled into place he becomes a shark ravenous for clothes, he could eat his own underpants in his desire to get away. Was a man ever dressed so quickly and gone?

And now at last a shower, a long, long, everlasting shower. I will be cleansed once more. I will stand beneath those jets of hot water and be cleansed.

I was brought up to be good, to walk the path of the righteous and the virtuous, so of course I have had to travel a long way in the opposite direction. This lad I was with at one time, Barry, started off calling me love and finished screaming *whore* in my face, as if he had any right to moralize; but his legacy, his gift to me, was the Blues. Before I met him the game was a like some weird male rite I could make no sense of. But then I saw how a victory brought the purest joy to his face, saw also how real was his pain when Everton got run ragged, turned over, taken apart. And then I began to feel it too. So I went with him to Goodison Park. And seeing a wonderful goal scored and then feeling the roar of the crowd as my own voice soared, feeling that roar all around me and inside me, I knew that I had become part of it, part of Everton Football Club, and that I always would be and that it would always be part of me.

That was his real gift to me; that was what I was left with when our little disaster had been suffered through, when I had walked away from the ruins. For, we were, in truth, a pair of kids who didn't understand what they were signing up to. But he was a quiet one. In a crowd he was a loud noise but alone he could be so quiet. On Saturdays, though, he was Blue, and wild enough to die for them. And at first he was desperate for me, full of need and desire, bursting with passion and joy.

Before I had him it was a long wait, as if I was always waiting for the sound of footsteps, of someone approaching who would be – The One. But all I could hear was the wind in the branches and lonesome romantic stuff like that. And then there he was, not quite like I'd expected, but there he was: the one I'd awaited – in a blue and white scarf. And for some time he seemed like everything to me, everything. Everything I wanted and needed was through him or with him or of him or by him.

And then I started to wonder where he went when he wasn't with me. Who was he with when he was out so long? Another she? Another blue girl? So then I wasn't sure. Quite suddenly I wasn't sure any more. I was no longer sure what I wanted. I had had certainty, but here, once again in my life, was doubt and confusion. Why should I have wanted something and got it and then not be so sure after all? It all seemed too tangled to make sense of. So I grew familiar with his body-scents, and how the words from his mouth would sound, and how the steps of his feet would sound as they mounted the stairs and crossed the carpeted floors, and I realized that I had some of him only, I had as much of himself as he was prepared to give me and that was all.

So I began to wonder what was beyond this, to feel that nothing was fixed and certain, and to understand that there were things happening inside me of which I could not speak. Maybe a baby would happen, though, and fill the gap and settle the turbulence that was in my thoughts and heartbeats. Because it seemed to me we were like two trees standing side by side and only the tips of our branches would ever really touch, that each of us was really standing in our own space, our knot-eyes gazing at the horizon looking for something different except those odd moments when some wild wind hurled us, our hands and fingers, closer together. For, he had given me Everton but had not given me himself – and probably never would. I was mere furniture in his life, an ornament on his shelf, and would never be truly joined with him, united; we would never share a duet in the most romantic opera of all because the closest we would get was chanting side by side with the crowd at Goodison Park.

And so, my eyes began to wander; although some days I promised myself I would not walk that path my eyes had picked out. But if I loved Everton more than I loved him, just as he loved Everton more then he loved me, then why did I need to promise myself that I would not walk along that path? For if I was careful I would leave no trail that could be followed, and whoever I allowed to lay hands on me would leave no sign that could be identified. And the moment I thought that I knew that it would happen, that I would be new again for somebody and would no longer be a piece of furniture, an ornament.

So then when I heard women say that women are not like that, that men are men, a pack of dirty dogs, but we are different, then I knew otherwise. But maybe I was odd and strange for I, once the prim girl who must read the Bible, was now Everton like a man, and loud with it on matchdays – my banshee screech cutting through the masculine rumble. If that made any difference how could I tell? But like a flying winger I was beyond the fullback and away, uncatchable – or that's how it seemed. I was in that space beyond the fullback and I was revelling in it. Limbs were a jungle and the forest was hot, and even if I was besmirched with mud why would I not be there?

And so, at home we still shared Everton and fish and chips and spaghetti and wine and the flickering box. The days made weeks, one season became another, we were there and yet not there, he coming and going as he liked, carrying backwards and forwards his separateness. And we, both of us, together but separate, took ourselves to Goodison where all the voices joined together and filled the gaps.

And so I went back, back to the thing I had discovered, was pulled there, drawn there even though I was no longer sure why, and was still trying to puzzle it when I let my caution slip and was trapped in a net of eyes and pointed fingers and accusations. I had outlived this other thing and had not buried it in time. Here was my error, my downfall. *Whore*, he called out, and again, *whore, you whore*. And I could not deny it, and anyway would not try to preserve what did not deserve to be preserved. But I said to him, oh I told him, I said, 'What gives you the right to point the finger, hey? You think I'm dumb? You think I haven't guessed that you go calling on some Miss Pussy Fucking Willo with your fucking dick hanging out?!!!'

And so on and so forth – as they say.

I did get quite excited, I must admit. Occasionally you realize how much venom you carry in some gland that no medical technology has yet managed to detect.

But, enough of that now, enough. Enough of that nonsense that is lust. Like the sensible ones I will set out to find the thing I want now and I will not deviate or hang around wasting any more time.

The water runs over me, down me, through me; its warmth, its hot wetness, courses over me, racing over curves and into crevices, purging me of pollution, corruption. Clean. Clean again, and ready to begin.

The phone begins to ring.

I am standing in the hall wrapped up in a bright towel, listening to the words that were always going to be said. How did I know that Ada would never live to tell the tale?

If it was something I needed to know then I will have to find out for myself now – unless I have just found it out. I need to settle down and give birth to a little boy blue, or girl, or both?

Is that it?

Anyway, I am clean again and ready, ready for the FA Cup.

12

Sky Blue Thinking

Solid John Sanger

The FA Cup. Even all those years later it was like a film I was watching for the first time. Way back I watched that game on TV– Everton 3 Sheffield Wednesday 2 – and the next day the city had turned blue.

I can still see it. Everywhere is blue, royal blue. I'm no longer a little kid who believes in magic – although thirty years on I have cause to wonder about its darker side – but back then, seeing how the city had turned blue, it was as if something magical had happened. And from that day on I'm Blue, Blue and only Blue. It's like on that day I first start to find out who I am. Because never for one minute after that will I waver, not even for a second when it seems like all the lights are out and the wind is blowing in off a cold, cold sea to harry the ghosts of Goodison Park.

And in a couple of hours I was due to be heading back to Goodison. But before that I took the kids down to the Cast Iron Shore. Joe kicked his ball along as I pushed Stephen in his wheelchair. The tide was almost in and the gulls were stood on the rail eyeing the high water. I can watch water for hours: the swell, the surf, the push and pull, even after so much time spent watching it from the deck of the *Britannia Princess* – that boat which used to be partly mine.

Then a ship appeared heading out to sea. 'Look,' I said to Stephen. And his eyes turned bright as he gazed at it. It reminded me of so many similar vessels I'd seen out on the oceans. So I started to tell the kids – Joe really, because a lot of it goes past Stephen – but I couldn't quite make it sound how I wanted it to sound. The old boats keep on sailing back to me. They're forging back through the foam. They're coming in convoys up the river. I can see flotillas of the damned things, bloody armadas.

I couldn't hold it in. I had to talk it out. The words I needed to speak were bursting inside me. Once I was down round the Philippines, Indonesia, the Spice Islands. I went ashore and that place was so wonderful it was hard to believe it was real. I've never smelled such natural perfumes or seen the sea so clear. And the fish were like floating colours: stripes and hoops and zigzags and all kind of patterns. And the plants, it was like everywhere was the winning prize in a show for hothouse flowers, but really you'd just turned up there on an ordinary day. It was a real fantasy place, a daydreamers' paradise, as far away from all the hurly-burly and aggravation as you could get, and I was walking through it and suddenly this thought came into my head: I wonder how the Blues are getting on.

You can't escape it, no matter how far away you go, no matter how strange the place, you can't leave the game behind. The Blues, they're in your head, you carry them with you in your blood, your heart.

But no, the lad didn't want to know about all that old stuff, he just wanted to kick his ball. I'd started, though, and I couldn't stop myself. 'And another time,' I went on, 'I was in the middle of the Atlantic. The lad who was looking after the wireless was a Blue. He came up on deck and said, "We won! We won it! Everton have just won the FA Cup, lad!" And we threw our arms up and danced on the deck.'

That was eighty-four. My mate old Marty. Ex-Royal Marine. R.I.P. Marty Dodd.

'Do you think we'll win the Cup this year, dad,' asked Joe.

No, he didn't want to know about the oceans. But it was my life, the life I had to give up. 'The Cup?' I said. 'You never know, son.'

'We might, mightn't we?'

'Until someone knocks us out we've got a chance, that's for sure.'

'Coventry won't knock us out will they?'

'If they do,' I said, 'we're in worse shape than I think we are, son.'

And then he was away after his ball. So I turned to my other lad. 'We'll win the Cup this year won't we Stephen, son.'

As soon as I said his name he was there with me even if it takes him a little time to understand the rest. But he will. He'll have to think about it, and then he'll know what I've said. A bit slow, that's all. For years there was hardly a word in the whole world that seemed to mean anything to him. But love can be a miracle worker. Talk, odd words, anything you say lets him know he isn't forgotten. And maybe they could prove to be the key. Even if his legs can never be fixed maybe now his mind might grow and grow.

I gave him the thumbs-up. And he replied to that straight away with his own – his hands are not a problem.

Then I said to the other lad, 'Come on Joe,' I said. 'Let's move. Let's get rolling! Or I'll be late for that match.'

Scholar McColl

Just setting off when I see Frank Brigstoke, who definitely isn't on his way to the match. A few years ago he would have been, but not any more. He comes striding along like a man with a mission and one eye on the clock. When he spots me he does a quick side-step and grabs my hand as if he could tug me away with him.

'Can't stop, Frank, got to get to the ground.'

'You still at that lark, are you?' He gives me this look: sadness mixed with vague amusement, a dash of smugness. Because he is the man who turned his back on football, who waved goodbye to the game, the ground, the gang of yellowjackets he'd worked with for years – the whole big football caboodle.

'What would I do with myself on matchdays?'

He can think of plenty, he says. But doesn't he ever feel like coming back? He must do sometimes. 'Don't you ever miss it?' The banter, the boozy post-match analysis, those odd rare moments of brilliance that stay with you?

'Not me.'

And he's still got a grip of my hand. 'I need to go, lad,' I say, pulling it free.

'Here, listen, one minute, one question.' He has the look of a missionary, full of intent, design, certainty. 'Do you not think that there are so many important issues that face us in this city, on this planet, and that they should have our full attention?' His hands are held out towards me as if I might drop a *Yes* into one of them.

A minute? If I stop for one minute I'll be here for twenty, 'Look at it one way, your way Frank, and I'm sure you're right.' I'm leaning away from him. 'But-'

But he's leaning towards me. So I take a step away from him.

'Okay run away, but don't forget,' he's laughing now, but he means it, 'when you're ready for the real world I'll be here to show you the way.'

Do I not know that there is a big mess that needs sorting out? How could I not? But I start walking backwards.

He raises the finger of certainty. 'I'll catch you another time.'

'You can try!'

But for now I'm away.

How can that happen? After a lifetime of worship you turn from the shrine and walk away. And you don't look back. Could that happen to anyone? Me? The question lingers, stays with me all the way to the stadium. Could I? Surely not. I've walked away from plenty before, turned my back, packed my bag, jumped the first bus out of it, but this, the Blues, Everton Football Club, no this is different. This is for ever.

And it's matchday again. And as the old blue stadium comes into sight a car pulls in up ahead of me on the other side of the road, a figure steps out, waves to the driver who turns away down Florence Street. That's himself: Solid John, the blood brother of my early days, striding the pavement. He shifts his wide beefy form lightly though with something of the squaddie's rather stiff gait. At the little alehouse on Tetlow Street he half turns to wave to someone I cannot see, but he does not stop. He marches on towards the ground and his afternoon on duty. Solid John Sanger – a man as conscientious as he is robust.

As I turn the last bend I see that cantankerous old codger Archie Block talking to one of the ground staff. The Blocker Man flicks his eyes my way as I pass. Neither of us speaks. We both give very slight nods, the most minimal of acknowledgements. I am not of that man's world and he is not of mine, though we must work together inside the stadium to ensure the safety of the thousands.

Into the coatroom – and my signature takes its place on the sheet. I shed my own coat and take on the yellow. In the chiefs' office at the far end the chief of chiefs sits at the table nodding to the man on his left, Harry Cluny.

I pass them and head for the cupboard-room at the back, seize my talkie – a little leather-coated busy-body through which I can be controlled from afar – that sits waiting in the rack. As it slips into my big yellow pocket I feel the tug, the weight.

A thin, very upright, fuzzy-faced man marches in – that's the brush-like face of a man keen to sweep away any lingering bad habits from around here. George Gnomes, once a naval officer now a professional grey-suit, has been brought in from down south by the local council because the old certificate man is on sick leave. So now it is within his power to close down both Goodison Park and Anfield. Although he is, the rumour fiend will tell you, an out-of-town Red, a Kopite with a southern accent. Is that correct? I have heard not. I am told that, despite the large red birthmark below his right ear, his true allegiances lie with that monolith of English football, Torquay United – a team that plays much of the time in blue. But once that little fiend Mr Rumourmonger sets a little bird like that free in this city it very quickly becomes like an escaped parrot: loud and gaudy and difficult to get back in its cage. So some of the lads are already calling that man The Anfield Gnome.

Now Mechanical Mike appears and sits down. He's one whose heart really is across the park in Anfield – although his expertise is a crucial part of the operation to keep matchdays safe in Goodison. An electronics engineer by trade, he's an ace technical man up in the control box to which the High Command will migrate as soon as this meeting ends. He's called Mechanical Mike the Pieman by some because what he loves most apart from LFC is hot pastries and old cars, old buses, old railway engines. He's a squat, chunky, stubble-faced former scrum half and amateur boxer whose nose was long ago flattened by some fist or boot – a snout to which his allegiance to the old enemy seems to have given a distinctive red glow.

The Craphouse Poet has taken a stab at the Pieman. His creation could once be read above the cistern in one of the toilets on Section Four:

> *Mechanical Mike the Pieman*
> *For the Anfield Reds he'd die, man*
> *Oh I wish he would*
> *Choke on a hot pie*
> *And then he'd lie*
> *In a box of wood*
> *So then we could*
> *Have a blue-blood man up on high, man.*

But this anonymous rhymester's pen is no sword. It has failed to strike a telling blow at its intended victim. No one is fonder of reciting that little ditty than the Pieman himself. It has given an anonymous technician a little celebrity and he enjoys that like a hot steak and kidney pie.

While he and the other bosses spread their restrained bonhomie around the table a filing cabinet offers a shoulder for me to lean on. George Gnomes then produces his hobbyhorse the Code of Conduct which since the mid Eighties has transformed the rag-tag casuals of old into a smart and disciplined in-house security force. But he's a keen man, is George. Very keen. Keen to make his mark while he can, perhaps, so that he's the natural successor should the sick man fail to return to his post. He wants to ensure that *all* yellowjackets turn up *every* game in a club tie and a pair of smart kecks and polished shoes; he wants to see *none* of them *ever* show any sign of celebration when the Blues score. And it seems that he is determined to address the masses about these matters this afternoon.

The Blocker Man shoulders in. Small mobile ratty eyes in a face like crumpled newspaper. A moustache scribbled on it. His hair all different shades of grey that have been chopped up and sprinkled on to his scalp.

The cop crew arrive, three of them accompanied by that ex-cop, Fred Gutteridge. He's a burly, but well-groomed, slightly dapper (but only very, very, slightly dapper) strong and silent type who once built a reputation for being a policeman who was very cool under pressure, so when he bailed out of the force he found a niche here as an officeman with big responsibilites on matchdays. Most men in the room only work part time or on the days of a match but this one has a proper job despite having, so they say, polished a little patch with his elbow on the bar of the Liverpool Supporters Club. Some days you could fall over the old enemy here if you weren't watching where you were walking. And you do like to think you know where you're going – even if you don't.

More boss stewards arrive. The room fills up – chock-full now with beefiness and mantalk; crammed with yellow jackets, blue coats, blazers, suits, uniforms, stuffed with biceps and testicles, bursting with masculinity and status. Len Hatman Knox, now adds his own bulk. A sharp-suited, poker playing, security consultant with a penchant for headgear that hints at film star fantasies, he eases his full size through the door, and, all the key men now gathered, the big chief taps his pen and begins the briefing.

Knox and Cluny do most of the talking. We're told that Mr Safety Certificate himself, the bearded one, George Gnomes, will speak to all stewards before the gates open, and then we hear about the usual stuff: special arrangements, estimated crowd figures, likely problems...

Then Cluny has one or two other matters worth mentioning.

Harold H Cluny – now a personnel man, a former captain in the redcaps, the military police, who finished his military career in Army recruitment, he's a fleshy, dome-headed, rigorous layer-down of rules; a man for correct procedures, the giving and receiving of orders. He stares dark-eyed and pink-skinned over a greying yardbrush moustache. A very clean-cut man – hard-scrubbed, sharp-shaved, bright-polished – he mouths his carefully measured phrases. Yes, he is extremely tidy in everything, this man: in how he looks, in how he thinks, in how he speaks – if a word isn't necessary then swallow it. That thick but neatly clipped moustache of his hints at old traditions, old values – military values perhaps that can seem foreign to some of us casual urban types. At times he points to the whiteboard at his back which is a map of his mind – floating numbers and instructions, wide empty spaces: no clutter. A fact for this man is like a big green cactus in the paleness of the desert: strong and spiky, nourishing even. We will not survive for long, thirty years spent in the troublespots of this earth has taught him, on flowery thoughts that fall apart when you try to grasp them. Manpower is his province here (there are few ladies in yellow jackets) but safety, as for other big bosses, is his obsession. No punter shall perish inside Goodison Park while Harold H Cluny is part of the High Command – that is his determination. Understand your tasks, perform them to the utmost and, most importantly, ensure that those in your charge do the same, is the mantra of his closing lines to the section bosses.

Len the Hat, though a student of security matters, the nuts and bolts, the tiny screws even, is bigger and showier: a man who wouldn't be out of his depth standing out front somewhere hearing the sound of his own voice ringing – singing even – in the ears of others. A man who can talk the talk, so they say. Like myself, some would say. And that is exactly what he's now doing.

At his shoulder stands a serving cop, an inspector with a long shiny stick of authority who'll be running the force's operations today. With him is his sidekick sergeant and another rather wooden-looking one whose fixed frown does look as if it's been carved out of very durable timber. He reveals that, acting on information received, his unit have tailed two car loads of suspected troublemakers from Coventry and that as he speaks they're in a pub in town under the watchful eye of one of his men.

Amid the dullness of the meeting this tale of tracking and surveillance pricks my interest like one of my Ma's embroidery needles. The cops seem to have a sharper act these days than when I was on the road watching the Blues.

The meeting over, I head out into the stadium, now a big echoey emptiness, a den of ghosts. The fragmented utterances of gatemen and ground staff float down deserted gangways. Beyond the red track the pitch seems brighter than last week. Rumours of spring have reached here at last.

I lift my talkie to my cheek and look up at the glass box, the chiefs' command post. I say, 'Section Six to Match Control, Section Six to Match Control, radio check, are you receiving me?' The Controller's thin, drained voice is affirmative. I switch him off as a programme seller trolleys a box of his wares along the gangway.

A gang of gatemen, each with a wooden chest under his arm, go past, gabbing and bantering. Yellowjackets begin to wander in. The first players arrive in their Saturday suits. Swinging handbags, they stroll across the pitch on the diagonal that takes them down the tunnel to the dressing rooms.

Down below in the musty zone, grey concrete land, women on the tea bars are filling up their great steel urns, stuffing hotboxes with pastries. All over the place the matchday routines go on. Groups of cops are getting their briefing, the match commentators are sorting out their gear, more gatemen pass by, disappear down below, the flagman halts at a corner and drops the white pole into its hole.

Maggie May

As I sign in for the stand-by team Mick Molloy, Head of Jackets, who is calm now but in an hour will be like a heart attack looking for somewhere to strike, tells me, 'You're on Section Six today, Mag.'

Oh Section Six? That's Mark McColl territory.

Mick seems like he's about to say something more but somebody calls him and he turns away, and someone behind me says, 'Wemberley!'

Billy Whizz

Ya can't buy that feelin. Ya can't buy it with a fistful of bluenotes. Yer up behind the goal watchin yer team run out on the Wembley turf with the sun shinin on them. I wouldn't sell that for notn. That memory will go with me to me grave. And even then al still think about it from time to time.

But I want more. Am ready for it. Av seen enough of de other side of it: the Blues scrappin for their lives down in the snakepit. And maybe the worst is behind us. Av got that feelin. The word is that we've found a kid oo can score goals. That's the key. That's the way ya gerrout of jail. That's what ya need to win cups. And silverware sure would put some shine back into Goodison Park.

When I turn in to sign on Archie Block says, 'There's a meetin in Section One.'

'A meetin? Wha? On a matchday?'

'Yeh. Now. So shift yer arse.'

'What's it about? '

'Mr Nomes will soon tell ya.'

'Wha? That redsnouted f - '

'Don't start, lad!' The Blocker's already in his big bossman mood. 'Just get yerself down there. Ya wouldn't wanna disappoint the man by showin up late.'

'Disappoint im? I says. 'Ad like to shove a very sharp point up his red arse. Ees a pest that fella.'

Old Archie just jerks his ed towards the big iron door to tell me to get movin.

So I go and sit down with all de others, a big crowd of yellerjackets. Then de Anfield Nome shows up on the runnin track with Mechanical Mike and Gutache Gutteridge. But Mechanical Mike doesn't hang about, ees probably got another pie in the oven.

Yeh, if ya wanna know oo scoffed all the pies then start askin questions at his office door. Check out the greasy fingers. Clock the pastry crumbs on his chin and shoes.

De Anfield Nome steps forwards. Arl fuzzy face. Ee would look well sat in someone's front garden with a red hat on, ee would. Then ee starts up. The same old rootine: tellin us that we have to wear the club tie at all times when wees on duty so that the public will have confidence in us and blah blah blah. Boy, can that karacter spout. Straight out of The Bullshit Book of Rules and Regulashons.

Ee says that when we started on this job maybe twenty, maybe thirty years ago, we was supporters, and what we was really interested in was watchin the game, and that that was probably no different from any other ground in the country, but now as we've been told many times all that has changed becoz when we put on the yeller jacket we cease to be a fan and become a club offishal with specific duties and responsibilities, we become in football terms a nootral.

Nootral? *Noootral?* Nootral, my arse! The day I become a nootral will be the day my arse learns to sing *Y'll Never Walk Alone*. But never mind that becoz the bullshit machine is still pumpin it out, tellin us that what happens on the pitch is of no interest to us becoz the only thing that concerns us is the crowd, that they watch the match in complete safety and that when it's finished they leave the ground in safety, and if Everton are winnin three nil, or if Everton are losin three nil, that is no concern of ours, and if Everton score the winner in the last minute or the last second we don't dance around with everybody else becoz we must remain nootral and ensure that the crowd celebrates in safety, we must remain imparshal…blah-blah-blah-blah-bullshit-blaaah.

And ya can just see him thinkin: I know ya don't score many goals at this ground but…

Bollocks to this. I shout out, 'Worrabout a rise?'

Ee glares in my direction and says ees come to address us about very serious matters and it's in our interest to take note of what ees sayin. But oo wants to listen to that bollocks? I says to the lad next to me, I says, 'A trip to Wembley has kick-started this club in the past, no reason why it couldn't happen again.'

John Sanger, Solid John the old soldier man, turns and does a big tut, and says, 'The man's only doin his job.'

Solid John doesn't like me gabbin while the Nome is spoutin. Ee takes the job very serious, ee does. As if the yellerjackets is some kind of crack regiment. But I don't shut up for no one. I says, 'If we beat Coventry today weeze in the last eight, and if we can get that far I can't see no reason why we can't go all the way.'

Why not? To stroll down Wembley Way and lift that pot. It's happened before and it can happen again. And a good cup run will carry us along to safety in the league. Ya get used to winnin. Just what the club needs. And me too. Ya can't beat that: bein up there behind the goal at a cup final singin yer heart out. Somebody starts the song off, and away ya go: We shall not, we shall not be moved. Yer up there in yer blue and white and all the faces around yer are tense and concentrated followin the ball and then the song breaks out and all the faces are alive: Just like a tree that's standin by the wa-a-a-terside, weeee shall not be moved. And yer lost in the sound. And the need to win. And ya do win. Like we done against Sheff Wed and Watford and Man United. And then ya walk back down Wembley Way in triumph singin We shall not be moved. And whatever little things are nigglin away in yer life, and whatever big things are loomin, they don't matter, becoz that is one day when notn matters but the game. I want that thing ya get watchin a cup final at Wembley, or wherever the final game is bein played. Aye. Someone tells me I haven't lived, I tell them: Av been there, av felt it.

And what? Can ya believe it? The Nome is still at it. A woolyback Kopite from cider country layin it down to blue-blood Scousers? Nah. Enuffathis. I shout, 'Why don't ya gerr over to Anfield and tell them shower instead of pilin it all on us?' Yeah, spread the shite around a bit!

Ee says ees in no need of advice about how to go about his profeshonal duties. But some lads near me ain't so sure. They start givin it too him, wackin his red bottom with the sticks of their wit.

Worra laff.

But Freddie Gutache down there beside the Nome is startin to twitch his voice ready, and Solid John Sanger is sat there shakin his ed, lookin disgusted, sayin this isn't no way to carry on. And Maggie May, oo I reckon is no angel in her own way, isn't happy neither – shakin her ed like we is actin ignorant.

Am just about to remind her that the Nome is a Kopite when Old Gutache decides he has to jump in, sayin ees ashamed and disgusted becoz ees never witnessed such a shockin display of bad manners from one or two people. Which makes ya wonder where ees been all his life, all them years in uniform. Has the tough old cop actually been policin teddy bears fokin tea parties all that time in the force or what? Eh? A firm presence to make sure no bun fights break out! A-ha-ha-ha. Anyway that's de end of the meetin. Or the High Command Comedy Show, which is what it's turned into. For me anyway. But old Blocko is wearin his bossman face, sayin to our crowd, 'Okay you lot let's have yer in ya posishons.'

And Mr Solid John Sanger is still givin me that big frown.

Solid John Sanger

Fred Gutteridge felt ashamed? That's nothing to what I felt. I'm an Evertonian, he's not. Ashamed and disgusted, I certainly was. I had words with one or two of them about their loudmouth nonsense. I said, 'George Gnomes is only doing his job. I don't care which club he supports, or whether he doesn't support any club at all. He's got responsibilities and he's only doing his job. And I for one am glad to see that a man who carries all the responsibilities that he does is doing his job properly. If he doesn't have faith in us doing our job properly he won't issue a safety certificate, and rightly so. And without that certificate the ground gets closed. And where will you be then? Eh?'

A few home truths, I imparted. Which is not what one or two people want to hear. But it shouldn't have been me having to tell them. Old Blocko should have had words with them. Or his deputy, who's never short of an opinion or two, the Ginger Scholar over there.

Scholar McColl

The turnstiles begin to click the first fans through. The programme seller peers from his cage in the dark corner below the stairs. Speckies feed him round pounds and bluebacks. The teabars have the smell of hot pies on their breath. The turnstiles click faster as if some great machine is being wound up ready for use. The undertone turns into a buzz.

Solid John stands erect, watchful, his arms straight lines down his sides. He steps away to go on patrol, moves into his stride, his measured paces, shifting his solid bulk lightly, each movement displaying his fitness.

And the turnstiles click on and on as the crowd-trickle becomes a flow. Men and boys, daughters in blue, are talking the game to come: the team, the tactics, the likely result.

More and yet more spill down the gangways, filter down the rows. I reckon we could be looking at a full house in half an hour. And why not? This is Everton Football Club and it has a history some inspired weaver could work into a startling new tapestry. It is a church with a massive congregation. From Seaforth to Speke, Scotty Road to Norris Green new young Blues are growing into the faith, discovering a creed that will last a lifetime. Unless, that is, like Frank Brigstoke, they begin to muse on the idea that football clubs that grew out of particular communities are becoming, have already become, global corporations that are more interested in pounds and dollars than the local people, and whether you wouldn't feel rather ridiculous to find yourself investing so much emotional energy in the equivalent of an international oil or agro-chemical company in which you had no financial interest.

Nevertheless, still they come from all over the city to gather here, from tower blocks and tight old terraces, from dog-eared council estates out on the fringes, from the cherry blossom avenues of the south and the seaside neighbourhoods of the north, from over the water and out in the sticks, and even the woolyback lands beyond. Those who yesterday would not pass the time of day with each other will now come together and shout, sing even, released briefly from the closed boxes in which they pass their days.

And their gabble goes on building up around me. The experts are holding forth: the Blues need to sign two new players, three, four, but most of all they need a man who can score goals, or how else will they get back to their rightful position at the top. They need to change the tactics, they need shaking up, they need... What else is like football? If a rockband played music like this team has played football this season their gigs would be deserted, they'd be back on the dole, scrambling for day jobs. But, this? You can't keep the speckies away. The worse it gets the more they come back.

The Blocker Man appears in the gangway. A man hacked out of granite or cast in some foundry, his shoulders fill the space. His head swivells from side to side. He patrols his patch like some shipyard foreman of old – surly and watchful, ever ready to crack the whip of his tongue at feckless underlings.

Billy Whizz, more on walkabout than patrol, is still cursing Gnomes. But he needs to take note of what the cursed one has said. He needs to remember that everything he does can be observed by the High Command from their high glass box. And I tell him so.

His response is short, quick and predictable, 'Bollocks to them.'

Billy Whizz has an ability to get himself into places, into situations. He's pulled pints down town and in the South End, he's captained darts teams and, his playing days over, 'coached' alehouse football sides; he's fronted the karaoke in that drinking den they call the Thieves Kitchen, and he's earned himself free pints for giving out pencils and collecting the papers on Quiz Nite down at his local. He can tongue a good yarn and bang out the jokes and is a popular figure anywhere that the people are rough and ready. But he is also reckless by nature – a recklessness that others have grown out of.

'If I were the worrying type, Bill. I might be inclined to worry about you.'

He laughs. Naturally he laughs. What else would Billy Whizz do?

To my left Maggie May appears, she who floats from job to job. She stops at my side, 'Did Archie tell you I'm with you today?'

'No, he didn't,' I say, 'but that's fine with me,'

'What's fine?' she asks in that bright way of hers. 'Not being told, or me being here?'

I have to smile – at her more than the words she speaks. She has got something about her this one, and once you start to take notice you see that, whatever that something is, she's got lots of it.

Maggie May

A deep voice calls him. Duty takes him away – the Ginger Scholar. He walks with his head high, comes to a halt further along the gangway. Ginger? No, that's just to mock him. More a slightly faded sort of auburn, I'd say. I've never slept with one of them.

Wake up to a head of short reddish curls.

A fan blocks my view – a big beerbelly. He moves as if he's carrying the whole world under his belt, and he's looking lost, too; like someone who sets out for Croxteth Park and finds themselves at the Albert Dock. He stares at his ticket as if it's written in Chinese, looks vaguely around.

Now he wants my attention.

Hold on there you great barrel of beer.

Scholar McColl

Her task completed, Maggie May paces the gangway: alert, confident, and… available? Is she? She's taller than most women. My size. Gleaming cat's eyes. Attractive. But no pussy cat, I'd say.

That first girl I went out with was a similar build. But Michelle Hayden had much less about her. And her old man was a Red. Said there was only one team in the city and meant it. No man for playful banter, him. War, and no prisoners taken. That little scene didn't last long. How long might it last with Maggie May? Hmmm?

The Blocker Man's eyes dart in my direction and stick. Has he been eyeing me eyeing her? The old stager casting a critical eye on me, trying to read my thoughts? He's no scholar, that man, but there are boxes in his mental loft packed with a certain kind of knowledge. He's one of the old school, connected with the city's past and proud of it. He has built ships and if you let him he will name them for you: the this, the that, the other; fine names all of them, grand and mythical, but meaningless now to most ears that hear them.

A ravaged figure, him. Over the years he has lost teeth, ear-power, the tip of one finger. The weather has been at him and washed the colour from his hair. And fashion is a bus that has passed him by. But even so he has a sort of presence, the presence of a statue maybe, or a heap of old iron, something that hints at history, but a presence all the same.

Maggie May too. She has that. And a lot more besides. And while the Blocker Man stands still she is walking towards… Towards what? The future. But what future? What will the future offer Maggie May? And how will she respond to that?

Interesting.

Archie Block

Lot of use he was, Scholar McColl, standing there eyeing up the female talent when we had the certificate man on the prowl. But no nitpicker was going to find fault with my section, not if I had anything to do with it. I checked the teabars and the lurking places and made sure there was no skiving going on. I went through the place like a dose of salts. I said, 'You and you, move! You lot, thin out, move it! You're not here to gossip and have pre-match conferences to pick the team. You're a body of men with a duty to perform so shift. Now!'

They were in no doubt of who was in charge after I'd been up and down a couple of times. There was more than one ear with teeth-marks in it and a few arses with boot-marks on them. I said to one of them, I told him in no uncertain terms, 'You stand there and make sure no one brings booze up from the concourse because if they do I'll have your balls on a spike.'

Oh, I told them, I had to. Crack the whip. That's all some of them understand. Otherwise they'd stand around all day nattering like a load of old women.

And if that fella McColl didn't want to put his boot on their necks he shouldn't have been wearing the deputy's badge. But he is a weird one with his book-learning and his damned opinions about this and that and everything. A good war book, that's all a working man needs. You work your shift, you earn your coin, you have a bet and a pint and a good war story and then a little dabble under the nightdress at the weekend – your conjugal rights. That's what life's all about. Simple.

But not for him. He'd turn a simple idea into as load of quibbles and clever talk to bamboozle a working man. But you get weird characters everywhere. Oddballs. Misfits. Awkward arses. Weirdos. Oh aye, we had our share of those back in the shipyard. The ones who wouldn't stand in line. That fella who worked in the painters' shop, what's-is-name, Elizer, Elizer something. Loner. Didn't know what the word team-spirit meant. Teetotaler, he was, and vegetarian. A bird-watcher. Head on him like a buzzard. Wore green wellies. Green, aye. In a shipyard. A man in green wellies is like a pig in silk stockings.

A man who couldn't enjoy a pint, though? Something wrong

there. Or a nice steak. Aye, preaching over a brew to men who built ships, men who worked outside in all weathers.

Give up meat? I'd as soon give up my conjugal rights. A slice of pork loin. Lamb cutlets. Beef on the bone. A dinner without meat is like a team with no leader. A body of men is a team. Or should be. And any man who wants to stand apart will stick in my craw like a nasty little bone. Teamwork is basic. They said the Everton team in sixty-six was a gang of individuals but out there at Wembley, two goals down, they showed what kind of a team they were: the greatest comeback the place had ever known.

And when we scored our second goal, the equaliser, that lad jumped out of the blue end, from right near where I was, and ran across the pitch. Just pure joy, that was, making him do that. What was his name? I even forget his name now. I saw him go and I felt like going with him. I nearly went. I've never done anything like that before. Nothing show-offy. Only that once the desire was on me, telling me to go, go with him. But then he was away. The moment had passed. The moment was his. They couldn't stop him. Not until they dragged him down. But he'd had his glory by then. The cops were falling all over the place at first, they dragged off his jacket but still couldn't stop him. He kept on running, running and running across the wide green grass. What was his name? Scholar McColl would probably know but I'm damned if I'm asking him. Bookworm.

And he reads the posh newspapers. If the Liverpool Echo is good enough for me it's good enough for him. I told my old Ma about him. She had a look on her face like the milk on her corn flakes was sour. She'd always liked corn flakes, since way-way back. That was before her teeth went. She ate them any time of the day. She was too old to care. I've felt like I was going that way meself sometimes. But I have duties, I have responsibilities to shoulder, and shoulder them I will.

And by the time I'd swung my boot at a lazyarse and whipped a pair of chattering deadlegs into life I could feel a pain in me chest – like being jabbed with a hot knife. But it was just a passing nuisance. They built men sturdy in my day. Like ships, they were made to stand up to the storms and hurricanes and anything else that got thrown at them.

I was just about to set off on another inspection to make sure there was no slacking going behind my back when Mick Molloy, the jacket man, showed up with a sheet of paper from the Captain. A list of names – those who had to attend on Wednesday to practise the heart-attack routine. When I showed Solid John his name on the list he said, 'I was in the last batch to do it.'

I said, 'What's the matter with them people, you could put a rocket up their arse and it still wouldn't wake them up?'

He said, 'No problem. A bit more practice won't do me any harm.'

'You're keen lad,' I said. 'Just make sure you're around if I ever keel over. I can think of a couple of them here who'd never remember whether to suck or blow if they seen me stretched out on the deck.'

And then I realized what I'd just said and added, 'Not that I've got any intention of being hauled away on Old Joe Knacker's cart for a long time yet!'

But the thought won't go away. One day all the whole show will go on without me. The clicking of the turnstiles and the shouts of the players out on the pitch and the supporters cursing and then jumping up to join in the roar of celebration when a goal goes in. Without me being there. Season after season there will be no Archie Block. One day the floodlights will blink on and light up the green grass and the royal blue jerseys and I won't be there, and I won't be there for all the seasons and the centuries to come.

A tough one to swallow, that: the glory days back here and me gone to the land of my fathers. The glory days, aye. That roar at a night game when Goodison is a bearpit, and the stand above us is shaking with the stamping feet, the iron girders trembling, like the night we put fear into the Krauts of Bayern Munich, the night we bombed them out of the Cup Winners Cup, blew them apart and then sent in the cavalry led by Andy Gray. Aye, we put the tingle of fear up their arses that night.

Another of them knife-jabs of pain in me chest. So sudden. Jab-jab. Something I'd eaten, that was all. That pie I scoffed before reporting for duty. You tuck into a tasty steak and kidney pie and then the damned thing turns around and bites you. But that's all it was. Or was it a bad sign? How bad? Bound for Joe Knacker's yard? Me? Never to go back to Wembley? Never go to another European final? Eh? Never to walk down Wembley Way with the massed ranks of Blues in all their pride and all their glory? Aye, the thought of it happening and me not there, that's hard. But even if a big spear came falling from the sky with my name on it right there I knew that there were worse places where I could finish my days. I'd be in good company. Some great men had passed away in Goodison Park. Harry Catterick, for one.

I was there to see it. Worked up there for a while at that time. That was a Cup game: Ipswich Town. Aye, the great man passed away right in front of me: our greatest manager, a man who built a truly great team. He was a hard man, though, Catterick. They took no liberties with him. He let them know they'd be on the first bus out at any sign of it. But he lost his grip, he built a team of champions and then he lost his grip. In nineteen seventy, that was. And the Blues were on a long slippery slope. A team that was on the road to greatness just fell apart. That was a tragedy.

History repeats itself as farce – that's what that smartarse McColl said once. I told him: 'Bollocks, absolute bollocks.' And I told him for why. Because when Harry Catterick's team fell apart that was history repeating itself as tragedy because the same had happened to the Everton team of nineteen thirty-nine, the champions of thirty-nine – the Second World War blew them apart. Oh, I know the meaning of the word tragedy alright. I'm a Blue. I've watched it happen twice. I was only a kid first time, but I saw it happen.

And years later I saw Harry lying there. He'd come back and died like an old king where once he'd ruled with a rod of iron – and let that rod slip out of his fingers.

But that was the way to go. Sudden. No farting around, lingering, becoming a nuisance to all and sundry. Switch the lights out and goodnight. Aye, there in Goodison like Dixie Dean and Harry Catterick and those supporters that I'd knelt over as they breathed their last. And I'd done that more than once over the years.

I thought: I want them to say, *He died at Goodison Park and what better place could it have happened.* But I want another ten or even fifteen seasons first!

And anyway that pain was gone. Nothing, it was nothing. I'd had worse pains in me arse – like George Gnomes and Scholar McColl.

And the players were in position now and ready to kick off.

Maggie May

The ref blows his whistle and the ball starts to roll, to be pinged about. Our players are pushing the opposition hard. Will they break through? I sense hope here today, more than that, belief, real belief. There's more noise than I've heard for weeks, months, all season. This game has stirred up all the fans, and they seem to have done the same to the team. Could this be the start of something? Out of the wilderness and into…whatever. No more tribulations and end-of-season agonies. Turn pressure into goals, like water into wine, and you're on your way, down to Wembley and up the league. And this team is showing the passion for it today.

   Passion. Genuine passion. I could do with some of that. No more of that other thing. Weird how your mind strays.

   But the Blues come again. The ball lands at the feet of this new kid, Franny Jeffers. He looks up. You will him to score but feel that he probably won't; the boy is no more than a bit of skin and bone. And then he does, he goes and does it. Oh put me to shame lad, put me to shame for doubting you!

Scholar McColl

And the whole stadium trembles. A kind of blue chaos. The carnival is in town. The happy hordes are leaping again, leaping and bouncing on the concrete steps as if they might grab handfuls of sky. Thousands of people squeezed into a single bundle of celebration, intent on shaking every tingle of pleasure from the moment. And who set them discoing on the terraces with that first and crucial goal? Who turned up the volume? A kid with big ears, and very quick feet.

Billy Whizz

Yis, this is the kinda Everton display we been waitin for. All season watchin that team has been like spendin an afternoon on Death Row, but all of a sudden they've busted outa jail. Coz we've found a lad oo can score a goal. We've maybe, just maybe, found a proper pearl in de onion bag. Ees like an athlete on the startin blocks, that kid, always watchin for a bit of space, a gap to dart throo. Ees light and ees quick so ee shapes up like ees never gonna get trapped in some dead end if the ball comes to him. That lad has got them in that much of a tangle they look like they're runnin after a ghost or a phantom or a willowdwisp as the Ginger Scholar would say. Worrever a willowdwisp is. Av never seen one in a football ground yet, and av been in a few stadiums in my time. But ees give them Coventry centre backs a bad headache all afternoon, every time the ball goes out of play they swallow another pill.

'Go on, lad!' I shout. 'Gerrin to them. There's a bagfull of goals waitin for you here!'

'Eh!' says Archie. 'Button ya mouth Bill or you-know-oo will be on yer case. And ya need to cut out that dancin nonsense. Av told ya before: save that for ya big nite out.'

'Big nite out?' I says, 'We're on our way to Wembley, mate. And we'll chuck the Nome into the Watford Gap as we go!'

But ee ain't laffin. Ee says, 'Al tell ya what tho Bill. Ee didn't like that bizzniss earlier on.'

I said, 'The day I start worryin what that creep likes or doesn't like will be the day I check out.'

Ee stood there shakin his ed like am a lost cause. Yeh. Hahaa!

Solid John Sanger

I was seeing smiles around me for a change, and feeling a little bit brighter and prouder myself now that the team was shaping up, when two punters approached me waving tickets, saying they'd been delayed in traffic getting to the ground and now someone was in their seats. I took the tickets, checked the numbers, scanned the terrace and eyed the seats they referred to right in the middle. Sure enough they were occupied. So I made my way over there. I had to disturb half a row of punters, and those behind them whose view was blocked when they stood to let me pass, but that was how it had to be if the job was to be done.

I arrived next to a large chunky character in a white mac, the kind of thing you see characters in films wearing. At first he seemed to be pretending that I wasn't there, which was my first clue as to what was to come. 'Can I just check your ticket please?' I said to him.

He took his time looking up, 'Why?'

'Why? I've got a problem with this seat, that's why.'

'There's other seats around isn't there?' Talking to me as if I was stupid.

I am a man who has travelled widely and shouldered many responsibilities and what I am most definitely not is stupid. 'There may or may not be empty seats, but what I'm concerned with is this seat. So if I could just see your ticket. Please.'

He looked at his mate next to him and they both shook their heads. So now they'd had a good headshake what about the tickets? I told them, 'Look, we're disturbing a lot of people here.'

'You're disturbin them.'

'Can I see your tickets please?' I said, like I meant business, which I certainly did even if this was becoming an awkward situation.

Finally he reached into his pocket and waved a ticket at me and as soon as I glimpsed the number I told him, 'That's not for this seat, that ticket is for a seat that is down the end of the stand. And the people who've bought tickets for these two seats are waiting to sit in them. So if you could make your way to your own seats…'

'Put them in other seats! That's what you're here for.'

'That is not what I'm here for. So I'm asking you now to leave these seats, and to move to the ones you should be in.'

I was getting in the way of other punters and they didn't like it but I'd started this job and I intended to finish it. You can't let the riff-raff get away with this sort of nonsense. You have to act. Once you start dithering around you've lost it. It's like a test. You can score high or low, pass or fail. Some qualify for the F grade every time, others acquit themselves with distinction. So I repeated myself, but in a firmer tone, 'I'm asking you now for the final time to leave these seats.'

Mr White Mac did a big huff-puff and climbed to his feet, as did his mate beside him. If the one in the white mac looked like some kind of TV gangster, his mate was one of the tracksuit brigade. He looked like the kind who keep those nasty little dogs with jaws like mantraps, the kind who walk around like constipated gorillas beating their chest trying to frighten everyone out of their bit of jungle. Okay, they were both big and they both seemed unpleasant characters but they weren't so big that they didn't have to live by the same rules as everybody else – even if they had other ideas.

I turned and made my way back along the row, apologizing to the punters as I went and making sure that the two big silly boys were following behind me.

From the aisle at the end of the row I ushered the two latecomers towards their seats while the bad boys lingered like a pair of lifetime loiterers. Job done, I turned to them. The Man in the Mac gave me the hard stare. But said nothing. The type who make threats with silence? Possibly. So, okay, this was a scary beast, but I wasn't going to let him put the frighteners on me. I'd be a lying if I said it didn't have my ticker in a bit of a sprint, but I know I'm a strong lad who can handle himself if need be, and one who knows that you will encounter the scum of this earth from time to time. Unfortunately. The first principle is: you stand your ground, you don't flap, you have confidence in yourself.

I've never been one to look for trouble, there's no box of murky secrets locked away in my cupboard. I never kicked around with the scallyboys and ne'er-do-wells – unlike someone else who was standing not so far away with his eyes on the pitch. But a man doesn't have to be a street brawler to find himself every once in a while challenged at the muscle game and drawn into a bit of a showdown.

Out of the corner of my eye I saw Archie Block moving towards us but this was my little scene, my High Noon. Maybe I don't wear the sheriff's badge or even a deputy's but that didn't mean I wasn't qualified or well entitled to – one day.

As old Archie Block arrived, that pair of overgrown, sullen-faced adolescents turned and moved on along the gangway to the end where their seats were located.

'Everything okay?' asked Archie.

I nodded. Of course it was. I started a job, I finished it. 'All taken care of,' I said and returned to my position, stood there amid thousands of fans who were in fine voice for a change.

Scholar McColl

Here is where all the small lives are pooled into something bigger. Here is where a man reaches out of the smallness of his life and touches something larger, something that can seem grand, awesome, enduring. Here is something that has not been stamped and coded by Mr Hum-Drum's faceless operatives. Here is where those long habituated to overcaution might poke a toe into another more turbulent pool.

Like fingers that have been feeling around in the dark all the voices find each other once again, discover common notes: the simple and joyous sound patterns that make up the club's name – Ev-er-ton! A repeat, a variation, then back to the start. And here we go again.

It feels like it could go on for ever. But the big wind that blows long from those lungs does subside. The chant shrinks. What was a grand opera becomes a short story, a bit of doggerel some drunk is reciting. But it will be recreated, as it always has been. For we watch from where so many have watched before us. We have taken their places, others will take ours. These voices are the echoes of those who were once here but have now passed on. Their history, their myths, their tales of triumph, are now ours. And if we move on, if the Blues one day find a new home, then that big royal blue bundle that is Everton's past will be carried away with them.

And another success for the boys in blue is never here in doubt. The minutes are so easy to live in today – let the game go on and on. But it must end, and does. The final whistle sends another victory into the memory box. And the crowd is upstanding to applaud most gratefully.

Some are in a sprint to beat the traffic or to be first at some bar, but many are slow to leave. A win, and a good one – here now is a fruit to savour. From the aisles and the gangways so much smacking of hands, all those elbows and wrists that will not be still. So many have supped at last that potent hooch of victory and must celebrate. And the final shout of the day – a few big round words – comes from a man dressed in dull colours, the greys and pale browns of those who live invisibly in the quiet margins. And there close by, another: one who wears the club shirt, a blue warrior who fears no winters and no foe, who would scoff at all worriers, flings high his knuckles as if a hole might be punched in the air above. And beside him another trooper, even bolder, who must give the whole universe a shaking for doubting us, for thinking that the Blues were ever anything but great.

And now the mass exit. So many backs and bottoms. So many shoulders edging in the direction of the big gates. But there is one who must linger, studious and alert, taking in all the breath he can manage for what might be filtered from it, giving his eyes as long as they need; a tourist of the richer human experiences maybe, or one who will never come back and must wrap up his memory in stuff that will last: in the green and the blue, the detailed patterning of divots and skidmarks that the game has left on the pitch, the print of studs on the long white line. Into the large bag of memory all of this will go along with all the other fragments of a single afternoon: that sudden bursting out of the crowd, like the speeded-up film of a flower blossoming, when the ball bulges the net; the simple repetitive rhythmic chant where over thirty thousand people speak with a single celebratory voice; the mass gasp and groan triggered by a near miss and the encouragement of applause that follows. The large scraps and the small, like torn-out pieces of newspaper, are falling through, settling in the large bag.

After releasing all the yellowjackets, and checking down below, I lift my talkie to my mouth, 'All clear on Section Six. All clear on Section Six.'

The voice from high up above in the control box acknowledges my signal. I am done, on my way out.

Another day in the long history of Everton Football Club. The day the old family found a new son, a goalscorer, who might, or might not, of course, have a big future and help them regain their rightful position. Coventry couldn't keep hold of him: like trying to hold water in a string bag, like trying to tie smoke up with a length of twine. How good will he turn out to be? Who can tell? But this is how hope will plant a seed in people's lives. Here is, perhaps, a player of the future – and that hope might feed a man when nothing else does.

You think of all the stuff that goes into your head in a week. All the faces on the screen, all the spokespersons and special correspondents, all those radio gabblers and paper columnists, all the pictures and quotes from all those people and all those places from Tashkent to Timbuctu, from New York to New South Wales and what do you remember? A single goal scored by a scrawny flap-eared kid in Goodison Park – that's what. And if anyone ever tries to tell you that it's just a game then you tell them that they don't understand and that if they don't understand then they don't know what they're missing.

I shed my bright outer skin. The comfortable murmur of success fills the coatroom like new upholstery – you can sink into this stuff, lounge a while. We're all winners here, we have smiles to throw away, our great yellow pockets are bulging with the stuff of satisfaction. We are all repeating what will bear repeating so many times. There is all next week to stuff with our repetitions: all our insights and analyses, our jokes and clichés. Because everything seems to make sense, for a change. Both history and the future are comprehensible. You can see how we got here and sense where we're going now. Those threatening mysteries, those ominous shadows, you can forget them now.

For a while at least.

We are dressed for our other lives in the Winslow or the Blue House or alehouses or kitchens or bedrooms far beyond. We have shed the yellow and are made ordinary again.

Billy Whizz

A pint after a good win. What more can yer ask? A shag, maybe. But first things first. A good pint of bitter just tinged with coolness from the cellar. Nectar. Yeah. We won. We shoved Coventry out of the cup and stroll on to the next round. I take a good swallow of ale and then draw on me ciggy, take that smoke in deep down, deep, deep down – and then let it go nice and slow and easy. Yeah. Everythins o-kay, just right. Yeah, I tilt me head back and take another good deep gulp.

Then Cally comes in. Old mate of mine. Ees carryin a Racin Post, and a lorra good that will have done him. Ee spends all day studyin form but it never does him no good. Eed have been better off spendin his coin watchin the Blues like in de old days. I can see ees lost again but I tell him, 'We beat Coventry easy,' I says. 'And now ya never know, it could our year for another trip to the final. I mean it could be me not you.' Aha-ha! Am poking meself in the chest and seein meself strollin down Wembley Way again.

Cally never went to the match no more. Cally was a loser, ee was addicted to failure like them needle-boys to their white powder. Women, work, motors, his body, his flat, his cat, his cooker, his cock: everythin give him gyp, or give him the elbow or left him stranded or fell down on his ed. Eed even watched the Blues right throo the nearly years of the seventies and early eighties and then thrown in his season ticket just as Kendall's eighties team was about to step on to the launch pad. Ee never made a decision in his life that didn't turn round and smack him in the gob. If ever a fella was born to lose and to be for ever reminded of it by his mates it was Robert Augustus Callaghan.

Ee tells me some of his latest woes which I can't help laffin at. So then to cheer him up like, I says, 'Remember that time we went down to the Smoke to see the Blues.'

'Arsenal,' ee says noddin, smilin, because that was one of the few times in his life when ee managed to score.

We travelled down by coach overnight. We got there at eight o'clock in the mornin and went straight to Covent Garden to that alehouse that was open at dawn for market porters. I had two pints of bitter for me breakfast. What better way could yer have to start a day? A couple of nice golden pints. The game wasn't one for de istory books but that night I copped off with a cockney girl. We all did. They was rampant them cockney girls that season. We was all in one flat. I was on top of a chest of drawers with mine. The beds was already burstin. But ya don't care when yer young. Yad do it anywhere just so long as the cock bird makes it to the nest. She kept sayin, 'Slow, go slow.' They don't like to rush things them cockney girls. A shag to them isn't like knockin back a quick pint. They might be rampant but they still like to take their time over titbits and nibbles. We got there in the end tho. The land of honey. Aye, a shag, that's another part of the set. A good bareback shag. I can't stand havin a balloon on me cock. Like dancin in wellies. A good shag on top of a chest of drawers while yer mates are trampolinin on the bed. Yis. No wonder de old codgers and fossils start harkin on about de old days. I can hear me footsteps startin down that street already!

I says to Cally, 'Ya lucky yve still got mates oo cn remember ya back in the day when every horse ya backed didn't turn out to be a donkey!'

Ee turns and looks at me, like ee doesn't usually look at me, and says, 'What makes you so sure you ain't gonna take a tumble one day, lad? Ya wanna maybe think about that sometime.'

Think? Laff, more like.

Then I says, 'Well one thing's for sure, we weren't put on this earth to sit around with long faces thinkin about the meanin of life and all kinds of doomy-gloomy crap.' I says, 'De effay cup, ya never know, ya just never know, lad. Someone has to win it, someone has to lift that pot in May.' I says, 'But first we got bread and butter bizzniss in the league.'

   Middlesboro next up. Bring em on.

13

Chemical Men from the Wild North

Scholar McColl

We've got that Middlesboro tribe in town again: bare-chested barbarians beating their fists on their chests and shouting their battle brags in an echoey stadium an hour before the match kicks off. They're going to send us down with the dead men. That's what the massed grunt is saying. But they'll be lucky if they're not down in the underworld themselves come the end of the season.

I always did like a night game. So much more atmosphere than the middle of the afternoon, even if the Northmen have brought some miserable wet weather with them. Floodlights make the pitch look perfect, and illuminate that royal blue.

Down along the gangway the Blocker Man is holding forth to an old speckie. He's looking older himself these days, more crumpled and creased around the eyes – those eyes that dart briefly in my direction when he sees me clocking him. But they don't stick. I'm not his favourite viewing material. And I can find more pleasant things to look at, myself. Maggie May is back with us today. A bit of that female scent and smile makes all the difference in a big box of blokes – those femme curves and painted eyes. Yeh, she's a smart dame, that one. The sexy nurse type. You could have a laugh with her, I reckon, that and a little bit more maybe.

But for now we have the wild men of the north to deal with, they who are deep now into their routines – flaunting their nipples and doing their tribal chants.

I went up to their place to watch a game one time. The local cops locked us in for half an hour after the game ended: suddenly you're a prisoner, can't walk out like a free man. Then when you are let out you haven't gone far before you walk into an ambush, a big mob of Northmen: real wild men, the progeny of Viking plunderers and rapists, pirates, marauders, cannibal tribesmen from the banks of the Tees, chainsaw murderers, torturers, men who on moonless nights offered up blood sacrifices to the dark gods of Cleveland.

They must have thought they had me and FreddieB cornered but we dodged the trap and dashed into the glare of a creeping cop car. When it halted we jumped into the back seats.

'Wot d'ya think this a taxi?' was the response.

The officers, it seemed, were being inconvenienced. I told them, 'It'll be a hearse if we go back out there, you'll be taking us in dead.' I said, 'We ain't getting out till you drive us away from this mob.'

'Arrest us if you like,' says Freddie.

So they dumped us a long way from where we wanted to be but but thankfully a long way from those ugly ambushers of Ayresome Park.

Happy days on the road with the boys in royal blue.

A speckie leans towards me as I walk the gangway. Staring at the pitch he says, 'Can you spot the deliberate mistake?'

I obviously should have been able to.

'Look in the corners,' he says like some cheery uncle with a slow kid.

'Flags,' I say flatly. Puzzled, a little worried.

'What's happened?' A very good question from a very observant man. A man as puzzled as I am.

I shrug. 'They should have been there long ago.'

It's getting close to kick-off. This is football at the top level. Corner flags are not an optional extra. So…like the man says: Where are they?

I'm on my way to the tool shed where the groundsmen hang out. On the concourse I spot one of the maintenance staff. 'Where's yer man?' I say jerking my thumb at the pitch. 'He hasn't put the flags out.'

This man who serves the club grins, 'Say nothin.'

'But…'

'Say notn. Leave him to fall face-first in the brown stuff.'

Say nothing? I love this club. I've come through the Valley of the Shadow of Death for displaying that love – a love that is the one unbroken thread that connects me back to my childhood. This isn't just a patch of grass surrounded by rows of seats, it's a chamber of myths and dreams, a shrine. The ghosts of the great still walk in the place. Or that's how it seems. But what is it really? Is it just another place where people work day after day and grow to hate the sight of each other?

'You seen the flagman?' I say to the big fella on the big blue gate.

He shakes his head. 'Not for a while, I haven't.'

The tool shed doors are padlocked. What to do? We were founder members of the Football League. Over a hundred years ago. Are we now beginning to lose our grip on the simple things? Oh what bucketfuls of scorn would be thrown at us if this match was delayed. And what future for the flagman? Ridicule and disgrace – the sack?

When the little inset gate swings open yer man's lanky figure appears, bending to butt a bald head through the gap, straightening as he strides, his jacket flapping to keep up with him.

I'm just opening my mouth, my finger extended towards the corner of the pitch, when he says, 'I know! I know!'

As he strides on past and I swing around he says, 'Old fella I know took ill out there. I stayed with him till the medics came.'

He pockets the padlock, flings open the doors to this cavern of hoses and grass cutters, 'Here,' he says shoving two flags at me.

I cross the grass and drop the first one into its hole and a fountain of muddy water spurts all over my boots, my legs. A big laugh erupts from the punters in the front row, somebody claps.

Archie Block

I looked across and there he was out on the pitch. Scholar McColl. What's he doing out there? Strolling across the grass, he was. Strolling – like he's out for a walk in the park. Who does he think he is? He might wear stripes but that doesn't mean he can't be put in his place.

I said to myself, I'll have words with him. You are my deputy, I'll tell him, no more and no less, and do not forget it.

Scholar McColl

I'm just turning back towards the section, my flag mission completed, when I spy this bearded figure come through the little iron gate: Mr Gnomes, the certificate man. He's back again, marching as if he's about to go on parade, or to the rendezvous point for some particular mission. Back again? I'm still pondering that when the Blocker Man approaches. His walk is stiff and march-like too – that's what two years of National Service, and a lifetime of war books, has done for him. It makes him look strong, impressively authoritative? Nah, makes him look as if he's got clockwork arms, it makes him look like he's got diarrhoea and is desperate to get to a bog without making it too obvious. And to add to that, he has his zip pulled right up to the chin, making him look like a tightly-wrapped parcel.

His head shifts backwards and forwards on a wrinkled tortoise-neck as he scans his little empire. The creases in his brow ripple back to his stubbled scalp. His voice comes ahead of him, gruff and demanding, as a stiff finger wags in my direction, 'What was you doing out there on that pitch?'

'Serving this club as a loyal servant should, that's what.'

'Eeehhhhh? Just cut the clever talk! That's not your duties to be out on that pitch. You stick to your proper duties in future, no more posing out there where you shouldn't be and getting yourself noticed!'

'Never mind me getting noticed,' I retort. 'Guess who I've just spotted – and looking like he's on a mission?'

Two wiry eyebrows ascend.

'And casting his eyes towards our section,' I add with emphasis.

Those eyebrows fall, settle on top of a puzzled sort of frown.

'Mr Safety Certificate himself,' I tell him.

The frown collapses as the jaw falls open. The Blocker Man stares at me – slow thoughts shifting in his old brain.

'Yeah, he's back!'

That old head goes from side to side. 'No. If he was here I'd know about it.'

'Don't kid yourself.'

He doesn't like the sound of that. But he isn't stupid and he can read the look on my face that's telling him to take notice.

Archie Block

Another inspection? Already? And this one not announced. To

find fault on my section? Oh no, no, no. Not while I'm fit for active service. So I was in among them, and woe betide anyone I found slacking. I said to one of them, I said, 'Where's your tie, why haven't you got your club tie on?' I said, 'What kind of advertisement for the club are you if you can't even be bothered to throw a tie around your neck and put a knot in it?' I said, 'In future don't bother to turn up if you've got no tie on, and that's an official warning and it's going in the book, so don't say you weren't warned when heads start rolling and yours is one of the first to hit the deck.'

By the time I'd made sure there was no one letting the side down it was time for kick off.

Billy Whizz

The ref blows and away we go. And we're lookin sharp tonight, we're lookin very sharp. Hutch plays a choice pass, and our new lad in blue, dartin like a whippet again, gets inta the channel between full back and centre back and gives them stooges an early dose of the shakes. And it's the kid himself oo spots a ghost in a blue shirt driftin inta the danger zone and plays a perfect cross inta its path.

And there's the ball whizzin just inside the post.

Ye-e-ess! In less than a minute we've grabbed a goal. And am stood in the middle of a blue and white volcano. Everyone is flung up out of their seats in the roar of celebrashon. And why not, why not? The Blues have surged inta form, ya cn see it. And I do see it. A few minutes later am watchin the ball float over their goalie's ed and drop inta the net. Ye-e-ess! Two-nil. Ere we go! Ere we go!

Scholar McColl

No, Billy, no lad.

Away to my right he's just thrown his arms up and done that little dance again – acting more like the raver than the doorman. And then, looking directly across at Section Two, I notice in the gangway that familiar bearded figure. Inspecting them? Or having a look at us from afar?

And seeing what? A dancing man in a yellow jacket?

How many times do you have to warn these lads? He dances too close to the wind, our Billy Whizz. Because the wind of change has blown through this place since the informal days of the past – all this Dress Code and Discipline and Code of Practice that's turned us bunch of casuals into some kind of regiment. And soon, very soon, the High Command will make an example of someone who reckons he can buck the system here. That's the way power works: hang a few rebels, crucify the odd nonconformist, call a feisty woman a witch and toss her on the bonfire, that's the old routine designed to put fear into the lower orders, and ensure compliance, stability. It's in the books and you need to know your history. And laughing, dancing, Billy Whizz obviously doesn't.

Billy Whizz

As the Blues sweep forward yet again Archie Block comes down the gangway towards me with a very busy-busy expreshon on his face. 'Yer wanted in de office,' ee says.

'Office?'

'That's what yer man said.'

'Eh? Now?'

'Now. Get yer arse down there right away.'

'Why? What for?'

Ee shrugged and says, 'I don't know what you've done but whatever it is you've done it, lad. The call just said send steward number 132 to de office immediately. Eell be there now waitin for ya.'

Eh? De office? While the game is still goin on? A ripple of worry goes over me skin like when I was a kid and got sent to de headmasters room.

When I get to the coatroom it seems so empty. And it still smells of the fish an chips that some of the lads was eatin before the game. I go past the counter, throo to the back room, the office. Captain Clueless is sittin at the desk with his pen in his hand, doodlin on a pad. I look down on his baldy ed. Ee looks up at me and drops the pen. Ee looks grim, ee looks like an angin judge. Even his tash looks like it's in a bad mood.

And then ee starts to drone. All stuff eed said an undred times before. And then ee got to the point. And a sharp point it turns out to be. Ee says I was seen jumpin up and down after the goal was scored.

'Me?' I says. I couldn't have sounded more innocent.

Ee says ee had it on video. I pull a puzzled face and shake me ed like I don't know what ees on about. Ee says that the camera shows me dancin around, that number one-three-two is clearly vizible.

I shrug, 'If it was me I didn't realize. I must have got carried away.'

Scorn. If ever a man had a scornful look on his face it's him. Then ee says that am not there to get carried away, that am there to be alert, to be responsible.

I says, 'It's just de abits of a lifetime. Ya can't change that in five minutes.'

'Years!' ee says. 'Seasons!' ee says. 'Not five minutes.' Then ee says that the deadline was long passed for everyone to start conformin to the rules, but that some people just won't get the message until they see an ed roll.

It clicks then. 'So ya mean…?'

Ee says, 'You're finished here. I have to do it.'

I says, 'But av worked hard for this club. Av done a good job out there. For years. Long before any of youse bosses was on the scene.'

Ee says, 'Am not sayin you haven't.'

I says, 'I worked for notn for this club on the section I first started on here. A match programme, that's all I got for an afternoon's work. For years I done that.'

He's not interested. I said, 'But that counts for notn now?'

Not interested. All ees interested in is his stupid rules. So then ee tells me to remove any personal belongins from the jacket. Ee sits behind that desk, like hidin behind it, like ees hidin behind his desk and that muzzybush under his nose, and tells me to remove the yeller jacket and leave the premises.

I says, 'Ya can't do that to me. Ain't right.'

'You knew the rules,' ee says, 'you were told enuff times.'

I felt like I was bein ripped apart. It was just a job to him. Ad been a Blue since ad first drawn breath and ee just sits there tellin me am finished and there can't be no arguments about it, no discushon and that's that. Ees just waitin for me to go, me ood been loyal to the Blues every second of me life, me oos got Dixie Dean for a middle name. Ee was just waitin for me to walk away and never come back, like it was notn.

I says, 'But ya don't understand.'

'No, it's you oos failed to understand. And the quicker everyone else understands the better.'

Ya can't talk to a man like him. Ees just a placeman, an old army cop, oos probably only there becoz of oo ee knows. Ad die for this club. But would ee? Eed just sit there and watch it sink. Just like ees sittin there lookin at me, his eyes like little beads, like as if just becoz ee has a desk and a blazer and a stupid mustash ees important. About as important as a boil on my arse. Yeh, ee just sits there waitin for me to give the jacket back and go.

So I unzip it dead slow, take it off even slower, and at the same time give him a long stare. Then I let it slip down me arms and just when ee thinks am gonna let it fall to the floor I fling it at him. And when ees flapped it away, when his baldy ed pops out, I tell im where ee can stick his fokin code of conduct.

Archie Block

And then the Captain came on the radio telling me what had happened. I said, 'But he was a good steward in his way, he was good at working with the crowd, sorting things out. It's a shame to see him go.' But that cuts no ice in the cold zone of the High Command and I can't say I expected it to. Even so, I did what I could for the lad, I said, 'Is there no chance of a reprieve, a final warning?' And then I hear what I expect to hear, 'There've been enough final warnings.'

And the Ginger Scholar must have been listening in because he comes up to me and says, 'That's stupid – when you think about it. We need experienced people on this job.'

I was in no mood for a discussion with Professor Bollocks McColl. I said, 'Aye, and we need people with the sense to see which way the wind is blowing.' I said, 'You tell them, and you tell them and you tell them again, but will they listen?' I said, 'You kick their arses and you crack the whip but will they take notice?'

I shook my head. You do what you can for people but if they want to stick two fingers up at authority then they have to pay the toll when the coin-man calls. Simple as that. Without discipline there's nothing. The regiment. The shipyard. The football club. A body of men without discipline is like a ship without a rudder.

He said, 'Surely someone can put a word for him in the right ear?'

I told him straight, 'Well don't you be getting ideas. Anyone puts a word in for people on this section, it's me.'

Who does this character think he is? I said, 'There's nothing we can do. If there was I'd do it. But the lad's gone. And that's that.'

And out on the pitch the Blues were running at the Northmen without letting up. All season, bar Saturday's game against the Sky Blues, they've lumbered around like carthorses, but all of a sudden they're like thoroughbreds, they're like Arabian stallions – and I know a thing or two about race horses – they're swift, they're mobile, they're damn near impossible to catch, and they're making the Northmen look like a herd of pantomime asses.

And the Scholar was still stood there mouthing about the sacking.

So I said, 'I'm sorry for the lad, but he's brought it on himself and that's that, case closed.' And then I gave him a very firm look.

I give him a look that old Bulldog, that ruthless tyrant of a shipyard foreman, would have been proud of.

Scholar McColl

Cluny appears on the section, asking for Archie Block. I point down below to the concourse. And then just as he's moving away I say, 'I heard we're a man short now, that Billy's been sacked.'

He turns and looks at me like it's none of my business. 'You won't be seeing his face again.'

I say, 'We've lost of a lot of experience there. Billy had worked in this ground longer than nearly everyone.'

He doesn't like it. He frowns and says, 'There are ways to behave here and there are ways not to behave and the sooner everyone here gets that message the better.'

Then he moves away in search of the Blocker Man. And as soon as he's gone the Blocker comes bouncing over, 'What's going on here? Eh? I've told you before. What colour is this coat,' he says tapping his sleeve. As if he actually expects an answer.

Archie Block

'Blue,' I said 'This is blue. And that one of yours is yellow and that's because I'm the boss here and you are not the boss, you are only the deputy. And I, and no one else here, do the talking.'

'Why? What did I say?' he asked with that smartarse look on his face.

I told him, I said, 'Whatever it was it was it was out of order.'

So he says to me, 'Well if you can't give specific examples.'

Specific examples? He could stick his specific examples up his arse. But you can't tell with that type, they might enjoy it.

Know-alls, barrack room lawyers, alehouse bloody philosophers – pests and nuisances sent to annoy the common man.

And bugger me, that damned pain was back, stabbing through the ribs. The last thing I needed was more nonsense from Professor Bollocks.

Scholar McColl

I can hear a minor explosion taking place deep inside him, probably sending shrapnel very close to his heart, so he's got the sense to take himself off. Just in time for me to enjoy seeing the Blues weaving very bright patterns out on the pitch, pushing the ball around like artists instead of labourers. Verve, skill, precision, it's all there tonight.

'Dacourt's had a good game,' says a voice from out of the crowd.

And you can't argue with that. Him and Hutchinson have been dominant tonight, and classy with it – just what you look for in midfield. But at times the Frenchman has looked as if he could control the game all on his own, going past opposition players like they're not there, dropping every pass on to the exact spot. He surges, he stops, he lays the ball off and then takes it back again: he does what he likes. And then he touches a brilliant performance off with a goal, taps the ball in after the goalie drops it.

'It'll be bad news if he goes,' says that voice when the cheering subsides. For the word is that Olivier Dacourt wants to leave.

But Solid John Sanger is not so concerned. I can hear him behind me sounding off. 'I heard that rumour,' he says. 'I heard that he doesn't like it here. Can't settle. Doesn't rate the city, apparently. Because the restaurants are not up to his standard!'

I turn to him, 'But it is just rumour and gossip! And the man's from another country, a different culture, he -'

'So what?!' That tacky stuff is bubbling up within him once again. 'So that entitles him to go around saying our city is no good, does it?'

I don't bother to answer. So he turns to the Blocker Man who has just arrived. 'If it's not good enough for Olivier Dacourt here he knows what he can do. What's wrong with the food here, anyway? I took Mary out the other week and had a fine piece of sirloin, a perfect piece of cooking, with mushrooms too. And I'd definitely slam a pan of my ma's scouse on any darkie frog's table and defy him to cook up a better meal than that. And then I'd show him what culture means, I'd show him a thing or two about the culture of this city.'

Maggie May

Why argue on a night like this? All the players between them have killed Boro off and buried them. Slick passing, smart running, sharp finishing – beautiful, it's made me giddy just watching it. And it's not only me who's affected by what we've seen. It's all too much for a scoreboard that's got so used to games without goals. When the third one went in it came over all confused and dizzy and now it just needs to sit in a darkened space.

But old Archie is still looking busy, and a little worried. He stops beside me and gives me the news. There's been drama on the section. There's a vacancy and they're looking for someone experienced to replace Billy. My name has been suggested in the office. Me? Settle down here after all those years of moving about? If that's what serves the club best, okay. 'But this isn't really the way I would have wanted it – taking someone's job who's been sacked.'

'Nothing you can I do about that now, my dear. Billy always was one of them characters who walks close to the edge. Everything's a big joke until you take a tumble.'

Billy Whizz

Am stood in the park across the road, stood there lookin down at the lake, the dark water. Stunned. Gutted. Then the roar. That's another goal. Four-nil. But oo scored for us? Am out in the dark and there's goals goin in at Goodison, how can that be? Me, Billy Whizz, don't even know oos scored.

My grandad once walked to Wembley to see the Blues play in a cup final, walked, aye. My family has supported Everton since the ground was built and now they've just kicked me out, just like that, for notn, just for bein a good Blue and showin me support for the team. Sacked. Booted out. Me, Billy Whizz, kicked out by that clueless baldy-eded bastid in the blazer.

Another goal. Five-nil! The game goes on and am missin it. Booted out of Everton Football Club and into the dark. Sad, that. A sad, sad fact. Ya could drown in yer own tears if ya let them flow. Or drown in that lake. Take the plunge, lay a soggy corpse on someone's conchence.

Nah. Better off swallowin booze than that dirty water. Yeah. I need booze. I need to float away on a river of ale, I need to drown in that. Get meself down to The Brick. Wash me sorrows down with the first of many.

But after a few swallows of ale am comin outa the doldrums. Av still got that first pint in me fist when I realize it's not booze I need, its revenge – vengence, yeah. That clueless ex redcap fired me, yeh, but ee was only the execushoner. It was his finger on the trigger but oo give him the bullet? The Nome. That fuzzyfaced arl sailorman from across the park. I could kill him, cut his fokin ed off and then al hurl it all the way back to cider country, or maybe over the roof into that piss-ole the Kop where it belongs. But ee ain't worth a long stretch in the dungeons. Nah, am seein revenge that ain't blood colour, am seein revenge that's the colour blue, royal blue, yeah. The royal blue of that tin of paint av still got in the van. Yeah. Yea-ea-ea-eahhhh.

Ee lives over in the posh, that nome. Over the road from Caldies park. Seen him. Done a roofin job nearby. That's it: a plan. Am bangin me glass down on the bar an edin out. Am on me way. The booze can wait. Ave gorran important matter to deal with – with a paint brush.

I leave the van on de other side of Caldies, thinkin crafty, like, put the paint and the brush in me shoulder bag and move on throo the dark, over the green stuff, round past the lake, and on to de other side. There's a handy gap in the wall over there, brings me out not far from where I want to be.

I cross the Avenue and am almost there, goin sneaky, walkin light. But it's all quiet in the leafy suberbs. And the Nome's motor is on his driveway and the bedroom light is on. Ees busy doin a shag with Missus Nome, maybe. Well roll over and sleep tight ya woollyback interloper and then see what ya wake up to.

I nip the lid off the paint and go to work, daub the blue stuff on his front door – Take that ya Red. And that. Big strokes of vengence. But I do a proper job of it. That door is well and truly decorated.

Just finishin when I hear somethin. Someone comin along the road. So I have to dodge behind a bush. Fella with a dog out on the pavement. Ees speakin to the hound. And from the way ees talkin the mutt is sniffin somethin suspishus – like paint, like Billy Whizz at one of his capers. And I sure ain't plannin on payin no fine for criminal damage or whatever the Nome's buddies in the force might slap on me.

I think the fella is lookin at the bush and maybe wonderin is someone lurkin in the garden. Lurkin? I sure am. But luckily ee ain't so sure. Ees tuggin at the lead, maybe wants to get home for his shag. As soon as they move on I'm away in the opposite direcshon. Just in case Mr Suspishus gets dragged back by his hound for a second look.

Just back on the Avenue, edin for the gap in the wall when I hear the siren. Did that fella spy me lurkin, has ee gone home and called the cops? No, surely not. But it sounds like it's speedin my way. Take no chances, Billy Boy, the crafty voice is sayin. So I jumps the wall instead of dashin along for the gap. But –

Ahhh. Fok me, it's lower on the other side – a lot lower. I ain't landin, am fallin. And the bag on me shoulder ruins me balance. So as I land on the grass I go over on me ankle one way and twist me knee the other way and even manage to bang me fokin ed on the wall when I topple backwards. Ahhhhhhh! What!!! Am crocked. Worra bastid. And if that ain't enuff, the damned paint tin's come open. Ohhhhhhhhh. All down me leg. And it's in me shoe. Ohhhhh. Ohhhhhh, jeez.

Yev just been booted out by the club yev loved all yer life. Ya lyin there, a twisty ankle, a nackered knee that's killin ya with the pain, a bump on yer ed, and paint – royal blue fokin paint all over ya. And ya might, ya might just start to ask yerself – Could it be that Billy

Whizz ain't winnin no more?

Part Five

14

Billy's Own Goal

Billy Whizz

Done me knee, yeah. Bad. Very bad. Try and put all me weight on that leg and it's torture. So I can't gerron a roof to earn me coin. So, like many a time before, al av to look elsewhere for some earnins for a few days. Worra mess. Lost me yeller jacket and now am half crippled. Worra bastid. Al survive, like. But.

Jane

Am lookin at him across the kitchen and seein a fella oo looks like ees been booted out inta the wilderness. But oos fault is that? A player tries doin fancy tricks in his own penalty box and ends up jugglin the ball inta his own net. He gets dragged off the pitch and dropped from the team. Oos fault is that?

An on top of everthin else ees gone and made a clown of himself, gone and painted a man's door blue oo turns out to support a team that plays in blue. All the Reds are laughin at him. Fool.

Even so, I must do what I can to cheer him up. 'We could go to the match together like in the old days,' I suggest, and the idea does have a big appeal to me. But no, it's as if ee doesn't hear that. Ee hardly seems to notice me these days. It's like somethin has gone and you didn't even notice when it went, like somebody closin the door really quietly without sayin goodbye, a guest at a party makin a silent getaway out inta the night and only later ya notice they're not there.

But once it was different, so different. Once we used to stand together in Goodison, right in there among the faithful, with all their voices risin around us, and the sun shining on the blue and the white, and the pitch lookin like somebody's back lawn. And the day we got married we went to the match before settin off for our honeymoon, but the Blues lost at home to Norwich so maybe that part of our life began with a bad omen. If that's what it was I wasn't takin much notice. But after the boys were born Billy went off to the match on his own and put on the yellow jacket. So we no longer went to Goodison together like I wish we could do again but somehow know deep down that we never will.

It's as if you open your purse and see there isn't as much in it as you thought there was. Yer countin the notes again and again. Did ya lose one? Did somebody steal it? What happened? It's like you buy a potted plant, it's all in bloom like a bride on her weddin day, you come down one mornin and it's keeled over, it looks like a dead ballerina. Did you kill it? Did you give it too much or not enough? Oos to blame? How do you find out? Am I different from everybody else or just the same? My two boys have gone so early, straight out of school and into the Navy, leavin what seems to me like a lot of empty space.

Some days I blink and then realize av been stood gazin out of the window and not even started the washin up or the sweepin or the moppin. I make the bed, I peel a pan of spuds, I wipe the surfaces, I head off out to work, I sit down at the checkout and that's it: another day gone. And what do I feel? What in the whole day do I feel inside? Like something has dried up – a fruit with no juice, a stream with no water. Is that my fault? His? Oose? And what happens now? You have made your bed so now lie in it, that's what they say. But not everyone does, some ignore what they're supposed to do and go their own way and do what they choose. Would Billy miss me if I wasn't here? He would, of course ee would, but. But.

But maybe the Blues can go all the way to Wembley this year? Maybe for such a special day me and Billy could get tickets and go there together and the passion of the occasion would bring everythin back to where it once was. Maybe.

The first time I ever seen Billy ee was playin football in the park. I was with Laura Foster oo had come to watch her boyfriend but my eyes were on this lad Billy oo looked so fit and light on his feet. I watched him runnin with the ball, so quick, so strong, so tricky, and such a powerful shot in those fast feet of his. Oo was this lad? I had to find out. He was Billy Whizz, a joker, I discovered, a smart lad, and ee was a Blue. And there ee was one Saturday afternoon on the bus goin to the match. Not only that but ee seemed to notice me and was maybe givin me the eye as everyone jumped off the bus and crossed the road to Goodison. So next game I hurried me dad up to make sure we caught that same bus, but Billy wasn't on it. But ee was in the park a couple of days later with other lads playin in a kickabout. I was with some other girls so we kept walkin past and then hung around and then when the game was over we all got talkin and Billy, yes, recognized me – the girl eed seen on the bus. And then after it got dark ee walked home with me, and we talked about the Blues, and I felt then that we were meant to be together. I did. I felt that. So that later times when ee started to put his hands on me I didn't try to stop him. I knew I wasn't supposed to let him do that but I didn't care because there's what people say you should and shouldn't do and then there's you in your body and they're two completely different things. One thing is just the voices of other people which are a long way away and the other is what you can feel really close up, what makes you tingle and turn hot, and it's obvious which one is goin to win. And then I realized that whatever you'd been doin in the dark didn't show so no one would know anyway. And love can't just live on kisses for ever, that's why your heart gets wild the way it does and your body gets full of fireworks with the blue touchpaper twisted and ready for the match to be struck because it's time to move on to do things you've never done before but were always meant to do from the moment you slipped and slithered into this world especially now that you've found the right boy who loves you even if he won't say so in three words. So in our little corners and hidey-holes I let him undo me buttons and touch me underneath me clothes, makin me feel warm all over and while that was happenin nothin else on earth mattered.

So I was a girl without a cherry and Billy was overflowin with juices. But what are cherries for anyway if not to be eaten? And oo wants to be a little sweetie all her life even if it is for a dad oo is the best Evertonian in the whole history of the world? I just could not be his little darlin for ever and now I wasn't. But I said to Billy, I said, I told him, 'Do not dare ever take me for granted or you will definitely regret it.'

But what he did do, he took me to the match with him. And Saturday nights when me and Billy made love that was born of victory that lovin was as sweet as it comes. And sometimes, naked, we would wrap ourselves up in a big blue flag and then it was like all the power that was in that flag was in us too, like all the world was blue, like Everton and love was the same thing. We even had our own little chant about those oo had missed out. He was deep inside me and we chanted together: *Never ad a shag in a big blue flag? Oh worra bore, oh worra drag!* And then we laughed and kissed and then it was bang-bang-bang all the fireworks goin off inside me belly and down me legs.

But that was a long time ago.

And you can never know how things will change, a little bit changin one year, another little bit the next, and it all addin up in the end to a total you could never have believed when you first started out together. You can never know in the beginnin how the big empty spaces open up in a small livin room, how days become hollow things fit only to be thrown away. Because what was one thing becomes another, what was the thing you found becomes a lost thing, so that maybe only Everton and children is all that holds you together, and then if the children leave early to start a life on the big ships then there is only Everton and maybe that is not enough, it is only a reminder of days you can't get back to – the land of the big blue flag that is forbidden to us now for ever.

But am still half there at the match through the radio because we need these things, like me dad says, ee says we need things, somethin at least, outside ourselves and our loved ones, so that we know we belong, so that we know we are not just a tiny group huddlin in a corner and not connected with what has strength. And I still have that, but I have also these hours when am waitin for somethin to happen, somethin that is not part of what I already have, somethin new and fresh and alive because that's what me body says I need and if our bodies are a weird bag of needs and desires then that's what they are and they can't be ignored for ever. I need to have someone close so that I won't sit around broodin on me own. I want to be noticed, I want to be the important thing in someone else's life so that our days are wrapped up together, twined so tight that they can't be separated, because this is my life, the only one al ever have, and one thing's for sure, nobody will come along when am seventy, when av gone all bent and creaky-boned, and say that things haven't been fair to me, that av missed out on a lot so I can have another half a life to make up for it. Oh no. And I would not like to discover in years to come that av walked in the footprints of the livin dead. Not that. I want to be touched and taken with a passion. And if Billy will not do it then it will have to be some other.

Somebody else? That shocks me.

So I decide to try again, to save meself from what's in me head, to keep meself off the path I see meself strayin down, so I say again, I say to him again, I say, 'Why don't we start goin to the match together again like we used to before the children?'

But again ee doesn't answer. No ee doesn't want that. But ee doesn't realize, ee doesn't realize how much depends on this. No, ee doesn't want me to go to the match with him. I know ee doesn't want that but aim to give it just another try just in case. I decide to have one last go to save us, to save us both from whatever lies ahead which is different from anythin that we have been through before. I tell him that I don't mean every game, we could pick our games, the ones we want to go to together.

But ee looks at the floor. Ee looks at the window. Ee doesn't look at me. And still ee doesn't answer. And I know now, I know for sure that am wastin me time. I know that av tried me best but that I can't save us from what's to come. Not on me own. With his help I could. But ee won't help me to do it, ee won't even try. And if ee won't try then what else can I do?

But should I try once more? One last try?

So we're sittin there with the chatter from the telly soundin so loud in our silences, and it's like as if that chatter contains a message you'd rather not hear about you sittin there night after night with this man and the red and purple carpet, and the grey armchairs and the grey settee. So I say, 'Can't we do somethin different for a change?'

'Different?'

You'd think ad asked him had ee noticed pigs flyin past the window.

But it wasn't always like this. Once ee would come home from whatever work ee was doin, and describe what had happened and the people eed met, actin it out, givin me the whole tale with jokes and different voices like a little private performance. And I would listen and laugh and just enjoy the sound of his voice, and sometimes ee would even sneak in and put his hands on me shoulders, and ad spin around, actin more shocked than I really was, and fall into his arms, and then ad say, 'I love you doin that.'

But it's a long time since ee last did that. Such a long time ago.

I say, 'Different, yes. Ya know: go out somewhere together.'

But am wastin me time. And I know it.

Then on the way home from work I see a notice in the shop window. *Fit for All - Self Defence For Women. Come and join us, get active, build your confidence, have fun ...*

No I couldn't go to that. Or could I? Bounce and shake meself out of the doldrums? At school I was good at netball. Maybe I could just go once and see. But what would I wear?

15

The Lilywhite Assassins

Jane stands in the hall in the Old Police Station in the middle row of seven amid women of various shapes and ages. 'Okay, let's loosen up! Let's get fit,' calls Rosie Rodgers, the very bright and fit-looking figure out front as she begins to move. 'Shake! Yeah shake! Shake the stiffness out! Shake your leg, your arm, your...'

Like the others around her Jane, after beginning slowly, hesitantly, a little shy, is eventually flinging out her feet and hands as if she doesn't need them any more.

'Now jump,' calls Rosie. 'Jump-bend-stretch until you're good and loose!'

They leap and they bounce, and Jane is like a kid again, the girl who tied a skipping rope to a lamppost and bounced on the paving slabs, the one who played leapfrog with her dress tucked into her knickers. She leaps and drops, bounces back, grabbing for the roof, leaping higher and higher, as if she is getting lighter, as if the years are falling off her like unwanted clothes. As she leaps and ducks again it is as if she is throwing off the stiffness of the years, becoming again the girl who danced, the one who was always dancing: in the playground and the alleys and the doorways where she clapped and shimmied and twirled around.

The assembled ladies pause, most panting lightly. Some wear leotards, others sport track suits or loose cotton trousers with T-shirts, Jane wears a summery yellow vest and a pair of grey jogging bottoms she picked up at work and is pleased to see that she doesn't look out of place. Most are in their thirties with just a few older or younger ones among them. There is a hint in the air of hot bodies, anti-perspirant.

Rosie tells them, 'You might be small, you might not be small, but you have strength, even if you don't yet feel that you have it, you do have strength, and that's what we're going to draw on here, so that you can go about your life, wherever and whenever, with confidence. So… Okay, listen to this, and then we'll all do the words and the claps together:

Reclaim the night (clap)
Reclaim the street (clap)
Claim your rights (clap)
Move those feet (clap)
Be set to meet (clap)
And yeh defeat (clap)

Whatever threatens danger!! (clap-clap-clap-clap-clap-clap). Now,' Rosie, commands, 'let's do those words together. Let's get the rhythm and do the words as one. Let's really open up our throats so we hear our own voices. Let's go.'

After several stuttering attempts she has them roaring and clapping and stamping in unison.

For Jane, at first, it was as if her voice was stuck in her throat, as if all the skitting boys she'd ever encountered were hiding at the back, ready to leap out and laugh and point and mock. But by the third attempt her voice had wriggled free and was out there with the loudest.

'Excellent,' calls Rosie. 'Now let's really do it. One last time…'

And so they do it, those rows of women chant and they clap; and from Jane's throat her voice rises, it soars.

'Perfect,' Rosie tell them. 'So let's move on. First of all, a point about breathing, a reminder: If you're ever taken by surprise try not to panic, try to keep control of your body. And breathing is the key to that. Because you conquer fear through controlling your breathing. Remember to breathe from the diaphram…'

Jane follows the instructor's words and movements, breathing through her nose from deep in her chest, keeping her back straight and her chin tucked in.

'But once you've stayed calm what do you do?' asks Rosie striding over to her right and lifting a hardboard man to his blocks. 'Now this,' she says stepping back and stretching out a finger that points to the area between his legs. 'Now this, what he's got down here, might be to some of you the funniest thing you've ever seen, or it might be something you have fun with.'

'I should be so lucky!' That voice sets off a burst of cackles and giggles in which Jane joins as she looks around at all the bright eyes, the wide toothy mouths.

'But today,' Rosie smiles also as she puts her hands up for quiet, 'I can assure you it's not a joke, because that for today is our target. There are lots of names for the thing he's got there but today's name is *target*. It's where this man is vulnerable. It's not the only place, as we know. But every man that attacks a woman is vulnerable there. So, for you, maybe having to defend yourself, it's one place you might aim for. Today we're going to concentrate on the kick.'

She throws her right foot up to demonstrate, one, two, three times. 'So, start by getting your foot up into an easy kick, gently at first, and then, as you get into it, higher and higher… stronger… more confident…kick-kick-kick. Think of yourself hitting a powerful shot, scoring the winning goal in a football match, if that helps, but at first just kick and then we'll look at the technique of the front kick and the side kick that will stun a man and give you time to escape or raise the alarm.'

Jane has never kicked anyone in her life. And she's never scored a goal before. But she is now. Here she is with her foot up, lashing with it. Her teeth are clenched, her skin is getting more and more flushed. Kick. Kick. She's Andy King scoring that goal against the Reds in nineteen seventy eight, Andy King who was her dream lover before she did the real thing with Billy. Andy King – with his fair hair, his handsome cheekyboy's face – oh how she adored him from the terraces and in her bedtime fantasies: raunchy escapades she would also go on in later years when she felt some lack, that lack she has begun to feel, most powerfully, again. But for now she kicks. Kicks. Now she's scoring great goals herself. She's scoring them in Anfield, Goodison, she's scoring them against Leeds on Saturday.

Archie Blockley vaguely scans the papers pinned to the wall of the bookies.

'Leeds on Saturday,' says his old mate Jim Waddington who's stood at his side.

'Leeds!?' Archie appears to almost choke. Is that phlegm in his throat, or bile, the bitter old frog of loathing? 'Don't get me started about Leeds United. Gives me a heartburn just hearing the name.'

'Get it off your chest, lad,' Jim gives the grunty, wheezy chuckle of an ageing man. 'Better out than in.'

'Hate them. Hate the bastards. Always have and always will. That bunch of scoundrels that came to Goodison in sixty-four.'

'And they were encouraged to play like that by their manager,' says another man, looking up from the betting slip he's scribbling; one whose face they recognize but whose name they don't know.

'Play? That's not football.' From the look on Archie Block's face he could be looking at a turd on a dinner plate. 'That's plain thuggery. If they'd done out on the street the kind of things they were doing on the pitch they'd have got locked up. And rightly so. Never hated a team like I hated them. Not even the Reds,' Archie winces. 'Told you it'd give me gyp. Got a pain now.'

'Just the one?' asks Jim. 'That all?'

And the ageing ones laugh the laugh of old timers who've travelled life's circuit and seen the wreckage on the way.

'Actually,' Jim adds, 'not been feeling too good myself.'

'Let's hope you're not feeling any worse after the final whistle on Saturday.'

Jane is sitting at the table studying one of Rosie's self defence sheets, a scene that Billy seems to find amusing. So she says to him, 'Maybe you'd prefer it if you had to visit me in hospital.'

He scoffs at that and asks who on earth is likely to attack her going backwards and forwards to work.

'Maybe al start goin out more,' she says. All those evenings she's sat here, all those years, watching TV, reading the paper, drinking tea, having scraps of conversation, trying to help the kids with their homework. Is she done with that now? Is it time for something else?

Billy clicks the lid back on his tobacco tin, pockets it, and pushes himself up as if he's going to go out of the room, but when he gets to the door he turns and grabs her, holding both her arms tight against her body, locking them there with his superior strength. 'Gerrout of that!'

Her head bobs from side to side as she struggles against the hurt of that grip, and then she just sits there absolutely still, staring ahead with her cheeks drawn in, breathing out through her nose a silent indignation. When Billy relaxes his hold she stays exactly where she is, breathing hard, filling the room with the hot breath of displeasure. And hearing him shuffle toward the door.

'Took you by surprise there, eh?' he says, trying to tackle the silence. But silence can be such awkward stuff to handle. And silence is all there is, silence through which embarrassment perhaps comes limping.

No, she's saying nothing to help him out. So this silence must be dodged, given the slip. So he shuffles, awkwardly, out of the room, and on out the front door and down the road on his dodgy knee to the alehouse.

Mark McColl is leaning, one elbow on the bar, with a pair of characters from his past in the Street End. Sledge Kavanagh, who he knew way back as a young demolition worker, is talking old times, old escapades. While he does so McColl recalls a bulky lad who spent his days swinging a big hammer, heaving lumps of concrete around, a lad with battered fingers, broken nails and blisters, a lad who in some ways was quite slow and in others extremely sharp, a lad with a deep ready laugh, loud and coarse, a relentless joker and mocker who could unnerve people just by his presence, a peppery character, unpredictable and quick-knuckled, who in seconds would turn from clown to streetfighter. His lead would be up, his shoulders back, his feet spread for balance. The wrong word, the wrong movement from someone, and his fists were on springs, his feet high as a stallion. And when he travelled away to see the Blues he never hid his colours. The scarf looked like a tie on his thick neck, but round his throat it stayed no matter what kind of territory he passed through – a habit that, despite his size, made him a target; but one who reckoned that whatever the assailants could dish out he could take and return with interest. And he was no slouch either, he could shift that big frame around like a dancer when the pressure was on. But he did have that gift for making people laugh. And the girls went for him – drawn by his bigness, his jagged presence, his quick tongue. If protection was what a girl was looking for, a strong wall to shelter behind, you could see the attraction.

And now McColl learns that Sledge Kavanagh has little girls of his own, three of them, a trio of lovely daughters and one lad. The bulky young streetfighter has grown into a family man with a garden to look after, a pet dog, a tank of tropical fish and a holiday caravan in Wales.

When the joys of family life have been extolled by Mr Kavanagh, the other man, Jack Duffy, shifts the conversation back to football. He is older than Kavanagh and McColl, a stocky fella with a pony tail, a fifty year old Jack the Lad of yesteryear. Now he looks like some big silent brave, a chief even, some modernday Sitting Bull or Crazy Horse, a warrior who would be up front when the territorial wars began. In truth though, Duffy, a lapsed Blue who only watches the occasional game on TV, is now a social worker, an obsessive chess player with an interest in astronomy – a thoughtful man who is talking now about Albert Johanneson. Who? Albert Johanneson the footballer, The Black Flash, the tricky wide man in that infamous Leeds United team of old. Jack Duffy says he went to Leeds once, Chapeltown, to visit someone, and while he was there he saw this broken-down figure on the street and recognized him despite the general scruffiness and the puffiness of the face: Albert Johanneson – a once flying winger whose wings were now busted.

He tells McColl how when Leeds came to Goodison in the early Sixties the sound of monkey noises would rise from parts of the crowd every time Johanneson got the ball and sped down the touchline with it. He spreads his hands for emphasis. 'It was merciless. And if it was like that every ground he played in is it any wonder the man cracked up in the end?'

'And did you join in?'

'Oh aye,' Duffy nods as he confesses, 'seemed normal in them days. It's all changed now, of course. People have changed. Not everyone, but…'

No, not everyone – McColl is well aware of that.

'But back then,' says Jack Duffy, 'You would probably have joined in if you'd been there.'

'Would I?'

Would he? Why not? He was, after all, coached in hatred in the living room.

Once he was mates with a lad, Howie Brewster, a goalscoring kid with a powerful shot; he brought him home on one occasion. His old fella told him not to bring him to the house again, told him to find someone else to play with, that Howie wasn't one of us.

In the jungle of George McColl's mind Howie's people were

coming down from the trees and jumping into anything that would float. They were coming across the seas in armadas, convoys, ramshackle fleets of banana boats to invade our island and to drag it down. He'd rather have had toothache than have to sit in a room with one of them. His lip was twisted as he spoke of them. They were scroungers, swindlers, sneak-thieves and house-breakers. They were pimps, womanizers, queers and dope fiends and they drove around in flash cars when they'd never done an honest day's labour in their lives. He said you could see the arrogance in them before they even opened their mouths. He said we'd have to fight them one day, that it was plain for all to see who the next world war would be between.

Family life: back in the day, when Scholar McColl was young.

And he said to his old fella years later, putting him on the spot, maybe, 'What about Howie Gayle? What about John Barnes then?'

And the man, who appeared not to feel that he'd been nailed to any particular spot, replied, 'Ahh, that's different. A spade is a spade in anybody's language. But if they're our ace of spades, that's different.'

Family life in good old England. Yeah.

But the man who was once Sledge Kavanagh looks at his watch, says, 'Better get back to me kids, make sure that lad of mine is keepin out of trouble.'

The trio drink up, go off in different directions, and as he walks away from the beery atmosphere McColl reflects on how people change with age and wonders whether the seed of that change is always there within them, ready, when conditions are right, to germinate. He recalls one Xmas when he and Sledge Kavanagh went to Leeds by train, away through the Pennines, the skew-whiff fields and scraps of old woodland, the green lands that must have appealed to him in a way that he didn't really understand at that time when he didn't know a kestrel from a buzzard, an oak tree from a sycamore, a fern from a foxglove. Lancashire became Yorkshire, the train raced through rough lands of England to that rough old city of Leeds where the Whites weren't giving away any presents. Three goals down and the players in blue were left looking at the ball like a gift they would never be given; though they did eventually snatch a goal when their hosts were looking the other way. But they continued like weary guests at one party too many, thinking not of dancing but of falling into bed, while their support subsided into scornful quips as a premature hangover began to set in. And then, just in case there was any doubt about whether there was more pain to come the irregular troops of Elland Road began to warn, to growl in unison: Yore gonna get yer eds kicked in!!!

And the visitors hadn't gone far from the ground before a pack of tykes showed up, yelping and barking, grunting death threats in that strange and barbarous tongue of theirs, spitting out fatty gobbets of vowel, the gristle of sibilants, and the half chewed consonants of a tribe long habituated to gnaw at the very bones of the language.

But that is years behind Scholar McColl now. No longer even on the team of travelling stewards, it's a long time since he ventured into the badlands of Leeds. And he has no intention of changing that on Saturday.

Saturday morning, and Billy Whizz is away with the travelling Blues, over the Pennines and into the little streets of Leeds. In a pub called The Britannia he says, 'This place makes the old hometown look like a city of palaces, seen bigger pigeon lofts!'

He's laughing, laughing and looking forward to the game. But he knows of old that this isn't a good place to come to, that the Blues haven't got anything at Elland Road for years. But maybe this time, eh? A pint glass in his fist and a laugh on his lips and hope in his heart, yeah he dares to believe that things might be different today.

Jane shifts the rolled up poster to her left hand and then lifts her right to press the bell. The green door swings half open. 'Hello, Frank.'

Frank Brigstoke steps back. 'Jane! Long time, no see,' he says, his face shifting from surprise to a smile. 'Come in. Go through. But Barbara's out, if it was her you wanted to see.'

'No, no, it was you.' And in saying that she looks at a man who appears to be as handsome as ever, if not moreso.

She sits down waving the rolled-up poster about the self defence group and asks him can he put it up at the centre where he works, where girls and women will see it. And Frank Brigstoke, being the man he is, will of course do anything he can to help. So that when, in telling him about the group, she says that now she has to find someone, preferably a man, to practise her exercises with so that she doesn't forget between classes, he says, 'So you thought you'd come round and assault me?'

'Oh no,' she laughs. And then pauses. 'Why? Are you offerin?'

'Oh I think I'd really enjoy being thrown around by a little lady.' The enjoyment is already on his face.

And she also must smile.

But he is a serious man, and will speak seriously. 'But if you do need someone…'

'There's no point in askin Billy, eed just…'

'Sounds like I'm the one then.'

Then it's not easy for either of them to think what to say.

After a moment he rises. 'I was just thinking about having a drop of my latest home brew. It's turned out rather well and it's just past two o'clock so I can I allow myself a drink. What about you? I don't suppose I can persuade you to try a glass too? Say yes because I haven't got anything else.'

'No, you can't persuade me.' She sits there looking playfully prim for a second and then adds, 'I'll have lots of it.'

'You haven't tasted it yet.'

'Am sure it will be lovely.'

When he goes out to the kitchen she sits there smoothing her sleeve and wondering what it is that she has walked into here.

'One glass of Brigstoke's Special,' he says, handing her a glass of dark beer.

She sips. 'Oh, that's nice, not too bitter, sweet enough for me to drink.'

'A light stout,' he announces, a man proud of his ability to mix the malt and the hops with exactly the correct amount of sugar.

After another swallow it occurs to him to ask, 'So…what's Billy up to these days.'

She gives him the story and then says, 'Anyway, ees away at the match today.'

'I don't bother with the football much at all now,' he says. 'More important things to think about.'

'I listen to the matches on the radio with me dad, keep him company.'

Frank Brigstoke talks about the *important* things that occupy his mind these days: the hard but necessary grind of community politics, the gritty struggle against the architects of poverty, the pressing task of preventing humans wrecking their home on earth.

As she looks at him she sees such a serious man, but, yes, a good-looking one, a smart man with important things on his mind. She has never before found such intense seriousness so attractive. Or ever thought she would. He had changed so much, from the boozy Frank of old. But wasn't that a good thing – to change, to allow yourself to be changed? He must be such an interesting man to be with; Barbara was so lucky – Barbara who was really quite boring. Very Boring. Poor Frank.

'All right, come on,' he says, setting his empty glass down and pushing himself out of his seat, 'if you need the practice.'

'I didn't mean you have to jump up right now and do it today.'

'Why not? Come on, let's see how much you've learned.'

'Really? Here? Now?'

He's there in front of her on his feet, waiting for her. So she says, rising, 'If I can remember anythin after this beer.'

'What happens if someone attacks you when you come out of a pub? You'll have to remember then!'

So she stands facing him and takes a big breath and then tells him to try to grab her hair. When he tries to do so she jumps out of the way, ducks and sways. It seems like a game. It really does feel like fun – nearly falling over the furniture, smiles turning to laughter.

'Okay, seriously now, you grab my hair.'

When he's, oh so gently, taken a handful of hair she slaps one hand on top of his, and with the other bends his pinkie until, 'Ow,' he says. 'Enough.' And releases his grip.

'Sorry if I hurt you.'

'No, no, that's the idea.'

'So now I'll try somethin else. Grab me again.'

Again she puts a hand on top of his, but this time she swivels, and with her free hand mock-punches him just above the elbow. 'I'm supposed to hit you hard there and make you let go of me.'

If he must let go of what he has of her he will. But stands ready to reach out for more.

The next manoeuvre ends with her grabbing his elbow, pressing hard, forcing him down. 'Got ya.'

And so she has. He surrenders most cheerfully.

'I didn't hurt you did I?' As she pulls him back up they fall into a loose embrace that might be just a little surge of old friendship. Or perhaps more than that, for there is a force that passes from his hands through her shoulders and on down. For a moment the two of them hold there – as if they don't know what to say, as if they both sense where this might be leading and don't know what to do.

She takes a step back. 'Oh, look at the time,' she says, 'nearly three o'clock, the match will be startin. Better go.'

'Call round if you need more practice,' he tells her. 'Barbara's away all next week. I'll be in on Wednesday.'

'Yes,' she says, 'okay.' And hesitates. 'Better go,' she says, looking a little bewildered, 'me dad will be listenin to the match and wonderin what's happened to me.'

Billy sits up in the West Stand at Elland Road watching his team play a tight game. Until, that is, the goalkeeper gives the Whites a present – that ball really might as well have been gift-wrapped with a big white bow on it. He gives it away and what does the Leeds striker do with it? He decides to put it in the net for safe keeping. The goalie watches it flash past him and land on the button that triggers visions of all the errors of his days.

And for Billy, looking around at what has always been a graveyard of a place for the Blues to come to, it's as if he's seen it all before.

'The goalie made a blunder by the sound of it,' says Jane's dad, a trim, balding man in a blue cardigan; a man with a tendency to set his jaw at whatever life might push or shove, or fling or hurl, his way. 'A bad blunder,' he tells her as they sit, a radio between them, at the kitchen table.

'We were doin alright up till then,' says Jane. 'We need a new Neville Southall in goal by the sound of it.'

'We need a new team by the sound of it, startin with a new centre forward,' says the old man, who has seen so many teams in blue, so many goalscorers, come and go through the decades. 'I can't see this lot comin back now. Nooah,' he mumbles, 'no way back.'

No way back? Words that shift Jane's thoughts in another direction. Is there no way back now from what she has started?

Billy, the game over, the points lost, disconsolate, waiting to get out of what he calls 'this shitepit of a place,' tells those around him, as if they wouldn't already know, that the Blues threw it away, that the goalie gifted the opposition the winning goal. 'Ee give that ball back to Leeds like a present, know worra mean, handed it over to em like a fokin easter egg. Some Kraut in a white shirt says, 'Tanks very much laa, and gobbles it up! Bastid.'

It stirs up a cluster of bitter little laughter. For they all will know that such things have happened too many times before, and that the little revival is over, that now it's back to those nervy games as they watch the players in royal blue attempt to grind the points out of extremely hard material.

And in the wide cold spaces of Blue despondency, for Billy dark thoughts are bursting. One worry sets off another. Money? He needs to earn, to feel new notes in his hand. What he has left will not stretch far through the coming days. So he needs to get busy. And he has always managed to get his fingers on some cash when the need was there. But he has an odd feeling, an unusual feeling that is becoming familiar, a feeling tinged with the darkness of the day and those that preceded it. Not winning, says the feeling, not winning any more. And his body twitches to shake it off.

16

Playing Away from Home

Jane

I hear me dad's voice and realize av been lookin out the window of his kitchen, me gaze gone far away as he talks about relegation, sayin the Blues went down in nineteen fifty-one because Cliff Briton, oo had worked hard for the club over the years, wouldn't open his wallet wide enough, so then it took them three seasons to get back up, but they did have the pleasure of passin the Reds oo were on their way down, which still makes the old man chuckle, and me too, but really av got somethin else on me mind, someone else, and it isn't some dream lover. Frank told me Wednesday, said ee would definitely be in today, that I should call round if I want, that Barbara will be away, but that I should feel free to call round. But what if I do, what if I do go? If I go back there what might happen? Or should I not go?

Ee opens the door and says, 'Ah, the lady not to tangle with.'
 So I tell him ee doesn't have to – but try not to sound too serious. Ee smiles and closes the door and follows me. As I walk in I feel like av definitely lost me bearins, not at all sure where am headin. I sit down and ee goes out to the kitchen to get us a beer, leavin me feelin like me thoughts are swirlin like leaves in the wind.
 Then ee reappears sayin, 'One glass of the usual for the fightin lady.'
 That makes me chuckle. Ee does have a funny way about him, and seems so easy to be with, and his beer tastes good like last time, and a taste of booze will calm me down, maybe, or maybe it won't and what's goin to happen will just happen anyway, coz av never, never, felt like this.
 Then Frank talks about his work while we drink. Ees just

managed to get two seventeen year old girls, oo have been in care all their lives, settled in a flat and lookin after theirselves, and now ee must try and arrange some work experience for them. I do like listenin to him talk. Ee is such a good man, wishin to do so much good in the world. Ee seems like a man you could admire – and I do.

So when ee asks me does Billy know am there I shake me head and as I do it I feel even more that somethin is goin to happen. Coz then ee says it's time to get started and there ee is on his feet in front of me.

I put down me glass and step towards him. And then guide him through some exercises, him pretendin to attack me, goin to grab me by the collar or the arm, while I fend him off. But every time I touch him to push him away I feel an urge to pull him closer. Coz I can see which path we're goin down, as if with every move we're workin our way round to it, and that I will do nothin, absolutely nothin, to stop us goin that way. So I tell him to grab me wrists, and when ee does that I take a long stride forward and then come straight back, bendin me arms at the elbows and straightenin me fingers. I turn me wrists outward and put pressure on his thumbs to force him to slacken his grip, and then turn quickly to deliver a back elbow strike to the side of his head to send him off balance, and then I go for the stunner. With me left as a knife hand I go for his groin, slashin slowly down until I can feel him. Oops. I tell him am sorry about that, it went a bit further than it was supposed to. And like me ee can't help smiling. Even so, I promise to go easy and tell him to grab both wrists again. Ee does. I step back, keepin me fingers straight and raise both me hands by bendin me elbows. Then I turn me palms face up and inwards and chop down at his thumbs to break his grip, and then go for his throat, choppin with both hands, but holdin back, and then ee just sort of flops forwards and we're in each other's arms.

It's just happened like dead natural but as if it was always meant to happen, and I can hear him breathin and feel me heart like a clock gone mad. And then we kiss. He has one hand on me hair and one on me back. It just feels so right to be all wrapped around by him, and it doesn't feel any different when his hands move inside me clothes and my fingers start to work down the buttons on his shirt. And then one thing just leads to another, and before I know it am steppin out of me clothes.

I stand at home and gaze out of the window where me tangled thoughts shift between yes and no. One moment I feel like av gone astray and must not, must definitely not, do so again, that I should avoid the street where Frank Brigstoke lives until what has happened has been forgotten so that it will be as if it never happened. But as the hours pass am not so sure. It's as if I can hear Frank's voice like it's callin me, callin to me to come to him. And then I get the feelin of being pulled to him whether I want to go or not, whether it's a big risk or just a little risk, and I want to go, all I want to do is go, but then thinkin about the risk of it I start to worry, I start to fidget and fret like am goin to drop things, cups and glasses, the spoon, the knife, the bag of spuds. I start to worry about what Billy will say if he ever finds out. What will ee do? Because most people get found out, they do, they get found out in the end, they get seen or make a mistake. I know that from films and gossip and magazines. But then I tell meself there's nothin to be frightened of, nothin will go wrong, it's just two people oo need each other, givin each other somethin that's good and natural in a world where there's so much badness and real wrong. And oo could begrudge me a little bit of pleasure and happiness and oo could begrudge it to him as well, him oo cares about others and the world we live in when so many are only out for theirselves and what they can get? So I shrug and lift the pan from the cooker and carry it to the sink and, holdin the lid, tip the pasty water out. What the hell does it matter if I don't know what al say if Billy finds out? Al think of somethin. And even if I can't think of anythin what does it matter if everythin does come crashin down as long as the roof doesn't fall on me head? What have I got to lose? What?

So I go. And it's as if am in a different world now, now that me and Frank have rearranged our work times to be free in the afternoon when we've got the house to ourselves. A different world now, a world where nothin seems to matter, a world where you stand naked with admirin eyes, desirin eyes, rovin over a body that feels like it's escaped after bein hidden away for years.

Another afternoon in bed. But what does it matter how many

times? A hundred or a thousand times, what does it matter once you've done it? A thousand times? My god you'd be worn out.

But you can do it as many times as you like once you've done it. Because it can't survive, this marriage can't survive now, not what's happened. Like a cat hit by a speedin car it's got no chance now, this marriage, no chance, no chance at all. It shouldn't end like this but when do things ever end the way they should end? And you can't tell your body what it wants, not when it's shoutin at you, screamin at you: I want Frank, I want Frank, now, now, av got to have Frank, got to have him, now, now, now!

Am either there with him now or wantin to be with him. Waitin for the next time, feelin like I want to see him, to hold him, to be held by him, my lover, Frank, and I want Barbara out of the way, and I want her to stay out of the way so that I can have him there in front of me whenever I like. I want him there before me, all solid and smiling and sayin Hello, and askin how I am and how av been and tellin me ee misses when am not there, and then throwin his arms around me, and me feelin his face on me neck and his body pressed against mine.

You don't have to be the same person all your life, av found that out. So av been stood in front of the mirror for the last hour. I could be a film star, am givin meself that much attention, tryin this pair of earrings then that pair because I want to look right, I want to look good, I want to look me best for Frank because soon, again, at last, al be with him, soon ee will be mine again. So then when av got the jewellery sorted there's the silk scarf to puzzle over. But am better than a film star because am not pretendin, am not playin a part, am livin it. Soon al be there with him, livin it, lovin it. Soon.

I feel like rushin but I don't, I go slowly thinkin that Barbara might be there, even though she isn't supposed to be, and so I rehearse me excuse just in case. Then I reach the corner of Frank's street and am turnin down it, gettin closer and closer to him with every step, countin the numbers, the front doors, the red one, the glass one, number nineteen, the one with the scaffoldin, the one with the brass lion holdin the knocker in its mouth.

And then I can see his house, and Barbara's too, her house. But that woman has had her chance with him all these years, and if she couldn't make a go of it in all that time then she never will. She has made her bed and will have to lie in it, except that she might find av got there first. Not funny that, but true. Life is hard and nobody is spared, and you have to be hard, have to become hard yourself or you get left out, and if you just sit there being good and feelin left out then no one will come along and invite you in, because if you want to be in you have to push yourself in, you have to.

And here is the green door openin, and here is Frank, the strong and serious man, my lover, standin back to let me pass. And as the door closes I turn to him. He wraps himself around me and buries his face in me shoulder. I feel his skin on me neck, on me cheek, I feel me blood rush, I feel meself start to swell, and I want to be without me clothes, to put them aside like a hat or umbrella. But first we sit down and have a drink of his strong brew, and ee tells me about three meetins ee went to and then ee says, 'Apart from that av been sittin here wishin somethin excitin would happen.'

And I say, 'Well here I am, am happenin.'

And then it happens. Am in his arms, and av got this warm feelin that starts in me chest and flows all over me body and out to the ends of me limbs. His hands are on me back, movin up and down, all over until they shift forward to unbutton me, to slide inside me clothes and touch a body that is longin to get out and be naked and free, to do what it wants, because it can do what it likes here. With his help I get out of me shoes, me skirt and all the rest, and at the same time I return the favour. I hold him in me fist and feel him swell, feel me own power to make him swell and rise, knowin that soon I will make him groan with pleasure, and ee will do the same for me. I will take him in me hands, his pale warm hard and swollen flesh, and put me lips to him. And then we will be ready for the two of us to be like one body. And nothin else in the world will matter even if the street and the city and the rest of the world is just outside the wall and the window – the world where I have become a different Jane and not the Jane that people know, or thought they knew, and say hello to in the street, but another that I never really knew about even if our bodies look the same – this body that will soon be lying in that gorgeous and wonderful place from where all the tension has flowed away.

17

When the Cash Doesn't Flow

Billy Whizz

Still can't gerrup me ladder, so am just thinkin that by the end of the week al be short of gelt to go to the match unless I roll me sleeves up and get busy. But I can drive okay and I can walk more or less okay, takin it steady, so I ed to the bookies. I feel a tenner in me pocket as I walk in. What to do? Al play the favourite, this ain't the moment for some loony outsider stunt. Play safe, Billyboy. A tenner on Blue Moon. Three to one.

And it's Blue Moon, Blue Moon, Blue Moon. And it's Blue Moon by five lengths. Yis, av done it. Av done it, av tripled me cash. Me luck is in, it has to be, I av to go with it. So I throw the lot on Lambergini. Name like that, gorra be a winner. Got the form, too. So they're at the startin line. And they're off. Samba Dancer makes the early runnin. As they come to the first bend Lambergini is in third place. It's Samba Dancer, then Dixie Belle. And Lambergini is closin the gap, Lambergini gets his nose in front. Yes, yes, you beaut, you cracker. Go boy, go! Lambergini is racin clear. Lambergini is at the last fence. Lambergini …What???

Can't believe am watchin it. The donkey. The assssssssssssss!! Can't believe it. That mule of a race horse with the race just about won, with only this one last fence to jump, goes hoof over bollock, near does a fokin somersalt, like it reckons itself a real ace at the horse gymnastics, and then. And then. And then it rolls over, like it's just rollin in the fokin clover, and then it gets up and trots home without no rider like it never had a care in this hole damned fokin world!

Aaahhhh. Fffffkkkkkk.

Walk away, I tell meself, walk away, lad, turn yer back and walk away.

So I do. Kinda limpin a little bit, takin it steady. And then I see this motor in the street with a note on it sayin, *Double Quick Sale*. The price looks really tasty. The profit I could turn around from resellin it looks pretty mouthwaterin to a cash hungry lad like meself.

So I knock at the door and say to the fella, 'Am interested.'

Ee says ees emigratin and the sale of the motor has fell throo so the first person to slap the cash in his hand can drive the thing away.

I look it over, bonnet to boot, and then go for a quick circuit to Seffy Park and back. It seems sound to me, and am no mug, I know a sick engine from one that's still in the prime of life. I says to him, 'Am definitely interested. I just need to raise the cash and then al be back.'

It means borrowin, venturing into sharky waters, but the fella is near givin that motor away and if I can't shift it at a very neat profit in a less than a week then my tongue ain't the silvery treasure it used to be. It's no kind of gamble at all. I reckon it's well worth goin to Denny Grant for a short loan. That fella ain't nice people to get tangled with but eel give you the gelt there and then, as much as you want, no questions, no messin about.

Can't find him. Takes me near half the day to find out ees away, back tomorrow. Loan sharks on holiday? What? What's the world comin to?

Nuisance. But no big worry. Al go back and explain to the fella oos sellin the motor. Ees been tryna offload it for a couple of weeks so will it suddenly be snapped up, will someone swoop in and grab it from under me nose? Nah. Al be able to sort it tomorrow. No problem.

But when I turns inta that street again I halts there dead on the spot. I stop like av walked into an invisible barrier. What? *What?*

The motor? Where's the motor?

Moody thorts passin throo me ed all of a sudden, very moody.

So I give the front door a hammerin. The fella comes out and says someone bort it an hour ago.

What!! The bastid. Ees gone and sold it to some arl dame oo only wanted it for shoppin. Ahhhhh! I says, 'Tanks very much.'

Ee says, 'But am emigratin. I can't hang around if a buyer shows up with cash in hand. Am emigratin.'

I says, 'Tanks a lot, mate. Tanks for notn.'

Ee says, 'Am emigratin.'

I says, 'An am in the shite now, but don't let that worry you. Don't let that disturb yer packin!'

Ee says, 'Am emigratin to Australia.'

I says, 'I know yer emigratin!' Am jabbin me finger at him. 'And if yer plane crashes in sharky waters - '

His eyes go swirly and then ee slams the door on me nose. Huh! I spin round and shoulder me way down the street like am bargin over anyone oo ever emigrated or bort a motor just to go shoppin!!!

Airliner crashes in the Pacific. That fella's voice on the black box as it goes down, Am sorry, am so sorry about that motor.

Too late, far too late for apolergees. I just hope them sharks enjoyed their Scouse breakfast.

I barge on down the street. I could kick a brick wall down – bad knee or not. I could elbow a car across the road. And then – they don't call me Billy Whizz for notn – I jink me way into a nice little earner.

But cash? It comes, it goes. Yer earn a few notes for a few hours decent labour and then yer back where ya started knowin ya never get nowhere if ya don't gerroff yer arse. But really I need somethin a bit solid, somethin that lasts beyond a day or two. I need to pick up some proper gelt to tide me over while the knee's bad. And then as soon as that's better I need a huge storm called Brutus or Ercules to come and scatter rooftiles like playin cards and keep me in work throo the summer so I can go and buy a season ticket to watch the Blues.

But for now I just need a couple of decent earners that don't give me knee a bad time.

I try Davy Mac the plumber.

Nah, notn doin.

I try Mal Butler oo hires himself and his van out. Sometimes ee needs an extra set of muscles. 'Nah. Notn Bill. Al give yez a bell if and when...'

The place is like a graveyard. The only things movin is dead leaves and litter.

Cruisin round, rackin me brains, I see Herbie Harper's van parked outside an ouse in Allerton. The front door is half open.

The floor boards in the hallway are bare and dusty, and there's cables and tools scattered around. Upstairs a drill is moanin. Downstairs an eavy ammer is buttin its ed against a brick wall. I can smell the plaster and the damp. I can smell work.

'Aye, aye, Mal.'

'Well, well. The Wizard himself. Long time, no see.'

We gab and gossip for a minute or two, and then I make me pitch. Ee shakes his ed. The work ee as in hand isn't enough for his regular lads. If ee could help ee would but…

It's time to refresh meself, time to take stock, a pint is called for. While am in the alehouse I pull an old bettin slip outa me pocket and see a number wrote on it. Someone give me that a while back. I can't even remember oo give me it, but I know it's linked to work, so I bell it.

This grumpy voice says, 'Oo?'

I says, 'Billy. Me names Billy…'

The clown at the other end says, 'That's your problem, pal.'

Some fellas must be just waitin for someone to buzz em up so they can have a nice friendly chat. Oh jeez. I says, 'Look mate, erm…someone give me this number, it's about work.'

Click. Bzzzzz…

What's wrong with people these days? Or is it yerself that's the problem? Sometimes, yeh, ya start to get that feelin.

Best remedy for that is another beer. While am consultin with that wise old man Joseph O'Booze I note three fellas come in. One of them is Bernie Taylor, Bernie the Boomerang. When we was kids ee was a pest, we couldn't get rid of him. Ee had no balls, no sense, no cash, no notn. The clobber ee wears now tells a different story. Whatever money cake ees feedin off I could do with a slice of that. Coz it won't be notn too dodgy. But from where am stood they seem like a tight little clan and not easy to crack open. But maybe, maybe, I can lever meself in.

Taylor looks my way like ee kinda recognizes me. I give him the nod. Ee doesn't exactly leap across and hug me like an old mate, but am not about to chuck the rag in yet. If I knew one of them others it might help. But av never scanned them before, they're pure mystery karacters to me. On one side, furthest from me, stands this sunbaked hulk with a polished skull. His arms poke out of the short-sleeved cotton bag ees dressed in like lengths of rusty steel cable. Ee licks his lip, bends forwards, and speaks to the others out of the corner of his mouth. Maybe somethin tasty is cookin around here. And if Taylor is interested then yd guess there must be profit in it. The transformashon in that fella in the last few years has to be witnessed to be credited. From a clueless scruffbag ees changed into a model for classy fabrics. But how ee makes his gelt av no idea. Now the third karacter is tossin a jokey little word in his ear. Ee looks like a cross between a spider and a hawk. Long limbs and hooked beak. Ee isn't a pretty sight now, and ees enjoyin himself. What eed be like if someone give him a bang on the beak I don't like to think. But ee isn't short of gelt neither if the message bein sent out by his jewellry is to be believed.

A race starts on the box. The horses are away and Taylor's little crew are scannin them. The braincogs, well oiled now, have begun to turn. I can talk a good race any time of the day or night and maybe that could be a start for me to blag me way inta somethin. The favorite in the race slobs it. Some 12-1 shot romps home without even a tickle from the whip. There's some moody looks on Taylor's crew. I pick up the negative vibrashons bein put out by their wallets, and latch on to them.

'Somethin dodgy goin on there,' I says, turnin to face them. 'Someone must have been shovin iron weights up its arse for it to lose that one.'

'You on it yself?' Taylor enquires. Ee doesn't sound all that interested, but it's a start. The ball is rollin.

I give the nod. 'But it's all piss under the bridge now,' I say takin a swallow. Lies come easy when them cogs is spinnin and grindin. 'Oo wouldn't have been? Looked like a decent punt, a very decent punt. The donkey.'

While Taylor lays out is own theories of skullduggery down on the racecourse am gettin ready to give this little crew me best racin tales. Five minutes and av got them stood there like an audience. A smile on the Screamin Skull turns into a chuckle. A chuckle from the Spider Hawk turns into a cackle. Taylor, playin the cool dude is, like they say, pleasantly amused, or seems to be. And while am in full flow I ease meself closer. When the racin show ends I steer the chat towards motors, another topic I can travel a long way with. I want to let them know am handy in there among the gaskets and spark plugs. A good spannerman or wheelman can be a useful member of any team.

But then I start to feel the old braincogs slowin. These karacters ain't shoved me away but they ain't shown signs of lettin me in neither. Before they move off, and they've all got half a glass left, I need to make some little link that I can work on and make bigger in future. But am runnin low on inspirashon fuel now. I need a bit of space to think while av got time.

The bog. Yeah, the bog. That's the place. It's amazin how much can shoot throo yer mind in them few seconds while the cock-a-doodle does its bizzniss at the troff.

I give a nod at the door and then make me way throo it. As soon as av turned the cocky boy loose I start to reflect on me performance. I ain't bombed but I ain't starred neither. I need to do more. Maybe I should invest in buyin a round when I go back out? And then the answer hits me, I can't believe av been so dumb. How come av had to go out to the piss-house to find it? But av done it. In this pissy little hole av found what am lookin for. Taylor used to watch the Blues sometimes, way back. But maybe now ees loaded ees started goin regular. Al find out. And if ee does go to the game now al find out where ee sits in Goodison and then al always be able to find him, maybe catch him on his own some time. That's it.

I slip the cock back into its bag, zip meself up and go back throo.

Eh? What??!! Gone. Three empty glasses on the bar. They made a dart for the door as soon as me back was turned. Scumbags.

Yeah, that's it – ya start to wonder. Is that it, is that really it – Billy Boy ain't winnin no more?

Halfway down the street I see a fella holdin a greyound on a lead. 'Dogman! Ow ya doin Davey lad?'

Ee does alright this fella, ee walks throo life with always a few bluebacks in his back pocket. Ee has ways n means, Davey the Dogman. Never publicizes them but one way and another ee does alright. And ees a Blue.

'Three points at Elland Road would have been handy, very handy,' ee says.

'And so would some cash in my pocket!' Why beat about the bush when yer arse will be hangin out yer kecks if ya don't get busy on somethin?

'Things not so good with you then Bill?' says the Dogman.

So I give him the story and then finish up sayin, 'But there don't seem to be no bits and pieces around at the moment. Too many cowboys on the scene, know worra mean?'

Dogman nods, lookin dead wise,

'Desperadoes,' I add coz I can't think of notn else to say. 'Outlaws. The bad, the worse and the ugly!'

Gets a laugh from him anyway.

Ee laughs easy, the Dogman. Always did. Ee has a very neat little leather on his back that tells you that times is still good on the dogtrack. Ees gorra map of veins on his cheeks, but ees always been a fella oo knew where ee was goin. And ee looks fit too from all them hours of walkin the dogs. Ee goes quiet for a moment with a look on his face like ees workin out how to do a bit of brain surgery. Then ee says, all of a sudden, takin me by surprise, 'Tell ya what Bill. Ya fancy a drivin job? Ya fancy showfferin us to the track on Friday? Al make it worth yer while.'

Now it's my turn to nod. A jaunt with Davy, a lad oo knows his way to the money chest? I coulda nodded till me ed fell off.

'I don't trust that thing,' he says pointin to his wheels. 'Just come and have a listen to this.'

We climb in and ee does a circuit up to Park Road and back. When ee switches de engine off I turn to him and shake me ed. 'That's one sick motor yve got there, lad.'

'It's just gone on me,' ee says lookin pained. 'I paid decent gelt for it, too.'

I say 'The best thing that could appen to this motor would be if a bunch of rascals nicked it for a spin and then torched it.'

Ee looks at me. Ee looks at me like I just said somethin very interestin, very interestin indeed. Ee looks at me while ee takes his brain for a little walk, and then ee looks around like very suspishus in case there's spies and snoopers hidin down the alleys and drains, then ee says. 'Ya fancy a quick bevy somewhere quiet?'

While ee stands leanin on the bar in the Bel waving a banknote at the barman I slide on to the bench at an empty table and watch the bald patch on the top of Dogman's ed and try to work out what is goin on inside that skull. Because somethin is. We ain't there to gab about the Blues chances of winnin the effay cup, that's for sure. Dogman is plottin somethin and my name is on the slate.

'So,' ee says, slidin in next to me, and givin his thorts a few seconds to settle down. 'Yer gonna drive me to the track on Friday. Okay. So yll have a few notes to slap on this dog al put yer on to.'

'Not your dog?' There's a little bit of surprise in me voice which ee doesn't seem surprised at.

Ee shakes his ed and gives a sneaky little smile. 'But that's not worra wanna talk about,' ee says, leanin dead close, so close ees near kissin me on the earhole. 'See, if that motor of mine did get nicked and torched then maybe you might find yerself with a fistfulla notes to bet with. Know worra mean?'

I take a deep swallow of ale. Shady business, very shady. But oo else is gonna come along and shove a stack of twenties in me hand? I take another swallow of ale and lick me lips.

Dogman's about to say something more but then the barman comes round collectin empties so we both sup a bit till ees gone.

Dogman's leans my way again. 'Tomorrow,' ee says, 'me and the missis is gonna see a film. So that's where you move in. I can drop yer a set of keys durin the day. I reckon I should be able to find a parkin speck with no cameras on it.'

No, it's not the kind of caper I normally gerr up to, but a fistfulla notes is handy money to a man oos been watchin the cash flowin in the wrong direcshon these recent days. 'Okay,' I says, crackin me glass down on the table, 'tomorrow it is.'

Dark, well dark, and time to move. The night is me accumplice so let's gerrit done. I grab me jacket, and then am on me way. There's a gang of rascals on the corner, a pack of crop-headed hyenas, evil little villains, the kind of kids oo don't know how to misbehave properly no more. This lot wear labels all over them that say *Nasty*. The days of laugh-lovin scallywags like we was are long gone. I flick a wary eye in their direcshon as I pass.

I move along towards where Dogman has parked his wheels but as I come up to it I spot a couple of people sittin in another motor. Me heart moves up a gear and starts knockin. Me impulse is to spin away but I don't, I stay with the job. I do a quick scan and see they isn't takin no notice of me so then I go for it. I key the lock, swing the door open and jump inta the seat.

Easy lad, I tell meself, and then grab the gear stick.

I keep off the main drag to miss the cameras. And I never see a single cop, all the way to Woolton Road, not one. And if there are any around I will definitely spot them becoz me eyes are all over the place, skimmin backwards and forwards across the windscreen like marbles on ice. I ed for the old peoples home and then bump over the pavement and down the lane next to it that leads to the golfy. About an undred yards along, next to a pile of dead wood, I pull up and give the pedal a few pumps to make sure there's plenty of juice splashin around. Dogman has left plenty of papers in there just to make sure, so I grab a sheet and screw it up and climb out of the motor. I stand there listenin, listenin and watchin this way and that.

It's still as a graveyard when all the ghosts are on holiday.

Holdin the screwed up paper in one hand I dip inta me pocket and bring out the lighter. I flick it on to full flame and when it blazes up I move the paper and the flame together. The paper takes the flame, I count to three and then lob it in throo the open window. In the same movement I turn to me left and move away in a hurry, but not runnin coz I don't wanna make me knee bad again. But I do go kinda quick between the bushes and trees for about thirty strides and then turn to see the motor and the wood blazin. Roarin, they is. Big red an orange leapin and dancin flames. There's somethin about flames that make ya wanna watch them. There's power man, real power and force. And smoke. Plenty of that.

And anyway this wasn't no time to dwell on the glories of fire. I could be in deep, deep, shite for this. And me heart knows it and me belly knows it too. So I shift meself along to the end of the lane then turn throo the trees on to de open grass of the golfy, edin straight across till I come to the fence and duck throo an ole in it and on down this little walled track. At the end of that am back on the tarmac, Yew Tree Road, and edin down to Allerton where me own motor is parked up.

Am startin to think more about ale than flames now coz I need a beer, I need to settle me arse on a stool somewhere safe and put some strong juice in me blood.

And by the time me second pint arrives me heart, me guts and me arse are well settled down. I sit forward in the seat and flick the old baccy tin open. I nick out a paper and then start to draw the fresh brown baccy along it. Calm fingers. Steady fingers. Fingers that done the bizzniss. Yeah.

Now the smell of the baccy reaches me nose. That's a good smell, that's a great smell, for a fella oo knows his way about the world: fresh baccy. I lift the roll-up to me mouth and lick the paper. Done. I nip the straggly bits from the ends and drop them back in the tin. I squeeze the lighter and watch it turn into a fokin flame thrower. Whoooah-Whooah! It near takes me eyebrows off!

I turn the gas down and light up.

I take in the smoke and breathe easy. A tricky job well done today, done neat, done smooth and tidy. And tomorrow the reward will ride on some rapid dog's back. And double up maybe, treble, oo knows. Coz Dogman ain't a lad ool steer yer bet towards some no-hope hound.

Then on Saturday al be there in Goodison to see the Blues win. We will. Av got that winnin feelin back, back where it should be: in the heart of Billy Whizz. Yeah. But first, yeh, first a winnin dog will carry the gelt from the burnin motor over the finish line and turn it inta plenty more! Weyhay!!

Am at the wheel with Dogman sittin next to me. Ees leanin over the back of the seat feedin chunks of black puddin to this hound called Nuggit that's gonna be one of the favourites in a race that it definitely ain't gonna win.

'Eel still be staggerin round the track when the next race starts,' I says as he lobbed another lump over the seat. That put a cool little smile on the Dogman's face.

And by the time we get to Blackpool that hound is flopped down in the back like a bloated thing that's fell off the seat at the banquit table. It's so stuffed with dogfeed and black puddin it can hardly shift its arse out of the motor never mind run a race. Some favourite! And am one of the few oo know it ain't gorra chance.

Mountain Flash has had the black puddin treatment for the last three races, so after a string of bad runs his price has stretched out nicely. Dogman and a fella called Burke, oo owned Mountain Flash, plus someone at the track, have been settin this one up for months. So tonight anyone in the know would be bungin everythin they could scrape together on Mountain Flash and expectin big rewards.

At eight o'clock the traps spring open, de electric hare whizzes past and the dogs was away, or rather Mountain Flash was. Ee had it wrapped up in about ten strides. Ee was movin as if ee had an extra pair of legs. The Nuggit was in the bunch it left behind. So our little caper wasn't obvious, like it would have been if the hound had totally slobbed it. Nothin like that. Smart operator is Dogman. So me and him was stood there for a little while pretendin we was just as sick as all the other losers.

Then we went strollin for the pay off. Yeah, more notes in me fist. I watched the money slide from the bookie's grasp, as the pile got higher, 'Eighty…undred…undred an twenty…'

And that's only the beginnin.

Yeah. Carry on my man, carry on. Take yer time. Pile it up nice n high.

When ee was done I felt the thickness in me fist. I touched the bundle to me cheek and smelled me wealth. Yeah! Nice one lad. Then with the cash stashed in me pocket I eded for the bar. A nice cool beer before we was back on the road, edin home for some serious boozin. Coz a man oo knows his way about this tricky old world is entitled to celebrate from time to time. Yeah.

I lifted that glass of ale and I was laughin, I was loaded once again. Money. Money for the match – Wimbledon. That crazy bunch from down south – makin a racket wherever they go, givin all and sundry the earache. But ad be there to watch the Blues shut em up.

Winnin? Oo ain't winnin? They don't call me Billy Whizz for notn.

Part Six

18

The Crazy Gang

Maggie May

By their nakedness you shall know them – or something like that. I swill the red wine around in my glass and wonder what this young doctor would be like when his clothes were spread around my bedroom floor, and what by then I would know about him, and what I might make of that. Just wondering. Myself and this young doctor – we make each other laugh. And a man who likes a giggle has for me a big figure in the plus column. His bright and attractive face is not so far from mine. Now that he has shed his white coat and his look of seriousness I detect someone inclined to mischief. But would I not, in the end, regret playing his little seduction game?

Although, I am in the mood to have my roots nourished by warm showers – as it says somewhere or other in some passage I read a long time ago.

Sarah watches him move away to the bar. 'So what's going on here then Nurse Maynard?'

'Nothing. Nothing at all. Nothing's going on.'

She laughs: that knowing cackle of hers. She's like a goose that I remember from this place I went to on holiday when I was a kid, she'd be very effective guarding a farmyard gate.

'Really, it isn't.' And my voice sounds very sure to me.

But she clearly has erotic plans for myself and the young specialist in rare cancers. 'No?'

'No. Nothing. I'm going to let that one pass.'

She pokes me gently in the shoulder. 'You should be flattered.'

Well, yes. Naturally. 'Oh, I'm flattered. I'm flattered, alright. I'm just not falling for it.'

I've got more exciting things to think about than dallying with a young Don Juan of the hospital wards – like hosting the Crazy Gang in Goodison Park. My new job – a permanent position on Section Six. I know it seems weird for me to take it so seriously. But I do.

So there I am on Saturday afternoon with the Ginger Scholar telling me how welcome my presence will be on the section. And he even has a little smile for the lady – a flirty little smile. So what's that about? I'm wondering, as I watch his yellow jacket recede along the gangway.

Above me the speaker crackles into life. Somebody or other singing about what they're looking for; like a voice without a body trapped in an echoey chamber. But the stadium has lost its pre-match echo now that it's filling up. The crowd murmurs all around me like little knots of conspirators plotting to bring the glory back to Everton. The players come out for a warm-up to a few handfuls of claps, more polite than passionate. A small woman waddles past in her blue and white knitwear – like a toy escaped from the Fluffy House.

The Scholar reappears in the gangway. Sharp features, he's got, and that seasoned look. A bit of a fox him, maybe, with that reddish hair and weathered skin. Those quick eyes. Grey, I think, they are. Grey with a touch of green maybe. Smallish hands. Archie Block and John Sanger have the big bears' paws, his are more like a monkey's – those cute things picking fruit in the jungle treetops. His reminds me of that surgeon I knew, Richard Kennington – he who acted like the star of his own romances. Something different about him, though. Here, there is. So they mock him – all the tabloid men. He's been seen reading the posh pages, so they say, the serious news. And that's more than enough in this earthy old city of comics and boxers, and popular songsters, to get anyone who studies the highbrow columns labelled the Professor, or the Academic, or …the Scholar.

A fan steps into the gangway with a beer in his hand. He's squat and dusty, wide-jawed. I must be assertive. 'You have to drink that down below, mate, not within sight of the pitch.'

His face tells me that he is nobody's mate. 'Why?'

I point to the notice on the wall. He flicks his eyes that way then back to me. Mates? He eats them with chips and gives their bones to his dog. 'So?'

I talk ground rules. Such an interesting subject. I could go to sleep just listening to myself. And who wants to drink down there on the concourse? Like going for a beer in your local subway. But it's a rule and I am the enforcer. In the domain of the testicle I must be firm and strong. Even if this character could scramble eggs just by looking at them.

He starts to shift himself back down to where he came from. A little victory for the lady in yellow. Now a stickman approaches, thin as a broom handle, spiky hair on top of a wide face, Mr Yardbrush, moving ever so slowly towards me in between pausing to stare at his ticket – another one of those with a look on his face that suggests the cock-up machine has done him a ticket in a foreign language.

I put myself forwards, 'You alright there, mate?'

Getting all the fans sorted out into the right seats is a bit like settling a big gang of kids in front of the telly: once the cartoons come on you can catch your breath. And by the time latecomers are seated the game is starting to look as if there's only one team in it. The Crazy Gang can't play because they haven't got the ball. The only time they touch it is when we give it to them. But we do that once too often. The first chance they get, Ekoku drops the ball in the bag from twenty five yards. Pretty stunning. Stunning but not pretty for the faithful here. So we are back in the Hall of Groans again. This team of ours is all scurry and chase and not much more. Here at Goodison where once the great men strolled and swept the ball about with such awesome skill the mediocre boys of today slip and stumble and skew that ball well wide of the target. But we are only in the Hall of Groans, we are not in the Vale of Tears, not yet anyway.

Scholar McColl

Here we go again. The mutterers and the grousers are back in position. I'm surrounded by the grumble and the groan. The players are trying, trying like labourers, like navvies on a hard dig. Their sleeves are rolled up, their sinews are stretched till they might bust, but every move they build collapses in the opposition box. All the goalie has to do is gather up the rubble.

The expressions on the faces of some punters suggest they might be asking themselves: What the hell am I doing here? And what about our new lady on the scene, what's she making of this spectacle?

Maggie May

The Scholar arrives at my side, sighs at what's going on out on the grass and says to me, 'What's a nice girl like you doing in a place like this?'

'Girl?'

He shrugs. A flirty shrug.

I mimic his shrug, 'I'm on a life sentence here just like you.'

He says with, yes, a discernible twinkle in those grey-green eyes, 'You never thought of going over the wall, escaping this?'

'Where would I run away to? Why, what about you?'

'I couldn't even imagine it.' But his eyes are darting away from me as he speaks.

And then he's gone again – starts a conversation and then flits away. You just begin to unwind a thread of thought and he leaves you there holding it, the end dangling in mid-air.

But then I see what took him away so suddenly.

Scholar McColl

Up by the rear seats a speckie staggers into the aisle. He sways and wobbles. But this is no drunk. I manage to catch hold of him and we go into a kind of grotesque dance. If I don't hang on to him he might tumble and split his head on something.

And so many eyes on us. The startled and the bored. Seeing more action here than on the pitch as my partner writhes as if he were being beaten about the head and punched in the kidneys. If only he'd tell me what's the matter.

But what is it that he's trying to say now? Is that word *diabetic*? So indistinct. Half-grunt, half-mumble.

Some know-all has the answer: 'Give him insulin!'

The suffering man tries again to say something but manages only slurred, bitten off sounds. Whatever possesses him contorts his arms – like a human corkscrew. He writhes and almost falls. I cling on, and turn my back on a shower of useless advice from all the would-be medics and ignorant wise guys in the crowd.

'He needs insulin.'

'Stick his head between his knees.'

'Give him some insulin!'

'All he needs is a goal. I feel like that meself.'

A few even laugh.

The man wriggles and mumbles in my arms. That shaking head is still trying to tell me something. But what? 'What? What is it, mate?'

He shakes his head again. His legs buckle. I feel him slipping down and out of my grasp.

Maggie May

By the time I get there they're both on the deck. The fan is thrashing around and the Scholar is trying to cling on to him but not quite managing it. The man slips out of his grip, springs to his feet and then crashes into the wall. The Scholar scrambles up and grabs him again. And then they both slip down to the ground again.

I can hear other fans shouting advice to him. And I can see from the look on his face what he thinks about those suggestions from the audience. The other man's face is contorted, twisted, constantly shifting around, but his eyes are those of a child who's lost its mother.

'He needs insulin,' somebody shouts again.

As I kneel down the Scholar looks relieved, pleased to have some assistance.

'Let's just try and calm him down,' I say, 'and then sit him up so he'll be more comfortable.'

One each side of the man, struggling at first to get him to be still, we manage it. As he sits now I put my arm around his shoulders and begin to administer the soothing talk I am well practised at, chattering about football, diabetes, nursing, anything. Then listening to his mumbly response I work out what's wrong with him.

'He's taken too much insulin,' I tell the Scholar. 'We need to give him something to counter it. Sugar would help.'

The Scholar is quick to comprehend. 'Go to the teabar and get some sugar cubes,' he calls to the nearest yellowjacket.

As we bend together over the diabetic our hair almost touches. Is he as aware of that as I am? I take a sweet from my jacket pocket and hand it to the man. He sucks it and begins to calm, to settle a little against my arm. The sweetness begins to take away the tortured lines from his face. When the yellowjacket arrives with sugar cubes the Scholar grabs one and places it carefully on my palm. Our eyes meet briefly. Are we not a good team? I unwrap the cube and hand it to the man.

Comfort – for the man who must endure his hurt under the gaze of thousands. And for me? That feeling of being useful, of being needed. But also of being close to the Scholar, of having shared a not unimportant experience with him. We coped. Together, under the pressure of being observed, we did our job.

The last of the pain starts to drain from the fan's face. His hair has been ruffled in the struggle, but his shirt, I'm sure, was already creased. Another of those men whose lives lack a woman's touch – so many lost in the wilderness, so many singing a lonesome song.

This one makes to push himself up to his feet, and with my help he gets there. I tell him, 'You can suffer with the rest of us now. This match is enough to make anyone feel ill.'

The crowd, hearing its cue, groans again, grumbles and gripes.

Solid John Sanger

'I see Scholar McColl has wasted no time introducing himself to the lady,' said old Blocko as he passed.

As if I hadn't already noticed that myself.

Blocko stopped further along the gangway and shook his head at the action on the pitch: another incompetent attempt to punish this team of Cockney villains who are stealing the points from us. The Scholar had settled even further along now that his little drama with Maggie May was over. His foxy eyes were on the game now, his clever mouth clammed shut for a change in concentration.

I could do both of their jobs: Deputy, Boss Steward. No problem. You organize and you instruct. You see potential problems ahead and you take steps to avoid them. When something unforeseen occurs you deal with it – like working on some army project oversees, like navigating on the *Britannia Princess*.

Simple. For those who are up to the task. And there are many who are not.

More groans from the crowd tell me what I can see for myself: that this is another one of those games. After the jamboree against Middlesboro we were back in the old routine.

But, wouldn't you know it, there was a new routine starting up not far from where I was standing – well that's what it looked like.

Scholar McColl shifted himself towards Maggie May again – one sniff of woman and he can't keep away from her. He moved with that slow idling walk of his. He either looks lazy or else he puts on this display of being so busy he can't stop for half a second, as if the whole show would suddenly end if he paused for a moment. But he did stop – next to the lady in yellow, and pointed out something on the pitch, probably something about the space we weren't making the best use of. Both his index fingers were outstretched moving backwards and forwards as if he was a coach giving instructions to players. The place was full of experts. It was the School of Science after all. It was either that or the Ship of Fools that was about to sink.

And it looked like we had a pair of those in the crowd. All moves made by the Blues seemed to end in the back of nowhere and what we didn't manage to mess up for ourselves the officials took care of. And the steam of frustration was building up inside some heads, and maybe giving us a little problem. So I took a step in that direction.

Scholar McColl

Two loudmouths are up on their feet in the middle of the stand. They're stood nose to nose mouthing off at each other. One of them looks as if his head has been boiling on a low heat all afternoon. The other's mouth is that of a guard dog that's about to burst its leash and bite.

This is what the dogfight of relegation does, it sets Blues against Blues, it has them snarling, ready to tear each other's throats out, or at least rip an ear off.

'Okay, lads,' shouts the Blocker from the aisle, making calm-down movements with his hands.

Just as Solid John arrives on the scene the whole crowd explodes on seeing the kid Jeffers loop a very clever header high and wide of the keeper's hand. Goal! And that tension on the terraces is clapped out, shrugged off, in the celebrations. The two contestants are no longer up for a boxing match.

Maggie shifts across to where I stand in the gangway, she pulls a packet from her pocket, 'Would you like a sweet?'

Sugar in my throat. And that sweet smile on wet lips is good to look at after what we've been watching all afternoon. So…would the smiling lady be up for a date?

Solid John joins us before I can make a move. But what he has to say is true enough. We have to be thankful for the point we seem to have snatched, but it isn't enough, nowhere near enough. We scratch around in the mud and crawl out clutching a single point and see, just below us, the mire into which big clubs have disappeared – and then, looking out, we see some nasty opposition appearing on the horizon.

'Where are we going to pick up the points we need?' says Solid John.

Nobody replies. Nobody knows.

Now two questions need answering.

And one of them only she has the answer to. So the only way to find out is to ask her.

Maggie May

So I'm being taken out: the movies. But the range of choice isn't great, so it comes down to a tossup between schmaltzy love and male heroics. The coin says we get buddy stuff and bonding, trumpets and gunfire, while the buildings burn. As the conflict booms and flashes we lean close together, press across the arm barrier. This very still and sustained contact is far more interesting than all the ducking and dashing and diving around on the screen: that sense that there is much to be explored and discovered.

Stepping out into the night we are both in the mood for booze.

'A man who enjoys good beer,' I say.

'And a lady who appreciates a good lager,' he says.

'Cheers' we say together, and make each other smile – which is a very good start because I've known those faltering beginnings from which nothing gets better. But not for us. As we drink we cheerfully carve up that dreadful movie with our blades of sarcasm. There's quite a mess on the table in front of us by the time we've finished: actors, theme, plot: the whole bag of trash.

We are an effective unit, it seems, a good fit for each other perhaps. The private bubble we float in fills with our laughter. And when we've done with ripping a lousy film to pieces we begin to trade excerpts from our back pages, swap small confessions, exchange our greatest moments in Goodison. And as we talk the past I glimpse the future in fleeting pictures. We will approach the bedroom at a leisurely pace – we are headed in that direction for sure. We will neither rush nor dally – let the garments fall at the appropriate moment.

My lips on his: Goodnight. And see you soon.

Soon can't come soon enough.

After a drink in the Bee Hive we move on to Duke Street – the place where you can see the pizzas go in the oven. I go for pepperoni, he orders anchovy. 'Unusual,' I say.

'Does that surprise you?'

I look at him. 'Actually no, no it doesn't.'

And when he passes a slim triangle to my plate I have to agree he made an interesting choice.

When we have moved on he talks about his work in people's gardens, funny little stories. I have my own about hospitals. And he does listen, I don't have the impression of a mind wandering back to Goodison Park or some other place.

Scholar McColl

We talk about books. After growing up as that Bible girl she appreciates a choice phrase when she reads one. But she also likes black grapes and black chocolate, avocados, red wine, fine lagers, the scent of wild roses, and she feels good wearing sparkly T-shirts and dangly earrings, but not necessarily at the same time, although she can recall with a smile a certain occasion when she was wearing nothing else. I tell her I wish I'd been there.

She does like a laugh, this one. And she does, on occasion, have a delightfully filthy little laugh.

Then we turn serious, talk of our favourite players and agree that what we like to watch is a team that can pass the ball like the

Everton side of the Eighties did: sweetly. And most possessively.

Maggie May

And obviously we talk about the trials and tribulations of now, about the tough games coming up – like the one against the old enemy.

Anfield: we both have stories of over there. And of course his father was a Red.

So then he tells me about him, and eventually he says, with a smile on his face, 'One day the old fella came back from the match with soggy socks. He used to stand on the Kop and he was cursing some other Kopites.'

And then my soon-to-be lover goes on to describe what he says was an ancient Anfield tradition there where a man, full of pre match booze and not inclined to push through the masses to get to the bog, would simply flick out his dangler and let gush where he stood. The more refined pissers would do it through a rolled up newspaper, apparently. And the really posh urinators would use their match programme to channel three pints of brown and bitter over somebody else's shoes.

He's laughing, saying, 'Imagine it: all that bladdered booze cascading so scenically down the hill of concrete steps that was the Kop – a proper postcard that is.'

And it is quite a picture. So I said, going with the flow of the idea, 'So maybe that Kop anthem is really just a reinvention of some old alehouse ditty: You'll Never Wee Alone.'

He grabs that thought and sings with it, 'Weeee on, weee o-o-onnnn.'

'With a belch and a fa-a-a-art!' I couldn't resist that. And there's nothing anyone can tell me about the excrescences and secretions of the human body. I've seen it all and I've cleaned it up and unfortunately on occasion I've had it all over me.

'And yoool ne-vere weeee A-ha-low-ow-ow-ow-ownnnn! Yoool…'

What a sweet little duet we made, though – our little singsong. Although we were getting some frowny stares from one or two who didn't appreciate the sugar.

Anyway, we kept ourselves amused. But then I wondered, 'Is it true, though?'

'According to the old-time Reds it is: back in the day, the Fifties, early Sixties. I grew up surrounded by them. They used to talk about it like it was their special folklore, and a joke too when they weren't actually squelching around like the old fella that day. Rivers of piss, they'd say, wet boots, soggy socks.'

Soggy socks? You do have to laugh, though. Put a pair of them in your *Global Brand* portfolio Mr Big Red Mouthpiece and see what the world makes of them! Eh? Picture it, though: some club ambassador is standing there saying, 'Gentlemen, you have all come from different countries, from very different cultures, and I see now one or two puzzled looks around the room. You'll be wondering why we asked you to bring spare footwear along with you, and why you also have before you a rolled up newspaper, and why I have here before me a pair of rather damp-looking socks that are giving off that intriguingly pungent aroma that you might have detected. Well let me now introduce you to the Authenic Anfield Experience, to a much valued part of our history here, a tradition much older than the singing of our revered anthem. Gentlemen, would you please follow me. And be sure to bring your rolled up newspaper...'

When we stop laughing Mark says, 'Does it ever occur to you that we have more in common with the Reds than we do with any southerner or Brummie or Jock?'

And it is true, when you think about it. We are like two halves of the same thing. The divided tribe. The Yin and the Yang of the city. Opposites making a whole – and once, briefly, at the time of Hillsborough, a chain of blue and red scarves was wrapped around that unity.

We are both of us, after all – us who for generations have filled Goodison and Anfield – the progeny of some of those men who serviced the slave ships, the local carpenters and blacksmiths and ropemakers, and those who crewed them, the ships that once sailed into the Bight of Benin, the Slave Coast, who dropped anchor outside Cape Coast Castle where I once stood: lads and fellas from Garston and the Dingle, probably, Bootle and Kirkdale. Like those who came later from Ireland and Wales, they are our forefathers, both of us: those men who manned the Liverpool Merchant and all the other ships that followed her out there to Africa. And sometimes I listen to us and wonder whether something from the squalor of those slave ships has seeped into our language and is there once again every time we say *shite*. Far-fetched maybe. Or maybe not. For their language has been passed on to us, those men who saw into the holds of those ships, the unspeakable horror of them, those who lived for weeks amid the weeping and the wailing and the shit – and then returned home with their pay-off to the cockroach hovels they themselves inhabited. We speak with their tongue, still, although some of their terms we have spat out and stamped on, many of us – though not all.

Sometimes, myself, I'm drawn back to the old Biblical lines, the purity of them, that wonderful phrasing I have never forgotten even if I have lost the faith:

Galatians 4.16: Am I therefore become your enemy, because I tell you the truth?

Corinthians 1.13: Though I speak in the tongues of men and of angels, but have not charity, I am become as sounding brass or a tinkling cymbal.

Those lines: when I say them to myself it's like drinking a pure juice, or bathing in a pool of clearest water – a pool of sound even. For me they are unsullied even by the sins committed in the name of Christianity. I can still speak them like the girl I once was, before boys and football and all the rest – but of course I am not her and wouldn't know how to be her again.

Us and them, though, the Reds: the waters of the River Mersey and the salt winds from the Irish Sea have nurtured us both – for better or for worse. Worse, it seems, at times. But not always. For the better, you feel, those occasions when the banter is bouncing like balls in the playground.

And when myself and Mr McColl have finished kicking those ideas around it's time to talk about us again. 'How do you feel about dancing?' he wants to know.

'Strongly,' I tell him, 'Where are we going?'

So we head down Mathew Street for a boogie. And out there, moving to the sounds, I'm thinking: I've found myself a partner who's not a bad mover, not bad at all. We are dancing towards each other, inevitably it seems. And it feels sort of right: him walking at my side towards Goodnight time. At the end of the road I tell him, 'Well, thank you, sir.' But he's not coming in yet, not quite yet. A little delayed gratification? Why not? But not only that: you start to get a very early feeling that this could become serious. So it's, 'Thank you again, and Goodnight. And we must meet up for the Newcastle game.'

19

Splashing Around with the Soggy Magpies

Billy Whizz

Bad start. Pissin down when we set off for Geordieland – a little convoy fuelled by the powerful booze brewed in that old trophy de effay cup. Ohhh Jeeez ! And it goes on pissin down all along the road. Kind of dampens ya that does. Ya start to wonder whether yer cup hopes is gonna drown in some big puddle further north.

Jane

Rainy day. Am dyin to see Frank but I know I can't go yet. Because Barbara might be still around and Frank's got so many things to do. But ee still wants to hold me, to hold me close to him. And that's what I want: to be needed. That's what I need: someone to lean on and share things with, someone oo can take some of the weight off you. Maybe I haven't been the best wife in the world but I have tried. I gave everythin I could to me children and they were welcome to it. All I want now is the basics of what's between a man and a woman: attention and love and affection and being able to say all the daft things that come into your head as well as the important ones. But it's not always possible for us to be good in the ways that we would want to be good if the world was like it should be because just thinkin about Frank's lips on mine, his hands on me, I feel that feelin start up in me belly until am achin, just achin for him. But I have to wait, I have to hang on and wait until Barbara is out of the way so I can get in there. Need me umbrella today, though. Still rainin.

Billy Whizz

And it's still pissin down when the game kicks off. And it's still pissin down when Newcastle steal a muddy goal. But then for the rest of the first half we was as good them. As bad as them actually. Coz we don't av no punch up front.

But we come out after the break and boss the game and manage to get level throo a crackin strike from Rhino that rips inta the top corner while their goalie stares at it like it's a bat outa hell. And this should be the turnin point. Should. But it's them that seem sparkier. Then the dummy of a ref gives them a free kick on the edge of our box. We don't need to go inta details of the farce that ends with the ball rollin into our net. That's a nasty kick in the plums that I never seen comin. We're chasin the game now like kids after bubbles. Newcastle are pullin us around and we're lookin as stretched as old knicker elastic. And some of our players are startin to look like they're about to lie down in a puddle and let them Geordie no-marks sail past them. But am not havin that. Am up on me feet. Me and a few others. Lettin fly a few choice lines. And then suddenly these clowns the Geordie cops appear and the big one with the stick is pointin towards de exit.

Scholar McColl

'There's no way back into this game for us,' I announce to Maggie, like a prophet in the Country of Booze, as we sit in the Albert before our half empty glasses watching this soggy game go on. 'No way back now.'

As if she can't see that for herself.

But that's football: you hear yourself stating the obvious because it's so damned obvious, while there really doesn't seem anything else to say.

Yes, the hopes we shared for this game only an hour ago are already like part of the past: distant and inaccessible. Like those old trips I made to Newcastle back when I followed the Blues everywhere. Like that time when I, and the travelling thousands had hardly left the ground before trouble came stalking in black and white stripes.

A shock of harsh voices and swirling fists: it was loud and yes knuckly, but it was very brief. Those raspy magpie assailants flew when the horsemen of the constabulary moved in. And I, along with two other lads who I didn't know, was suddenly looking at the inside of a meatwagon. The back doors flung open, uniforms spilling out, a face glared from underneath a peak. 'In thor yee lot! Cum on, move yoorselves!'

My dry breathy mouth hung a little open. 'But…'

'In! Neeo! Or wuh put yee in.'

We were surrounded. We were being herded, prodded, tongue-lashed.

'But?'

'In!! Scoose bastids. Git in!!'

But I knew there was no sense in making it worse than it already was. So when their cargo of meat had been loaded and the wagon driver had heaved the engine into gear I introduced myself to my travelling companions.

Pikey was a big lad with a smooth bum-fluffy face. The other one, Jack Moran, was round shouldered and bow-legged; he had a big monkeyish jaw, a fist-flattened nose, and a voice that, powered by the fuel of injustice, rose as high as a schoolgirl's.

After reflecting rather vehemently on the lack sanity, reason, common sense, and fairness in this part of the world we gradually quietened into an anxious silence in which I tried to concentrate on ordering little groups of words around my mind, laying out the pattern of our innocence.

At the door of the copshop we were ordered out. A surly, smarting little crew, we filed into the lock up, and were led up to the sergeants' desk. I was in unfamiliar territory now – this place seemed like a cross between a school and a dole office with an element of something more sinister – but the big bony sergeant looked us up and down like he was sick of the sight of us already, as if we were familiar old lags, boomerang offenders. I felt like protesting but the large man before me was king of this little castle and down the corridors were dungeons, the torture chamber. The sergeant's skin was red, stretched tight over his bones and his chin looked like an offensive weapon.

Hearing noises behind, I glanced over my shoulder and saw three more Scousers being herded on. But they looked like they'd had a rougher time. One of them had taken a real pounding, his face was already in bad shape and it had obviously only just started to swell and colour. By the morning he would probably look like somebody even he didn't recognize.

'Look what they done to him,' protested a girlish-looking Blue with long blond hair. 'Put the boot in. And then walked away while we get dragged in ere!'

'Tell that to the magistrates,' said the sergeant. His heart was an ice box, this man, he had seen too many, far too many, on the way down, too many of them crying innocent. 'We nivvor had a Scousor lodging wi us yet whe wasn't a decent chorch-ganin lad whe got mixed up in trouble by complete accident.'

Now I felt the need to speak up, 'What's a fella supposed to do when he's attacked?'

His response was to demand my details and the contents of my pockets. Not since I took a catapult to school had I had anything confiscated. That was the scale of my sudden diminishment. I was reduced to a little kid with his name sown into his blazer, scabbed knees, snotty nose, skidmarks on his underpants. This wasn't fair, this wasn't right, but like the stony jailer said, 'Tell that to the magistrates.'

I was led away to the cells: a place to myself; a slab of wood for a bed.

I looked up at the window. The glass was as thick as the bottom of three milk bottles and about as clear as milk. I sat down on the bare bed, and then tried lying on it. And my body, drawn into itself, adjusting to the hardness of the surface, finding what comfort it could, resigned itself to numbness, and the cold that would sneak up on it those long hours before dawn. I shifted my aches this way and that, sorted my limbs out into what seemed the least painful arrangement and tried not to move in case I couldn't find it again.

So now I was a criminal, would carry an official blemish, a minor one maybe, but I had stepped across an important line, it seemed, or been shoved over, to acquire it. An injustice – but what would that count for in the end? On that rough bed I grew cold where many had become chilled before. All over the world, in all kinds of languages, dialects, men, kids, had thought that: Here I am a prisoner; why me?

It's like falling into a pit. And you are like the one who would be asking: How come of all those figures walking that territory I was the one who had to place his foot into the wrong spot and take the tumble?

And so I lay on, lay and ruminated, where many before me had lain, millions, in the hard place, the cold place. For one man a single night is all, for another he has entered with steps he will never retrace. Life. All the world contained inside some soaring razor-ridged walls. But this was just how things were, how they'd always been: some held the keys, the whip, the gun, and some were doomed to become slaves, convicts, the occupants of concentration camps. And the earth goes round the sun and the moon goes round the earth and it all goes on just the same: somewhere in the middle of Africa, somewhere to the north of Brazil, somewhere just around the corner. And those who manage to stay clear go about their ordinary pursuits: earning a coin, chatting a girl, watching a game of football.

Sometime later, those seemingly endless hours of incarceration, a chorus of bangs and broken sentences brought me back to Sunday morning Newcastle. With a clatter of keys the door of my dungeon opened. Here was the jailer with two cold rubber eggs and some pieces of supposedly edible cardboard.

What would happen now? Were they going to keep me in? Would I need to get a solicitor? What?

At ten o'clock I stood once more at the sergeant's desk – stiff and sour tongued – and was told, along with the other two I'd been brought in with, that if my face was never seen again on the streets of Newcastle no charges would be brought against me.

One thief escaped being crucified. Was his relief any greater than mine when I stepped through the door of that meat-house?

Outside in the breathable air my body re-connected itself with life. I was off and away with a bounce in my heel.

But the next time I saw the inside of a police cell my exit wasn't quite so joyfully bouncy. The Birmingham cops bounced me into court one Monday morning and when I left there I did have a criminal record and was in debt to HM Govt by almost three hundred notes. The lads who'd surrounded me and some other Blues, the Villains of Villa Park, had gone strolling away smirking when I was snatched. So, despite the blemish and the fine, I strolled away from that court, so that anybody eyeing me (nobody was) would see that the weight of the state hadn't crushed me. Yeh,

I went strolling away into the zone of forgetting in which unwanted experiences are discarded. Or that's what I thought.

Anyway, years later as I sit with Maggie May I see that my team aren't strolling anywhere, they are slipping meekly out of the FA Cup. Four-one. They've conceded four goals in front of a big audience and now their Cup dreams are lying tattered in the mud, like scraps of soggy newspaper.

Billy Whizz

Got thrown out. Yeh. Suddenly the cops show up sayin, 'Yee, yee, yee an yee: yeut!'

I says, 'Wha?'

The one with the stick says, 'Yeut!' Then ee spells it o-u-t, spits it out, more like, the weirdest gobfull of chewed up nonsense yev ever heard in a football ground. O-u-t: Yeut! Yeh, am not jokin. And then he announces, 'Yuet is a very simple ward aroond heor.'

Simple wards for simple minds, eh? Ever heard anythin like it? A Geordie cop tryna talk clever? Fergerrit ya dope. Learna fokin langwidge first!

Then the babyfaced one says that they don't tolerate that kind of langwidge in their ground. And the one with the stick says that next time we'll know to moderate our langwidge but this time we're gannin yeut in the street.

'Yas gannin yeut,' ee bawls. 'See moove!'

I says, 'Swearin?' I says, 'Swearin? Worr else can ya do when ya watchin a shite team like ours, worr else can ya do but swear at the useless shower of -'

'Yeut!' shouts the clown with the stick near poking the thing right at me gob. 'Yeut! Neeo!'

They're not very understandin up there, somma them cops. They lack understandin, and they lack tolerance, and plenty more besides. As me arl fella used to say, coz ee had a problem one time, 'Got some decent mates in them parts but yez gerra certen tipe up there oo ain't notn but Scotsmen with their brains bashed in: the wreckage what the Vikins and the Romans left behind.'

And when they'd booted us out, when we gorr out, guess what? It was still teemin. Bucketin down, it was – the world turned to piss. So am sat there in me damp clothes all the way back. All that long wet way back home.

Yeh, am sat there wonderin about the week ahead and feelin that somethin ain't right. Me kecks are all clammy on me legs but me knee seems okay now, so I should be able to go back on the roofs, and anyway av still got dosh left from what I picked up at the dog track, so I should feel good about that, but somethin ain't right. The Blues ain't in good shape, not good shape at all, but it's more than that what's givin me this feelin. It's like somethin else, some nasty little bug is bitin at me brain.

Jane

'Oh Frank,' I say, Oh Frank, I want this to go on for ever…'

Scholar McColl

We talk on the phone about the Newcastle debacle. Maggie says, 'So now it's back to the real business of the season.'

Yep, now all we have to contemplate is that desperate old struggle to dodge one of Mr Relegation's three bullets. So now we have to drag ourselves out of the muddy puddles and shower away the self-pity and then we have to open the tin of optimism and inject some of its contents into our veins. Or something like that.

When we've said all we can about the mess the Blues must not slide into we turn to other happier matters. 'Would you like to come round and have something to eat,' she says.

So it's not long until I'm on my way round.

When she opens the door my heart goes over a bump. She looks fine and rosy and very welcoming. Am I about to fall, to tumble into the lush grass, or is that just imagination, the re-hashing of old plots? I settle my lips lightly on her cheek, and fill up with her scents.

She moves in soft shoes and wears brightness like an actress claiming centre stage. Her decorative ideas are simple, restrained, tasteful. The place is comfortable, predictably woody with plenty of foliage and means of illumination.

We eat pasta with Chianti, fruit salad and cream, the coffee and chocolate comes and goes, the words flow along merrily on a current of alcohol.

We ease into her choice upholstery. We are close and being drawn ever closer. I inhale her presence, take in of her as much as I am able, a mixture of consumer scents and others more natural. Now her shape is against mine, her inner structures and softnesses. Hands, lips, cheeks, tongues find each other. Buttons, clasps, buckles, laces are manipulated, unloosed, left to hang. If we were neat, ordered, carefully groomed when we entered the room we are not so now. What had been two separate immaculate figures is now a single bundle of dishevelment, but now is the time for the real feast. Half laying on the untidy couch, she suggests it is time to climb the stairs.

Naked, lying on the bed, she stretches back her arms and offers her nipples as a choice hors d oeuvre. I begin at the high table and then move on. Her tongue is happy, keen even, to reveal its own deft skills.

She licks me like a child its ice cream and I am entering the lushest regions of summertime – to which I return most keenly in the following days.

As we lie still, and most content, yet again, she wants to know about the marriage that got broken and ditched. Okay. There are no big secrets locked in that little box. I should never have got married, should have realized what kind of a dame I was teaming up with back then – that football would have no place, absolutely no place, in her scheme.

I bumped into my beautiful future tormentor when I went away to study how to lay out a garden, to blend stone with the green stuff, to balance bright colours with those less so. She was very fair, and perfectly proportioned. At first it was like she was playing at the cautious girl, putting up barriers, prohibitions, tests. As if I had to prove my staying power, my dedication to the task. If that was what I had to do to gain access then that's what I would do. Over many wanders in the woods the barriers were pushed back, her defences overrun, until I arrived at that place of her deepest secrets, her most delicate constructions. The wait had charged everything with a special kind of power. The conclusion of the chase left me feeling towards her a special kind of gratitude. And laying there beside her it was as if I had just watched the Blues score one of their best ever goals, a blend of intricate teamwork and individual brilliance.

I was constantly aware of her breath, her scent, her curves, her heat, and was drawn into her leafy world, seduced down its unpeopled paths, and if there were lurking dangers, pitfalls and traps then I was ready to be reckless; if there were risks I would take them – for I reckoned I had found there something strange and rare.

She could name a bird from its song, an animal from its tracks, or even its shit – she was no damsel, no pale and queasy princess. And she was no fake peasant girl either, she had ideas, she had the pickings of large minds at her fingertips: theories, references, astute observations. She reasoned that two people bound by the twine of powerful emotion could build their own world apart, could make of their lives a statement that denied the essential grubbiness of the human world.

Her idea was that when we finished the course we would set up home and business together. And when it came to the detail she was no woman for tinsel and fancy patterns, she knew very well what nuts and bolts were for, and how to apply a spanner to them. And she could screw down tight too; you'd notice the sinews in her arms. She sold her little terraced place to raise a decent deposit for our love house and work van; we would buy some tumbledown unmarked by suburban trashiness and make a thing of our own.

We found a stone relic over the water from the city, a place with apple trees out back and bats in the attic. There were flat fields around it, and a scrap of woodland where bustling rooks found a refuge. The wedding was modest – our long-term plans didn't include a lot of people. I stood beside a radiant and passionate woman who looked like she'd been feeding on electricity all night and echoed the words of the scared text. I walked with her through the confetti cloud towards our shared future. She was so easy of movement, so comely and elegant. And I was so well groomed and turned out that I looked like somebody else. Looking back I might say that I felt like someone else – but I don't think I did.

So we set about constructing our secluded ideal. We went forwards always, everywhere, or so it seemed for a while – a perfect partnership. Until I became aware that she rather than I or both of us was the motor that powered us on. And if I had been before in the position of sidekick, running boy, I had never been prepared to remain like that for long. And if she was the engine, I began to feel that the wheels were rolling towards a place called Discontent, and might be about to fall off.

She had ideas for the house which maybe I didn't share, but it was to all intents and purposes her place; and that was a problem. I was paying the price for those years spent in my monk's cell of books when I might have been out accumulating capital. But if my homemaking instincts were underdeveloped, hers were in their prime. She sensed in me a lack of commitment, a detachment, almost a casualness, and she was not pleased. The alchemical processes were in reverse, gold was being rendered into brass. Small poisons were brewing up. The collision, the explosion came, probably inevitably, over football. I became a yellowjacket. And as such I was committed to going to all the games and this got in the way of some jobs we did because I would stroll off to Goodison and leave her to work on alone. Everton Football Club was the last enclave of my independence and Tricia clearly had plans to overrun it.

'I don't see how you can go on with it,' was her opening line.

'But I need something like that,' I said, and the implication was clear.

'Then can't you just go when it fits in with other things? If you're trying to run a business surely that must take precedence over a silly game.'

'It's not a silly game and it can't be occasional. I've made a commitment.'

'I rather thought you'd made a commitment to me. At least that's what it sounded like the day you married me.'

I felt myself digging in, all of my bodyweight settling on my heels. Maybe some men will concede, capitulate when stood in the fierce glare of the Queen of the House, but I was too deep in with Everton. I had given up my days, my evenings, to her and her project. I rarely picked up a book now, or my guitar; evenings were to be shared, given over to plans, to talk of all kinds. I had given up all other pursuits, but my place in Goodison Park I would not walk away from.

We had done more than a little sparring around this subject since we'd set up together but this I realized was the showdown, this was to be a bareknuckle contest to find a winner. The set of her mouth spoke of unhappiness, displeasure, grievance. I felt as if I'd been summoned to the head woman's office. 'You haven't got time for football any more,' she insisted. It was no longer a debating point.

'I've made time for it ever since I was six years old.'

I tried to imagine myself as an ex-Blue, an armchair Blue, a television Blue, keeping up with the club only through the papers, the radio. No. People did. I'd met them, I'd known them. There was always a slow drift away as the new punters, new yellowjackets, arrived. I could have said that maybe in the future I wouldn't feel so strong on this issue; that as some men grew older the game could start to matter less. For I knew that to be true. But I didn't say it. I sensed I was fighting for something more than just my football rights here and I was placing no concessions on the kitchen table.

But there was a strain of regret entwined with the wariness, the frustration, the anger. As an outdoor team planting perfumed gardens, mixing up conifers according to bulk and shades of green, we shaped up well; and we were heading in the direction of a very decent income – but I could see no way that our landscaping partnership would outlast a domestic explosion.

Sensing belligerence, more resistance on my part rather than less, she moved for compromise – I should give up the football for a few seasons until everything else was well-grounded and solid built. But I reckoned she wasn't above a trick, a ploy, and would not hear of it.

'So, what's happening to us,' she said suddenly, as if a little shocked, 'would you really rather have football than me? I'm your wife, doesn't that mean anything? Is that what you're saying, that Everton means more to you than I do?'

I knew, obviously, that that wouldn't be very flattering for any woman, let alone one like Tricia, 'I didn't say that.'

My answer wasn't unequivocal enough. She was summoning her considerable energy for another charge. And she could be a fearsome presence too with her wildcat eyes, those claws set to slash at my face. But part of me wanted this now, was geared up for the scrap – if shit and fur was about to fly it wasn't all going to be mine. Every now and again things will get like that; it's rough and tumble time whether you like it or not. But life isn't a pre-season friendly, and wouldn't be much of a game if it were.

'People who don't know anything about football will never

understand — some of them don't want to understand and some of them just can't,' I said looking beyond her at the door. She would never be any different; she would always want everything from me or any man: absolute devotion, submission to her and her ideal. She believed in love with a terrible passion — but love on her terms, nothing less. She would never be at peace as long as there was part of me that wasn't hers. I looked at the door again. I looked at her. She stood in my way. She was set for a long hard battle. I wanted this to be over now, I wanted to get out. But we slogged and slashed for a while longer, sometimes not so unpleasant, sometimes distinctly nasty, circling around, going over old ground.

And then she said, 'If the only thing you've ever really been committed to is a football club, then you must have led a pretty pathetic life.'

And hearing that I knew it was time, I knew with absolute certainty, with total clarity, that I'd had enough.

And seeing me slipping from her grasp she wanted me to hit the ground hard, to be damaged, broken.

She told me how conceited I was, that I was full of conceit as fraudsters are full of shit. She said that what had attracted her initially was that she sensed in me something different, that as well as knowing much, having travelled a long distance over land and through books, she'd sensed in me something a little bit wild, uncultivated, but now she could see that all it was was shiftiness, that I was full of evasiveness and conceit and I was unreliable too and shabby because worst of all — incredibly, unbelievably — I rated a little boys' game above love which anyone but a fool knew is the greatest thing in the world.

Were there any strands of truth in that knotty little bundle? In her desire to mangle me, to leave me a mess for anyone I met after her, she had surely gone in with her studs showing. But could I dispute with everything? Romantic love — the greatest thing in the world? Was it? I was no expert, no connoisseur, that was for sure. Was I even out of junior school? I couldn't answer that for myself. Was I, like she said, not what I seemed? A fraud? Was the fact that I worked for Everton Football Club after having a history of minor lawlessness a proof of something?

Maggie May

Sometimes we don't make it to the bedroom. We do it on the living room floor. And it's as if the wind has blown off all the washing from the line. And sometimes we do make it and spend many passionate hours there. And sometimes he hums out his orgasm and lies in silent contentment. These days are most pleasant. He turns to me and says that.

But what of the future? Does he see me there in the years ahead? I am not sure.

I could talk to this man for a very long time but will I get the chance?

His words linger in my memory like scraps of an old and important text. The smell of sex is left in the room when he's gone – those moments of our deepest intimacy. But does he love me? I kneel on the bed and give him soft sweet pleasures. But does he love me, will he ever love me?

I give him the hard sex of wild animals, sex without roses or silks. I give him the musky, rutting sex of the field and let him climb like the stag on my back. I give him all the sex he wants.

Maybe in time he will love me. Maybe one day he will speak the words.

The words on his tongue, though, are: Blackburn Rovers.

20

A Darkness in the Heart

Solid John Sanger

Another night of torture by radio. It is so painful listening to a game you can't see, especially a game you need to win. But us fans have made our choice and must take our punishment. The match was on my mind when I got home from work, naturally. The Blues were close to the edge over which the dead men topple but with three new points in our pockets we could take a big step away from it. Maybe.

'After that performance in Newcastle we shouldn't build our hopes up too high, I'm afraid, son,' I said to my lad. 'But if they've got any kind of backbone, if they've got any pride at all, they'll have sorted themselves out and be ready for this. You need backbone in this life, son, and you need pride.'

Then the wife came into the room looking worried. 'Mrs Mason at number seventeen has been broken into.'

'Ah no, 'I said. 'Poor woman.' These sly figures creeping around dipping their grubby fingers into other people's lives and making a mess of them – they make me want to vomit. I could break them in two.

Instead I went round to see what I could do. The fingerprint man was just leaving. Mrs Mason was slumped in her chair.

It looked like a quick job to me, they hadn't hung around to make too much of a mess of the place before they got on their filthy way with their pathetic bag of swag.

'We never used to have this sort of thing,' she said with a sigh, in almost a whisper.

'They've got no morals,' I told her. 'They've got no standards.'

She said, 'They took my ornaments. They took my grandfather's fob watch. They took my mother's wedding ring. They took everything that meant anything to me.'

What can you say that will ease the pain of losing what matters? 'I'll see what I can do to patch things up for you. See if we can't keep the villains out.'

You can't let them get on top and destroy everything and turn our streets into a damned jungle. I know what real jungle is. I've been out there.

I phoned home and got the missus to send the lad round with my tools. I might be a spanner man but I can turn my hand to a neat bit of joinery when the need is there. By the time I'd finished the key turned smoothly and the lock slid home and sat there tight and secure. 'That should keep them out Mrs Mason.'

She couldn't stop thanking me. It was a relief when she returned to an old theme of hers, 'The area has changed. It isn't what it was.'

And how that makes her shake her head. And what can I do but join her in that?

'It's the people,' I told her. 'It's the kind of people who've moved in.' And, glancing out the window, I noted a pair of disreputable bothers hanging around down at the end of the road. I didn't know which part of the dark continent their family bailed out from, but one thing I did know was that they were a pair of pests. 'We'll just have to keep our eyes open Mrs Mason.'

She squinted at me. 'Mine aren't so good any more.'

'Well I'll certainly be keeping watch from now on. But I must get going. I've got a football match to listen to Mrs Mason. You take care now. And any problems you just come and knock on my door.'

When we got outside, sure enough I could see a whole bunch of hangabouts on the corner. Seven, I counted. White trash and the other sort. A mixed rabble. The culprits? Well I certainly had no thoughts of looking further.

But I noticed the look on Joe's face. Something was wrong. I only had to look at the lad to see it. I know my sons. I knew when something was wrong and when it wasn't. I hadn't given up my life in the military to finish up not knowing when a lad of mine had a problem. 'What's the matter, son?'

'Nothing,' he said in that feeble kind of voice that children use when they want to avoid talking about what needs to be talked about. But talk about it is exactly what he was going to have to do sooner or later. 'Are you sure?' I could see in his eyes that he was looking at something nasty. But what it was he wouldn't say. 'Is it that lot?' I jerked a thumb in the direction of the rabble, letting him know that I was in no mood to let the matter drop. A splinter must come out if it's not to fester and infect the finger, and then maybe the whole bloodstream.

When I began again my tone was firm. 'Come on, what is it?' I didn't want to upset the lad but a little pain now and the poison would be cleaned out.

This feeble voice replied, 'They say things about Stephen.'

I could see the broad picture immediately. I was in no need of the details. I hadn't pushed my son around in a wheelchair without being aware of a thing or two. 'It's them brothers isn't it, they're the main culprits?'

He waited a second and then nodded, and then he added, 'And the rest of them.'

So it was the whole hardfaced little crew that we had to tackle. And tackle them we would. I said, 'You have to keep your head up in this world, son, you'll encounter scum from time to time, but you always keep your head high.'

And just at that moment I turned and spotted the rabble on the move. So what were they up to now?

I said to the lad, 'You go on home, take the tools, and tell your mum I'll be back in a few minutes.' And as soon as the scum were round the corner I went after them. Maybe they were going to smirk over their bag of loot or maybe they were thinking of going over somebody else's wall? Whatever they were up to it couldn't be good. As I rounded the bend I couldn't see them anywhere. Then I heard them in the yard of the end house where one of them lived – like a pack of hyenas. And then I caught the whiff. I smelled the drugs they were smoking. I knew the smell of illegal narcotics when it came wafting my way, I'd been about the world enough to know what was what. We never used to have that sort of thing in our green and pleasant land. One time, that was a sign of the rank and putrid places on this earth, that stinking weed. Not any more, though. But would the police be interested? Not a chance.

With one thing and another, by the time I'd eaten my dinner it was getting close to kick off. The lad was already sitting with the radio. A good young Blue, our Joe. And I was confident he'd grow up upright and strong, knowing right from wrong, good from bad, gold from brass. He'd always walk a foot taller than the riff-raff, the crew that will drag us all down if we let them.

I was just saying to him, 'Well son, if they don't get something out of this game they're in dire straits I'm sorry to say,' when the team was announced. I couldn't believe it. I said to him, 'Bakayoko's playing. Bakayoko!! He should never be allowed near the pitch never mind be given a team shirt.' I said, 'What kind of madness is this?'

That wasn't a question a lad could answer. Nor me.

He'd left out young Jeffers, who had been shaping up like he could be the Little White Hope of Everton Football Club, and given his shirt to this failure from the Ivory Coast.

Even the names of those places bugged me.

I'd sailed that coast in the *Britannia Princess* right down to Cape Town. Giving most of it a wide berth, dodging the pirates – that was the idea. But a storm out there left us damaged so we had to put into port for repairs. Had no choice. Monrovia, in Liberia. Bad place.

While we were waiting for the boat to get sorted a couple of us wandered into this booze den. There was a fella in there with a red hat on – a Liverpool hat. Him and his mate must have heard where we were from. They came up to us and started saying, 'Liverpool great. Liverpool great team.'

I was with Marty Dodd, another Scouser, an ex-sergeant in the Marines. He was a Blue like me. We said, 'No, no we're Everton.'

We turned away. We didn't need that kind of company. We were neither of us the kind who needed amusing. We didn't need to be entertained by a pair of clowns. But their voices went on behind us. And then the point was reached where we had no option but to turn around and face them.

'Everton shit,' said the one in the hat. Aye, this was an African telling us, a pair of Scousers, born and bred, what was what, telling us about football.

Marty said, 'Who plays for Liverpool? Name the team.'

The clown in the hat looked like he'd just had a very stiff examination paper placed in front of him.

Marty said, 'Name them. Go ahead. Give me the names of this team of yours.'

Two names we got, two, from this pair of so-called supporters who were looking dumber by the second.

'Don't try and tell me about football. You don't know nothing,' said Marty. He didn't suffer fools, Marty didn't, no matter what kind of stupid headgear they were dressed up in. And he made that very clear to them. But the atmosphere in that place wasn't one we wanted to linger in so we headed for the door leaving behind a few home truths for our hosts to chew on.

We'd just got outside when – would you believe it – this character in the hat, who is such a passionate supporter of Liverpool Football Club that he can name *two* of their players, appears in the doorway and – I kid no one on this point – puts a curse on us. A curse, yes. A curse – some kind of ju-ju or other mumbo-jumbo. As we walked away we couldn't stop laughing. What else would you do? A redsnout in a silly hat with an arse the colour of coal had done some witchcraft on us. As we sailed on, glad to be well clear of that place, we kept on having a laugh about it. It became a joke with all the lads on the boat.

But a year later Marty, who'd never been ill in his life, dropped dead, just keeled over, stone dead. He walked out of a bar where he'd been on high form and fell down in the street and never spoke another word. The post-mortem said heart failure, but the officials didn't know what I knew.

'Maybe Bakayoko will score a goal dad,' the lad was saying.

I couldn't in all honesty encourage him in that belief. But here we were going into a game relying on him for goals – a striker who had to kneel down and pray to Allah all hours of the day and night. Sometimes it was a shock to realize how far the mighty had fallen.

'Bakayoko should have scored at Newcastle,' I said to Joe. 'The ball falls at his feet with only the goalie to beat and he makes a hash of it. Any striker worth his salt would have gobbled that chance up. I wouldn't feed him,' I said. 'Never mind his fasting. I wouldn't give him the bone from a Sunday roast,' I said. 'And he's not the only problem. It's not just that he's the wrong man in the wrong place in the wrong shirt. But we've got seven defenders out there with him. Walter the Wizard, our manager, has put out a team with seven defenders in it. Seven. Has that man flipped his pancake or what?'

Joe laughed, that laugh only a child can laugh, bursting free from his throat.

I said, 'Bakayoko up front and defenders all over midfield – what kind of a team is that? It's like old Archie Block would say: Hasn't the manager ever heard about square pegs and round holes? I can't believe it, son.' I couldn't. I know I was going on about it but what else could I say. Flabbergasted. I was. But seething, too. Quietly. Quietly seething at the state we were in, I was. The club, the city, the nation. Seething. Quietly.

'And this is a game we have to win,' said Joe.

'Well let's be realistic. We have to take at least a point home with us. Because if we slip up again there's no time left to recover.'

The whistle went. First thing the commentator said was that we'd lost possession. Yes, we give the ball away, and then what? Bang! One-nil to Blackburn.

A minute, we couldn't even stand strong for a single minute!

'Bad start,' said the voice on the radio. 'Big holes opened up down the right side of the Everton defence.'

But ten minutes later he was getting excited. 'Bakayoko denied by the goalkeeper!' And then a couple of minute later, 'Bakayoko denied again with a fine save! But he's getting closer.'

I have to admit I had a laugh at that, a bitter laugh, of course, what other kind of laugh could it be? And then, would you believe it, the voice on the radio was saying, 'Corner to Everton, taken by Hutchinson, flicked on by Weir at the near post, and Bakayoko, Bakoyoko heads in at the back post!'

Joe was looking at me. I didn't know what to say, it was hard to believe what I'd just heard was true, so I just said, 'Well now we need to go on and win this game.'

But we were hanging on for a point, giving them too much of the ball. You could tell even though you weren't there. And then you could see the opposition pushing us back at the start of the second half. But just after the hour the commentator's voice was getting high again, 'Wonderful pass from Hutchinson sends Bakayoko away... a neat little cross-shot...'

'Bakayoko's scored again dad, Bakayoko's won the game for us.'

'Maybe,' I said. 'Still a long time to go, son.'

A pair of goals in our situation were worth their weight in stardust. I had to admit that. But it was about time; the time for Mr Ibrahim Bakayoko to start earning his corn was long overdue.

The lad said again, 'Bakayoko has saved us dad.'

I said, 'Need to hear the whistle before I believe that.' And a long wait it was, too. That referee let them play on and on and on. The opposition had more than enough time to mug us and rob our points – if they were capable, which thankfully they weren't. But if I hadn't been the man I am I would have been uttering foul language in my own home, and before a young lad. Fuming, I was, at all that added time, livid.

Anyway, when I'd calmed down I saw that with those three vital points we'd made a bit of space between us and the pit at the bottom of the league.

I said to the lad, 'When you come from behind to win a game, son, you start to believe in yourself. So maybe we can build a couple more wins on a foundation like that.'

Then he reminded me, 'Arsenal next.'

The Arsenal? Tough one, that.

21

When the Gooners Came Gunning

Archie Block

Just getting ready to go out and report for duty when she comes back from the shops with a fistful of rhubarb. I do like that stuff. When it's in season it keeps my bowels turning over like a Rolls Royce engine. I sit on that seat in the morning and I couldn't ask for a smoother ride. She says. 'You look off-colour Arthur. Are you sure you're fit enough for this today?'

'Off-colour?' I said, 'That's just my complexion.'

She looks at me like I'm a fool. Hasn't got a clue. Fusspot. Makes a decent rhubarb crumble and a fine pan of scouse I'll admit that; she can hold her own with any group of gossips and chatterboxes, but about a man's world she's clueless. Women and football? They go together like trifle and ale. If that game was a gift from the gods it was only intended for them with balls. It's a sport for bravehearts and Alamo men, lads who'll stand tall and say: They shall not pass. And that's what we were going to need against the Gunners: guts and spunk. Balls. Real balls. Balls that swing between the legs of an Alamo man.

I said, 'Anyway I have duties to perform. The club looks to me to lead my section and that is what I intend to do.'

I got into the ground and found some kind of secret policeman in the office, part of an operation to catch some gang leader from London. Smart looking fella, or so he probably thought. Kind of fella who'd starve if he had to earn a living with his hands. Like some of them big bosses we had in the shipyard.

Scholar McColl

As I walk into the coatroom I note an unusual presence, see this character in a smart grey overcoat standing by the wall: a squat, square shouldered, upright figure, prematurely greying into its coat. Like a human filing cabinet: stood there immobile and impassive. His grey eyes scan you as you pass. Who is this man? Turns out he is a human storehouse – of visual information. Once he's seen a face he's got it stored like a photo. Works for the secret police, but he's been seconded to some gang-busting unit based in the big cop headquarters down in Scotland Yard.

As the briefing is about to begin in the office he enters. When his moment comes he speaks in a low very even voice of this gang he has been tracking. He says that some, including its leader for whom an arrest warrant has been issued, are believed to have been heading to the game. He says his colleagues are very keen to execute that warrant this afternoon and put an end to this character's violent escapades.

His words are so carefully measured, so clipped and smooth, and coolly delivered: a voice from elsewhere, from the higher echelons, from the quiet corridors of the secret state. He has the assurance of those born to power, this man in the grey overcoat. Confidence: he exhales it with words he speaks. The job gets done – he gives that off like man-scent. And with that whiff of efficiency in your nostrils you are not inclined to doubt. And might there be another such Mr Memory and crowd-scanner who has my face locked away in the storehouse of his brain?

Weird the thoughts that might go wandering through your mind as you stand in the chiefs' den in Goodison Park.

Finally he tells us that we might become aware of some unusual activity in our part of the ground as his squad goes in for the snatch, because these characters are elusive and are not to be found in the obvious places, but that whatever happens we just carry on as normal.

Normal, what's that? Normal for me once was encountering a gang of Gooners, a proper Goon Squad, a large and very well organized crew.

The worst kicking I took on my football travels was from those North London Cockneys. We were down there for a night match. Before the kick-off, full of ale and recklessness, I hopped on to the pitch, me and FreddieB, and strolled over to our goalie, Wee Georgie Wood, shook his hand, and gave him some advice, a few tips, just for a laugh, then dived back into the crowd before anyone could collar us. It must have been the cocky way we swaggered over their turf that got up some Cockney noses. Their nostrils were still twitching when the game was ending. They sent spies out, sharp-eyed observers, who managed to finger us. So the group of lads we were with had a whole regiment on their tail, the Highbury Hoods, or some other daft name. But they were no jokers them goonerlads when they caught up with us.

There was a black lad with us, Dessie the Diamond we called him, a lad from Lodge Lane, worked on the oil rigs, good footballer when he was around, handful for any pair of centre backs, a lad for the girls who took a few kicks in the bollocks that night. They were some very angry boys who waylaid us.

We had no idea we were being tracked. We'd parked our wheels a bit of a walk away, over by Stoke Newington, and were well on our way back to them, going down this quiet street, past a park. We were away from the big surge now so there weren't many people around. It was that night time quiet, most people on their way to bed probably or already bouncing on the bedsprings. Then we heard a different kind of squeakiness from somewhere behind: voices, squeaky Cockney tongues but kind of rough and challenging. We turned and saw a couple of lads with red and white scarves, another pair behind them, come swaggering towards us, beckoning us to come on, defying us to scrap with them. They're outnumbered more than two to one? We scanned them for a few moments and then dismissed them as no-mark fantasists. But when we turned round again we saw more of their crew spreading across the road in front of us, a lot more. And then on the left flank even more appeared, facing us on the park's dark green horizon. The right flank was boxed off by brickwork. By now the original four had become more like fourteen. And so from three directions they were coming on now like some warrior tribe of the Cockney Nation. And there were we, a tiny band of Scousers, boxed-in for a beating.

'Get the clowns and the coon,' that was the enemy call, the battle cry. So that was me fingered as one of the circus buffoons: me, FreddieB and Dessie to be made into mincemeat for Cockneyburgers.

A lad called Boner, a big lad who worked on the buildings and could bend a scaffolding pole like it was a bar of lead, led the charge for escape.

A kick in the thigh, and then a fist in the mouth pitched me deep in the ruck, the Valley of Pain. It was like I was tangling with some huge many-booted beast. I tried to roll myself up to protect my face, but one of my arms was tangled up with something. I managed to drag it out, to pull myself together. My nose was against the road, the rough cool tarmac, my head was wrapped up in my hands, and the boots went in with a terrifying fury. For the first time on my travels the scary message was being sent out: You might not come out of this alive. Through it all I could hear one of their voices, screaming, cursing Scousers as the shit of the land, the scum of the earth. Would they be the last words I ever heard? No, for then came the wail of a cop siren. The storm of blows suddenly ceased. I pushed myself up a few inches to see the knuckly many-booted beast withdraw, heading across the grass, back to its cave, its Cockney underworld. I felt like my mouth was a bowl of mashed fruit and my body was a bag of broken bones. Was that a piece of broken bone digging into my brain, or some foreign body? I saw Dessie sitting up against a wall like he was trying to make sure one of his legs was still attached. Freddie was groaning, making kind of animal sounds that turned into a groany sort of laugh – sometimes it's fun just to know you're still alive. Mickey Roach, blood on his fingertips, was leaking the red stuff from somewhere in his head. Boner and a couple of others who hadn't gone down under the battering were hauling others back to their feet. And the cops were sitting off at a little distance inside their squad car watching us drag our battered bodies back into shape. When we were all off the ground the squad car slid down. One of the faces inside emerged through a window, 'Cam on, move yorselves, clear awf aahhht of it before ya get locked ap.'

'Eh?'

Yeh, like we were the offenders. A familiar scene that, though. Back then it was.

But the last time I was down there I was as in a yellow jacket. I was one of the first travelling stewards employed by Everton, to liase with local cops and stewards and make sure there were no problems, that no one was bringing our club into disrepute.

And what about those lads who ambushed us, had they changed?

Later, when I'm out on the section, I take a walk to where the opposition support is gathering. The sound of those voices, those old Cockney vowels, echoes in my past once again. Are any of them still at it, that nonsense? Surely not.

I stand there in my big yellow jacket with its deputy's badge and I'm scanning the faces of the Arsenal fans. Many of them are too young, but what of the ones who look older? Did any of them not grow up yet? Is one of them the character that the secret policeman is hunting down?

As I move away a punter calls to me. 'Who's the ref today?' As if know everything.

Solid John Sanger

I said to Archie Block, 'Don't like this referee.'

He started going on about the ref for that Blackburn game who added all that time on. I told him, 'But that's in the past. Now we've got this fella to contend with.'

And I was using the word contend advisedly.

I said, 'I don't like him at all. Fancies himself too much. And that's not his only problem.'

Scholar McColl

This tall ebony figure with a polished head blows his whistle and sets the game off. But soon it's not looking good. The Gooners are strolling. And the Blues are doing rough and tumble, bumbling around them, that now familiar huff and puff. Arsenal are sauntering in the sunshine of Goodison Park and stroking the ball around as they go, and we are struggling to stay with them – grabbing at their shirts and being left empty-handed. But the voices of the crowd are strong, they're big and boisterous and they're ready to will the lads on, to roar them on to achieve the seemingly impossible – to beat a full-strength team of champions who haven't lost in sixteen games.

Yeh, the blue multitude believes, or at least they sound as if they do.

Until Arsenal's Flying Dutchman delivers. His pass is long and it's right on the spot – he could drop that ball on a top hat from five hundred yards. The teammate he picked out runs clear, away into enough space to land a helicopter. Our defenders stand and stare, as if they have come only to watch the maestros. One touch and their man fires it in at the near post, while the goalie does a flapping routine. The shocked scoreboard blinks several times before it is ready to come to terms with its task of illuminating a very stark truth.

I move down to Maggie, stop close to her so our shoulders almost touch.

Maggie May

'Well it was a wonderful pass,' I tell him, and lean his way.

'Excellent,' he says, 'Brilliant. Exquisite,' and sighs. And if there weren't all those thousands around us I could give him some comfort.

Scholar McColl

She's wearing a touch of that perfume – a very subdued scent that is very subtly seductive. But if we're not up Shit Creek now it's some other place that doesn't smell good. There is a big whiff of Danger around us. And we are about to be enveloped by a cloud of stinking injustice.

Hutch fends off Keown who takes a kick at him, real mule kick, Hutch breaks free…and the ref is flashing a red one. What!? Red!?

Don Hutchinson is thin and tall, wiry. He lopes, he prowls, stalks, never rushes. His brain is slanted to the crafty side, and that allied to a sockful of skill means that his passes rip open the best quality defensive covers. He is very determined, both to win the ball and to retain it. Very determined. So he has gathered quite a collection of yellow cards from referees. But, reds? No. Is his elbow quick to trigger? No. No historical evidence. And not this time, either. Is it against the rules of the game to use your arm to fend off the opposition – defenders who'll happily give you a hefty boot on the bone if they can get close enough? Is it not reasonable to push an attacker away to make yourself a yard or a few seconds?

Not according to this referee.

Mr Rennie might be a pioneer in the land of officials. In the Olympics of Life he has, perhaps, run the hurdles, breasted the tape and worn the medal. A fit athlete he may be, but infallible he is not. Red? Never.

Solid John Sanger

A red card? What was that character trying to do to us? Hutchinson couldn't believe it. I couldn't believe it. And almost forty thousand others couldn't believe it either.

A wronged man, Hutchinson disappeared, and whatever hopes we had of getting anything out of this game vanished with him. Some of these refs love being out there on centre stage, as if they're the stars of the game. Well if what Mr Uriah Rennie wanted was attention he was certainly getting it. There was plenty for him to get his big ears around. It was like I was standing in the centre of a storm of human fury. And it was still swelling. So much anger. Like a force that's building all around. I was looking around thinking: This crowd could erupt. I could picture some of them out on the pitch set on cornering that bastard. And the truth was that my heart would have been with them. But my head said different. I had to be ready to intervene. I had to be ready and prepared to do my duty, to be alert for hotheads and their reckless heroics – just like the stewards who had to escort that damned referee off the pitch at half time.

Archie Block came by just as the match was kicking off again, telling all the team to keep their eyes open for anyone invading the pitch – as if I needed to told. But it looked like the strain was starting to show on him. Getting too old to take the pressure. Can't be far off retirement now. Time to hand in that blue coat soon. Scholar McColl would take that, most likely. And behind him would be a vacancy – and the deputy's badge. Which would surely be handed to me, if there was any justice in this world. But judging by the goings-on on the pitch there wasn't.

Scholar McColl

The sun lights up the grass but in the shadows we lose our way. On the horizon some dreadful spectre looms. It comes creeping like a huge insect built of cold statistics. But we must not fall prey to it. One punter is on his feet hollering. A fist is clenched tight, raised high and shaken. Now another. The rousers stir up a stew of voices: the rough, the gruff, the shrill, the squeaky. Palms are smacked together. A rhythm begins to thump and build. The chant repeats our name over and over again as if some of those present fear that it might die away into an echo and never be heard again.

They will not let it die. They have been too much goaded by injustice. Battered they might be, worn and bruised and very weary after seasons in adversity, but they will not be silenced.

All along the stand the punters rise, give vent to vocals. As if they've broken open the emergency chest and shared out the brew of survival. But the players they would lift are navvies and journeymen in a land where the artist is king. The man with clay feet is doomed to lag. You cannot make goals out of dross. We are the also-rans. We chase the games and they run away from us. We arrive too late or at the wrong place. So that even if that referee does send one of the Gooners off late in the day this game is beyond us. And finally, mercifully, the whistle brings it to an end. Another door is slammed in our faces. Inside they are giving out the points we need but we stand outside and bite at the nails of our empty hands.

All those vocals, all that hot breath, all those hearts beating for the Blue – and nothing, nothing at the end of it. Not a single scratchy point. We finish with nothing but anger and pain. We are falling, and I see no hand reaching out to save us.

Below is the trapdoor of failure and the mire beneath. So we must stand now stripped of all claims to greatness and slug it out with the bareknuckle fighters of the relegation zone.

Leaving an empty and silent stadium behind me I enter the coatroom and learn that the secret policeman caught his prey. His camera team scanned every face in the stadium and he picked his man out immediately, found him not among his own crowd, but sitting quietly among the blue masses where he probably believed he was safe. So now he needs a lawyer.

And me? I know what I need.

Where is she?

Part Seven

22

A Bedside Tale

Archie Block

I seen Smartarse McColl leaving the ground with our Maggie. Together, they were. What's going on there then? The old hanky panky? Or is he chewing her ears off with some of his nonsense talk? I was still smiling to meself about that when I went into the bookies to catch the last race and pick over the bones of that terrible game with me old muckers from the shipyard. George was there as usual but where's Jim?

'He's in hospital. Been taken in for tests. Didn't make it to the match.'

'But he's never been sick in his life,' I said. Not real sick. Jim always looked like he was built to last. Like me. Never mind the odd twinge now and again.

'Had a bad turn, apparently.'

'Tests?' I said. 'So he could be back out in a couple of days.'

'I've known some come out the next day,' says George. 'And I've known some never come out at all. At least not to come back to the land of the living.'

Dark thought. Very dark. When you've just come from watching a match like that.

I worked with Jim for over forty years. A damned good plater, he was. No finer man with a bag of hammers in that shipyard. Apart from meself of course. He was salt of the earth, a stalwart, a man of the people and a lifelong Blue. So me and George head on down there to see how he is; but he didn't look like the fella we knew. I've never known the life to drain out of a man so quickly. 'Jim,' I said, 'you still there, lad?'

His head turned slowly on the pillow. 'I'm going nowhere yet.' His voice had a bit of a croak in it like it needed oiling. I cracked open a can of ale. But he made no move for it.

'How was the match?' he asked, raspy as a file worked across a length of rusty angle iron.

'Best forgotten, lad,' I told him.

'You was the lucky one,' says George, 'well away from it.'

'Bad day?' goes the rasp.

'Bad day,' me and George said, like a duo of doomsters.

But it doesn't do to dwell too long in the dark when a lad's in his sickbed. I had my little rant about the referee and then George had his. Then I said, 'Get some of that Guinness down you Jim, lad.'

It wasn't like him to be off his ale. He was never shy of entering an alehouse. Especially on a Friday after clocking off at the yard. A pint in the Castle and then the Britannia. And that was just to clear the dust out of his throat so that the real bevvying could begin.

What days they were. What days. Us building fine ships and Harry Catterick assembling a great footballing side. So I started talking the old times to give him the glow of those days gone by. And we had plenty of them between the three of us.

'What days,' I said as Jim, holding the can a bit shaky, managed to tilt it and swallow some of the dark stuff.

He gulped and then he wheezed, 'Aye, but that's all a long time gone now.'

It's like yesterday and years ago at the very same time. All that water under the bridge. All those ships passed in the night.

A man with no memories is a like a bag with no onions.

'Things not looking too bright for the Blues now, though,' Jim mumbles like he's chewing his tongue.

And then himself seems to fade.

'Jim,' I said, 'Jim? Jim? You still there?'

His head was turned sideways on the pillow towards me but his eyes were gone away from me. Then his voice comes back, not strong though, like a cough and a wheeze mixed up together, saying, 'I've told you: I'm going nowhere yet.'

'Good man,' I said, 'good man. And we'll be here to make sure you don't!'

So it was us back at the bedside next day trying to keep the lad's spirits up and watching him turn ghost.

On the way out George showed me a grim look and shook his

head. 'He's sinking isn't he? Sinking fast. He's going down like he's holding a toolbag full of lead.'

And I feel this shooting pain, and it's like George isn't only talking about Jim, it's like he's talking about all of us who grew up in the war years, all of us who built ships and saw Everton fall into the Second Division and then rise again to glory. It's like he's saying something is ending, an era, an era is ending. It's like he's saying: Something there was that will be no more. It's like he's saying: Soon we will all be history.

Is that it? Life? Is that it now: done, all over? Are we through to the other end, the messy bit, the falling apart, the falling away, the leaving, the going?

But where was the recognition? We built the ships, the finest ships: submarines, aircraft carriers, destroyers, tankers, and the finest liners ever to sail the seven seas. We built them, we did: the Ark Royal, the Devonshire, the Renown; the Opalia and the Opina – them tankers with those grand spiral staircases; and we built the Windsor Castle too, a beautiful, beautiful boat. But where was the recognition, the salute? It wasn't right. It couldn't end like this.

I said, 'Jim's only a young man yet, he's no age at all, none of us are.'

'Aye,' said George, 'but when did that ever stop anyone booking out?'

I said, 'No, he'll pull through, our Jim will. They made them tough in our day – you've said that manyatime yourself, George.'

We were no mollycoddled generation. We grew up on rations. Plus whatever you could get on the black market – which was quite a lot if you knew where to go.

I said, 'He'll rally. He might.'

George shook his head.

I said, 'He will, you watch.'

George says, 'He's on his way out. He'll soon be in that hospice out in Woolton.'

Perish the thought. Oh perish that thought and cast it away. So many good lads departed early to go to the land of their fathers. And how far were the rest of us behind them?

Jim lay there just the same. I looked at him and wondered: Where has the life gone? Where does the life go when a man succumbs?

He hasn't moved for what seems like ages. He hasn't uttered a word. So, then I had an idea. 'Here comes the Bulldog!' I said, kind of hissed.

Jim twitches. George grinned.

It worked the trick.

Old Bulldog, the real Blocker Man, the old bowler-hatted boss of the shipyard – he'd make any man spring into life. A fearsome breed of boss, he was, the bane of our working lives. But not any more. Now we could laugh.

'Here comes Bulldog!' said George, joining in the game.

And, yes, Jim was still there. The old shipyard warning had struck a chord deep down in him. Hearing those words back in the day – it was like the sound of an air raid siren. Everyone scattered. But you couldn't let Old Bulldog win every contest. Discipline, aye, but pride too. A man has to have his pride like he has to have his pint. So you boiled up a secret brew just to defy him. You rolled up a fag and lit it and blew that smoke out like you were blowing it in his scowly old face.

'You couldn't beat getting one over on Old Bulldog, though, could you,' said Jim in a whisper, remembering the glory of that old shipyard. But then he seemed to slump again like he was slipping way down.

'But the job got done,' I said to boost him back up. 'The job got done, Jim.'

And it did. I bent down towards his ear and said, 'We built ships, lad. We built great ships.'

Was he stirring again? Maybe. Was the old stalwart rallying? It was hard to say. But I carried on, 'We built fine ships and no one can ever say any different. We built fine ships, grand ships, and we followed a great team. And we've seen some fine players, great players. Tommy Jones. Remember Tommy Jones. He was good, wasn't he? A great centre half. He was, wasn't he Jim? Jim, I'm talking about Tommy Jones. T. G. Jones of Everton and Wales. The man was a prince and you saw him. The greatest footballing centre half in the history of the game. And you saw him Jim, you had the privilege. And Roy Vernon, he was another Welshman: the Welsh Viper. He was some player too wasn't he?'

So little back-lift when he shot at goal and yet so much power and so cleanly struck. Like a rapier, he was. A blade of Welsh steel.

So quick. And so lethal.

A striker without speed is like a bike with no chain.

George said, 'Remember in sixty-three. He came out into the directors' box smoking a fag when we'd just beaten Fulham to become champions.'

'He did George. Used to smoke in the shower, so they said.'

'Killed him in the end, those fags.'

Not a thought to dwell on, that. 'And Tony Kay!' I said almost shouting in the excitement of the sudden memory. 'What a player he was.'

A great midfield battler. A steely fox of a player with an eye for the crafty pass.

Then Jim stirs again. His eyelashes flicker. His lips make words. Tony Kay has stirred him like he stirred many a man with his fearless play. 'He was a leader,' says Jim, in a gaspy sort of way.

'A general,' I said, 'a midfield general, a leader who led by example.'

A team with no leader is like a ram with no balls, a dog with no dick.

I said, 'It was a tragedy when that man got banned. A tragedy.'

A terrible shame, a terrible, terrible shame. A career in ruins. Banned for life. But he wasn't the first man to have his past catch up with him, and as sure as kippers are kippers he'll not be the last.

But tragedy wasn't the kind of place we should have been dwelling in. I said, Ray Wilson, he was another wonderful player, and you loved the bones of the lad didn't you Jim.'

'Aye, Ray Wilson,' says Jim. It's not much more than a whisper, but that love was back in his eyes.

George said, 'He could kill the ball stone dead with just a touch of his boot, in mid air too, three foot off the ground.' He sat there seeing it again, marvelling at the sight of it. 'I've never seen a better left back than him.'

Jim moved his head a little in agreement and even managed to say in a croaky whisper, 'Nor are you likely to,' and then added, 'nor me. Definitely not me.' And he might even have been laughing a bit at his plight.

'Aye, Ray Wilson,' I said. 'He's an undertaker now.'

And then I wondered why I'd said it.

But Jim was always a man to see the funny side. So I went on,

'Well if he lays those stiffs out the way he played on the pitch he's doing them proud. And there's not much chance of them getting away from him is there, because no winger ever give him the slip!'

Yes, even Jim laughs. Well, he sort of smiled. But he was there with us, he was there alright. For a little while he was.

We sat on a while longer watching the man fade out, trying to think of something to say, talking more of the old days. But that only brings you face to face with the fact of where you are now. 'We've got no one to stick the ball in the net, that's our trouble,' I said as if I was telling them what they didn't already know. 'It's like the bad old days again, like a return visit to when we were lads.'

All the great names had gone then. My old fella told me that. After the war, this was. He'd watched them: Joe Mercer and Tommy Lawton and Dixie Dean. And they were all gone.

'We went six games without scoring a goal that season we were relegated. You remember?'

'Aye,' says George, not wanting to remember.

But no man can hide from the hard truth. And only a fool will try. We couldn't score goals, and we paid for that. I was an apprentice in the yard at that time and I watched it happen. We needed something from the last game to have any chance of staying up. And Sheffield Wednesday tore us apart: six-nil. We were destroyed. The Blues were wreckage that sank into the Second Division. And here I was back at the same place. All the great names were gone again. Gone where old ships go. And the Blues were sinking once more. Sinking like Jim, like Jimmy Waddington, as fine a working man as you could wish to have stood at your side at the workbench.

I realized how long we'd been sitting there without speaking. So I said to George, just for something to say, I said, 'Does it ever seem to you like we keep saying the same thing over and over again?'

'No,' George says, 'no.'

I said, 'You are listening aren't you?'

George says, 'What?'

We laughed. Like they say: You have to. It's either that or weep. A life without laughs is like a ball without bounce. You either bounce the ball or you reach for the rag. But even that can leave you feeling wobbly some days. I said, 'I think I'm going to have to go George, I don't feel so good.'

'Aches and pains, aches and twinges' said George, 'they're just part of life.'

'Well it's nice to know I haven't missed out,' I told him.

But heading home it was a struggle for me to put one foot in front of another. I had to stop and lean against a wall on the way. But I was in no mood to lie down and be counted out. 'It'll take more than a couple of stabs around the ribcage to lay me out,' I said to nobody. And then, rousing myself, I laughed from down in my throat and said, 'I'll slap Joe Knacker's horses on the arse and send them galloping!'

But back home I hear the clock ticking in a way I've never noticed before. The old brass bugger keeps on ticking like it's ticking my seconds off one by one in some little notebook. 'Shuttup!' I told it. 'Shuttup your noise.'

Then the missus appears. And I know what's coming. 'You keep rubbing your chest, Arthur. Are you feeling alright?'

I said, 'Oh fine, fine.'

She slides me one of her looks. So I told her, 'The odd day under the weather, what's that? Life. That's all it is.'

Course she pulls one of them womanish faces. And that damned clock ticks and ticks.

I said to her, I said, 'Maybe there is a place with angels or maybe the only glorious place is Goodison Park and we all finish up in Old Joe Knacker's place, and if we do then so be it.'

She says to me, Arthur Blockley, 'Don't talk such nonsense, man!'

So I said no more. I let her know how quiet silence can be for a good few hours. A man of my years isn't used to being spoken to like that by anyone in a dress even if she is armed with a pair of knitting needles.

The sounds of the old brass clock fill the room. The wheels of his cart grind ever nearer. But when I can hold him at bay no more I'll look Joe Knacker in the eye and say: 'I have sowed my seed but no wild oats, I have been true to my wife and my wedding vows, I have shown my children the right and the wrong and I have placed food on the table for them, shoes on their feet and shirts on their backs. I have worked my trade and earned my coin and come home to my fireside with my strength used up, and I have enjoyed the fruits of my labours: Everton Football Club, and a pint of good ale. Oh, and aye, my conjugals too.'

But I'd hold him at bay for while yet, and maybe Jim could too, maybe, maybe he could pull through with a couple of stalwarts at his side.

Another day at the bedside. Talking football. Talking of ships, of back in the day. Because that's all we have. Because at the end of it all that's all we have. Because all the welders and the boilermakers and the chippies and the sparks and the old Blocker Men are all scattered now – scattered to oblivion, some of them. But a shipyard, when you're in it, with all them cranes, all that gear, all those men, looks like it will be there for ever – like Goodison does on a matchday, like the Grand Old Lady of Goodison Park does when she's in her royal blue glory, aye there for ever, for all eternity with her memories and her new generation of Blues gathered there.

Camel Lairds, aye, when she was a real shipyard, not some scaled down model of the real thing, when she was an asset to the city and the nation and the working class, launching fine ships on a grand scale. So much life in a place like that. Back then there was, when it was in its glory. All them hammers and drills and grinders and saws going at the same time. Aye, you breathed in welding fumes and fog off the river and the farts of a thousand men and you cracked on with the job because that's what you were there for. You were up to your ears in shite and grease and gunge and iron filings, but out of all that filth you watched great ships grow – and then sail away with our fingerprints on them. You watched the champagne bottle shattering on the bow and some fine ship you'd built slid away into the water and you filled up with pride, right up to the brim.

A life without pride is like spuds without salt.

But then it was all over. For us it was. No more banter. No more ships. No more launch days. Just a few lines on a piece of paper to tell you you were finished, you and all the others who weren't being kept on. I walked out through those gates feeling like someone had taken a big hammer to both my hands so that I'd never work my trade again. You could have stood out there and wept for your working life, but no ship was ever launched on a river of tears.

And I had something to cling on to, something that told me I was wanted. The day after they finished me in the shipyard I was back on duty. It was a ragbag of a game. We let a bunch of no-hopers from Oldham snatch a point after we'd wasted a sack-full of chances. But I was in Goodison and I was needed. I was feeling my own importance even if those shipyard bosses denied it. And there I remained to inherit the blue coat while Time wreaked its havoc on many a good man.

I must have gone drifting on a sea of thoughts. George was poking me, and saying, whispery, 'I better give Vera a call. Jim looks like he's on his way out. That lad won't last the night.'

We walked away in silence.

'Here comes Bulldog!' said George suddenly.

We laughed. Tried to. But my laugh turned into a cough.

'You all right?' said George.

'I'm okay,' I said, 'I'm alright, I'm fine.'

'Good,' he says, 'because I'm not sure I am.'

And then we laughed even more.

But as usual George was right. Next day he was stood outside the bookies waiting for me. As I got near he shook his head. He didn't have to say a word. He did though, he said, 'I had a phone call just before I came out.'

I said, 'Jim's gone?'

He says, 'A couple of hours ago.'

Jim was gone to the land of his fathers. And we who survived him took refuge, like many a day before, where the ale flowed strong.

It was my last chance to see Jim before they closed him in. I said, I said to him straight out, 'You were a credit to your trade, mate. Always worked to the highest standards, never let things slip, even when you was balanced high up on icy trestles.' I said, 'You were one of the best Jim, the very best. And between us, between me and you Jim, and George and all of the rest of them, we built some of the finest ships ever to sail. Because we were the cream Jim, we were the cream of the working class. We were the cream of shipbuilding men and our like will never be seen again. We were the craftsmen of Camel Lairds. And in a seafaring nation the yard that built the best ships will never be forgotten. Never. Never Jim. Never.'

It better not be. Or my old ghost will be back to kick some arses.

'Aye,' I said, 'so this is it, lad, the last goodbye.' And then I said,

'But I'll tell you what Jim: at least you won't have to listen to the match on the radio tomorrow, at least you're spared that, because if they don't get something out of that game they're in dire straits.'

There was a click at the door and George comes in. So I slipped out and left him alone with Jim.

The air outside was chill. But such is the real world and we must live in it. And when George was done we headed off with the scent of ale in our nostrils.

Old Barney, another section boss, was in the alehouse for a birthday bash with his matchday crew: Tommy the wood man, another of our old shipyard lads, Steve the spark and Gerry the cleaner and all the rest. It didn't seem like a very highspirited party, and we soon found out why: the football results. George said, shaking his head, 'As if we needed more bad news! Coventry, Southampton and Leicester all won.'

I said 'The dark clouds are gathering George.'

'So that leaves us fifth from bottom.' He shakes his head and makes his mouth like he's going to whistle, but makes no sound. And then we both lift our glasses at the same moment to sup, exactly the same moment, as if we've been rehearsing, the same moment exactly, as if one of us is the mirror image of the other.

I said, 'We have to go to Old Trafford and be strong George.'

He says, 'But them players, are they up to it?'

That wasn't a question I fancied answering.

And on top of that I had the old hen at home pecking at me when the Man United game was kicking off inside the radio. 'Are you feeling alright, Arthur? You don't look too good.'

'I was never here to win beauty contests,' I told her. 'I was here to build ships and support my team.'

And by the sound of it we'd got a team of centre halves out on the pitch. Setting out to hang on to a point: risky business, that. Another afternoon of torture. And sure enough, the Blues are under pressure from the start. And I can feel this spanner tightening the big bolt that's screwed into me chest. 'Get the ball up the pitch!' I'm telling that little talking box, 'you're asking for trouble!'

How did they expect to survive, playing like that? Too much pressure. They were bringing it on themselves. And on me. 'Get that ball up the pitch!'

The missus appears again in the doorway, saying, 'Turn it off, it's making you ill, you look terrible. It's only a game! Turn it off. '

Since when did a woman know anything about football apart from how to wash the kit? You could educate them for fifty years and they still wouldn't know what off-side meant.

I said, 'I will not. The Blues have got their backs to the wall and I'm sticking with them. Never deserted them yet and don't intend to start now.'

'You silly, silly man.'

Yabber-yabber-yabber. Same old woman-babble you've been listening to for a lifetime. I was leaning towards the radio, but all I was hearing was odd words between the fussing and tutting and yabbering.

'Arthur, it's just a game and it's not worth making yourself ill over.'

I said, 'Will you be told woman, I am *alright*.'

She huffs and gives up. But that's only a womanish tactical retreat. She'll be back, ambushing me with that tongue lash. Anyway, I had more important things to worry about. I'm telling that radio, 'Get that ball upfield. Put pressure on! Give them something to think about!'

But nobody hears. Only herself banging about in the kitchen.

United were rampant. Onslaught: that was the word. But we were resisting, by the sound of it, standing tall and tight. So far. Like warriors with their backs to the wall and their balls hanging strong in their bag.

But wouldn't you know it!

Buckled. Buckled under the pressure. One-nil. And then the collapse. Two-nil.

Enough to make a strong man weep. Clowns. Clowns pretending to be warriors.

And then wouldn't you know it: Mother Hen is back, poking her beak round the door, squawking at me like I'm the fox in the henhouse. Oh go and lay and egg, woman! Give a man some peace in his hour of darkness.

Three-nil.

And then we got the consolation. Thanks for nothing.

But hang on, I was telling myself, hang on there Arthur Blockley, we might need that goal come the end of the season, we might have to survive on goal difference again the way we're shaping up!

And then the referee put an end to it. And leaves you sitting there feeling the pressure. Feeling the pressure turned right up. Because there isn't much space between us and the pit at the bottom of the league – two points that's all. Not much space to breathe in now. Not enough air. The old airbags showing signs of wear and tear.

But the years go so quick. All those ships, all those games in Goodison, all those pints on the bar. So much behind you and so little in front. Old Joe Knacker lurks in the background waiting to cart you away, calling out your name. Your name echoes down the street, over and over, so it can't be ignored. What does it all mean? One minute you've got two feet in life; the next, some other bugger's stepping into your boots. As if you're no more than a name. As if you're no more than a fish in the sea. Like a cod. For an example. Ferocious predator living like a shark, gobbling up everything that moves. Hauled out of the ocean in a big net by a bloke who wears wellies up to his bollocks. Next thing, it's wrapped up in hot batter and lying on a mound of chips having salt and vinegar thrown all over it…What does it all mean? Where is the meaning?

When the missus started up again I said, 'When my time comes I'd like my coffin to be drawn through the streets on a carriage pulled by plumed horses. I want to go like the old boys.'

She says, 'You'd do better getting the doctor to have a look at you instead of talking like that. It wouldn't do any harm to make an appointment.'

I said nothing.

She said, 'I could make one for you when I go past.'

'Ill? Me? I'm not ill. Never been ill, and you know it. Never been ill and don't intend to start now.'

'I expect Jim said the same,' she huffs.

'Well I expect I'm made of sterner stuff.' Was I ready for the scrap heap? Joe Knacker's cart? Nah. All I needed was a drop of lubrication from a pint glass. I said, 'I need a doctor like I need a damned fashion consultant.'

She tutted.

I told her, 'Will you be told woman, I am alright. No-one's carting me off any time soon.'

But Monday morning the man in the top hat was walking before the long black car. Me and George and four other lads shouldered the coffin, walking steady, never a stumble, before a gathering of old shipyard lads. Some of them were bronzed and looked like the sun had burned years off them, but some were creased and bent and looking like they were shuffling through an airless room.

When the time came I strode to the front to say a little piece. You can't leave the important stuff to a man in a frock who doesn't even know which way to put a collar on. I felt like I could crumple up but I didn't. I said to all present what most of them probably knew already, but I told them anyway, I said, 'Jimmy Waddington always did the job exactly right, no matter what. Every plate, every bolt and rivet, had to be spot-on – and it was. Because that's the nature of the man. Because that ship might have to ride out a hurricane without breaking up, and men's lives depended on that. I can see Jimmy at his work and I can see them ships on the oceans, their bows forging through the waves.' I turned to that long shiny box and said. 'They're out there because of you Jim, your workmanship, your dedication to the job, because you took pride in your work, and no finer thing can be said about a man. You were one of the best Jim, the very best.' Then I felt like I could say no more. But I did it. I had my say and I hope I did him proud.

Out in the graveyard I stood beside George watching the coffin being lowered, lowered out of a world that will never see our like again.

And then a beer, and I was in need of that, a few ales with those still in the land of the living – even if some of them are Reds who don't waste much time before they start sounding off.

Aye, a good man passes away and life goes on, the game goes on, so it's us and the Reds over in Anfield next and I'm trying hard, trying very, very, hard, surrounded as I am by a bunch of ranting Reds, not to fear the worst.

23

Over on the Dark Side

Scholar McColl

News, big news: the Blues have found a striker – in Turkey. Kevin Campbell has flown in to score the goals we need. And he believes in us. He thinks we are in a false position down in the depths of the division. And he will be there to lead the line for us in Anfield. And I have managed to get a ticket for the match. But only the one. So I start to get the excitement. Maybe, just maybe, with a new man up front, we can get something over there on Saturday.

Maggie, of course, won't be there, though I tried my best to get two tickets. But there's something else, some other problem lurking; lurking around us, between us maybe.

The strands of her plans are drawn together around me. I am being invited to share the rest of her life – or at least indicate a willingness to consider. What? Already? This is both flattering and seductive. Here is something warm and precious that might render my life from now on simple and clear, secure. She is not the kind, she stresses, who expects a man to give his whole life over to her as long as the commitment is there, as long as he is truly there for her. She has seen plenty of lovers come and go – those who arrive big with promise and then shrink away into shadow – and knows now the importance of rock-solid companionship. And so, she is in a hurry now to find it. If you drift too long, wander unattached, the spectre of age will come to haunt your sad and private space – that is the way her thinking goes now.

I am split between wariness and abandonment. Here is my chance to visit that place where humans pair off, sing duets to the joys of throwing off selfhood, individuality, isolation. But do I not know already the dangers that lurk there?

She brings up her knees and lets the covers slide off. Here I am naked, she seems to be saying, I have nothing to hide from you, you can put all the trust you have in me. Would I dispute that? Her nakedness has stories to tell of vulnerability and pain, of brashness and joy, of warmth and abandonment. And I am drawn to it – to stroke, to hold, to kiss. It invites from me what is natural, what is not tied up by nerves or the urge to restraint.

I can't help but tell her how much I like her, which is a very great deal. I feel her magnetism, the pull it is exerting on me. And it does have a definite force. And there might be rewards on offer that I have so far gone without. Out of mutual concern might come more than generosity – a kind of lavishness. But I haven't been around for this long not to know that even that would come at a price. I know myself well enough to realize that however contented I might feel there would still be a voice asking: Isn't there something else?

Yeah, that old restlessness, the impulse to move, to go, to seek something else, something other, something better or more interesting or just simply different.

Sometimes when I'm out in the high blue air, where my hands are close to the elements of earth and air and water and fire, where I have a grip on textures: sandstone, leafmould, bark, where I'm able to observe the passage birds and the nest-builders while I earn my coin doing what I have chosen, bossed by nobody, taking on what work I choose – an enviable position perhaps – I am tempted to walk away, not only to look over the fence but to jump it.

But she is no ordinary find this one. If not spectacularly beautiful or fabulously breasted or over-trimmed at the waist she is all of a piece, one part proportioned with the rest, and you can't really find flaws. Sure, she has done some service, she has been round the course one or two times and paid the normal visits to the funfair and the graveyard, but she occupies her space without apology or apparent thought of retreat.

She reflects light and heat, both. She is smooth of skin and sharp of mind. When she has something particular to say she does so with emphasis and when she meets resistance she is inclined to be sparky, but her smile is rather fetching and her laughter, rising rapidly from deep down, is unrestrained. Her body is not a vessel of shame or embarrassment that needs to be quickly hidden in sheets, gowns, silky scraps, nor will she place obstacles around it to stop you getting near. And she possesses the power to make you feel extremely comfortable, unfettered, expansive, as if she were applying to your skin some sort of balm, massaging it into your muscles, those places where the aches and twinges lurk.

But she does have an aim, a particular destination in her sights: the Wedding House. And though she is gifted with considerable stamina she no longer has vast resources of patience. She makes no attempt to conceal her objective. Marriage has become for her a denouement with Shakespearean riches and resonances. Two characters could find each other in act five and pledge themselves in beautifully-fashioned couplets. The couple is the thing. Mutuality and respect. The long embrace. Till death us do part.

I am lying under the cover with my eyes closed but I know she is looking at me, that she is lying on her side with her eyes wide open.

She breathes with some force. Down in the street a car screeches past. Her words swirl around my skull, 'Do you always hold back from becoming too involved?'

To this I have no snappy answer.

She asks, a thread of irritation drawn through her words, 'I mean, how long do you think this might last?'

She gives me a lot to think about but not long in which to formulate answers. She slips from the bed and pulls the cover up around me patting it carefully down – as if she were putting to bed her child. And then with hardly a sound she opens the door.

But though I lie there, apparently comfortable, I feel that she has pushed me into that corner where a decision must be made while she is now positioning herself a little closer to the exit.

Maggie May

There are things I need to know. There are things we need to talk about, things that cannot be skirted around for much longer.

He is eating breakfast at my table. He is crunching the nuts in my cereal. But as I enter the kitchen in my short silky dressing gown which shows off to very good affect my rather fetching legs he does not look up. Does he really find my muesli that interesting? Is he a connoisseur of breakfast bowls? An expert in yoghurts? Or perhaps I should have come down wearing only a necklace of Brazil nuts, dried apricots over my nipples.

And this is the man who said he could eat me!

Morning. I'm Margaret. We have met actually. You're Bastard aren't you? See, I did remember.

This is the man who said that if I had milk he would drink it. I obviously misunderstood. He meant milk in the fridge.

Was it really only twelve hours ago that he arrived and wrapped me up in his arms, that his lips were on my neck, my ear, that his tongue slid over, under mine, that his breath and mine were one?

Was it me who said I wouldn't let this happen, or was that in a film I saw?

When we stand I place my hand on his arm. I kiss him – but he is not all there. Part of him has shifted, migrated, gone who knows where.

He stands and says to the window or maybe the sink, 'I'd better get going.'

When he is ready he opens the door and turns to me looking vaguely puzzled, confused, as if he's unsure whether he should kiss me or not.

Can this, will this ever, work?

He is walking away. His figure shrinks as he strides off down the street.

In this house with no clocks to tick and everything switched off there is only silence now, there is only the silence telling me that I am alone, that I am alone again.

That old weepy song. That ancient text.

In the bedroom those old bodily aromas linger. I will throw back the curtains and unlatch the window. I will let in the morning, I will let the breeze clear out the remains of a day that has died. But must not give up on this, not yet anyway.

Scholar McColl

New growth is all around us, shoots and early bloom, the air is laced with a taste of things to come. And she persists. 'We look right together. We seem proud of each other.' And then her desire for permanence is quietly emphasized, her belief in a common future free of the extremes of worry and longing.

'But,' I caution her, 'you can't rush into that sort of thing. I know, I've got it wrong before. And so have you.'

If someone you care for is to be let down, why do it brutally?

Kevin Campbell, though, might he uplift us all? Will he be our saviour? Will he step into that space once occupied by the great names – those now long gone? Could he? Could he possibly be the man? Why not? Wherever he's been he's scored goals.

'I'm very sure this time,' she counters, 'I am certain I am in love with you. And I'm talking about love that is restrained by nothing. I don't hold any back and I don't want to and I just wish you would be the same and then…'

The violinists are ready to play for us but I don't have the right kind of something – a suit or speech or mind-fix, something. I am trampling on the flowers in her Elysium Garden, I am blurring her vision of Paradise. I feel guilt like some cold damp substance on my skin. But also that something vague, bodiless, silent-pawed is creeping up behind me, a presence I must be ready to deal with. What is that? What spooks me? I am not making the correct response here? I am acting in a way I will regret? Or something else? Kevin Campbell will fail us? Might he? No. It is not that which I fear. I have hope. I have to have high hopes for him. And do: the man scores goals. I keep repeating that to myself. He has scored them for everyone else he's played for so why not us?

What, then, stalks me? What is it that is spooking me?

The door she has opened for me will not remain so indefinitely – is it that? I am making a huge mistake – is that it? She is too certain of what she wants to stand for long holding out to me my own key. Even her breathing tells me that, her fingertips rolling spilled salt or sugar across the tablecloth she puts out especially for me. And I know also that if I have made one kind of mistake in the past I hold no insurance policy against making errors of another nature now. I might carry through the rest of my life a kind of regret? Not a cheering thought, that. So there is no sign to a place of easy resolution.

Without this large and serious issue we would have been strolling in our new summer outfits. Ten years back that's exactly what we would be doing: untroubled by the worries that time might bring. But this isn't a decade ago. We have both seen the days and the months pass by. We are both those years the other side of thirty and approaching the next timestone. If she is to bear a child it will have to be soon.

This uncertainly squeezes from her a tear. But her pride only allows a few weepy moments before it takes a grip. Her emotions are wrestled into order. Restored to her still self she says, 'I would like to be married, and I do intend to be married. That might sound terribly old fashioned but I don't care, it's what I want and that is that. I want to be married and if it isn't to you then it will be to someone else.'

It has to have been rehearsed. She says it so beautifully, with such feeling and dignity. But I have not been practising the appropriate next line. I have practised nothing. I say nothing. I follow her eloquence with silence, dumbness.

There is no more gaiety in the air. All the bunting has been taken in. And I am the tongue-tied villain now. I am the destroyer of dreams, and some dark fate awaits me off stage.

Awaits only me, or all who gather at Goodison Park?

Or will Campbell be our man? And we do share that, me and her, we share that, at least: that he will indeed be the man.

Maybe he will not disappoint us. Maybe he will turn out to be the man and all will be well.

Maggie May

I have no ticket for the match, so of course he will go alone. Whatever will happen will happen now. He will cross the park and enter the house of the old enemy alone. But Kevin Campbell will be there in a royal blue jersey – to bring us what? The goals of our dreams? He has to. If he does not do it there is no one else who can.

Scholar McColl

Sunshine Saturday over in the Darkness. The whistle has only just set the ball rolling and the game explodes. Dacourt swings his left boot from way out and the Reds' net shakes. One-nil to the Blues. Sensational.

But can we hang on to that lead? Stupid question. Fifteen minutes, that's all. And it's one who turned his back on us, walked away from us, who does the damage. Fowler. Him. He grows up as a good Blue, and then he defects and pulls on the red, and how does he finish up? Doing a clown's routine after scoring against us:

on his hands and knees snorting at the touchline. Sad sight, that.

And it's even sadder watching him put a second past us. Because once the Reds get themselves in front they tighten their grip and try as we might, and we do huff and puff, we cannot loosen it – although we have them in a panic at the end and we do get let down again by the referee. Another injustice. Tell me an old, old story. Sing me an old, old song. It's like everyone and everything is against us – prime time for the conspiracy theorists. But one thing is for sure, we're deep in the brown stuff now. We've got four more games at home and if we don't win at least three of them we're down. Simple as that. And how many games have we won at home all season? I can hardly bear to answer that even to myself. But the truth withdraws from no man who stands with his eyes open. So the fact must be faced. Three. Only three league games won at Goodison since the start of the season.

So can we now, under great pressure, win another three?

A wise man would be sceptical.

Unless he had seen what I've seen.

I have seen a new player in a blue shirt, seen him fronting our attack: busy, powerful, and with a presence that no opposition defence could ignore – a man with self belief in whom you can truly believe. We lost another game, in a season of many loses, but we look so much better with him out there leading the line. We have shape, we have purpose – and, yes, I do have that belief.

But I have still to face what cannot be avoided.

So I walk into the alehouse and find myself facing a whole chorus of Reds. They look at each other giving smirky little glances as they limber up for a session of blue-baiting. The mob mentality. Not a pretty sight. They tell me that Everton are going down and won't be back for a long, long time, maybe never. They say we're going where we deserve to be, where we should have been years ago.

I tell them, though, I warn them, I say, 'You ain't seen the last of us yet.'

One of them retorts, 'But next time we see yez at Anfield yal be playin at giantkillers in the Cup!'

'Or trying to! Aha-ha!'

And then another adds his six penneth worth of shite, and you get a lot of shite for six pence off some of these Reds. He says, 'Yeh, because you've got left behind. The show's moved on.

Liverpool's a world club but oos heard of you lot? You won't be able to keep yer best players. You're the Tranmere Rovers of the future. And we'll be up there with Juventus and Bayern Munich and Real Madrid. We're takin off again, but there's only one way you're goin.'

'Yeah,' this big Redsnout joins in, 'Yer wasting yer time tryna cling on, lad, coz we just stamped on yer fingers!'

And it's like the rest of them have never been treated to such hilarious entertainment. Kee-kee-kee-kee!! Ak-ak-ak-ak-ak!!! It's like I'm stood in the Anfield Zoo: giggling hyenas, snorting pigs, cackling geese – what a beasty bunch this lot are.

'Don't forget yer istory, lad,' one of them tells me. And then the punch line: 'Becoz soon that's all yooo'll av!' And then here we go again: It's…Zootime. And the loudmouth is stood there like King Pig in the Farmyard of Fools as those chuckles at his own line make his belly wobble.

As soon as it's quiet again I say, 'And don't you forget your history. Don't forget your hooligans stampeding through the Hysel Stadium. Because you have tried very hard to forget it!'

Grunting now: big buffalo grunts. As well they might. Mooing and snorting.

I say, 'And don't forget who paid the price!'

'Bitter!' They're spitting the pips of resentment at me. 'Another bitter lemon!'

And then a pair of them are breaking into song: 'Bitter lemons in blue. Ah, they ain't gorra clue. Boo-hoo-hoo-hoo…'

And then the rest are joining in. Singsong time in the zoo of redsnouts. Ahhh, let me out of this place!

But where is the justice in this world? If you set off looking for it don't expect an easy journey, don't be surprised to find yourself surrounded by a pack of redsnouted hyenas, jackals, wild pigs, geese, parrots, apes and assorted creatures from the lower zone right down to the depths of the swamp.

Anyway I can't linger in the alehouse jungle. I have another tricky encounter to think about.

Maggie May

We are walking in the green of the park. His voice is talking Blue, speaking, naturally, once again of yesterday's defeat, for it is not possible to dodge the fact that we have dropped points into the pockets of the Reds, points we did so desperately need ourselves. But I also have other serious thoughts in mind, thoughts of a more personal nature, as he speaks of Kevin Campbell and of hope.

If only he shared my hope of what we might be together. If only he would open all the doors and let me into his life. But you can't build a life out of if onlys, you can't build anything out of them. He's like a house with closed rooms. Does anyone have the key? I don't think I do. But the world is big and beginning to blossom. My life is not barren because he steps out of it.

The path curves round past the lake. Two ducks fly over, their wings whistling. Do they mate for life? Chance would be a fine thing – to wear a wedding dress and then fly away to somewhere hot and exotic leaving behind a trail of confetti.

Whatever it is that this man is after it's not what I'm looking for. If we once seemed the same, we do not now. So I have to do this, despite the defeat we share. I have to do what I am about to do. I have to make myself do it otherwise in time I will regret it. He will string me along this man, he will string me along for months, a year, maybe even two and then he will tire, get bored, dump me. I know he will. I have read the script in his eyes, in his heart. So I have to do this. 'I've been thinking,' I tell him. 'About us.'

The tone of his 'Oh?' suggests he's half expecting something. And something he certainly gets.

'I don't want someone who turns up to seduce me,' I tell him. 'I want something serious. And what's wrong with that? I'm looking for a serious man – a man's who's looking to make a life with someone. I want someone who I can really get to know – in the fullest possible way, so that we have something special between the two of us. I'm looking for loyalty and trust and commitment. And I don't see myself getting that with you.'

Scholar McColl

So I am dealing with two heavy blows. And that defeat over on the dark side of the park: that does linger. It opens up the door to the darkness and lets the old demons out. You see again what you thought you had shut out.

Once we were swift as the eagle and strong as the lion, but now we have fallen. Our bows are broken and our arrows have no wings. And so we must stand now in the pit and slay the beast. Our new leader, Chief Campbell, with the help of his skinny sidekick Franny Jeffers, must slay the Beast of Doom – or else we will be devoured and our bones left to the creeping things of the night.

But this second thwack, that bang on the ego from Maggie May – if she thinks that blow will floor me she is about to read a fresh paragraph in the Book of Love.

But when the phone rings I cannot stop myself from grabbing for it, thinking it will be her. No, it's someone calling about a gardening job.

I'm not used to this. But I do know that these womanish moods come and go. She'll think of some pretext to call. That's my best guess. And if not we will be face to face at the ground tomorrow.

24

When the Steelman Came to Steal the Show

Scholar McColl

We cannot fail today. The Blues surely cannot fail us. But I have other things on my mind. I feel like I'm trapped in a net of knotty thoughts and need to find a way out. And that doesn't seem like a good omen for the day. This is a day that needs to start well. So it is I who must pick up the phone.

Maggie May

The phone calls. I reach for it then hesitate, but then go ahead and lift it. His voice is in my ear. And it doesn't take him long to smalltalk his way to the main point. 'Are you really serious about what you said in the park?'

He is giving me a chance to turn back? My reply is quick, 'I wouldn't have said it if I wasn't, Mark.'

'I just wanted to make sure.'

'This isn't going anywhere. That's what I said, and that's what I think.'

'But are you sure you've given it a decent chance…?'

'I'm quite sure. You'll never want me enough.'

'I don't see how you can be so certain of that.'

'Maybe not. But in my own mind I am.'

There is one of those pauses that seem so very long on the telephone. But I really don't want to prolong this conversation.

'Okay,' he says, finally, 'Okay. I thought we should talk before the game. So that everything's clear before we meet at the ground. That wouldn't be the best place for this conversation.'

'Obviously.'

Then there's another lengthy pause and I sense that we have not quite done yet.

Finally he says. 'But we could still be good friends, meet occasionally...?'

Ah no, I have travelled that way, that ever more casual walk. So I take a long breath. 'I'm not sure about that, Mark. I've been down that path before and it didn't really seem...didn't seem to go anywhere that I wanted to be. All I can say at the moment is that it isn't what I'm looking for.'

'But it takes different people different time to see whether something or isn't what they're looking for. Don't you think?'

Some men?! What would you do with them? Where's the best place to send them for treatment? 'That's not enough Mark. You see you're -'

'I've got to go.' His voice has changed. 'I'll see you when you report for duty.'

Ohhhh? Will you now, Mr Deputy?? Ha!!

And sure enough, he's gone.

I stand staring at the now silent phone. This is puzzling. I wonder: Is he trying to shock me into falling back into his arms? Does he imagine that I'll come over all regretful and tearful and then fall into his arms hot for him once again?

It almost makes me smile. Almost. Who does he think he's dealing with? Some little Cinderella in a blue and white scarf? I feel again that mocking smile almost take shape on my lips.

Then I realize I have to face him in a couple of hours.

Scholar McColl

On the terracing of an almost empty stadium three gatemen on their way down to the turnstiles turn off the gangway and leave me face to face with her.

Are there any signs of conflict, regret, desire even, in her eyes? She appears to be floating on a cloud of calm. Is this poise, this self-possession, this oh-so-composed a presence, an act? Is what I'm looking at just pretence? She looks as if she's just spent the last couple of hours in the hands of some masseuse and guru whose claim is to be able to extract and dispose of all personal problems.

But what goes on beneath that tranquil exterior? I will put her apparent serenity to the test.

So I take a brisk step forward, as if I have many other matters to deal with, 'How are you?'

She is, she says, fine. Only that. But that is a cold word which she utters. She speaks like the Icicle Girl come straight from the freezer. The Maiden of the Icebergs: there is frost in her hair and ice in her eyes.

Were we so recently on the highway to somewhere special or was that just a detour? But what does it matter now?

A new and different light shines on her. In it I read an old tale of an Arctic Maiden who sought to capture a man, a traveller, and keep him prisoner in her ice-house so that she could eat his heart and drink his blood at the Feast of the Long Darkness.

Was I not always adept at escape? But are we really that pair which were so rampant in their nakedness? So abandoned? So intimate? Can this Cold Maiden really be the one who was recently so hot?

The past is voracious. It gobbles up our lives and leaves only bones behind.

The past is a great cave down which a hollow laugh is forever echoing.

But this is the present and the present is a stadium in which the voices of the faithful call for deliverance.

The present is a game that the Blues can win and must win. The points are there for the taking if our fingers are light and our feet are quick. We can stroll away with three in our pockets and there'll be nothing that the Steelman can do about it. And if we can beat Sheffield Wednesday today then that could be the springboard we use to bounce away from the old trap-door. And why shouldn't we beat this shambles from Sheffield? Almost everybody else has.

What does she think – Missy Ice Lips? What is she thinking?

Maggie May

I absolutely refuse to think about that man. I have much more important matters to consider. Easter Monday. The day the one presumed dead emerges from the tomb. The tomb of relegation worries?

We have lost the last three games. Big birds are gathering on the roof of the stand again. The dark clouds hang low over the stadium like the smoke that lingers around those who play with fire. This club is now risking being consumed in the flames of ignominy one time too many?

We cannot think like that. Winning: that only can be on our minds. Three points, and the wellbeing of the fans around me, is all I am concerned with – nothing and nobody else.

Oh, and of course my first glimpse of our new man.

Scholar McColl

The flag goes up, the whistle pipes, Kevin Campbell is caught off-side. But he's the one; if we are to survive he is the one who must lead the charge.

Charge? Us? This season? Scramble, more likely.

The Maiden of the Icebergs stands with her chilled hands crossed before her. She is thoughtful, as if she's watching a documentary about the clitoris or the solar system or…the life of icebergs. She lifts her finger and hooks her hair around her ear. That fetching little habit that used to touch me below the belly.

The Chief climbs as if the air has rungs, hangs as if the sky has bars and waits…but the ball does not arrive.

The Maiden moves off. Those slow measured paces with her small chill feet.

But Kevin Campbell is more worthy of attention. He is too strong for the steelmen's defenders when they come hustling and barging.

Maggie May

Oh, I do like the look of that man.

He leaps and wins once again the duel for the ball. And he calls on other players to rise to this occasion with him. But more than that: he calls on the crowd also. He is saying: Support me, and I will deliver you.

He is a leader. He is a man born to this task. And he is indeed leading. He is with us, he is of us, we who can only watch. He is ours in our time of need.

Scholar McColl

On the roof of the stand the doom-birds are back. But Campbell and that young whippet Franny Jeffers seem determined to defy them. Campbell leaps for yet another high ball. The Sheffield keeper is Mr Butterfingers. The ball drops at the young lad's feet, and with the most beautiful, most glorious lob he dispatches it like a veteran into the net. Almost effortless, and yet so expert. A goal you could watch a hundred times. Like something pure discovered in a messy place. A little dash of excellence amid the slowly-shifting dross.

So we are away now down Victory Road, surely we are. This opposition don't look capable of tying their own bootlaces never mind putting together moves that will bring them the goals to win this game.

And now the Ice Maiden is about, busy and headlong, snatching some brat as he makes a run for the pitch. The Blocker Man also is on his way. As he reaches the aisle she steps out of it holding her captive by the arm and telling him, 'You're not going to spoil this game for everyone.'

When he wriggles she tightens her grip. The kid curls his lip – that adolescent mixture of defiance and scorn that my own face once wore.

The Blocker takes charge of the prisoner and then marches him away while commencing a sermon. The Maiden turns back to the crowd, slips into the empty seat next to the culprit's little mate. He won't hang around for long now that his accomplice has been ejected. The Blocker returns smacking his hands together as if he's rubbing dirt off them. The lad beside the Maiden looks from side to side. His head tells you he's not watching the match. He has his own little game to attend to. He's setting himself to copy his mate and try to do a runner on to the pitch, to claim his few seconds of attention. The Blocker Man growls, an old lion in his concrete cage. The lad slips forward on the blue plastic. The Maiden seems distracted by a punter on the other side. The mischievous kid slides to the edge of his seat. The Blocker Man sets off to take control. At the crucial moment, as the lad is about to leap, the Maiden reaches out without turning around and puts her hand on his shoulder. He crumples back into his seat.

The Blocker Man turns back, pulls out his record book, his stubby pencil. His mouth shifts and twists as his hand moves across the narrow page.

The Ice Maiden talks to the lad. Is she smiling? What charms does this scallywag possess? No, it is she who has worked hers on him. He is no longer a cat set to spring.

He watches as the Blues concede free-kicks; around him the crowd begins to murmur, anxious that the precious lead should not be lost. It is as if some creature caged by anxiety waits for someone to let it out of its cramped and unappealing space.

A volley of shouts is aimed at dallying players: words of chastisement and of warning from jack-in-the-box figures – especially for our defenders, and for Big Marco Materazzi in particular. They don't care how elegant he is supposed to be, they don't care if he could dance a tango, or the Italian equivalent, on a ten pence piece, what they want now patrolling the penalty box is a yard-dog not a ballerina.

But, too late the warnings, too late.

Why? Why with a goal in the bag do we begin to play like a gang of fumblers and duffers? Why do we turn slapdash, scatterbrained, hamfisted? This game can be as cruel as the sea, and with players like we have in the crew we'll sink for sure.

Big Marco, deep in our half, has plenty of time to boot the ball into the opposition box, into the stand, over the roof, all the way to some vineyard back home, anywhere, but that's not elegant enough for him, not stylish enough. He obviously thinks football is a game for princes, not labourers and journeymen. So what does he do, our Italian Prince? He clips a delicate little ball to Rhino Unsworth, a chunky journeyman who gets in a panic as he's got nowhere to go with it when the hounds of Sheffield come snapping. What he then does with it you wouldn't want to watch again, and neither no doubt would he, but once this darting little figure in stripes gets on to it there's only once place it's going to finish up.

We've just torn up a priceless lead and flushed it down the boghole. But that isn't the end of our foolishness. The thousands of appalled spectators must endure more of the same, a repeat performance of such sad drama when Marco the Impetuous, who clearly does want to do well for this club in a foreign land, drops a horrible pass into the path of the same little predator who plundered the first and then must stand and watch him stick it in our net again.

You could weep at watching it. And some almost are. What did we do, oh what have we done, to deserve this?

The boos rise to a furious crescendo. The players squat, hang heads, stare into the grass, peer through the green into the darkness, that pit into which they are about to topple dragging us all down with them.

How could this happen? How? We're faced with a team that can't create a single chance for themselves, not one. So what do we do? We present them with gifts, two goals on a plate, on a silver platter, garnished with olives and a garlic dressing. And with so much at stake! With everything at stake.

Maggie May

Old Archie sighs at my side, says, 'You could see it coming after the first twenty minutes.'

'Maybe.' I'd prefer to believe that wasn't the case but he is probably right. Yes, you could feel the crisis building up darkly, grumbling like an approaching thunderstorm.

Kevin Campbell, our great hope in this time of need, shoots and misses.

'That fella,' says John Sanger, shaking his head, 'I never rated him. He always looked second rate to me.'

So I tell him, 'He doesn't look second rate when he's giving their defence a hard time. And it's not his fault we've messed this up.'

'He tries,' says Archie, 'I'll give him that.'

'Give him nothing,' says Sanger, in that tone you hear from him sometimes. 'He's not good enough and he never will be.'

So I tell him again, 'You'd better hope he proves you wrong because if he doesn't there's no one else around who can get us out of this trouble.'

And we are in trouble. We are right down in the depths of it. And who, of those around me here, isn't feeling that? Shock, disbelief, fear, dread: they're all there in the murmurs and mutterings, and the silences also, the pained silences of this gloom. And it is real gloom. A sense of impending woe: it surrounds me, weighs on me. I've never known a mood like it here.

Scholar McColl

It's like a mist, a chill grey fog has settled over the place. Here are the faces of the desolate, the bitter and the frustrated. Some look sad and pale, as if some bloodsucker has been at them, siphoning off their vital juices – they're like the faces of the living dead. Some wring their hands and some breathe back tears. And some, who only have anger, must cast their curses on to the pitch. But some have seen quite enough, some cannot bear to watch any longer. And some, the odd ones, go so far as to offer encouragement. If a lone vocal might fortify the players then so be it.

Maggie May

But we still have the time, and games enough to save ourselves. And we have been through this before. We know as much about survival as anybody. And aren't the people who give up the ones who get trampled on? Don't the ones who keep their heads up, who have some kind of view of where they're aiming for, have the best chance of getting there?

 We have played with fire before, and we have dodged the inferno. We must remember the Wimbledon game, remember the Coventry game, and be ready. We did it then. We can do it again.

Scholar McColl

The crowd shuffles away like an army of the doomed. It's as if finally after so many seasons of dodging away from the awful truth we have suddenly walked into it, as if that truth is a door that has been suddenly, violently, slammed in our faces and left us only one way to go: down.

 Have we used up our luck? Is there a limit to how many times you can pull off the last-minute escape?

 The end of our world is, at last, nigh? We await, now, the apocalypse? The four horsemen who operate the trap door are on their way, galloping to Goodison Park? Babylon fell. Jericho fell. Carthage finally fell to the Romans. But the mighty Romans could not be sustained by past glories, could not hold back the Barbarians for ever, their fate could not be put off indefinitely. Is this so in our case?

Finally the weeping and wailing, the funeral music.

Or the brass band of celebration that leads those who come to bury us, to lower our coffin down into a deep dark hole, cheering, and chanting: Going down, going down, going down…

We must not let it happen. And we can confound them. There are clubs above us who are in no better shape than we are. We must do the messy thing now. We have to scramble up and push others down into our place. We must grab them by the bollocks – oh this is such a grim sport at times – and shove them through the trapdoor and let them fall, not us, no never us, into the mire below.

25

Billy Whizz on the Wing

Billy Whizz

Am still broodin about that match. Another dream start. Another bad endin. But there's somethin else. That bug in me brain. The woman am married to is upstairs and gettin ready to go out. Again. To where? Where to? Am stood lookin out the window tryna puzzle this out. She is upstairs in front of the mirrer again suckin her cheeks in like some kinda film star and doin the lipstick rootine and then makin like she's kissin someone. And it sure ain't me.

Jane

The splodge of me face starts to shape up into a portrait. I must make meself look nice for Frank because it cheers him up, puts a lovely look on his face when ee sees me. Because ee has to deal with lots of pressure Frank does, bein so busy and so involved in important things, but ee says that seein me takes all the pressure away. Which makes me feel important too. So Barbara better not be round there gettin in the way. Earrings? Al wear the turquoise ones. Ee likes them.

Billy Whizz

Av been thinkin for a few days now – Why does she spend so much time in front of that mirrer and where does she go when she's all dolled up sayin she's goin to see her arl fella?

When I take another walk up the stairs there she is, still at it. She's spendin all that time gettin painted up to go and see her arl fella? Oh yeah.

And suddenly it's like I know somethin that I wish I didn't know. Somethin is goin on here. Somethin is goin on behind my back, somethin underhand and sneaky. And it ain't gonna go on goin on much longer coz sparks is gonna fly and shit is gonna hit the fan and the can of worms is gonna get chucked throo someone's window and them worms is gonna be all over someone's face and neck and all down their fokin back and everywhere.

Jane

He looks at me a bit strange. He looks like a tomcat that's heard a weird noise and is tryin to puzzle out what it is. Does ee know? No, there's no way ee could know. Me and Frank are the only ones oo do know. But should I maybe not go today? No, no, av got to go, av said al be there and Frank will be expectin me. And all I want is to be there with him. And, anyway, how the hell could Billy know?

Worry, that's all that is. Silly worry. Like av been doin all me life. Even so, it's makin me a bit giddy, me legs gone wobbly and me head in a spin. But in the middle of a fuzzy, flashin, fast-whirlin room I see one thing very clearly: I have to go to Frank. Ee is my lover and I must be there with him. But I need to talk to him about this. Again. Like av told him, Frank needs to make a decision and then we have to come clean. Or we could end up in a terrible mess.

Billy Whizz

So I make me mind up what to do. I goes out and waits on the corner for her to leave de ouse and then I follow her. I stay well behind but all the time I have her neatly combed ed in me sights. Round the corner and over the road, down the street. Av walked this way an undred times before – down past de ouse with the bright yellow door and the one with scaffoldin, on and on, past de ouse with the brass lion for a knocker, so I start to get an idea where she might be edin. No. Surely not. But it feels like me skin has suddenly shrunk till it's too tight for me bones.

And sure enough she stops at de ouse with the green front door. No, can't believe it. Frank Brigstoke. Me old mate Briggy? No. This cannot be. Can it? Frank? Frank Brigstoke a lousy rat?

I dodge back and see the door swing open and that familiar face appear. I watch him nod to her and give her the big smile and then she's swallowed up inside de ouse. And am out here with only the closed door to stare at. I turns away and chews on me thumbnail. I have to do somethin about this nonsense and I have to do it now. And at the same time I want somethin to tell me it isn't really like this, that Jane oo av been married to all these years isn't in there with Frank Brigstoke me old Goodison buddy. But no one and notn is gonna tell me different. Av seen it. I know it. I have to deal with it and that's that. This minute or the next or the one after that am gonna have to cross over to that green door.

A motor crawls up the street with a trailer on the back. The fella on the passenger seat is lickin a roll-up. There's an upturned wheelbarrow in the trailer. I blank for a second the mess am in as the van passes. But soon, too soon, am back seein the shitty fact of what's goin on.

So that's it. I have to go and face them. I have to do it, I have to.

As I steps out me heart wobbles like av gone over a bump but I keep goin. One by one I pass the doors, the green one gets closer and closer, like it's the doors that's movin and not me, like am walkin on the spot becoz I never want to arrive at that last place where the devilman and the devilwoman are up to their abominashons.

Am starin at glass, at lace curtens, but seein notn throo them. I grab the knocker and give three big raps. Bang. Bang. Bang.

Jane

Bad news. Frank is just tellin me that Barbara might be back early today, and I'm thinkin what a nuisance that would be, when there's a knock on the door and we think it's her, forgotten her key maybe, but no. Oh my God! It's Billy. What? And you can tell by the look on his face that ee knows. This is a trap, a terrible trap, and am caught in it. It's like av not been lookin where am goin and av walked straight into somethin I should have stayed well clear of. I want to be out in the street, walkin away from this but I can't, am stuck here. And me heartbeat seems so loud it could fill the whole room.

Billy glares at me, ee glares at Frank, ee glares at me again. 'So what's goin on?'

I don't know what to say.

'Nothin, nothin goin on,' says Frank lookin shocked, just like you'd expect, but tryin to sound innocent.

Billy's not havin that. Ee knows. Ee looks wild, like a hurt animal, like a dog that's been pelted with stones. It's like his heart is pumpin all of his blood into his face and that any second it will explode.

'Goin on? What d'you mean?' Frank, the fool, is still playin the innocent.

'I mean this,' Billy says movin his pointin finger backwards and forwards between me and Frank.

And then Frank starts makin up this story about some of the girls ee works with bein interested in Rosie's self-defence class and me comin round to give him some details. Once ee gets started ee just keeps on goin maybe hopin that if ee talks for long enough his words will work some kinda magic.

And Billy is startin to look a bit confused. Maybe Frank has talked us out of bad, bad, trouble. But now there's a noise at the front door like the sound of a key. No, not Barbara, not now. But oo else could it be?

Frank goes quiet as Barbara enters the room. Her coat and her face and her hair are in the room, and her eyes are fillin it with their stare, and now her voice, that quiet and dead slow voice of hers is sayin, 'It looks as if am disturbin somethin.'

It's too much. Frank looks like an actor oos forgotten his lines. And I can't think of any. And Billy doesn't look so confused any more. Seein Frank go weak ee comes on stronger, 'Looks like yve been well and truly caught out, Mr Fokin Goody-Goody.' It's like his voice is from deep in his throat, and there's a kind of growl in it.

Barbara turns to Frank, 'Well say somethin. What's goin on, Frank?'

Frank can't face it. There isn't an eye in the room ee wants to look into. It's like ee looks at the floor for some excuse, some plan, some idea, some anythin that will get us out of this. But there's nothin down there, so ee can only mumble, 'I don't know what… I mean… what I mean is…'

Av never seen such a clever fella have so much trouble with a single sentence – not that am performin any better meself. Barbara, though, is definitely buildin up to somethin. She tuts and huffs.

'Just tell me will you!' But that woman oo might be borin certainly isn't dim. She knows. 'Well?'

I would like to help him out, but am still havin the same trouble with words as ee is, 'You see it…it…It's not what…' I want to tell the truth and be done with it but it's like the truth about this is a foreign language that I haven't learnt yet.

Somethin is gonna happen now, we can't go on standin around like this. But Frank's goin nowhere because Barbara has got him fixed in a fierce glare and she isn't goin to let him out of it. 'Is it so bad you can't even say it?'

When Frank doesn't answer her Barbara turns to me. 'Have you been comin round here when I was out?'

Frank does a tiny headshake at me but I haven't got the strength to deny anythin now. What's the point? Lyin will just make things worse. 'Yes,' I say. 'Yes I did.'

Billy spits the word bitch at me.

'Some people get lonely you know,' says Frank, realizin ee can't bluff any longer. Ee says to Barbara. 'You might not understand that but they do. Jane was lonely and so was I.'

And all Billy can say is, 'Bitch. Fokin bitch!'

And then Frank sighs a sigh fit to mark the end of the world and says, 'But whatever has gone wrong is in the past now.'

What? No it isn't! Is it?

Billy doesn't think so. He calls us a pair of bastards, hisses and growls, hawkin the words from the back of his throat.

No, this is insane. We need to sort this out. Now. We can't keep hidin the truth, we have to tell them how we feel, that's the only way now. It's wrong to be sayin it's all bad and over and done with when it isn't because I love him and ee loves me, even if ee never says so I know ee does, well I think ee does, I hope ee does.

Barbara's lips are tremblin and her chin too, but she isn't goin to shed any tears here if she can help it. 'You're no good Frank,' she says in a weary sort of voice that's got plenty of contempt in it. She sounds like she has had enough. She doesn't want him. So ee can be mine now, mine. But before she dumps him she wants to put him in his place. 'Despite all the fine sentiments you mouth you are clearly just another worthless cheatin bastard.'

'No!' I say. I can't let her talk about him like that. 'That's not true. Ee loves me. That's not a crime. Ee loves me'

I look at Frank, all ee needs to do it admit it and then whatever she says will not be true because real love can't be a bad thing even if people get hurt while it sorts itself out so that the two people oo really want to be together can be together. But ee won't, ee doesn't, ee can't admit it, ee says, 'No, no look - '

No. No. If we both tell the truth, together we can be strong enough to get through this, so I tell him, 'No, don't deny it Frank.' I turn to the others, 'We love each other, that's the truth. Everyone has to tell the truth now. That's the only way. Because you didn't want him Barbara.' And then I turn to Billy, 'And you didn't want me, not really.'

'Bitch!' he growls. 'Slut. Dirty little slag.' He looks set to explode, gone almost purple.

'Well you can sort it out between yourselves,' says Barbara, 'Because I - '

But before she can finish, Billy, with a look on his face like he's a wild beast, and his fists in tight knuckles, takes a swing at Frank oo turns away and lifts his arm and dodges the punch, but Billy, swingin the other fist upwards, catches him on the face with it. And then me, seeing my lover under attack, launches meself forwards and just in pure instinct kicks Billy, a side kick on the hip, just like Rosie taught me, a big and true kick she would have been proud of havin taught me. I can't hardly believe av done it. But it staggers Billy, coz ee wasn't expectin it, and in staggerin ee grabs this glass vase and busts the top of it against the wall makin the lumps and splinters bounce and tinkle and everybody jump and jerk. Ee holds out the remains like a shattered torch, pantin and hissin and jerkin and jabbin.

I can hear his breathin comin in gusts through his teeth as he says, 'You didn't have to do this to me.'

And I feel so sorry for him now, I feel as sorry for him as any human being has ever felt for another, and I wish so much that it wasn't me oo has brought this on him.

'No,' I say to him. 'But we can sort things out between us without…'

But I don't finish because suddenly Frank grabs a cushion and charges at him. I run forward and grab Billy's free hand while Frank pushes the cushion on the vase. It's the cushion I used to put under me arse when we did shaggin on the floor.

'Billy, please, please,' I say as I wrestle with an arm that seems much stronger than the whole of me.

Frank forces Billy's hand and the glass against the wall. But Billy throws me off, and then kicks Frank on the knee. So I, just instinctively, kick him again, another side kick on the hip, but this time it doesn't stagger Billy so much, it just jerks him into pullin the hand holding the vase free and in the same big wild movement ee swings it and jabs it into Franks gut. Frank crumples forwards and groans and staggers backwards at the same time. His blood is out in the room. The carpet is changing colour. Then there's all kinds of screams and gasps and grunts and shouts and some of them are mine. I can't believe that am seein this and neither can Barbara oos stood against the wall with her eyes bulgin like stunned frog.

'Yoo stupid bastards,' shouts Billy. 'Look what yve done now!' Then ee drops the vase. It doesn't break but it's got blood on its spikes. Billy spins round and out the door.

'Al get an ambulance,' says Barbara pantin her words.

'Frank, Frank,' I call, kneelin down, 'Frank. Don't die Frank. You'll be all right. The ambulance won't take long. They'll sort you out.'

There's blood all over me and Frank and the floor, but how do you stop it? I grab another cushion and press it against where the blood comes from. A sheet, maybe. 'You'll live,' I say. 'I won't let you die Frank.' And then I turn to the door. 'A sheet!' I scream to Barbara. 'A clean sheet. Or a towel. Bring one!'

Billy Whizz

Blood on me hands. I legs it away, full pelt, like the flyin winger I used to be. I reach de end of the street and then I slows as I go round the corner so I don't draw attenshon to meself with the blood on me. Am pantin, swallowin hard, as I move along at what seems like a normal pace, cursin under me breath and even out loud. I can see Brigstoke stagger backwards after I give it to him. I can see the blood soakin inta his shirt. It's on the glass as I pull it out. But ees brought it on himself. Ee had it comin to him and no one would deny that. But the cops ain't gonna look at it that way. Nah, but they won't catch me, not now they won't.

The streets look strange, like I don't belong to them no more. Al clear out, that's what al do, al move away across the city to where no one knows me, away up the North End, Fazak maybe. Al keep me ed down and blend in. It's their fault anyway, doin their filth behind me back. Well that's learned them an ard lesson alright. Now they know they can't mess me about and gerraway with it. Av done him, but it's his own fault for makin me do it. Him and that bitch, that dirty little hore av been married to all them years. Slut. She took the best years of me life and spat on them. And then she put the boot in on me. Twice! The filthy little scrubber. Twice!

I cross the road, slowin down, not drawin attenshon. In a few hours it'll be dark and then no one will find me. Al become a night hawk for a while only movin in the safety of the darkness.

Key? The key? Where de ell is me key? I plunge me hand in me pocket and wrap me fingers round it. Back at de ouse I shove the door open and slip inside like a burglar not wantin to be seen. I close the door quick and stop. I need to think, more than anythin I need to think. I need to think clearly, very clearly, but for a second me willpower drains away. I just freeze with me back to the door. I wanna fold up and curse her, to curse the both of them for what they've done to me and I wanna let the tears flow over me ruined life. But no, not that, I won't buckle, they won't crush me so easy as that.

I bounds upstairs, wash me hands, then inta the bedroom where I throw the bloody clothes off and jump inta clean ones. I grab a bag, the black leather holdall. Me holiday bag. Holiday, ha! The thorts are goin thick and fast throo me ed now. Cash, I need all I can get me hands on. I stuffs me pockets, like a thief in me own house, as if am grabbin what belongs to someone else. Then I starts shovin things in the bag. Blanket. Kecks. Jumper. Then me team shirt – can't disappear without that in the bag. Worrelse? Swiss blade. Protection, yeh. Goin inta de unknown. Then I thinks of somethin else in that bracket. The rattin gun. De air shooter what the lads have left under the bunks. Worrabout that? De idea sends me scrabblin. Am pullin the rifle out and thinkin yeh, makes ya feel kinda stronger just holdin it even if it don't shoot bullets. Could maybe bluff me way out of a dark corner with that in me hands. So I wrap a woolly jumper around the barrel and shove it in the bag.

Back downstairs I grab biscuits from the kitchen, cans of fizzy from the fridge, chocolate, whisky, me stash of baccy. Enough. I have to call time now. Av been here too long already. Out, I have to gerrout, I have to shift me arse before some clown from the constabulry grabs hold of it. I snatch up me van keys and then am out the door and on me way. But as soon as am rollin away I have an idea, a crafty one. If I stay with the van they'll track me down. I have to dump it. To fool them. So I drive to that little deadend road that leads to Prinny Park. They won't find it there, am thinkin. But while they're lookin for it al have plenny of time to scoot clear.

Nah, they won't catch me. Am away across the grass. Am leavin me life behind, puttin distance between. Am finished with all that now, finished with that bitch and her fancy man, that gobshite Brigstoke. And if ees dead it's murder, manslaughter maybe with gross provocashon or somethin like that. But they won't catch me now. Am away inta the streets, goin careful, kickin no cans, makin no sound, leavin no trace, like as if av never been here. I ed on down an empty street. Am just thinkin – Unless someone is lookin from a window av got in an out of that one unnoticed. Then a cop car. I jump back. It goes cruising past. Did they clock me? Nah, I reckon not. I get me ed down and press on, cross pavin slabs, tarmac, grass. I can hear me breath rushin out. I can see me feet going step-step-step as I keep me ed down so me face isn't showin. I see the kerb, the tarmac. I look up to check it's clear and then I cross it. And then I hear de ellycopter. A glance over me left shoulder – and there it is. Out for me? Surely not. Not already. Even so, take no chances Billy Boy. So am lookin for somewhere to hide now, before it gets too close.

There's a dead street in front of me. That's the one I need. Abandoned ouses with steel curtains nailed to de outside of the downstairs windows. And the gate to the jigger at the back has been left open. I glance over me shoulder again, de ellycopter is still a way off. I look this way, that. Go.

I slips down the jigger behind de ouses. I pause at the back gate of an ouse halfway along, look round again. When I see that alls clear I step forwards. I take a sackful of breath and throw me shoulder at the gate. The old wood is in no mood for a fight, it can't get out of me way quick enuff. I step throo the gap, drop me bag, and shove the wood back in de ole. The yard is a mess of rubble, scrapwood, old tiles. The back door and ground floor window are sheeted over. But there's a spare metal sheet leaned against the wall. So I duck in under that and get crouched down as I hear the copter judderin closer. It goes wham-whamin overhead but doesn't hang about above me, only passin over. So when am sure it's well gone I scramble out and find a wedge to give the yard door some backbone and then build a barricade around it. Across the jigger de ouses are still lived in but there's no sign of faces at windows over there. Every one is a little picture of stillness. Even so there's no sense in advertisin meself so I settle into a brick armchair and wait. I take a swallow of hooch but don't guzzle it coz I need to keep it for maybe worse times to come. I get me baccy out and roll one, reckonin I can risk a smoke. And once av got that ciggy burnin I hear cop sirens come close then go distant. So am smokin some strong thorts. Too many cops on the prowl. I need to keep me ed down for the rest of the day and throo the night, keep off the streets till they start to think av slipped them. Al have to use this ouse as a hideout. No choice. That's it.

So when darkness covers me I make a move. Up the wall, and on to the drainpipe. Then I throw me bag throo the window and follow it. Damp. Ya can feel the damp shovin its fingers up yer nostrils as soon as you hit the boards. It's like av fallen into a big mouldy cheese, an abandoned piss-ole, but it'll do as a den for a few hours. I crunch over a carpet of crumpled plaster, throo to the front. I take a peep out of de ole where the window used to be. De ouses across the road is empty too. So the street is like a filmset before the crews and de actors show up. Notn moves out there. That's gold to me. If it stays that way there'll be no gripes from my direcshon.

I do a bit of spring cleanin and set up camp. Then I settle down and wrap the blanket around meself, and allow meself another swig of the strong stuff and a smoke.

I sit and watch the dark take over. Worra mess. What's my life now but a cupboard full of junk? Where did it gone wrong? How can I sort it now? If only things could have been different. But what's the point in sayin that? That's just how life is. Ya never walk out of de ouse and find flowers sproutin everywhere throo all the cracks, and birds singin their little bollocks off, and cops dancin in the street. Life's never like that, never has been, never will. Life is a dagger in the back, right between the shoulder blades. Life is a sudden blade in yer guts. That's it, that's what it comes down to. It's an apple with a bug in it.

But at least av done somethin about it. At least av trod on them pair of maggots. At least av give the gossipers somethin to gabble about. De only trouble now is that me world has collapsed. The girders have give way under the strain and the roof is about to fall in on me ed.

No, no lad, cheer up, I have to tell meself, yer a smart fella, yerll find a way outa this mess.

As the minutes go by that damp seems to creep up on me. It gets right to me bones, me guts. So I wrap meself up in more clothes. But the ground is hard and cold so I try sittin on a brick but that's no better, so I sit on me bag instead. The minutes creep past in slow motion, and as they do pass they let in more chill. But that's just somethin I have to get used to now that I don't live nowhere, now am a foogitive. And it isn't even my fault. It's her fault, it's their fault. And if ee dies it's even worse. How badly have I done him? I don't know. I don't wanna go down. I don't wanna get locked up at all. Worrabout the Blues? Al miss seasons. I won't be able to go out for me pint. Needa plan, that's what. A plan. Ain't makin no move till av gorra plan. A plan yeh. A Billy Wizard of a plan. Don't contact no one, so the gossip don't spread to the wrong ears. That's first thing. And stay clear of the van while the big sniffers are out for me. Gerranother. Yeh. In the mornin al jump a train to Blackpool, go de orkshons, buy another. Come back and find meself a place up in the North End and start lookin for earners. Then put the new number plates on de old van to drive it to Blackpool, switch the plates back and flog it.

Av gorra plan. So I treat meself to a swig of hooch. And then close me eyes on the whole horrible mess.

I wakes up feelin like av been dragged throo a warzone and dumped de other side. Still dark. The damp and the stink and the emptiness starts to get to me. And the cold. Av got scrap wood lyin around and a chimney hole gorpin at me. Why not? Oos gonna see a bit of smoke in the dark? So am playin the happy camper starin at a little bit of flame that's shiftin the cold outa me bones. And feelin the rats of hunger nibblin at me guts I cheers meself up even more by munchin some biscuits and then rollin a smoke. But when me little campfire shrinks I leave it to die. And then I doze again.

Then as the light comes creepin in, and am startin to think about when I should make me move, I hear a motor in the road. I take a peep and see a squad car outside de ouse. No! No!!!

But yis!! They're there. But how come, how come this?

What's the point in askin? They're out there.

One of the cops is lookin up. I dodge back and then have another glance. Now the two cops is lookin up at me and one of them is holdin somethin to his mouth and talkin into it.

I dashes to the back of de ouse. Maybe I can jump and run. But there's a motorbike cop sittin on his machine in de alley. How did ee get there without me knowin? Sneaky bastid.

No chance of doin a runner now. They got me in a trap. They're gonna lock me up. For years maybe, years and years. They're gonna shut me in a box not much different from the one am in. Why me? Why did that bitch have to pick on me to ruin my life? Why did she have to do this to me? But she has. And am done for. Am doomed. The court is there and the judge is there and the cell is there and the screw with his bunch of keys and his eye all squinty from ogglin throo too many Judas holes – they're all there ready and waitin to push me throo the system like a sausage throo a machine. They'll talk their legal gabble and go throo their rootines and then they'll bang me up and forget about me.

I hear movement out front. I jumps up, looks down and sees the two cops walkin towards de ouse. They're comin to get me so they can shove me inta the machine. Oh no, they're not. I grabs the rifle and stands in the window space with it down the side of me leg like am good and ready for my High Noon shootout but so they can't see what kinda shooter it is. And that works the trick coz when they clock it them cops dashes away like dogs with their tails on fire.

Am just startin to think about maybe borrowin their motor and zoomin away to Escape Town when de ellycopter comes rumblin throo the sky and starts circlin above the roof. Then de other reinforcements start to arrive. And soon there's bluebottle figures duckin and dodgin all over the show, and the gunners is among them, yeah the shootin squad is out there now, behind the cars, at the windows of de ouses opposite.

No way out now.

Once I had a ferret. I made an old orange box into an utch. Soon al be boxed in meself like that. Yeah, that's all al be, a ferret in a box. A rat in a cage.

Nah. Am not goin. Not me. I take a big swallow of hooch. I stroll across to the window space and let them know. 'Am not comin down. Yor gonna have to come and get me.'

Nah. Not me. Not Billy Whizz sat in a box day after day after day.

I sees a cop stick is ed round the back wheel of a motor and peep up. I glimpse again one with a rifle at the window of an ouse opposite. Eel kill me, that one, if ee has to, or if I make him do it. His finger will tighten on the trigger and al be blown away – no more worries for Billy Boy.

I feel like a cold damp claw has been laid on me neck. I pull me collar up, take another swallow from the bottle, and then lookin out again to my left I see a cop behind the wheels of a van settle down with the barrel lyin on the palm of his hand.

No, they'll never put me in a cage. Al go down in a burst of bullets. And maybe one day some kid will write a song about me. The ballad of Billy Whizz – the betrayed lad, a simple roofer and royal blue, oo turned avenger and then got gunned down rather than let them lock him up. Yeah. That sounds like it.

Then this cop in a suit shows up, standin behind a squad car, tellin me throo a voice trumpet that I don't wanna make it no worse for meself.

'Fergerrit!' I shout back, 'It don't get no worse than this.'

Ee says that all everyone's concerned about at the moment is makin sure that neither me nor nobody else comes to any harm. Ee says I haven't pointed the gun at anyone yet and that counts in my favour and if I throw the gun out now that will be even more in my favour. Then ee says ees put off goin on holiday this mornin to try and sort this out.

Put off his holiday? 'Ya daft twat!!' Ee could have been headin out to the sun and instead of that ees stood in a broken-down street shoutin bullshit at me. I had to laff. I thort to meself, I hope it pisses down when ya do go away, I hope the showers don't work and ya get the shits real bad.

Then I move back and sit there for a while studyin the brickwork, the rubble, the grot.

Ya take yer chances and where does it get ya? Ya do what ya need to make a livin but where dy finish up? It's like the main fuse blows and yer standin in the dark not knowin where yer are but certain that notn will ever be the same again. Why does everythin turn out wrong? Why? Why does everythin get screwed up?

Then I hear that cop again, come back for another shout. Ee says his lads are gonna throw me a telephone so we can talk easier. So I tell him ee can stick his telephone up is back passageway and talk to himself. So ee carries on throo the trumpet. But I just blank that blag.

Ees determined to get me gabbin but am not playin his game which is to get me locked up, banged up in a tomb that stinks of old socks and unwashed underpants. Better off dead. Life's not worth it. Not at that price. Av had me life, but it's all changed now – the Blues in the shite, the women gone to horedom. It's all changed out of recognishon. But av seen some great matches. Av had some great seshons in alehouses near and far. But that's all over now. Them lads is all scattered now. Some have snuffed it already. McReadie. His ticker couldn't take no more. Okay. Fair enough. That's life. So where's the problem? Ee had his life and then ee checked out. Wise fella. What's the point in hangin around? Av had me ride on the merrygoround and now it's time to jump. But no one can take back what av had. Av been far and wide with all the lads in blue and felt the feelin of the tribe. Av seen the blueboys lift the big silver cup. Av stood right in among the flags and banners and seen a girl up in the stand flash her tits when the goal went in. She got her tits out for the lads and danced on her seat. These are the great moments and no one can take them back. Ya couldn't buy them with a million notes, with a pot of gold. Av been a rich man, I have – in me own way.

But it's all over now. Av had me time, it's time to check out.

So I take another big swallow of the strong stuff, and another, and then put on me Blues teamshirt and grab the shooter and stand up there at the window gap with it next to me leg and shout, 'Ya don't frighten me.' And I feel stronger from shoutin it so I goes on. 'Coz av got blue blood. Coz am Ev-er-to-o-o-onnnn. Ev-er-ton F C…' Yeh, I give it the big voice and feel like am livin me last moments big and strong, not like some little no-mark.

When I stop the cop with the trumpet starts up, tellin me to put down the gun, to put down the gun and lie on the floor.

'No chance!' I tells him. I points to me shirt and tells him, 'I don't lie down for no one, not when am wearin dis!'

And then I start to sing, We shall not, we shall not be moved, letting them know that sooner or later they gonna have to take me out with a burst of bullets.

And then when the bullets have laid me out and set me free they'll pick up the rifle and see it's only an opeless slug-gun, but by then it'll be too late. Al have slipped throo their fingers, al be well gone.

And still that damned cop is tellin me to put the gun down and lie on the floor. So I know al just have to sing it again. And then next time the sheriff with the trumpet shows his ed al take aim at it and then his possee won't have no choice but to blow me away.

Archie Block

I was sat there reading in the Echo about how Kevin Campbell was trying to encourage the Blues' fans to inspire the team with their support when there was a knock on the door. This pair of cops was stood there. One of them was Inspector Flapper who knew me from Goodison. Straight away they started asking me questions about Billy Whizz, wanting to know what sort of a character he was and what is he likely to do if he's cornered. I knew straight away that something was going on. I said, 'Why, why do you want to know?'

They didn't seem to want to tell me at first. But I'm not the kind of bloke who enjoys being left in the dark. I said, 'You play straight with me and I'll do the same with you.'

So then they told me.

I said, 'I never ever heard him say anything about a gun. He didn't seem the type to have anything to do with them. But he is a bit of a reckless character, in my opinion.'

And I told them why I thought that. Then they started getting ready to make a move. But I could see what would happen when they'd gone. I'd be sat here not being able to think about anything else. I'd feel like I was sitting on a nest of cockroaches. There was only one thing to do so I did it. I said to them, 'I've known him for years, that lad, I'll sort this out for you. He'll listen to me. Let me talk to him.'

They looked at each other. But said nothing.

'You know me well enough,' I said to Flapper. 'When did you ever hear me talk just for show?'

The pair of them sat there weighing me up and exchanging more looks. I was thinking, You can take as long as you like doing that because I weigh plenty, I'm a solid man, I'm a stalwart.

Then Flapper said with a nod, 'We'll take you along. But it's not my show so any decision when we get there won't be mine.'

So I slipped the Echo in me back pocket and grabbed me jacket. Then when we got down there I saw the whole scene decorated with orange tape as if they were making a blockbuster film. There was a little audience of rubbernecks and there was sentries posted all over the show. What a load of nonsense. No one was allowed past, but I got walked through by Flapper and his sidekick.

They brought me to the edge of the action zone and then the sidekick waited with me while Flapper went and talked to the kingpin of this stupid operation. I saw him look towards me and shake his head. Detective Inspector Bungler.

Flapper came back and told me to wait where I was. Wait? For what? While they turned a bit of nonsense into a disaster movie? How long had they been at it already?

Cops with rifles all over the show, and the helicopter turning circles overhead – aye, they had the air force and the infantry out, and for what? For something I could sort in five minutes.

I could hear Billy's voice, shouting and sort-of singing further along the street, on past where some police cars were parked with the cops crouched behind them. But was he a gunman? Billy Whizz? I'd done my stint in the army. I'd seen how a man might change when you put a rifle in his hands. But Billy Whizz? A blagger, I reckoned, a blagger all day long. But one thing I was sure of, very sure: he wouldn't shoot me.

Then I saw a flashback: Wembley in sixty-six. That lad whose name I can't remember running across the pitch when we scored the equaliser. He made a dash and then just kept on running. So I unbuttoned me coat. Me fingers just did it while I watched replays of that lad in Wembley dodging the cops all those years ago. I was long past running like that but I reckoned I'd still got a decent pair of legs on me. Then, without another thought, I went. I started walking fast at first, sort of scurrying. No one was expecting this.

The surprise of it gave me a few seconds to get some strides in. I passed a police van with two cops squatting behind it, staring at me, gormless. I glanced back and saw Flapper on my trail. Picking up a bit of speed now I reached back to fend him off and he fell for the trick. He grabbed my sleeve and I pulled away and slipped out of the jacket, and as I left him stood there holding it another cop was about to step out from behind a squad car when a loud voice shouted, 'No! Back! Everybody back!'

So I was clear. I was out there on me own. I moved on along to where Billy was stood up in a gap where a bedroom window used to be. I took a second to get some breath back and then 'Billy,' I shouted, still panting, gasping, but I had a job to do, I had to show what could be done by a man who knows what's what. 'Billy,' I shouted, 'get your arse down here, lad!'

He'd stopped that singing racket. So I was making progress straight away.

There's a way to handle a tricky situation – common sense Scouse diplomacy. And there's those of us who understand that. I said, 'Get your arse down here now, Daftbollocks!'

I said, 'What d'you think you're playing at, eh? Eh? What kind of nonsense is this? Eh?'

He stood there in the space where the window had been staring down at me.

Billy Whizz

Eh? Archie Block? Am all set to go to Oblivion and then that old bugger turns up and stands in me way. I says, 'Go home Blocker, go and polish ya memories.'

Ee takes two steps forward and stands there in that wide-shouldered bent-armed way of his and shouts, like as if ees in charge around here, 'Get your arse down here now Billy.'

'This isn't none of your business,' I shout. 'This is between me and them.'

'It's between me and you now and a bit of common sense, lad,' ee shouts up. 'Come down, and stop actin daft.'

I could have been lyin dead in the street with no name, bullet holes in me royal blue jersey, a big picture for the news reports, if ee hadn't showed up. Me glory moment. Bang-bangbangbang!! The outlaw Billy Whizz blasted away, bites the dust and enters the country of legends. Instead of that am havin this stupid conversashon with an old fart of a redundant shipbuilder. Ad have been riddled with bullets, me blood runnin down the wall for all to see. Me, Billy Whizz, gunned down, defiant in me Everton shirt. Billy Whizz on the news. Front page of de Echo...

Ee says, 'Am goin nowhere till you've got yer arse down here,' pointin at the deck, jabbin down with a stiff finger like the bossman of old.

I says notn. I turn me back on him. I reckon eel soon get tired of shoutin into an empty space.

But ee doesn't. That voice keeps comin up to me, won't leave me alone, so what else can I do but speak to it? Ee says, 'Ya wanna get yerself some edlines in de Echo is that it, is that what this bloody circus is about? Edlines?' ee says. 'Ya dope. Ya clown. Where will yer edlines be by the end of the week? Answer me that!'

Archie Block

Authority. Some had it and some didn't. A figure of authority is a like a grandfather clock, no one can ignore its chimes for long.

I said, 'I'm going nowhere while this daft game is going on.' I said, 'There's people in this city who'd thank you for shooting me but most of them have got red snouts and since when did you do that lot any favours?'

I turned around and saw one of the infantry peeping out at the upstairs window of a house opposite. I jerked my old thumb at him, 'Go and put the kettle on, lad! Make yourself useful, will you!'

Then I had Jeronimo, aye Crazy Horse the Blue, the Dingle Apache, telling me, 'Let them come. I don't care no more Arch they can shoot me if they want.'

I said, 'Don't talk soft! Shoot you? Where will you go to watch the match then? Eh? You telling me you don't want to see the Blues no more? Yeh? They're not that bad are they? Eh? And you're telling me you don't care whether they go down or not? Eh?'

I pulled the Echo out of me back pocket and waved it at him so he could see what it was. I said, 'It says here, New Blues striking star issued a rallying cry to Blues fans today.'

'A what?' he said.

I said, 'A rallying cry.'

His face was all screwed up in puzzlement. Even at that distance with my mince pies I could see the confusion on his face. He said, 'Eh?'

I said, 'A RALLYING CRY, you know what I mean, like to get behind the boys in blue. Kevin Campbell says, "We need all the support we can get, but if Blues fans get behind the team and everyone pulls together in the same direction then we can survive." The man thinks we can do it – if the support is there. But if you're telling me you're not bothered any more, okay.'

I give him a few seconds to think about that, and then I said, 'It also says there's some injury doubts for Saturday.'

'Who? Who's doubtful,' he said.

And then I knew I was winning.

Billy Whizz

'Think about the Blues,' ee shouts. 'They won't go down. They'll stay up and be a great club again. But you won't be there to watch them if you're not careful.'

Ee had me thinkin now, de old fossil had cranked me brain into motion, it was startin to turn, steady and regular, as the power of the booze began to drain.

Ee says, 'Get yerself down here, face the music, and then count the days till yer back in Goodison where ya belong.'

Where I belong? Belong, yeh. Where I've always belonged. The royal blue of the shirts. The blue iron crossed against the white of the stand. Goodison. Aye, Goodison Park.

And it's like somethin has happened to me willpower. It's like it's runnin down like an old car battery. If am gonna go to Oblivion now am gonna need a push.

Coz in the silence I hear it, like Kevin Campbell says, all the crowd gettin behind the team, the roar of it, the Goodison faithful. My crowd. In me real home. The home I shared with the Blues. Aye, that was where I should be, not in Oblivion. That was my destiny, to be there with the Blues, the Blues on the pitch and the Blues all around me in the stand. My beloved Everton. To go to Oblivion in a blaze of bullets an edlines was all very well but it meant missin an awful lot of football. It meant no more football, ever. Ever. Ever is a long time if yve spent ya life followin a footy team. Oblivion is just a big empty space with notn in it, like the inside of some Kopite's ed. What kind of a place is that to spend the rest of yer days? No place at all.

No balls ever bounced in Oblivion. That's what they call a soberin thort. A very soberin thort. That's enough to shift all the whisky out of yer blood straight off.

Never to see the Blues again – that does make ya think. All the lads gabbin the game in some alehouse and me long gone, long forgotten, just a throwaway edline in de Echo that no one remembers no more.

Nah, am not havin that. They aren't gonna get shut of me that easy.

But if am not gonna go to Oblivion after all what's the point in stayin up in this broken down piss-ole any longer? I might as well be locked up now and doin me time and gettin it outa the way like the Blocker says, rather than put it off and miss more matches when the Blues are back where they belong.

And lookin down at the old bugger I realize that one day eel be dead and al be free again and goin to the match, walkin with the crowd, cheerin with the thousands. In Goodison Park where I belong.

I stand up at the window and drop the gun and raise me arms, 'Am comin down Blocker. Am comin down.'

Archie Block

So then I had this fella from the Echo knocking at the door, wanting to know my side of the story, so I told him I'd say it once and once only and then I'd put me boot on the seat of his pants and close the door. Then when I'd finished he said another fella with a camera would be round to take me photo. So I told him straight I wasn't going to pose for him or anyone. I said, 'I've never posed in me life and I don't intend to start now.'

I didn't need all that nonsense. A man of my age, even one as robust and as stalwart as meself, needed a bit of time after a carry-on like that to get his breath back, to let his ticker get back into its normal rhythm.

And sure enough after the cameraman had finally left me in peace

I went to put the kettle on and started heating up. And me finger ends were tingling. It was like this hotness took over all of me body. The sweat was running off me like I was melting. And something felt wrong inside. I wasn't on full power. The engine was struggling, like the gas was running low, like it was almost run out. I had to sit down, me legs were set to buckle. I sat down in me chair and I could feel meself starting to shake, like I was sitting right at the centre of an earthquake.

I knew if I didn't put a stop to this I'd be in Old Joe Knacker's yard before the hour was up. So I told meself quietly, 'Get a grip on yourself, lad. Calm yourself down. You've got plenty to live for. You've still got plenty of living to do. A good stout man like yourself.'

It was like I was talking meself down from a suicide attempt. But I just kept on talking until normal service started to restore itself. And then I realized I was sitting there in a soaking wet shirt. It was. It was wringing wet like I'd kept it on in the shower. So I said to meself, I said, 'From now on you take it easy, lad. From now on you watch your step, you've had a bit of a warning there, you need to heed it or you're heading for the edge and George'll be left stood at the bar talking to himself and a right sad sight that'll be.'

Good job the missus wasn't there or she'd have had me away in a damned ambulance.

Billy Whizz

So they take away me belt and laces. They make me drop me kecks and do a pirooet with me T-shirt held up and then they make me bend over and pull me cheeks apart to make sure I haven't gorran acksaw and a grapplin hook hidden up me arse.

And then they remand me in custody. And as am marched along de echoey landin the cons is sayin, 'What's ee done? What's ee in for?'

I roll past sayin notn. They'll find out soon enough. What else do fellas do here all day but blag and gossip? I thort to meself, Am in for a revenge job, a crime of pashon, am in becoz of the sins of a woman, am here becoz some people don't know the meanin of the word loyalty.

Oo needs friends like that? But that Brigstoke, ees a weird one.

Any fella oo turns his back on football and walks away must be missin a few onions from the bag. Ees bound to be edin for strife because ees cut himself off from what's important. I just wish ee could have dumped his load of trouble in someone else's yard because then I wouldn't be in this shitepit of a place.

Worrit is. It's a big shed of keys and door-bangs. All de air is second hand and the big dungeon-keeper has gorra big lardy belly inside his uniform and a face that wouldn't be outa place on a pig farm. In my dungeon av gorra sleeper, a table, a chair, and a steel throne with an andle that sets the waterfalls gushin down. You haven't a clue how bored a fella can get till yve been inside.

The fella am supposed to be sharin with is in the sick bay. That's no shock. Every poor prick in here seems sick, one way or de other. Screws and cons, the lot. Dunces, desperadoes, and swaggerin dudes, the whole sad crew seem like they're in a bad way, like I say, in one way or de other, even if they do try to wear a bold face and give it the big blag.

The walls are like the faces of people oo pretend you're not there. They blank you out. They just stand there all day and all night actin like ya don't exist. But they listen inta yer thorts. Ya can almost hear them listenin. And I have a tiny window with bars in front. It opens up a mean little gap. But ya can gulp some outside air that doesn't taste like yd sucked it throo some sweaty old sock. And with me ed full of outside air I know that every day I get done in here al never have to do again.

So that's how I do it. Minute by minute, day by day, tellin meself al never have to do that day again. That doesn't make it no stroll, oh no. Even a second can be a long space to walk throo in a place like this.

How long is a second? That might sound like a daft question, but in a dungeon yve gorr all the time ya need to chew over every daft question ya wobbly mind can chuck out.

How long is a second? It depends how ya feelin.

And when ya feelin dead low, when ya right down there in the pits and lookin up, then a second isn't no piece of string. It's as long as a mile. Each one is a marathon course on its own.

Yeh, ya mind does some weird kind of contorshon tricks when it's got notn but a blank wall starin back at it.

So you have to be strong and not buckle or break. And you have to keep tellin yerself that over an over – I must not buckle and I must not break. I must not buckle and I must not break. Over and over. And over and over again. I have to keep me ed down and do me time and not buckle or break.

And then I say, how strong is a second? And then I say, Am I stronger than a second? Am I stronger than a minute? Am I stronger than an hour? Am I stronger than a day? Have I got the muscle to wrestle with a second that's as long as a marathon and as strong as a steel bar? Because if I haven't I better start doin press-ups right here and now, I better start runnin on the spot and doin press-ups and sayin to meself – I must not buckle and I must not break. Over and over. Over and over. I must say to meself – They will not send Billy Whizz home a broken man, they certenly will not. And that's what I do say. And then I sit there and think about the great matches av watched, and the great sights av seen, like that Bluegirl oo got her tits out for the lads.

26

Down With the Dead Men?

Scholar McColl

The Story of Billy Whizz begins its short passage into history. The Blocker Man returns from his few moments of fame. We are back in the Now – the Now of needing to score goals and win a game of football or face the consequences of failure. After all the calculations and the permutations, all the adding up and taking away, there is only one fact, one answer: we must beat Coventry City or slip down among the has-beens. One point would be about as much use as a bar of gold to a drowning man.

Goals, yes, are the only answer.

Step forward Kevin Campbell please. The story of the future is ours to make. This day is yours to seize.

Maggie May too is up for grabs again. For any who would risk getting frostbitten fingers. Best wear thick woolly gloves when handling that one methinks.

Maggie May

Scholar McColl regards me cooly. I return his coolness with some added chill, an extra ice cube. I am walking again through love's minefield alone, while he is, I guess, back in his hermitage. But I made a difficult decision and acted on it and have the sense of power that comes from that.

Old Archie's radio is making the sounds of gibberish as he holds it by his ear. That man himself doesn't look good to me. As if all the attention he's had recently on top of the drama of today is starting to take its toll. He seemed on fine form a couple of hours ago but now it's as if he's ageing before my eyes, the colour being wrung from his face, leaving only greyness. And his breathing seems heavy, as if he's hauling his breath up a big hill. I need to say something.

He translates the radio gabble for me, saying, 'The cavalry is ready outside in case we lose and there's a pitch invasion that turns into trouble.'

Yes, I look at his face and I worry for him. I'm seeing a man who I think should return home to his armchair. 'Are you feeling okay,' I ask. 'You don't look-'

That's as far as I get. The silly man growls at me: what's really making him sick is being asked these stupid questions. He walks away shaking his head. But he hasn't heard the last of me. If he still looks the same at half time I'll have another word with him – or somebody else with more sense maybe.

But if Archie looks rough the early signs out on the pitch are not bad, the players have got their heads in gear and their hearts on their sleeves.

Archie Block

The old trooper Watson cools the hotheads, boosts up the faint hearts. This game is the battle we have to win or the war is lost. And the defeated fall into the darkness like the vanquished in any war. Us? We can't give a thought to that now. If we think like a defeated club now then that's what we will be. We must fight them on the halfway line and we must fight them in the corners and we must fight them in the danger zones. We must concede nothing, nothing. And the Blues are shaping up, they're scrapping for every ball. But this battle is hard, so hard. So hard. Exhausting. So exhausting.

Scholar McColl

You can feel the anxiety like the closeness of an airless day. The crowd are like those gathered to celebrate the second coming who secretly fear they might leave bearing news of the end of the world. Yet the Chief looks formidable up front. When he gets buffeted he holds his position, once again muscles defenders into the background, then as the ball falls from the Walton sky a flick from his head touches it into the path of the skinny boy. When it is neatly returned the powerful one makes the strike he has been threatening –

Go-o-o-o-o-o-o-o-o-o-o-alllleeeeeyyessssss!!!! The sound of it is all around me. The jamboree has started. And the one who declared it open stands with arms raised, swaying until he is swept away by a deluge of blue and white kisses.

You see the scoreline in bright flashing lights. And then when you're no longer dazzled realize how slender is that lead, that the fuses might suddenly blow, as they have done before, and leave us back in the dark. So now we must chase, chase everything, the ball, the opposition, those fingers round the clock. If only our tall and elegant Italian didn't, in his desperation to do well, look like a man playing on a new pair of feet and the referee wasn't an insect that was born to irritate.

The ball flies toward the church that long ago squatted in one corner of the stadium as if waiting its moment to reclaim lost ground from this religion of the masses. As if. We'll do without divine intervention if we can only keep our concentration steady and cling on to that goal. And we don't look as if we're about to let go of it easily, so why are there three punters stood in the gangway with looks on their faces as if it's the opposition who have scored and sent us on our way to the Land of Doom? What's the problem?

The one with the most funereal face observes, 'It's hard to concentrate on the game with a corpse lying in front of you.'

'Corpse?'

'Yeh, one of your crew. Down there.'

His finger extends towards the far end of the gangway where someone lies stretched out on the concrete with the undersides of his shoes looking back at me. Corpse? Who? Who is the one that couldn't take the strain? Old Doughnut, whose belly is an overloaded sack of guts? Excitable Eric? The Nark? The Blocker? Whoever it is there are three yellowjackets bent over him.

And then, moving closer, I see. The blue coat contains the figure on the deck and Solid John is giving him the mouth-to-mouth.

I click into emergency drill. 'Has anyone called the medics?'

Someone has gone looking. But my talkie takes a short cut to the control box. Solid John gives the man's chest another pump and then looks up and shakes his head. And the Blocker – that great lump of worn and weathered man – seems a long, long way away.

His face is grey and slack, blank, lifeless.

I turn to a jacket, 'Get Maggie May over here.' Then I kneel down to have a go myself; pinch the Blocker's nose and put my mouth to his. He tastes of old meat pies, old news, old traditions. But I knuckle to it. Blow him up like an airbed. And again. Then go bouncing on his chest.

The Ice Queen arrives. 'You want me to have a go?'

'You're the professional.'

I move aside as she bends into my place, watch the curve of her yellow back, her hair slipping forwards. She is a house I have lived in. A country I have travelled through. Some of my snapshots might be deemed porno. Bed games. Now we must tussle with death.

The Ice Queen, palm on his chest and pushing, performing like she's scored victories at this game in the past, must haul the Blocker Man him back from the other side.

Maggie May

The fool, the silly silly fool. But I begin in hope as always. And I have had my successes. There is a kind of magic in watching someone come back to life on the strength of your breath, your touch.

But this one, this feels like one of those that slip through your fingers. This man is so grey now, so heavy and limp. I can feel his moustache on my cheek when I put my mouth to his but his nose already feels like part of a thing that has gone, given up the ghost. I blow my own air into him, place my hands on his chest and try to shove him back from the death zone, and at the same time I feel all the eyes on me. I hear the silent voices willing me to push him back into the land of the living but I know I'm going to disappoint them and that the only hope now is for the medics to come and connect him up to the machine. Maybe they can kick-start his exhausted heart because I'm definitely feeling like I'm going through a pointless routine now, that there is nothing I can do to stop Death claiming this man as one of its own, nothing, nothing at all.

So when the metal case crashes down on the concrete beside me I'm relieved to be able to scoot out of the way.

'Come on, give us a signal,' the chief medic coaxes, feeling for a sign of life in that wrinkled old neck. When he gets none he wires up the fallen one.

Archie's body jerks, jumps a little off the deck, every time a belt of power goes through him. Again. Again. Again. But when they cease the old Everton loyalist just lays there like the dead man we know he is.

The medic, though, is not yet ready to accept. He switches back to manual pumping, his actions getting more and more frantic. But he must now know what I know, what probably all the watching yellowjackets know.

Scholar McColl

Then the doctor shows up with a big spike. This will be the last shot. There's quite a scrum of us now. All I can see of the Blocker is his feet. But there is no sign of them moving anywhere. And they won't either. Even if the medical man fills that spike with whisky and injects it into the Blocker's throat he won't taste it. He's raised his last glass, he's swallowed his last pint. What they're doing now is like taking a whip to a dead donkey.

That beast has carried its last load, leave it be.

And the message is very soon clear to all. It's time to pack up and move on. 'He's history now,' the medic announces, slamming his case shut – a big, final, metallic k-chunk.

Thus a man passes over to the other side and enters that very crowded country called History. This is how it ends: on the grey and grimy concrete with the crowd screaming for a throw-in, howling at the linesman who denies them, advising him to stick his flag up his arse. This is how it ends.

The professionals are turning away, pulling out. There's a sense of hurry. As if the last bus is due, the train is set to pull out. And the Blocker Man lies among the busy feet like he's wondering what all the fuss is about.

His stretcher arrives. Two medics struggle to haul him up. Dead weight. As they land him the ball is wellied from our goalmouth to growls of approval.

They are wheeling him away with a blanket over his face. And the game goes on: the sound-mix from the rows of seats, the hurly-burly on the grass. And so it's back to work.

The talkie crackles. It's Captain Redcap telling me to take control, that I'm in charge now and should make sure that all the jackets are back in their correct positions.

So that's it. You run around for this club, soaking up the pressure until you keel over and then the game goes on the same, the whole business goes on just the same. And come next match someone else will be wearing the blue coat. Maybe myself, maybe someone else. And by the start of next season it will be as if the Blocker Man had never been here. Except that he will have become part of the spirit of the place, at one with those generations that have been and gone, those who walked before us, those who felt as we do for the blue, the royal blue of those shirts on the players' backs: the tribal Blues, the Blue Tribe of this old divided city by the sea. Us. We who have known adversity as we have known the glory, we whose eyes have seen the glory, the glory of the Blues: Everton Football Club. The faces change and keep on changing but the game just goes on and on. It's a hard truth to look straight in the eyeballs, especially when it's staring at you like today, and telling you that you also one day will go that way. But the Blues will endure. In a world of wars, and uncertainty, and failed utopias we must have somewhere where we feel we belong among others. So Everton will go on, in Goodison or elsewhere on the banks of the Royal Blue Mersey, the Blues will be there, and Evertonians will know the adversity and the glory, both, as we have. This, we must believe.

But the Blocker Man got his wish. There is that. The cantankerous old stalwart, a True Blue to the end, breathed his last in Goodison Park.

Part Eight

27

The Coat

Scholar McColl

We could not prevent one man slipping out of this life. But we will not let this victory slip today. That feeling is strong. The faithful are you sense, yes, firm in that belief; despite the narrowness of the lead: that single goal from our new man who has wasted no time in showing what he can do. And the idea is beginning to spread that he can do for us a great deal.

However.

The match officials would, it seems, tinker with the confidence gauge in Goodison Park – by bringing down the red mist upon the royal blue once again. Another red card? What?

A tumbler from Coventry performs before the referee a circus routine – down in the grass he goes: the flying dolphin. And then the man in black, seizing his own moment of theatre waves the yellow card, and then…and then raises that red. And our Italian Prince, a much improved player in this game, is now a tragic figure in the wrong drama: he is the appalled, the distraught, the doomed victim.

He appeals, most theatrically, to the linesman for reason, for justice, but he is a man of flesh and blood pleading with a statue. Ignored, he slumps down to the advertising boards – such genuine human misery down there among the banalities of commercialism. And you do feel for the big man: so far from home and so little going right for him. And there is a good player in that large frame if he could only calm down and let him out. Calm down? He has to be lead away flinging handfuls of emotion at the sky while the crowd, only moments ago so calm in their quiet confidence, spit mouthfuls of abuse at those who have dealt both him and themselves such a diabolical blow.

So we are short of a man – again.

We are short of a man out on the pitch and, with the Blocker Man gone, on this section also.

Solid John Sanger

So a gap had opened up at the top. And if the Scholar picked up the blue coat then the deputy's badge would have to be pinned to somebody new, somebody with the right sort of profile. And who was that? Who was best suited to take on the responsibilities that went with the badge?

I looked around. I took a good look around me.

Where was the competition? Who was always there first when there was a problem that had to be sorted out? Who could possibly challenge me for that badge? I could see no one.

And I couldn't imagine that anyone else would either.

Scholar McColl

In adversity the Blues are resolute. Those three new points will, in a couple of minutes, be locked up in the blue box in which we are saving up, despite the predictions for impending doom, for a trip to a place called Survival. But the Blocker Man will never know that we arrive there. He has booked out of the land of the living. I'm thinking survival and its opposite in the same moment, of life's contradictory tendencies, as Solid John steps into the gangway, his head raised, slightly tilted back, like he's all set to say something. He's like a man on a rostrum about to make a speech when his audience quietens down. I'm guessing, being the man he is, that he might want to start a collection to buy a wreath for the Blocker.

But, no.

When I arrive before him he starts talking about something else. And he's straight to the point, 'What will happen about the blue coat now?'

That which still contains the cold corpse of a man? 'Not thought about it.' I nod towards the control box, 'But that's for them to decide. We'll have to see what they say.'

That is clearly not what he wants to hear. He looks stern, a little edgy, when he says, 'The blue coat goes to the deputy and then his job goes to the next one in line. That's right isn't it?'

If I've never thought about this, it's obvious that John Sanger has. I tell him, 'Sometimes it happens like that, sometimes it doesn't. There's no official policy, as far as I know. But if they were to offer me the blue coat I expect your name would come up for deputy. What others they might have in mind I wouldn't know. But they might not be thinking about that just now, with the game still going on, and yer man only just this last hour lying dead. And we haven't got a game for two weeks. So they might leave it till then. But I don't know. Just have to see what happens.'

But he is impelled, it seems, to persistence. 'That was the way you got it though, wasn't it.'

'The way I got it was that they had some special meetings to talk about all aspects of the running of the club, they were looking for someone from each section to go along. All hands here were saying, "Send the mouthy bastard. Send Scholar McColl." So I said I'd go. So then the High Command knew my face when they had to decide about a new deputy. But what they decide to do now, we'll have to wait and see. Maybe they won't give it to me, but bring in someone from another section instead. I don't know.'

He wants it. He wants it bad. I'm looking at his naked need, his desire, his ambition and, what I'm starting to feel might be, his obsession. But I've got things to do. 'I need to go and get everyone organized for the end of the game.'

Maggie May

Time almost up and Mr McColl is signalling yellowjackets from their positions to come and protect the pitch: his big command of the day. But some must be instructed, urged along every time, for it can feel so exposed out here with thousands of eyes on you.

The red track crunches beneath me. A glance over my shoulder and I see Kevin Campbell in a flash of powerful blackness as he dashes in through a gap for one last charge on goal. But the strong man stumbles as he shoots. The keeper dives, gets a hand to the ball. Then, as it falls, our man does a little dance of control and fires it towards a place called Victory.

Go-oa-oa-oa-llll! The one some are already calling the Chief stands before the admiring masses.

And maybe there are some here now watching him who will be breaking up the ill words they uttered about him, breaking them up into tiny pieces in preparation for having to swallow them.

Solid John Sanger

Well he knows now. He won't be going into that office in any kind of doubt. He knows what I expect. Just have to hope that with that mouth of his he hasn't talked his way out of the blue coat.

Scholar McColl

When I arrive in the coatroom everyone else has gone, Mick the Jacketman and a couple of his lads are just getting ready to go, but unusually Cluny is still around. He calls me into the office, saying, 'While we're all here we might as well sort something out.'

I hang up my jacket and go through.

In the office three large men, three sad-faced large men look me over as I take a seat. Only Cluny speaks. Shaking his head, still looking sad, he says, 'He told me he felt fit and well before the game. I took him aside. He was adamant.'

So I tell him, because the man shouldn't feel responsible, 'That was his way. So it wasn't only you he said that to.'

This he accepts, and moves quickly on. 'But we're professionls, and we've a job to do.' A slight pause, then, 'So…you'll be taking over the blue coat permanently.'

Oh? Already. When would they have removed it from the man who zipped himself up in it at five minutes to one o'clock this afternoon? Odd thoughts.

But, okay, life goes on.

Fred Gutteridge observes me coolly, which is his way, I guess, as an ex-cop, so I wouldn't expect him to be celebrating my promotion even if circumstances were different. Beside him Len the Hat scratches his large fleshy ear. Cluny taps his nose with a pen. He tosses the pen on to the table. 'So now we'll have to think about who should take over as deputy. Then we're all set up for the next game.'

The phone on his desk interrupts. 'Hi Bert,' he says. 'Possibly,' he says, 'I don't see why not.'

And then while he listens to Bert, the boss of bosses, I feel as if I've been stung – by another thought. What if they ask for my opinion as to who should be the new deputy? That sting is giving me palpitations. What do I say?

The Blocker Man has fallen and opened up a worm-can and I am going to have to put my hand in it. And maybe spill worms all over the bosses' very tidy table.

While I have a moment I must try and see clarity beyond the worms.

John Sanger has already put himself forward as the prime candidate – but is he?

In many ways, yes he is. But.

It is all in that *but*. Such a large dark **But**.

If not him, though, then who?

Who has the long experience, and a willingness to sort things out? Who could stand beside him for comparison?

Her? Yes, her.

There is nobody else I could think of recommending. If they ask me, that is – which I sense now that they will. It can only be her: of equal stature, with longer experience, much longer, and, on one particular count, she is more suitable. Far more suitable.

But would I want her around me in that way, after what has happened? The Ice Queen around me as my deputy? A chilly picture, that. Seeing her move to another section would suit me far more.

Whichever way I turn I see a problem. But what I have to think of is the endpoint.

What are the questions? If progress is made up of small steps, is this process that I might now initiate a small but important one? Are there certain attitudes that disqualify some people, however dedicated to the job, however competent, from holding important positions in football grounds?

I must do what I have to do. And the moment is perhaps approaching. Cluny is putting down the phone. He is saying, looking now in my direction, 'So we need to decide on a new deputy.'

He seems to be waiting for me to say something. I notice a nick on his neck where he shaved too fiercely and then, as I'm about to speak, hear Len the Hat say, 'I would have thought that John

Sanger was the likely choice. Seems like the type who'd respond well to pressure and responsibility.'

With that I won't argue. 'Yeh, he's very dependable.'

Detecting the flatness in my tone, they wait for more. But I must pick words carefully. Or else trip over them.

Cluny is giving me some very close scrutiny. How many faces those eyes must have examined across the table in the interview room. Captain Cluny: Special Investigator in the Royal Military Police. Anything you say may be taken down.

Evidence? I can foresee that it will come to that before too long.

My tone is judicious when I choose to speak again. 'Now that I think about it there is someone else who should be considered.'

There are six eyes on me, half a dozen expectant ears – some of them very large ears.

'Erm...Margaret Maynard.'

Who?

Three puzzled men scrutinize me most seriously. Have they just offered the blue coat to a nitwit?

Cluny has to clear his throat. Every wrinkle asks a question. 'But she's only just joined your section.'

If I have to state the obvious then I will. 'She knows her way around every section in the ground. Been doing it for years. There's nothing she doesn't know about the job.' A big sweep of my eyes takes them all in. 'And I'd say that if you spent a few matches on Section Six she's the one you'd choose.'

Gutteridge folds his arms now that he's taking Maggie May seriously. 'How good will she be at man management?'

Harold H Cluny has spent his life within command structures, he knows all about bossing and being bossed, 'If she doesn't score there she's no good to us.'

Now Len the Hat must speak as the wise man. 'And you don't do anybody a favour by pushing them further than they've a right to go.' And then this afterthought which causes him to focus on me a look of suspicion that would suit an old detective rather than an academic. 'You're not doing this because you fancy her are you?'

I need to stamp on this one here and now and kick it into a dusty corner. And that's what I do until there's nothing else to deny. And then this line comes to me – a line I'd never have found if I'd set out looking for it. I say, 'Maybe she isn't so familiar with everyone on the section like she would be if she'd been on it for years, but maybe that's a good thing when it comes to telling people what to do.'

Where I picked that up I don't know but it falls right into place. It falls right into Cluny's lap and he picks it up and pockets it. 'I'll go for that,' he says thoughtfully. 'And now that you mention her,' he goes on with a series of slow nods, 'I can see what you're saying: experienced, reliable, very good at the job.' He looks to the other two. Fred Gutteridge says nothing – which is often the way with him. Len Knox, who is never comfortable with silence, says, 'But John Sanger has been about the world, he's a very experienced man of in lots of ways.'

True enough, but. 'But so is she,' I tell him, 'in a different kind of way. And she's been doing the job twice as long. More. So you'd think that ought to give her some sort of precedence – in all fairness.'

I get the feeling they're starting to wish they'd never brought me into this. But maybe I'm wrong. Maybe it's just one of those things: you're expecting simplicity and then find yourself looking at complications.

'We need to give this some more thought,' Cluny announces in a tone that means it's time for me to go.

So I do. And as I get outside I can hear Len Knox saying, 'The final decision's yours Harry. And if you've got two people pretty much equal then go with your instinct, and your instinct, I'm pretty sure, would tell you to go with an ex-serviceman.'

But Harold H Cluny is inclined to be more cautious. 'We need to be careful here, Len. Now this has come up we don't want to be accused of....' He doesn't seem to finish. Probably he doesn't need to: the others would know where he's going with that line.

But their voices go on in the office as I move away. Outside the air is cool. I half expect John Sanger to be out there, but the streets are empty. The crowd has gone and left its rubbish behind. And I can see an even bigger mess beginning to spread out in front of me.

Solid John Sanger

I said, 'Eh?' I said, 'What?' I said, 'Say that again, Mick.'

Mick Molloy replied, speaking slowly, pronouncing each world as if I was half deaf, 'Yer man has recommended Maggie May.'

My fist tightened around the phone, I could feel myself crushing it. 'You're kidding me.'

'I kid you not,' he said.

'So is that it? She's getting the deputy's job?'

'That's what it sounded like to me. But she has been doing the job for a long time, so...'

'Not on my section she hasn't.' That woman, McColl's bit of skirt, was going to get the badge? Before me!?

'She's only been on the job five minutes,' I protested. 'She's only just worked out which end of the section is which.'

But Mick sounded like he didn't want to get involved. 'I wasn't in the office with them so I can't give you chapter and verse. I'm just telling you what I was told.'

'Well I can,' I said. 'He's shagging her. That's what this is all about.'

Mick said nothing. So I told him, 'I'm not having that. Something's got to be done about this.'

A kick in the mouth, a blade in the back, that's what it was. But why? Why would a figure who you've known all those years do that to you? So that he can keep on nailing a tart's knickers to his bedpost? 'I'm not going to let that go through without a word being said.'

'It's outside my province, lad,' said Mick. 'All I do is give out the coats and run messages for the bosses.'

'Well I'm going to speak to them myself about this.'

'They won't like it if you create a problem for them.'

'What about me?' I said. 'My job is been given away to a tart!'

'They make the decisions, not us. That's how the world is,' he said. 'So be careful you don't create a situation that's going to rebound on you.'

'How,' I said. 'Rebound how?'

'I don't know,' he said. 'I'm just telling you to go careful. That's all.'

I said, 'What's happening to the place Mick? What's happening to it? They'll be handing the *blue coats* out to tarts next.' I said, 'She'll be waggling her arse up and down the track: a blue coat and no knickers!'

I could hear him chuckling.

'I'm not joking,' I told him. Joking? I was in a mood to throttle someone.

Scholar McColl

Captain Redcap looks up. 'Come in. Sit down.'

I have this feeling: heading for a dark tunnel and not able to turn back.

Immediately he begins, 'As I said on the phone John Sanger contacted us about what's been happening over the deputy's job.' His old investigator's eyes study me for clues. 'So it seems as if there are one or two things that need clearing up.'

John Sanger has accused. I am under suspicion. But he is not doing himself any favours by shaking up the worm can. So if he finds them crawling over the finger he has just pointed and on up his arm to the region of his heart he will have himself only to blame.

Cluny wants clarity and neatness? Okay, so I lay before him a very simple sentence. 'Whatever might have happened in the past between myself and Margaret Maynard has no bearing on my decision to recommend her for promotion.' And then when he's had a moment to take that in I go on, 'That is over and in the past. So I have no personal interest here in doing this particular woman any favours. In fact, I'd be quite happy if she was moved to another section, but as she is on my section I would say, without question, she is the best candidate for the deputy's job.'

'Well that's your opinion,' he says doubtfully.

And opinions are something I've never been short of – according to some people. But my eyes are open and my gaze is steady. Look deep into me, I am saying, and you will see beyond 'opinion' to the truth.

But he still wears the old interrogator's face.

Then he sets off, clearly with some intent, down another path. 'Well, the fact is: I've been giving this matter some more thought, wondering whether it might sensible, and be simpler too, to give Sanger the job as he's clearly well capable of doing it.'

My body is doing the talking. His hand rises to make it still. His mouth takes over. 'You see, it is very hard to argue against John

Sanger's suitability. We could make her next in line for when a deputy's job comes up, so that she's ready to take it on when the time comes?'

'No.'

'Well, you're sitting there saying no.'

I'm looking at a displeased man, one who goes on, 'Let me remind you: You are not in a position to say no to me.'

'But that *is* what I am saying to you.' No, I can't accept what he's suggesting. Not now that John Sanger has made his intervention and cast his aspersions. I'm telling the man, 'Margaret Maynard is ready now. As ready as anybody could be. In fact, now we're where we are, I'm surprised she isn't the automatic choice.'

His moustache twitches, his chin confronts me. 'Whatever you say, the decision in this matter will rest with myself and my senior colleagues.'

He goes on jabbing himself in the chest until I reply, 'What you're suggesting might seem simpler but it wouldn't be right.'

'Right?' His face creases up around that thick moustache. Through the creases his eyes peer. And then his special investigator's nose starts to twitch. 'Why?' He's demanding now. He wants the hard point placed on his blotter for inspection. 'Why wouldn't it be right?'

So…here we go.

'John Sanger is very good at his job.' I begin, then pause. But cannot linger for long, sitting there looking thoughtful. 'He'll sort problems out all day long on that section no matter how difficult they are. But for certain reasons I don't think he's the best person for the deputy's job.'

He leans forward, 'Why? Why would John Sanger not be the right choice?'

He's pushing me. And now I've started there is no way back. Here is where we take a long step into that dark tunnel. 'There are aspects of his character, his attitude to some people, that make him…' How to express this? 'That make him not the ideal candidate.'

Cluny leans forward even further. 'Some people? What people?'

So I tell him.

And Harold H Cluny does not like what he's hearing. He's recoiling, staring into what could be a big mess. 'Hang on there!'

He's got his hand up now, his palm is high, it will not be ignored. 'You realize that nowadays this is amounts to a serious allegation.'

This tunnel is long and certainly dark. 'Of course, yeh.'

'And if you're going to start making this sort of allegation you have to deal in facts, real evidence.'

I've visited the law courts of ancient Athens in the company of Socrates. I know very well what the legal nitty-gritty is composed of. I need no introduction to clear thinking from Captain Redcap. 'Okay, I'll give you one example.' I pause to let him see that though I might appear uncomfortable I am in no way deterred by the weight, the density, of the problem we are now looking at. 'John Sanger has lines that he uses habitually about black people.'

Cluny's silence, the look he gives me, tells me he wants them. So I have no choice now but the lay them out very clearly before him. He stares down as if they are indeed there before him on his table. Then looks up and says through a frown, 'He says that sort of thing in this ground?'

'In this ground, yes, and outside probably.'

'And – let me get this clear,' Cluny leans towards me. 'He has said it *to* a black spectator or *about* a spectator?'

'He's half said it to the spectator and then turned to another steward and repeated it in full. But I think, on this occasion, the spectator heard what he said.'

'You witnessed this and what did you do?'

'I waited to see if the lad made a complaint. If he had I would have backed him up and said what I'd heard, like I'm doing now. But nothing ever happened so...'

'You're a deputy, you hold a position of responsibility at this club. Don't you think it was up to you to do something about an incident like that?'

This question I have seen coming from way over on the horizon but I still don't feel ready to deal with it. Cluny detects reluctance. 'Don't you?'

'I wasn't the most senior man present. Archie Blockley was there too. In fact, he was standing beside the one that John Sanger made the remarks to. And he always insisted he should be the one who made decisions.' I'm dodging now, but on the other hand what I'm saying is true. 'But apart from that, by the time we got into the office that day everyone had gone. And it was the last match of the season. So when we came back three months later it had kind of faded into the past.'

'But let me get this clear. You are suggesting that this was not an isolated incident?'

No, there is no way back now. Onwards into the darkness we go. 'Yes. That is exactly what I'm telling you.'

He waits for more, so I begin again. 'It's just part of John Sanger's everyday way of speaking nowadays. It's the way he is, the kind of man he's grown into.'

'He's said these sorts of things to you in the ground?'

'Not to me. He's known me too long. But he's said things to others that I've overheard. And I'll guarantee you now that if you brought all the lads on the section in here one by one and interrogated them, to the point where you got the truth out of them, as to whether they'd had heard John Sanger make those kind of comments about black spectators, players, referees, you'd end up with a long list.'

'Are you suggesting this is widespread? There is a look of what might be horror in the strong man's eyes.

'No. No, I'm not. John Sanger is the only one I've heard it from. Others just seem to accept it: that that's what he's like even if they're not. He's well-liked, generally. Much moreso than I am myself, I suppose. So…'

Solid John Sanger

Mr Cluny said he needed to speak to me in the office again. He wasn't the kind of man to put a lot of bounce into his voice so you couldn't tell whether you were about to be knighted or nailed to a cross. Although it had to be about the promotion, otherwise why would he bother calling me in?

But the face I saw when I walked in wasn't encouraging. It looked like he'd just borrowed it from a corpse. And his voice sounded as if it he'd gone back to his old job as Chief Interrogator.

Then the security man Len Knox came in and sat down. When Cluny turned back to me he said something very strange, he said something I was completely unprepared for, he said, 'If I got all the people who work on your section together and put them in a court of law under oath and then asked them had they ever heard you make remarks that were derogatory of people of certain races inside Goodison Park can you guarantee me that none of them would be able to say that yes, they had?'

What are you supposed to say to a question like that?

Knox sat there saying nothing, but taking everything in, and this look on his face like he's staring into your thoughts.

I was thinking to myself: All of a sudden I'm in the dock here, I'm having to defend myself. I said, 'I never discriminated against anyone in my life.'

The pair of them swapped looks. Then Cluny sat there for a moment deciding on the next line in this interrogation. Then he started throwing questions at me.

He said, 'Have you ever referred to opposition players as monkeys?'

He said, 'Did you once say, 'I'll bring a bunch of bananas for that baboon next time he plays here?'

He said, 'Did you once say in this ground that the referee Uriah Rennie should have been lynched?'

On and on like that, he went. Not even stopping for me to answer.

It was like all of a sudden I was a criminal and the law was coming crashing down on me like a big brick wall. And how should a man be judged – by what he does when the heat was on, or by something that comes out of his mouth? Words? What are they? You see these characters on the box mouthing it, spieling, they go on all day, gab-gab-gab, bamboozling people with their sentences, their fancy words. But me? By their acts ye shall know them – that's my motto. And always has been.

Cluny said, 'Would you ever use words like spade, coon, black bastard in routine conversation with other men? Have you ever used those terms in this ground?'

Enough. I said, 'Why? Why are you asking me this?'

He said, 'Because certain allegations have been made, John. And a response is required.'

Response, I could feel a response surging up inside me. That sly bastard, that rat, McColl had sold me down the river for a piece of stale crumpet.

And still Knox sat there saying nothing – him who usually can't keep his mouth shut – sitting there like Jimmy the Joiner had carved him out of an old railway sleeper, like he was a piece of broken totem pole, one of those idols you see when the television goes primitive.

Cluny said, 'I have in my possession a list of the names of others employed by this club on matchdays. I can interview these people in connection with this matter. I will have to interview them if I'm obliged to pursue this matter. I will have to caution them that if it is discovered that they have attempted to cover up the truth in order to protect another club employee that they will face immediate dismissal. You understand?'

I didn't say anything.

So then he asked, 'Do you wish me, in order to clear up this matter, to start interviewing other people - '

'Okay,' I said, 'Okay. Let the woman have the job. I'll accept that. And then just let the whole thing blow over. It's not worth the aggravation.'

I was all set to walk away and leave it at that. But he looked at me as if I'd handed him a form in a foreign language. He shook his head slowly. He said, 'It's gone way beyond that now, John.'

He said, 'I'm sorry it's come to this, John, I really am. But do you wish me, in order to clear up this matter, to start interviewing other people or would you wish to resign your position here before it goes that far?'

What? I felt like picking the table up and hurling it across the room. He said he had no choice. He said the accusation had been made and that it couldn't be ignored. He said, 'Everton Football Club cannot employ anybody about whom there is even the slightest doubt. We cannot, absolutely cannot, tolerate club employees using inappropriate language in this ground even in private conversations.'

'So that's it, I'm finished?'

'I have to act,' he said.

I said, 'There isn't a man in this stadium on matchdays that has worked for this club as conscientiously as I have.'

'That could well be true John, however - '

'However go and give that deputy's job to tart if you want. But that's what she is.'

'That is not the impression Margaret Maynard gives, John.'

There are times when even the calmest of men can't help losing his rag. 'They don't call her Maggie May for nothing. She's got tart written all over her. In bright red lipstick!'

He said, 'I don't think slurs of that nature will get us very far John, so - '

'So, okay,' I said, 'Here you are. See how far you get with this.' So I told him. I gave Scholar McColl a set of references that Satan could have put together for him. I said, 'Now you can work out what Everton Football Club is going to do about him.'

Then I walked out without another word.

I set off looking for him. I was ready to break every bone in his body, I was, I was in a mood to kill him. Really. I was ready to spend the next twenty years in a prison cell for what he'd done to me.

But then I stopped.

I heard my lad's voice calling to me in my head, a lad with a difficult life who needs all the help he can get. And then I heard Mary's voice and the other lad calling to me. Yes, people needed me, they needed me to be around, they depended on me.

Did I have the right to throw away the help and love I have to give to those closest to me, to trade it for the pleasure of stamping on a rat?

No. It wasn't worth it. He wasn't worth it.

And anyway Justice and Retribution were on his trail; the poison he'd concocted was in the tray, and soon, very soon, the rat would be forced to eat it.

Yes, I had a lad to think of. I had two lads to think of. Those lads were the future, even if one was going into it in a wheelchair. I owed it to him to be there. I owed it to them to be there. I owed it to Mary to be there.

I had to take the long walk home and calm myself down.

When I arrived back I saw bits of worry lurking in Mary's face. It was five hours since I went out saying I wouldn't be long. She put her hand on my back and her cheek on my shoulder. A man needs a good woman in times like these. Some people turn out to be rats who'd bite you in your sleep but others are the strong ones you can lean on.

We've aged together, myself and Mary, lost our youth together, worn our first age-lines together. And she's a good woman and an honest one, dependable and strong. And this was such a dark, dark day. I felt as if the darkness was clinging to me. I felt like I was carrying it around with me.

I'm not a lying man. Never. But it seems there are times when the truth is best buried. So I said, as if the words were saying themselves, I said, 'I'm finished down there at Goodison.' I said, 'I'd rather pay to watch the game from now on,' and saw her waiting for more explanation. But I couldn't bring myself to speak the true words and looked instead for a way out, wanted to run even from her who was my rock, because the truth can be cruel, the truth can be merciless. 'Yeh, I'm finished down there. I've thrown the jacket in.'

'You decided to leave?'

How could I refuse the opportunity she'd offered me? She had opened a door through which I could escape from a place of torture and torment.

'I told them,' I said, 'that they had the right to promote who they wanted but by the same token I had the right not to go on working under circumstances I didn't approve of.'

'Good,' she says, filling up with admiration, the most wounding kind of admiration you could be called on to endure.

Scholar McColl

Cluny calls me in again. There's a matter we need to discuss. But he won't say what it is. As soon as I arrive I can see that he's found a cockroach in the kitchen, a big one. He looks like he's spent a couple of nights in the Sleep Deprivation Unit. When Len Knox shows up and sits down without speaking Cluny fixes me clearly in his sights and then begins. 'Some rather serious allegations have been made about you.'

Yes, of course: Solid John Sanger.

Cluny shifts in his seat, takes a deep breath, 'My attention has been drawn to certain aspects of your past.'

I can hear the rest before he says it.

But that is so long ago. The lad who was involved in all that nonsense might be another person, might never in fact have been real, he might have been imagined.

Grimly Cluny states, 'John Sanger told us things that have made matters very difficult for us here and, I have to say, impossible for you. He has told me many things but most damaging is a headline in the Echo from years ago, a headline that read one Monday after you'd spent the weekend in police cells in Birmingham: *Everton hooligan fined for affray.*'

Nothing I can argue with there. Apart from the hooligan tag. As if having a quite normal urge to survive, or at least go down fighting, after you've been surrounded by a bunch of morons is a criminal offence. But like they say: Tell that to the magistrates. I did, actually. And it did me about as much good as I'd expected.

'But the really damaging thing,' Harry Cluny sighs, 'is a photograph also issued a number of years ago by the police down in London seeking information on people involved in serious violence close to West Ham's ground. One of those pictures, John Sanger claims, although you were never formally identified by anyone at the time, was of you. He says there are people you've fallen out with since then who would now be willing to identify you as the person in the photograph aiming a high kick at a West Ham hooligan.'

And a very effective kick it was too. Decked that brute who'd just kicked a lad in the head, and gave him plenty to think about over the next couple of days as the footprint on his jaw faded. But there are loads of fellas around the city, both red and blue, and in other cities too, most likely, who'll tell you exactly the same thing: *West Ham, we had some battles down there over the years.* You got so's you expected it. Back in the day, you did. And at West Ham it usually happened. And why the Metropolitan Police decided to make such a big deal of this incident I don't know. But they did. And there was my picture – the lad I used to be – but nobody coming forward to point the finger.

Cluny now wishes to explain, 'I'm not an unreasonable man. I'm not a man who believes that another man should be burdened with his past for the rest of his life. But in this case I have to do what I'm doing. I have to put an end to this matter now before it becomes damaging.'

And what can I say now that will change anything? I could try explaining to him what it's like to be in another city and to find yourself surrounded by a bunch of goons keen to decorate their pavements with the patterning of your blood; what it's like to be cornered, ambushed, hunted down; what it's like to see some desperado pull a knife, or hurl a half-brick in your direction; what it's like in those moments to have only your fists and your feet to defend yourself.

I could attempt other lines of reason also, for I am not incapable of thinking around the parameters as well as the very nub of an issue. But Harry H Cluny, as he has pointed out, has his responsibilities to consider, and John Sanger will not give up on this now, not until he has dragged me down with him. He has a grip on my ankle and is pulling with all his muscle. It seems that I must fall. So why bother trying to hang on?

Nevertheless I must tell this man who is dismissing me, and his unusually silent colleague, 'I've worked hard for this club over the years. I've taken flak for this club, I've sorted out its balls-ups – irate spectators fuming about being sold tickets for seats that don't exist, and…'

But what's the point in going on down that line? Cluny looks at me like the hanging judge who's allowing the doomed man a few words before the sentence comes down with a cold shock on his neck. Yeh, the game is up so what's the point in me sitting here making a big speech to him? It's exit time. It's time to walk.

But when I'm up on my feet and about to turn away he says, 'Just for the record, just so you know. This decision was made above our heads. In this case I'm only the messenger. And if the only problem had been the conviction and the fine I would have been prepared to argue your case. In twenty years a man changes. I've seen that many times. But that photograph makes it impossible for me to make a case for you. Even though it's a long time ago, technically you could still be prosecuted, and if somebody came forward and identified you now maybe the Met would make an example of you. This club couldn't take a chance on that: one of our most senior stewards, who already has a conviction, is up in court on a charge of violent disorder. I'm sorry, but no…'

No. So I'm walking. Like a long way through an empty space.

What will I do now? What else in my life has been as solid as EFC? What other bond can compare? Everton has been my rock and my refuge. But I am rejected now by the thing I love, cast adrift, thrown aside, like a bag of trash tossed over the side of a ship.

My old fella's ghost appears. Wearing a red scarf. And saying, ' I always knew that club would break your heart.'

I try to blink him away but the stubborn old buzzard won't be blanked so easily. He begins to sing You'll never walk alone…

No. Not this. I must get a grip on myself – *do* something.

My stack of discs draws me away. I need the old solo acts – some lone figure with only strings for support. How long is it since I tried to write a song? Did I ever have so much feeling to squeeze into a three minute lyric?

I pick up my steel string guitar and strum. This is not the moment to go classical. I need a rhythm that will carry my lines. Suddenly I walk alone and I need to get some words out as much as an old Delta Bluesman ever did. I'm hitting E chords. I'm doing twangy hammer-ons. And beginning to hear the words.

The city goes to sleep. My heart is a big as the night. I scribble and strum and scribble again until the dawn gives birth to a song. If everyone has a song or two in them then this is mine, even if the walls and the furniture is all the audience it will ever have.

I walk alone
I am away now through the door
I who have walked this path before
A rolling stone
I walk alone

I've had my fill
That song is sentimental crap
I heard them sing it on the Kop
We lost five-nil
I had my fill

I sing the Blues
I know the lyrics for the beat
For I have stared straight at defeat
But I won't lose
I sing the Blues

I walk alone
That song's an anthem made of kitsch
Life can be such an evil bitch
I'm on my own
I walk alone

I walk the shore
I hear the curlew's plaintive song
As darkness falls both deep and long
Been here before
I walk the shore

Don't cry for me
No not for me you dirty old town
I'll be back up like now I'm down
No damned pity
Don't cry for me

These boots must walk
Must tread the high and windy bank
Where ships of dream capsized and sank
These heels will talk
These boots must walk

I walk alone
I am the loner in the street
They say my ego's in my feet
I'm on my own
I walk alone
Don't cry for me
No damned pity
I'll sing the Blues
But I won't lose
I'll walk alone
I'm on my own
I'll walk alone

I've gained a song and lost most of the morning. But that song lifts me only briefly. I have lost the yellow jacket and the blue coat both and entered a vacuum.

Maggie May

The bathroom is getting its regular once-over. I'm Mrs Mop on a mission. Any germ that sticks its head above the parapet gets it.

Half the house smells like a pine wood, the rest like a lemon grove. Beyond the thick pimply glass people are vague shapes passing down the street.

The phone begins to buzz. My rubber gloves are cast-offs. My feet drum down the stairs. Sarah? Him? No, why would he? Who, then?

It's the personnel man. Can I come down to the ground as soon as possible for a meeting? No clue as to what it's about. His tone gives nothing away. Mr Neutral. The non-committal man.

I find him sitting behind his desk with a face on him like an undertaker who's just found out that a potion for everlasting life is about to go on the market. He talks briefly about recent events like a doctor delivering very bad news: names from a list of terminal cases. Mark McColl and John Sanger have left, are no longer employed by the club.

No? Why? I can't believe that. Why would they both do that?

'That's not something we need to go into here.'

But he hasn't called me in because he's got no one else to talk to. What is the point in my being here?

We seem to be arriving at that very point. He plans to transfer Jimmy Meagan to Section Six to be the boss and…and…and… after talking to him and weighing everything up he has decided to invite me to become the new deputy.

Me? I got the job. I got the deputy's badge.

'Well, yes of course,' I say, 'If you think…'

I am the new second-in-command. I got the job and I should be flying, fluttering around like a butterfly. But what has happened here? Why have the two of them gone? And so sudden? Mick the Coatman might know.

He does. He says I must take a vow of secrecy before he will reveal details. And then he tells me.

Scholar McColl did it for me? He sacrificed himself for me?

And yet he is gone: gone from me, gone from the club.

Last time the Blues went up to Newcastle he was at my side but tomorrow when the match kicks off where will he be?

How quickly it all changes.

Part Nine

28

Plundering the Magpies' Nest

Kick off time up in the northeast, and a bad day for Everton Football Club is foreseen by many who enjoy a gloomy prediction. So Maggie May is a bundle of knotted sinews sitting there on her couch staring at the radio. Can the Blues snatch some vital points from the Magpies' nest? Can they possibly do it up there where so recently they tumbled and sank so miserably?

She has a sharp thought to help loosen a knot or two: since that wretched show in the rain a new man has appeared; and he's already shown up as a big actor in this new version of an old drama.

And that man again has the answer for her.

In less than a minute he slots the ball through the gap between goalkeeper and ground. A goal: a word written in bold, a scorer whose name is already being written in gold lettering in the Annals of EFC.

And Maggie May has leapt from her cushions, and now that her limbs have broken loose she can't keep still. She's walking from window to couch to door to window…

Can Everton hang on to that lead? What if they don't? A one-goal lead – eighty nine minutes is a long, long time to hang on to something so slippery.

But she's trying to stay calm and to make sense of a game she cannot see, tilting her ear to the radio voices as if in so doing she might gain a clearer picture. And it does *sound* as if the men in Blue shirts are bossing the midfield, snatching the ball back whenever they're careless enough to lose it. And with that man in the team, so strong and athletic and once again making life difficult for opposition defenders, maybe…

In a garden off Queen's Drive, by the Fiveways, Mark McColl

continues with his weekday business. It isn't usual for him to work on a Saturday afternoon but these are strange times. And having to think about other people's quiet green spaces does release him from the tribulations of the world of the leather ball. But ten minutes after kick-off time he cannot resist a glance into that troubled sphere. Out in his van the radio announces the score – might have sung it with a silvery tongue. Winning! The Blues are winning. He returns to work with a clap in his hands and a bounce in his heels, a glow in his chest. How the frost of apprehension that will form around the human heart might be melted away by that blazing ball of the sun – bouncing suddenly out of the clouds – or some other round object that possesses the power to raise the temperature quite suddenly.

The knots of tension might be a little looser now but even so, there must be other ways to enjoy yourself – the thought almost makes her smile at herself. Then the phone calls to her. She considers ignoring it, then grabs it. It's Sarah. 'I'm listening to an important match,' Maggie tells her, one ear still on the radio and hearing that a penalty has been awarded to Newcastle. 'I'll call you back at half time.'

She drops the phone as the goalie parries the ball. Saved! She claps her hands into the form of one who prays. They've missed a penalty, so it's not their day, so it must be ours, our day. Could it be? Could this, against all expectations and predictions, against all odds that anyone came up with, be our day? Could all the pundits and prophets of our inevitable doom be wrong?

Could they?

Drawn once more back out to the van, the radio voice delights McColl. It's half time. It's two-nil!

A second goal for... It's as if he knew before he heard the name: Campbell. Again. The Newcastle goalkeeper fumbled Campbell's shot and watched it trickle into the net.

McColl might have been told a joke. First the fumble then the trickle – you have to smile at the thought of it. He's lingering a moment to savour such unexpected delight. He's watching the pictures through the suburban trees, seeing the ball trickle. Trickle. How entertaining! And what relief such clowning can bring. As if he's stepped out of the Theatre of Tragedy into the Comedy House. The Newcastle goalie fumbles. *Fumbles?* He'd never realized what a great little word that is. He could laugh out loud. May all the opposition goalies *fumble* for evermore!

But when the slapstick elation subsides he sees something other, sees a far more powerful image, sees something grand, a figure from some epic perhaps: he sees the big ebony man as saviour. Two goals for Kevin Campbell: two killer goals, surely, from the Dark Deliverer. Two more to add to the pair he got against Coventry. Four goals in three games! The man was called for, prayed for – a real centre forward, a big muscular striker who can shake up the opposition and stick the ball in the net. And this man has heard the call, and he has come, and he has delivered. And maybe, maybe, the Blues are saved.

'Am bored,' Sarah is telling Maggie down the line. 'Been out to lunch and had a few glasses. Now am bored.'

'Well I'm all excited. Everton have found this player in Turkey - '

'Turkey? Remember that fella I met out there. He was a proper sex god. I was in heaven, until we fell off the bed that time!'

'Well the one I'm talking about is more of a warrior chief, a leader out on the pitch.'

'Oh Maggie! You and your football! Here's a question for you. How many orgasms would you swap for your team to be able to win a game? I wouldn't swap one even if I was a supporter.'

'But you're not interested. So how would you know?'

'I mean, obviously it would depend how good the sex was. And we all know how different that can be. We were just talking about this over lunch. On the one hand you've got the multiple with fireworks and illuminations and more special effects than the Auraura Borrealis, and then you've got the one that's like a slap on the belly with a wet fucking kipper!'

'How many glasses have you had?'

'Enough. Enough to know I wouldn't swap one good shag for ten goals.'

'Well goals are what I'm interested in right now Sarah. And the teams are kicking off again, so...'

So the Blues, it seems, are now riding their luck. And the goalscorer – Twice!! –the hero in this hour of most desperate need, is hobbling. He has done all he can today. But he has surely done a very great deal for Everton Football Club.

Maggie pictures him, the wounded hero, limping towards the touchline. Oh how she would comfort him given half the chance – all her nursey charms. And in the lull of substitution her mind strays down the path along which Sarah was trying to lead it. Orgasms? She can think of one or two intimate experiences she'd swap – as if you'd get anything worth having in exchange. Some of the Romeos she's ended up with over the years: like the foul-tacklers of sex – jumping in three-legged. You're looking for the referee to send them for an early bath.

Mark McColl, crossing the garden he works on, turns as the woman he is working for appears in the doorway. 'There's a cup of tea here if you'd like to come in.'

They usually bring it out, but he'll be glad to sit down

She seems a bubbly woman with a swingy sort of walk, one of those middle aged ones who retain some of the prettiness and liveliness of girlhood. She's well set up in a substantial house in the leafy zone but there's maybe something missing, a bit like that other one up in the far North End who he did some work for, whose name he now forgets. Natasha something.

As he tastes the tea she comes up with another offer. 'Would you like a piece of cake. It's rather nice.'

Why not? Cake and chat. A break from bending his back to the earth.

Sweetness in his throat, the sugar and the fruit, as her words, her many words, drift around his ears. '… and my husband is away again with his work. He's always away. Sometimes I wonder whether he does it just to get away from me…'

Her cake is pleasant enough: neither too sweet nor too bland. And she herself is perhaps not without a little spice. Sweeping away a crumb she becomes inquisitive. 'Are you married then?'

That old female question. A piece of cake for every time he'd been asked that and he'd be a fat man making extra holes in his belt.

'No, no I'm not.'

She has just had a thought. Her eyes are on holiday. Or maybe at the supermarket. 'Would you like some more cake?'

Is there more to this offer? Or is he a fool? Vain and horny. Either way, he has travelled that territory before.

Here is her voice in a strong flow: '…I work three days a week now. My mother left me some money and took away all the pressure. I worked very hard at my job but I never seemed to get anywhere even though I had all the qualifications and experience. So what was the point? What was the point in going on for ever up a dead end? So I thought I might as well dedicate my time to enjoying myself…'

When she thinks of enjoyment what does she see? Might he be part of that picture? It can be so hard to be sure.

But if the offer was there? Would he? Linger in her bountiful garden, reaping the unexpected harvest? Pleasure beckoning with a fruitcake in one hand and a teapot in the other. Illicit home comforts. Clandestine domestic bliss. Going secretly to bed. That certain frisson. That extra thrill.

Two snags. First: he could be watching the wrong film. And even if he's not, would he really want a part in it? He's been there before – routine concealed in the fancy wrappings of disloyalty. He has unwrapped it before, that nonsense, and cast it aside. 'Thanks for the cake,' he says. 'I'd better get on and finish off out there.'

And check on the score.

The goalscorer is gone, will his two goals be enough? Maggie walks to the window then back to the door, turns, stands staring at the little black box, with its long black worm that crawls up to the plug, willing it to cough up another goal: a third goal which would surely be the beautifully pattered paper in which the three points might be wrapped up.

No. Something very different.

Another penalty given away.

She is holding herself together as if her bones might fall apart. She is praying, like the girl who once went to church, for another save. Please.

No.

She should have known better. The spot-kick is struck both hard and true this time, while our goalie seems intent on hurling himself as far away from the ball as possible. He catches only handfuls of air. And our lead has been sliced in half.

So now the onslaught?

No.

Instead: the retort, the sharp and very direct strike that volleys away all doubt and sends an arrow into the throat of the cackling doomster that has stalked us.

She falls like a tossed cushion on to the couch. But the knowledge of three points soon plumps her up. Maggie, growing ever lighter, is floating now, floating on radio waves, drifting, coming to rest in a land of blue silk, a place from which to look down on the zone of relegation.

McColl listens to the pundit picking over the bones of the game as he puts his tools away. And how he silently mocks the doomsters. Two weeks ago we were down so low and so many were saying we were out, gone, finished in the high zone. But we were only on the edge, and now we have scrambled back and up. We were clinging on while those who bear us ill-will were queuing up to stamp on our hands – but, five points clear now we are close, so close: one more win and we will be sitting on the safety ledge watching others slip away. We would not let go, we would not fall into the darkness, down there with the dead men, into which some would have delighted to see us disappear.

He slams the van door shut as if in their faces.

But there are other complications for him to consider. Will he go to the funeral? Should he go and face what will have to be faced if he is to pay his respects to the Blocker Man? Might there be trouble if he shows up?

But why should he hide? And, anyway, if there is any bother it won't be him who causes it.

29

The Send-Off

Security signs make the old Smithdown cemetery chapel look embattled. But there's a freshness about the afternoon. It's one of those breezy days, bright clouds on the move, gulls balancing briefly, wobbling on unpredictable currents. A decent enough day for a man to be laid to rest. Who wants to fade into drizzle or to go wrapped in a grey blanket?

A small brass band is there to see Old Archie off. Those heavy, slightly grumpy sounds that suit him so well. The brassmen stand inside the gates pumping and fingering as two fine dark horses with black plumes pass through pulling the carriage in which lies the coffin draped with a blue flag; on top of that is an old iron rivet set and a pair of work-worn hammers. The long black limo bearing the family comes slowly behind. Before the chapel a crowd stands waiting: the common people, the Blocker Man's folk.

The horses stand easy now, like actors between scenes, as four bulky men hoist the coffin on to their shoulders and move into a place of stone and almost silence. The slow feet shuffle and scrape among the pews, among the sniffles and coughs of bereavement. And then as he waits to take his place a puzzled face from Goodison is looking into Mark McColl's and asking quietly, 'Worr appened?'

So McColl tells the tale in short and simple lines – and is faced with a look of profound incomprehension.

But he does not speak on in the hope that he might be better understood. The facts are there as he has given them, others can make of them what they will – as indeed they are already doing, have already done.

John Sanger takes his place, calmly it seems, but shows surprise when informed that Mark McColl has turned up. Although he doesn't turn his head when the pair of Goodison men who stand with him do turn to look at the one who was so briefly Archie Block's replacement as Boss Steward of Section Six.

A hand is laid on McColl's shoulder. Given two light pats, he turns and nods to this one who seeks no explanations, who knows and understands, and who must give passing acknowledgment. And then, moving into his place, McColl stands alone, fends off a glance and then a stare from familiar faces, before he focuses his eyes on the coffin and ignores whatever looks might come his way.

He has offended: he senses that. In the eyes of some he has. He has failed to conform to that manly code which says you must never incriminate another, you must not reveal to Authority what it does not already know. He has broken the rule which says you must not, under any circumstances, *tell*. And he has, some would say, received his just rewards.

Up there in front he sees a lot of family: wrinkly women, muscly lads; a sturdy people, their heads bowed, in dutiful black. Behind him the Goodison men are scattered among the old shipbuilders and Archie Block's ageing Dingle cronies. And Maggie May, she also is there at the back of the assembly, aware perhaps of eyes shifting her way also.

The priest begins, goes through the usual routine: how the lost one was a much-valued husband, father, brother... Unpractised voices sing hymns with gusto as if worried the man himself is watching to see who isn't giving everything to his big occasion.

Archie Block's old mate George says a few brief words and then another old man from the shipyard speaks. He's a chunky survivor stuffed with industrial phrases, with the Blocker Man's sentiments about the ships of days past.

As if more than one mere man is passing away, he reads something out: *And they shall walk the way that multitudes have walked before them and their like will be seen never again...*

When all has been said, when the last note fades, the four bulky men step forward, hoist the polished box up once more and carry it slowly out. They bear Arthur Joshua Blockley to the graveside: a deep hole, neatly dug, the displaced earth in neat piles and covered with green matting. The black coats shuffle into position around the edge.

The polished box is hoisted on new ropes and lowered. The pale rope slips through the big palms. Archie Block is on his way, descending, going slowly back to the earth.

The final words. Ashes and dust.

Mark McColl takes his turn in the waiting line and drops a small handful of earth, the local clay, his last goodbye to a cantankerous old boss who was nevertheless a stout old boy who was royal blue through to the bone. The soil makes a dry sprinkly sound as it hits wood.

Done. All done now. The Blocker Man has entered the long house, is gone to the land of his fathers. The gravediggers will finish off when the mourners have departed.

Out on one edge a blackbird sings. Up above gulls turn, silent, tilting on the currents of the high air. And from behind white clouds, as those bright rags of vapour are drawn away, flung away and sent drifting westwards to the river, the sun shows up, spreads brightness where the common people of this old city, they who have gathered to see the old shipyard man off, begin to walk away into the future he left behind.

Mark McColl steps away from the graveside aware perhaps of more glances in his direction, more stares, and his movement suggests one unsure what to do now that the formal part is over. Before he can make his mind up one man who he used to supervise on Section Six has stepped into his path; and this one can't restrain a hissed, 'Why couldn't ya just keep yer mouth shut for a change?'

This? On such a day? Those still lamenting, feeling the loss, all around you.

'This is neither the day nor the place,' he replies. But will explain himself in one very simple, very clear line before he turns away.

He steps past a tearful woman, veers around a tight bunch of mourners, and then, sidestepping an ageing couple, finds himself facing John Sanger. They stand before each other, all the years between them, from the young teammates of so many years back and on to now. All of that.

'Why?' John Sanger demands. And then again: 'Why?'

McColl is impelled to sigh before telling the other man, 'You wouldn't understand, John. You really wouldn't. You haven't got the equipment to be able to do that.'

The solid man, the provoked man, glares; that face shaping down into a hate mask out of which a hiss and a grunt might have been the words, 'Shithouse rat!'

This? More of it. At a funeral? McColl, in that scornful way he's had since he was a lad, blanks the other man. But Sanger knows that look, has seen it turned on others so many times, and he is a substantial man and not one to be treated with disdain. Overflowing now with his own contempt, he follows.

By the time they're through the trees and beyond the other mourners McColl has heard enough. He stops and turns and as he does so feels John Sanger's huge fist smash into the bone above his eye and glance across the side of his nose. The bloody nose: he's got another; a reminder of those times way back down the years when he returned home stained with his own blood. But if he took blows on the snout back then he sent his own knuckle in the direction of one or two big gobs in return. And even, when necessary, turned stallion.

Knocked backwards, and ducking from another blow, he swivels to his left and then launches himself forwards. If one has the size, the bulk, the power, the other still has the speed, the lithe athleticism of one who earns his coin shifting earth, stone, resistant rootwood. Leading with a swift high-raised right foot he lands a fierce kick – a kind of flying stamp – bang in the centre of the other man's chest. Sanger, sporting an earthy footprint, a heelprint over his heart, is rocked backwards, almost falling over a gravestone. And before any further blows can be attempted the intervention is under way. Mick Molloy, Goodison's custodian of blue coats and yellow jackets, and two of his helpers are taking a grip of the solid man. 'This is not the place, John. You wouldn't want to go away feeling you've let yourself down!' Mick the Jacketman whispers, leaning close.

Letting yourself down: those words so sharp, jabbing at your heart, puncturing that great swelling of anger, letting out a huge sigh. And Solid John Sanger appears to slump a little where he stands.

So the jacketmen usher him away down the path.

Others, peering round the trees, stand there staring, muttering. A line of blood runs down the side of McColl's face. A scarlet drop falls from his nose on to the blackness of his tie, another to the whiteness of his shirt. He touches his fingertip to his nose and studies the blood on it as if he's never seen the stuff before. He looks up and for a moment stares back at the staring faces, then turns away, walks a few steps, touches his bloody nose again and then stops to flick away the blood on his fingers. And then, as he's about to move off, hears the hurried scrape of heels, a voice behind him. He turns back. Maggie Maynard is saying, 'Have you got anything for that?'

'Don't carry hankies.'

'Here,' she is reaching into her bag.

He takes a tastefully pattered and perfumed piece of cotton and holds it to his nose. That familiar scent is like another blow smashing into his consciousness.

'Oh, dear.' The exasperated woman surveys him. 'You've got blood everywhere.'

As if he didn't know that.

'Don't blame me,' he tells her while throwing up his bloodied free hand and lifting his foot to show the splashes on his shoe.

'My job is to tend the wounded,' she states rather formally, 'not allocate blame.' And then she pulls another hankie from her bag and, stepping closer, but still keeping a certain distance, she touches it to the cut above his eye. Withdrawing it, she peers at the wound, dabs again, tells him, 'You're going to need something on that.' After two quick dabs, and then another look, she goes on, 'I doubt that it needs a stitch but it will need something on it to help it close up.' She allows him a moment to consider that, and then dabbing once more, says, 'I've got a little patch for it at my place. Save you going to the hospital.' She shifts her gaze from the cut to his eyes, 'If you want?'

He looks, as if for a clue to the appropriate response, at the blood on his hand. He shrugs – the disorientated, wounded man – he nods.

'I'm in my car.'

They move away, walking in step, side by side, 'People might be watching,' he tells her.

'Does that matter?'

'It might.'

'Why?'

He doesn't answer. She puzzles over the silence for a moment and then leaves it at that.

As she drives them away she asks, 'Does it hurt much?'

'I've survived worse.'

'You'll have to explain that some time.'

'Maybe.'

The silence that follows doesn't last long, she breaks it with a thought that appears amuse her, just a little, 'At least it didn't happen during the service.'

'Two of the mourners rolling around and falling into the grave – a fine sight that would have been!'

She shows him a small smile. But then her face straightens, 'But it was a shock to see John Sanger acting like that. Even after what has happened.'

'It was certainly a shock to my nose,' he says with a wry bloodied smile. 'But I expect it will come a shock to himself once he calms down and realizes.'

Back at her place she plays the nurse beautifully – she cleans his wounds, positions a small butterfly patch above his eye, brings him tea and sympathy, football chat. She says, 'Sit here as long as you like. Until the shock of it all has passed.'

He seems set to do exactly that. So she studies him as he sits there. 'That was a wild kick you took at John Sanger back there, where did you learn that?'

'Oh,' he says vaguely, 'somewhere along the road.'

But not a place he is about to revisit for her just at this moment.

'I can guess the answer, but I'll ask anyway: Will you be wanting to go back and join some of the others?'

'You guessed the answer.'

'You think it's best to steer clear?'

'Wouldn't want to ruin it for everyone.'

'Or sustain any more damage?'

'Maybe that, too. But I knew all along that some wouldn't see it from my point of view. I knew that a lot of people would, but that for sure there'd be those who wouldn't.'

Resisting any inclination to request explanation she suggests, 'It's gone five now. I could think about cooking something – if you have no other plans.'

'Plans?' He even manages a chuckle.

'We could have a quiet and peaceful little wake of our own.'

'Quiet and peaceful sounds good.'

She cooks, they listen to sounds, drink wine, and, though they skirt around some large issues, the shortening distance between them closes even further.

But there are questions that must be asked. 'Are you going to the match tomorrow?'

He doesn't know, he says.

'You haven't got a ticket?'

'I heard it was sold out. Maybe that's a sign: that's the end of watching football for me.'

'Is that possible?'

'Maybe Frank Brigstoke's right: football is a drug, a narcotic for the masses, a slave industry for the wage-slaves, oh and either plaything or a money-spinner for the billionaires.'

'You don't really believe that.'

'Whether I do or whether I don't it's still the greatest game human beings have managed to think up. People all over the world can't be wrong.'

'So?'

'So I'll see how I feel about it all tomorrow. But I'll probably end up going down to the ground to see if there's a ticket on sale outside.'

She settles a very serious look on him, says, 'You lost your job because of me. And because of other things, but - '

'I didn't intend to lose it. Self-sacrifice isn't really my style. I expected to have that job till I dropped dead like Archie Block.'

'Even so, you did it.'

'I did, but you owe me nothing. Nobody owes me anything, and I owe nothing to anybody.'

'You are a strange one.'

'I'll take my strangeness away.'

'You don't have to.'

He looks at her. What is she really saying there? Reading his question she gives the answer, 'You could stay the night if you want.'

He doesn't seem so very surprised. However: 'Word gets around. People would talk.'

'Let them talk.'

'They'd say they were right all along: that I only said what I said to get you the job. And that's not true. And I don't want people saying it. I want the reason why I did it to be clear. So that I didn't lose that job for nothing.'

'Well, if anyone says anything while I'm around I'll make sure they know what they're talking about. But maybe there's a limit to how important that coat is, even if it has caused all this trouble. I'd rather give it up,' she says, 'than have it interfere with the rest of my life.'

'No. No, you can't do that, not now.'

'Then why don't we do what *we* want now, and then see what happens and deal with it when the time comes. And what's happening now is that I'm going to open another bottle of wine – because it is a sort of special day. Red or white?'

After he's considered that one he tells her, 'I'll go with your choice.'

'My choice? Oh I know what that is,' she says, fixing him with the big bright eyes of a connoisseur as she rises.

Part Ten

30

A Second Song from the Scholar

Scholar McColl

You cannot linger in the wilderness, alone in the stony places. You cannot do that. I sit alone yet am being drawn back – in different ways. I am hearing Z Cars in my head. I am hearing that and a scrap from some old hymn that remains from school assemblies.

I am feeling a surge of words in my head while Z Cars plays on. I'm grabbing my steel string and strumming the Johnny Todd chords. I am hitting the G and then the C. And then there's a D chord at the end of the second line. And then the words start to come, almost as if they're being dictated to me and all I have to do is write them down –

We'll Support You Evermore

Far and wide, or by the river
Where the royal blue waters flow
Side by side and blue forever
Where the Blues play we will go
We'll be there to let them know
Everton, Everton
We'll support you evermore
We'll support you evermore

We'll be there, like those before us
Who had blue blood in their veins.
For the lads who wear the jersey
We'll be there through sun and rain
We will sing it once again
Everton, Everton
We'll support you evermore
We'll support you evermore

Part Eleven

31

A New Coat for the Lady

She goes about her new duties as she did the old, ever willing, quietly assured; a slightly brisker stride perhaps asserting her right to wear the deputy's coat before those who might question.

Eyes of puzzlement do follow her – there are those who do not know the story. The tale seems to have been told in hushed tones only, so far; like a secret that must be kept by the few – but probably won't be.

For today there are other concerns: those three points that, like three rungs on a ladder, could take us to a height from which we will not be dragged down.

And out on the pitch Hutch, that crafty schemer, is probing for a gap in the opposition defence. Thin and tall, he lopes forwards, and finds it, finds that gap to set off a blue and white explosion, a swirling of hands and arms, a fragmenting of joyful words.

And if one is not enough the Chief looks the most likely now to add to it. Naturally. The opposition can't keep a grip on him. They're grasping at air, but he's away leaving them stumbling and tumbling. The ball bounces back off one of them – so what does he do, this man born to score goals, born to don the royal blue shirt and score the vital goals? He sticks that ball in the net. Like a postman slotting a letter.

Now the celebrations of survival can really begin.

And he, the one who heard the call and answered, answered most emphatically, gives the nod to that by glancing in another. His bearing is that of a king claiming his new kingdom, but his huge smile is that of a bright boy who hardly realizes his power, by his mere presence, to bring light and joy to the lives of others.

And then the real boy, Franny Jeffers, his willing assistant, nicks one like a lad swiping an apple from a market stall. He now raises his hands to the upstanding crowd, and the scoreboard illuminates our goal tally: we have four in the bank, our credit is good, our future is assured.

A woman wipes tears from her eyes. Today we can weep without pain. We are the scrappers who survived. We are the tightrope walkers that made it across. We are the dancers in the country of blue clapping the rhythm as the chant bursts out, as the celebratory words are released, flung out high into the air to rise like birds on the wing: Staying up - staying up - staying up!

Maggie May

It's a high time now alright for all those who were so recently down in the lower depths. And this might be the joy of people finally set free to celebrate that I'm witnessing all around me but the eyes of one man in a yellow jacket seem to accuse. Others seem indifferent or puzzled, some have sought explanation and got it, but this one man – do I imagine that? In time I will see more clearly. And continue to ignore it, if I have to. But would rather not have to. And who else, I wonder, in this stadium, might have the bad eye on me? Is there a familiar bearded face somewhere in this huge crowd? Does John Sanger, sitting in his own jacket in the middle of the punters, regard me from somewhere with the evil eye? Might he come to haunt me with that stare? Or try to. I'd like to think he didn't hate me, that after sitting quietly with some calm thoughts he has realized; that he understands now and accepts why things are now as they are. I'd like to think that this game we both love has not brought more hate into a world that really could do without it.

And what of the other? Where is he whose coat I now wear? Did he get a ticket? He is in the ground, the longer the game goes on the more I sense it. But where? Are his eyes on me as much as this game that is now won, observing me going about duties that were once his? And what might he be thinking about that – and other matters?

I stand on the edge of the pitch as the players stroll through the final moments and the crowd gives big voice to its final chants of the day. And in doing that they acknowledge him: the man, the Chief. Out of both relief and gratitude, all these people, who will be forever in his debt, acknowledge he who has saved them, he who these recent crucial games has done what was asked of him and in doing so shown others the way.

And as the last whistle sounds he who has come here and driven the bogeyman away from the Grand Old Lady punches the air like the conquering hero he is and leads the team in applauding the crowd that did not desert them.

And the many, of course, reciprocate.

Here now applause is plentiful, the ground is overflowing with it. Here on a sunshine afternoon, amid the warming brightness of spring, the Grand Old Lady is floating on these waves of mutual admiration.

But where is the one who will admire me – and love me? Will he who once was here in my place, who once wore this coat, turn out to be the one? Will the kisses of his mouth be my nourishment? Might he be the one whose love will make me fair?

For now, I stand alone hearing the Goodison anthem sound out once more in acknowledgement of the task that has been completed – Z Cars, the melody of an old seafarers' song that ends with a warning for the roving man, that he might not live forever in regret:

Do not leave your love like Johnny
Marry her before you go

Are you listening all you lads? Are you, in your moment of celebration taking heed of the burden of the song? Marry her before it's too late.

The applause patters down, as it must do, to a smattering of handclaps as the players and the masses turn to go their ways.

All the punters gone, I release the yellowjackets from their duties, set them drifting along the running track and back to the coatroom, and then for me a final task. I must go and check down below.

The gates are locked. Nobody lingers in the concrete zone.

I step back up and stand on the edge of the pitch. The place is deserted already, and so quiet. I am the last woman standing. But even in the silence, the emptiness, I feel that yes, this is the place, the place for me, the blue and the white, the wood and the iron, the ghosts of those who once graced the green in their royal blue jerseys, and these stands which have been home to so many through the generations, this is where I belong. And when we leave here, when we leave Goodison Park behind, elsewhere in our new home I will belong as a Blue, as a proud supporter of Everton

Football Club, through the high times as through the low, through the light as through the dark, as I have belonged here.

I take out my talkie, 'Section Six to match control, Section Six to match control. All clear on Section Six. All clear on Section Six.'

My job is done. And who can say I was not up to the task? Let those who would bite me in the back suck on lemons instead. Me, I will settle for a glass of fine lager.

So, that is it: another matchday is over, another season is almost gone. And we must now put these times of tribulations behind us. We must show those who would relish our fall the dust from our heels and let them choke on it. And we must believe that we will stand again one day on the high places, that our song will be bright with silver, and our colours will fly high once again, that royal blue will be seen upon the wings of the wind. This we have to believe, even in the face of they whose mouths are twisted in mockery. For we cannot keep on like this, we cannot play with fire again and again and expect to avoid the conflagration. Such dangerous games must be part of the past only. So now for the future – and whatever that holds.